CW00674619

Hope this scares
you!

Bill Davidson

The King of Crows

By
Bill Davidson

www.DarkInkBooks.com

www.AMInkPublishing.com

2016

Detective Chief Inspector John Dudek stood at the rendezvous point, close to the main body of officers, but maybe ten paces ahead. Blue lights washed over him as he waited, erect in his long coat; a tall, slim man, dark haired and sharp featured. An icy wind made his eyelids flicker as he stared. Otherwise, he did not move.

The university parking lot was half empty, just before term started, but it was poorly lit, and armed response was taking it slow, flashlight beams slicing the dark. Dudek recognized his old partner in the distance, Gerry Devlin, pointing with his whole arm as he directed the search.

Beyond the cars, the student's Union building was brilliantly lit, but people had stopped trying to peek out, not wanting armed police officers shouting at them, telling them to get down.

A squall of freezing rain hit Dudek's face, but he didn't take his eyes off Devlin, and so was watching when the man raised a hand and spoke into his radio, already walking before the bustle of activity started behind him.

Dudek angled quickly through the parking lot, leaving his new DC, Nathan Findlay, to catch up. Police vehicles were starting up, an ambulance being waved towards where a girl lay injured.

Dudek threaded through cars, coming to the open square in front of the Union, where Devlin was waiting. He slowed, well short of where the dead man lay, face up on the cobbles, turning to warn Nathan not to step in anything. But Nathan was already walking away, stiff legged and blowing hard. Dudek watched him for a moment, then turned back to Devlin.

"What have we got, Gerry?"

The expression on Devlin's face was almost pained, like he didn't know what to say, or want to say it. "One fatality, Sir. Suicide."

Dudek looked again at the dead man, the blood around him showing up black under the lights, thinking Devlin must have it wrong.

"Suicide?"

"Looks that way."

Dudek glanced towards where the paramedics were bundling out of their ambulance, several rows of cars back. "The girl?"

"Just a stray pellet, hit her leg. Doesn't look like she was targeted."

Dudek frowned and turned back to the body, trying to make sense of what he was looking at. The dead guy had been a very big man, big as Nathan, late fifties, wearing a long, black leather coat that had opened right up, framing him on the ground. Dudek thought he must have stood out, when alive.

Which was a good thing.

He had been shot in the neck, and again through the chest, a hole in there the size of a fist, jagged edges of rib showing. The back of his head was gone. The man's eyes were open, staring up into the night, and his jaw hung loose, something in there broken. He still held a pump action shotgun in his right hand.

Looking around, Dudek could see at least three positions where somebody had been shot by something like that shotgun, given the wide fans of blood.

Faces were appearing at the windows of the Union again, people speaking into cell phones or holding them up, hopefully too far away to get a decent image, in this light. With everything else going on right now, another murder, a shooting on the university campus no less, was the last thing he needed. Nathan, still looking pale, was back.

Dudek gave him a flat look. "We can't afford for you to be sick here."

Nathan compressed his lips. "I'm fine, boss."

He kept his eyes on his Constable as Devlin stepped closer, his voice low. "Doesn't add up, does it?"

Dudek indicated the mess, the blood splatters on the cobbles.

"Not for one suicide, it doesn't. Looks more like a shoot-out."

The nearest line of cars had been badly damaged, smashed windscreens and holes in the bodywork. Beyond them, scenes of crime officers were pulling on their suits.

Dudek looked again at the blocky Union building, noticing a second-floor window was broken, thinking maybe someone had shot at the dead man, and missed.

He turned to Nathan.

"Get a tent over this, quick. Keep these damn crows off, if nothing else."

Nathan, maybe relieved to get away, moved quickly towards where SoC were assembling their kit.

When Dudek turned back, Devlin was squatting on his heels, as close to the body as he could without disturbing anything. At one time they had been something like friends, Devlin at that time the guy who knew all there was to know about cars. Now he was the guy who knew about guns.

He pointed to a long shotgun cartridge, lying near a splatter of blood. "Look at those things. And you see the cars? The size of the holes?"

Dudek turned, seeing what Devlin meant, holes large enough to put a finger in.

"And the mess of *him*? Jesus Christ, that hole in his chest."

"I thought Nathan was about to lose his dinner."

Devlin wasn't listening, he was talking, working out what was in his head. "This guy, the gear he was using, Jesus. Massive shot, non-standard, magnum load. What did he think he was shooting at, a rhino?"

Dudek didn't want to tell his friend where he had gotten confused, but had to say, "Gerry. You're talking like the same gun did all the shooting. This guy was shot three times. And he's got a gun in his hand."

Devlin looked around, the same expression on his face, like he couldn't believe what he was seeing.

"I reckon the first few shots went into the cars. Maybe he was aiming at somebody in front of them, or in one."

He beckoned Dudek several paces to his left, pointed at a wide splatter on the cobbles.

"This looks like the first shot that hit anybody, though. You see the hair, bits of what looks like skull?"

"Somebody had their head blown off."

"Yeah." Devlin nodded towards the corpse, five yards away. "Him."

That stopped Dudek. "That makes no sense, Gerry."

"That's what I've been saying. The head shot must have happened with him on his feet, the spread of stuff back there."

He took a long step to the side. "And this is where he was shot in the neck"

Dudek shook his head. "Can't be. Whoever was shot here, they weren't on the ground."

"No, they weren't."

The two men stared at each other. Dudek had to make it clear. "I mean, whoever got shot here, they were standing."

Devlin nodded, so Dudek shook his head, like a reset. "We're getting ourselves turned around here. What do we know, I mean for sure?"

Devlin took a moment, getting his thoughts in order, then nodded towards the corpse.

"We know the dead guy took three shots, right?"

"Ok."

"And the last shot happened with him on his back, exactly where he is."

Dudek looked again at the blood surrounding the body. "Right."

"But the other two shots, the head and neck, didn't happen there."

Dudek, reluctantly, nodded once more. Then, showing his irritation, "What, so somebody blew the back of his head off, then picked him up, so they could shoot him again?"

When Devlin just shook his head, Dudek kept going.

"Then they drag the body across there. Shoot him a third time, and put the gun back in his hand. For what? To make it seem like suicide?"

Devlin threw his hands up and turned around, searching for an explanation. "Ok, I must be looking at this all wrong. Maybe he got into a fight with someone who had the same gear."

"So, there could be somebody else out there with a gun set up like this one?" Dudek tapped Devlin's body armor. "How would this stand up?"

Devlin smiled, no humor in it. "Close range? I'd be better off wearing my pajamas."

Nathan was back, trotting, out of breath. "SoC coming now, boss. Barry Batterham."

"Witnesses?"

"Uniform have a list, but nobody so far has seen the whole show. We've got a room in the Union to work from."

Stalled for a moment, the three men stood, staring at the body. They were a mismatched group, Devlin short, stocky in his armor, with a gleaming scalp. Dudek taller, late thirties. Tall as he was, Nathan's blonde head topped Dudek by a good four inches.

Nathan jerked as a crow dropped in a sudden flurry of feathers, scuffling amongst the mess on the ground. Devlin yelled, cursing, waving his arms, but it picked up a piece of something, dark hair hanging from it, and flapped into the air.

Dudek pointed a finger at Nathan. "Didn't I tell you to get a tent over this?"

Once Nathan had scurried off, Dudek turned to see Devlin had dropped into a crouch, sighting his semi-automatic on the crows, milling in the air. Saw his trigger finger tighten.

"Gerry!"

Devlin dropped his gun and straightened, walking away without another word. Dudek watched him go, replaying the moment in his head and trying to work out what he had just seen.

September 1976

The first time David Haddow saw Angela Murray was in the library of the University of Dundee, his first visit since starting the second year of his course.

He entered the foyer, hit as usual by the smell of wax and paper – he thought of it as scholarly – seeing how busy it was, newly hatched students milling around, looking lost or excited, or both.

David thought back to his own first visit here, how it had seemed overwhelming and loaded with potential at the same moment. He pressed on, appreciating the feeling of competence that went with knowing how the library was set out. He had enjoyed reading the set novels the year before. Enjoyed talking about Pinter and Defoe in tutorials where he could slump in his chair, open his mouth and find his thoughts take shape and walk as he spoke.

He didn't feel the same about actual study. Or assignments. English Lit came easy, because...well, because it did. Political Science (what was he *thinking*?) didn't come easy, and he had been relieved to drop it at the end of the year.

In the end he had only just scraped through, and had been intending to take Philosophy as well as Literature this year, his words to his friend, Neil, on the subject. "See me? I'm going to philosophize like fuck."

Then, first day in, he found himself signing up for Psychology instead. Psychology. How hard could that be?

A group of first years had crowded around an imperious, gray haired librarian who was explaining the index system in low tones. David surreptitiously checked out the females in the group, settling on a girl with full lips and breasts pushing against her cheesecloth shirt. He put the album he was carrying, Stevie Wonder's *Innervisions*, on top of the cabinet and pulled out one of the drawers. Now he could pretend to flick through the cards, getting a better look.

Her eyes flicked across to him and he quickly focused on the card in his hand, leaning so his long, dark blonde hair covered his face. When he risked an eye again, she was giving the gray hair her full attention.

A girl he hadn't noticed before shifted at the edge of the group, and he noticed her now. She stood slightly apart, and that seemed strangely fitting. The word 'apart' actually formed in his head before she too looked his way. This was no flick of the eyes, however. She turned to look at him and it took a full beat before he could haul his attention into the cards. He knew he was blushing and, annoyed with himself, kept his eyes down for several seconds before stalking into the body of the library.

He thought about what he would say when he and Neil got together in Rankine Hall later. Neil would probably have spoken to some new girls. Maybe, knowing him, had arranged to meet one in a bar up Perth Road. David felt itchy and dissatisfied, irritated with himself and girls in general for making getting off with them such a trial. If they fancied you, why didn't they just say?

He thought he might tell Neil about the girl, the one who was so apart, how weird she was. Everything about her was different. Whilst everyone else wore denim or cheesecloth, some tie-dyes and leg warmers in there, she was dressed not dissimilarly to the librarian. Actual slacks, polyester, and a cardigan. Short, dark hair, brushed straight.

Why would someone dress like that, who wasn't about thirty, David wondered. And then there was how she held herself. Nobody's back was that straight naturally. She had smiled as she listened, but not a happy smile, with her high tilted chin and long jaw.

She wasn't pretty, David decided, not like the other girl, but she was striking. He heard himself describing her, using that word, Neil saying, "Striking. So, she's a dog." And David, as he often did in his internal dialogues, taking the opposite view. Weird as anything but not a dog, come on, man. Striking doesn't mean dog.

He was standing with a copy of *Hard Times* in his hand, but not really looking at it. Not looking forward to reading it either; a book with such a miserable title.

The first years were being taken to the stairs that led to the lower levels and there she was, behind the librarian, but with a gap between her and the rest of the group. They felt her apartness too.

Watching her move, her posture was even more pronounced. She seemed to walk high on her toes, something approaching a bounce with each step and that straight, straight back. *Hockeysticks.*

The word came unbidden and, as these things usually did, unquestioned into his head. Her nickname at school, he'd bet.

David wondered if she was nuts. Probably going to spend all year studying and eating raw turnip in tutorials. Get a double first and become a lecturer and master of a hall of residence, like Brainiac 5, the exceptionally strange master of Rankine Hall. Getting older and weirder while the students stayed the same age.

He watched her head disappearing down the steps and wondered would she look around, even at this distance feel him watching. She didn't look.

2016

Dudek sat in a small office in the students' Union, drinking instant coffee and speaking to the first of the witnesses. This was a second-year law student, a tall dark-haired woman. He checked his notes.

"Morag, is it?"

She nodded. "Morag Jordan"

"I know you've been through this already, but bear with us."

"No problem." She looked at Nathan and smiled, "Glad to help."

Nathan smiled back, a bit too wide, a look from Dudek making him drop his eyes to his notebook, pen hovering.

"Where were you when you first realized something was wrong?"

"In here. Getting something to eat."

"What time did you arrive?"

"Six forty-five-ish. Got myself a sandwich at the bar. The place is dead at this time of year, so it was quiet."

"Where were you sitting?"

"By the window. My back to it."

"Did you see the person doing the shooting?"

"Once it started, yeah."

Nathan asked. "Ever seen him before?"

"I've been thinking about that! It might have been this guy, we called him El Perv. But I don't know if it was him."

Dudek had frowned when Nathan asked his question, but now he asked, "Who was this El Perv?"

"I only saw him once, in his car. That's what he did, see? You sometimes saw this black SUV parked out there. Sometimes the window would slide down and this big lens would come out."

"Photographing female students?"

"Well, yeah."

"So, the time you saw him?"

"I was walking towards the Union one night and I see this black SUV and I'm wondering if it's El Perv. Then the window slides down, just as I'm coming up behind it. He started taking photos and I walked right by."

"So, you got a good look at him?"

"Well, he had this huge camera and I didn't want to look *at* him, you know."

"But you think he might have been the same person?"

"He was big, and old, with lots of dark hair. A beard."

"The man out there didn't have a beard."

"No."

Then she said, "The funny thing was, though, there wasn't even anybody there. Nobody to photograph. And it was dark, not even during term."

"When was this? You know the date?"

"Actually, I do, because it was the night before I was *supposed* to go to Amsterdam. I got sick with something that exact night, knocked me flat for weeks."

She shook her head, sorry for herself. "I've not been right since."

"So, the date?"

"Oh yeah. July last year." She pulled out her phone and scrolled. "24th."

Nathan asked, "Anybody report this guy?"

"Nah. We just laughed it off."

Dudek looked at Nathan, back to the girl. "Let's get back to today. You were in the bar."

"Yeah. And suddenly there's this loud bang."

"Can you put a time on that?"

"About seven. I looked up at the barman and said, 'Was that a gun?' Then the next thing somebody is screaming outside and there's another bang and you could hear glass shattering. I go to look out, and the barman shouts, 'Are you nuts? Get down!' I dropped just as there's another bang, then everything goes quiet."

"So, three shots, then a pause?"

"It might only have been a few seconds. I creep under the window and the barman's getting upset, like if I look out *he* might get shot. I peep out."

Morag paused, blinking.

"What did you see?"

"The big guy, just standing there in his coat, with his back to me."

"Nobody else?"

"No. He had this shotgun, like in the movies. He turns the gun and shoots himself in the mouth."

As if that wasn't clear enough, she mimed turning a shotgun, putting the muzzle in her mouth and pulling the trigger.

"You saw all this gunk come out his head. That's what smashed the window, right beside me."

Nathan, surprised, asked, "Gunk from his head smashed the window?"

"No. I guess the bullet came right through."

Dudek nodded. "I guess the same thing. What happened then?"

"I was screaming my head off! Got down and stayed down till the Police came. Do you think I'm in shock?"

"I'm no medic. A team of councilors are arriving shortly, if they're not here already."

Dudek looked at Nathan, widened his eyes slightly, inviting him to ask a question. Nathan said, "Did you hear anything else?"

"Two more shots, seconds later. That's all."

Dudek tapped his pen, thinking. "The very last thing you saw, can you picture it?"

"He was falling back."

"The gun?"

"He dropped it. It fell onto the ground."

The next witness was Sally Wyatt, who had been walking away from a crunch meeting with her senior lecturer. It hadn't gone well, and she was out. So, she hadn't been paying attention to anything as she hurried towards her car.

She had noticed the guy in the leather coat, walking ahead of her, however. Remembered saying to herself 'Who does he think he is, Van Helsing?'

"Van Helsing?"

"Hugh Jackman, in that film. How many full length leather coats do you see?"

"You were following him?"

"Maybe thirty yards back, up the side of the Union. He was walking fast because I was nearly running, but not catching him."

"So, he disappeared, around the front of the building?"

"Yeah. And a few seconds later, bang! I know it's crazy, but I just kept going."

"What did you see?"

"He's running, shouting. He racks the gun, just like in the films, and shoots at the fucking cars!"

"You see who he was shooting at?"

"I figured they must be legging it. I did."

"What then?"

"He racked the gun again, and I got myself back around the corner. Started running."

"Did you see anything come out of the side of the gun?"

"The spent shells? Yeah!"

"What color?"

"Blue, I think."

"Did you hear anything else?"

Light dawned in her eyes and she said, "A girl, screaming!"

"Back to the man. Did you hear what he was shouting?"

"No, but he seemed pretty angry. Or scared."

The detectives interviewed two other students, but learned little more.

When they were left alone, Dudek said, "Maybe he just didn't like cars."

"If he hit somebody there would be evidence, boss, artillery like that."

"If there's something there, Barry B will find it."

The door opened and Dave Bowen, one of the uniforms, stepped in, his expression catching Dudek's attention.

"Dave?"

"We've found somebody claims she saw the person being shot at."

"Well, get her in here. Name?"

"Wendy Lawrence. A mature student."

When he left, Nathan blew out a sigh of relief. "Finally. A break."

Dudek looked at Nathan, dead pan. "You didn't listen. Dave said, *claims* she saw, giving it some, like he thinks there's something off about it. About her."

Lawrence was tall and very thin, with a lot of hair that had once been red, thick and frizzed and almost a foot wider than her head. She was wearing a striped jumper, red on blue, over a short black dress. When she moved, her bangles clattered. She shook, even her hair, so there was fairly constant noise.

She moved quickly to the chair and sat down, staring hard at Dudek.

"Ms. Wendy Lawrence?"

She didn't reply, so he had to ask, "Are you Wendy Lawrence?"

"I told the other officer."

Dudek managed a stiff smile. "We just have to confirm your details, then we can get to what you witnessed."

Wendy Lawrence, forty-nine, lived in the town of Markinch, and was attending a course on person-centered counselling. When they got through that, Dudek asked,

"Can you tell me, in your own words, what you witnessed this evening?"

Her voice shook, like the rest of her. "I was already late, but didn't want to cross the square in front of the Union. It disturbs me."

"It disturbs you?"

She stared, her hair trembling and her left nostril rimmed with blood.

"It's disturbing." She narrowed her eyes. "You understand. Or you should." Then, a nod at Nathan. "He doesn't."

Dudek glanced at Nathan who widened his eyes slightly but made no comment.

"What route did you take?"

"I come by train, but take the long way around. To avoid the disturbing effects of the students' Union."

"Ah. The disturbing effects of the students' Union."

"I come by West Port and cross through all the parked cars."

She leaned in to point at a map of the campus, already on the table.

"I was here, when it started."

"About a hundred yards away."

"That's right. I saw him, the big man, coming around the corner of the building and knew something was about to happen. I'm sensitive to things."

"What next?"

"He started shooting."

15

"Did you see who at?"

"The first shot, no. But, then, I was *looking*, I knew somebody was there and I knew if I looked hard enough…"

She swallowed noisily. "He didn't want to be seen. But, I saw."

Lawrence hit the sides of her head with her palms, not soft like someone trying to remember, but hard. Hard enough so that Nathan jumped, looking uneasily at Dudek. The hair dampened the noise to a dull thud.

"You ok, Wendy?"

"It hurt to see him, and it hurts to remember."

"Someone being shot…"

"That's not what I mean."

A line of blood started at Wendy Lawrence's nose. Dudek handed her a tissue, asking could she go on.

"Can I have a drink of water?"

After gulping down most of a bottle of Strathmore Springs, Wendy nodded, telling Dudek to continue.

"What did he look like? The man being shot at."

She screwed her face up. "It's hard to bring the image to mind."

Again, she hit her head with her palms and this time Nathan surprised Dudek, stepping around the table to take her arms. She looked up at him.

"Stop that, okay?"

"What?"

"The hitting. Stop hitting yourself."

She didn't take her eyes off his face, just nodded.

Dudek looked across at Nathan, dropped back to Lawrence. "Can you try? I can help you."

She grimaced, but nodded.

"Was he tall?"

She glanced behind her. "Not like him. Normal height."

"Like me?"

"Shorter."

Dudek gave her another tissue and she dropped the bloody one into the waste paper basket.

"Was he young?"

A shake of the head. "Older than you."

"Sixty?"

"Maybe"

"If we give it a range. Fifty to sixty?"

"I think that would be right."

"Caucasian?"

"Yes."

"You're doing good, Wendy. Hair?"

"I can't say."

Her face looked pained, and she suddenly looked much older.

"Are you alright to keep going?"

She nodded. "Let's get this over with."

"Build?"

"Skinny. But he was wearing…bulky clothes."

"What kind?"

"A suit. Not smart like yours. Old-fashioned. Light-ish color. Far too large for him."

"How could you tell that?"

"It was obvious. He was a slight man in a fat man's suit."

"Ok. You're doing great."

The woman was shaking even harder now, and she raised her hands to the side of her head before looking up at Nathan and dropping them.

"The second shot, I saw him being hit. He was spun right around, but didn't fall."

The detectives looked at each other, then Dudek turned back to Lawrence, not smiling.

"Will you give us just a moment? I need to check something with my colleague." He came to his feet as he spoke.

"Just relax for a moment, Ms. Lawrence."

Outside the room Dudek said, "She's crazy."

"You don't think there could be anything in what she says?"

"You know as well as I do that if someone was shot with that gun…" He left the sentence unfinished. If somebody had been shot, the evidence would be splattered across the cars.

Nathan said, "We didn't ask her to pinpoint the exact position of the victim."

Dudek nodded, thinking about it. "No, we didn't. Maybe the positions were closer than we first thought. Maybe some of the blood…"

The two men looked at each other, the same thought now in both of their heads.

Nathan said, "Maybe that could account for how everything looks wrong. We're looking at the mess left by two people."

Dudek nodded, but still looked unsure. "Let's hope Barry can make some sense of it."

"Do we think the description of the victim might be real? At least it's a description."

"Of what though? Let's see where she puts them."

Nathan checked his watch, hesitant as he asked was it ok to take a minute, phone home? So Sue would know how late he might be. He held up his cell phone.

"She tried to call me twice already."

Dudek had to look away. Couldn't even glance at Nathan as he said, sure, be quick. He watched him as he walked out of the building, though and his hand went to his own phone, knowing it was way too late to do anything about that now. About two years too late.

Wendy took a long time over the plan, finally placing her finger close to where the man in black was still lying. "Here's where he shot his gun." Her finger moved to edge of the parking lot, "And this is where the other man was."

Later, after Lawrence left, Dudek shook his head.

"Couldn't happen. Our shooter hit somebody there, it would be obvious."

Nathan tapped a finger on the plan. "But where she put the gunman. Right on the money."

September 1976

Neil Kerr had hurried back to his room in Rankine Hall of Residence and, first day of term, was already studying. He had done well in his first year, third best overall, and wasn't about to let that slip. His score in Anatomy had been less than dramatic and that little shit Bob Marjoram had beaten him by a mile.

Moving suddenly, he hopped noisily off the bed and dropped to the floor, popping fifty quick press ups. He stood and took a few deep breaths, thinking David might be back soon and not wanting to be caught working out. Then, he flopped back onto the bed, dragged his shoulder length hair into some sort of order, and re-opened the book.

David's father, who taught math at their old school, had told him the best way to make something stick was to go at it immediately after the lesson. Telling him this whilst handing a tea tray into David's room.

David, as usual, grabbed the tray then all but shooed his father out, slumping back before the television, Starsky and Hutch running up a stairwell.

"Why do you do that, with your old man?"

"Do what?"

"He comes up here with toast and everything and you chase him away."

"You want to hang out with my dad?"

"I'm just saying he's ok for an old guy. Into his sounds and everything."

"Yeah, if you like…" He pointed at the screen. "David Soul. Seriously."

"He's into The Who."

"Come on, he has singles by The Carpenters!"

Neil shook his head. Until he hit fourteen, David had no discernible interest in music. Had gone through a series of obsessions, lasting a year at most; tennis, Subbuteo, even the Air Training Corps. During his ATC year, he hammered cleats in the heels of his shoes, and took to marching rather than walking.

By fifteen, he was a muso. A hippy. Neil could annoy him these days, just by mentioning the Corps.

In those few years, though, David had built up a surprisingly large collection of albums, and, this time, there was no sign of the obsession disappearing. Even more surprising, given that this was David, he had developed a truly impressive knowledge of modern music.

That night in David's room, Neil, not wanting to get into a musical argument he wouldn't win, said simply. "He's ok for a teacher. That's all I mean."

David just looked at his friend, who had to say, "Don't start in about what it's like having your dad teaching at your own school."

Neil had taken the math teacher's advice and, every chance he could, put in some study on the day's work before David got back to the halls and sought him out. He even studied steadily across the summer break, getting to grips with cardio and renal.

Thinking about home, Neil wondered again about his sister Rachel and David. Something had happened between them, but neither was admitting to what. Neil was sure they hadn't actually *done* it, certain that David hadn't ever done it, but something had occurred. Maybe just a kiss, but for his sixteen-year-old sister and David, with his incapacitating shyness around girls, that was still serious.

He shook that away and tried to refocus on the function of the liver. David needed a girlfriend, and surely, this year, it would finally happen. David, though shorter than Neil, was six feet even. He had naturally wavy hair, dark blonde, that came over his shoulders and everybody said he was a good looking boy. Something like Bowie before Ziggy, when he still looked something like a hippy.

Neil himself wasn't just tall, he was *big*, not a fashionable look. He no longer had to look up when he spoke to his enormous Father. A police chief-super, in his uniform the man looked like he could blot out the sun.

Neil was struggling to concentrate. Out in the hall, a girl kept laughing in that loud way that demanded attention and somebody was playing Velvet Underground at volume. Neil sniffed, thinking somebody had lit a joint. All of which seemed strange. Last term, the Master of Rankine Hall, Brainiac 5, would have been all over that, roaming the corridors, keen to stamp his weird authority on the new intake.

His attention was taken by a sudden spray of rain, rattling against the window, and he stood to look outside.

The summer had been nothing short of amazing. Hot day after hot day, full weeks of unbroken sunshine even in Neil's Northern hometown of Aberdeen. David's dad had said the only other year that came close was 1975, the year before. Two exceptionally long hot summers, one after the other, in Scotland, how about that?

Now Neil, watching rain spatter the leaded window, felt a chill draught on his bare arms. From where he stood, he could see a huge stretch of the river Tay over the roofs of sizable old houses. The river, over a mile wide and widening fast as it emptied into the North Sea, was gray and roiling today. It was called the Silvery Tay, and he had seen it many times shining like burnished metal, almost blindingly bright in the sun. However it looked that was where his eye was drawn and held, whenever he stood here.

David was worse, tending to pause here and stand for many, many minutes, silently staring out of this window. He'd do that whether he was stoned or not.

Sometimes the great river could be as flat as glass, or as blue as the sky, or green and storm tossed. Neil had seen it home to slow moving ice-floes or brightly colored yachts. It might be gray and flat under rain or wild and foamy in a gale.

The grounds of Rankine Hall sloped down to a stone wall, ten feet tall, behind which was Perth Road, one of the main arteries into Dundee center.

Neil watched now as cars slid by, their sound muted, then a motorbike blatted past and a group of crows launched noisily into the air from the huge monkey puzzle tree, only twenty yards from the house.

Rankine Hall was a poor fit for a student residence. It was, Neil believed, hundreds of years old, built by a fat factory owner called Rowland Rankine, whose likeness still glared out from his portrait above the stairs. Whenever David caught sight of the painting, he would say the same thing, "Look at that miserable old bastard."

Three flights tall, with high, steeply peaked roofs, most of the hall's windows were high and narrow, with stained glass top panels. Large rooms had been partitioned into chilly bedrooms, much taller than they were wide, but the most striking internal feature was the staircase, six feet wide with a banister of gleaming walnut.

Now the grand hallway was lined by plastic domed payphone kiosks and Rowland Rankine's portrait was protected from felt pens by Perspex.

This September, every tree in the expansive grounds was crammed with rackety crows, forever launching into the air, like a feathery explosion.

2016

It was nearly midnight when the detectives left the Union. The journalists had only departed after Dudek agreed to give a short statement, speaking to a local television camera. Brief as it was, he had the feeling that, Mackie, the boss, would take it badly.

The body was gone, but the numbered markers and tent remained, behind Police tape. Two uniforms, bulky in their Hi-Viz, stood at opposite corners of the cordon, looking chilled in the wind.

As Dudek watched, two young men, probably students, definitely drunk, approached and were waved on. They went, but one mimed pulling out a shotgun and shooting the other, who staggered back in slow-mo at every shot.

The detectives walked through the near empty parking lot to their unmarked Ford Focus. Dudek opened the door but stopped when he saw the way Nathan was standing, turned to see what he was looking at. A black SUV, alone in the far corner. Dudek looked back at his Constable, shrugged and closed the door.

They reached the car and walked around. A late model VW, black, tinted windows. Dudek leaned close, shading his eyes. "What do you think?"

"Well. It might be his. Or it might be somebody else's."

Dudek gave him a flat look, pulled on a latex glove and tried the door. It opened with a clunk and the interior light came on. He opened it all the way. Leather interior, on the passenger seat, binoculars, food wrappers and a can of coke.

"What does this remind you of?"

Dudek leaned in, flicking open an unmarked carboard box open to show blue magnum shells.

While Nathan called it in, Dudek walked around and opened the glove box, coming out with an insurance document.

"Neil Kerr. Arthurstone Terrace. Here's something else, a bill from…Glen Property. His landlord maybe?"

Nathan broke the connection on his cell phone. "Yeah, Neil Kerr is the owner."

Dudek nodded absent mindedly, looking at the box of oversize shells. "I think we've got the name of our shooter."

September 1976

David returned from his first English lecture, skimmed his folder into the corner and wandered upstairs to Neil's room.

It was obvious that his friend has been studying, as usual, and as usual had slid the textbook under the bed when David knocked. The Who were on the turntable, Daltry shouting about his mother's squeeze box, but David avoided comment, restricting himself to a cool look at the album cover.

He glanced out of the window, but the river was hardly visible behind a rising mist, so he threw himself on the only chair and asked had Neil scored yet.

Neil shook his head, "The skinny guy that used to sell his own weed has dropped out."

Then he leaned forward to peer at his friend. Finally, he nodded. "You're looking unusually philosophical today, my good man."

David raised his eyebrows. "No, I'm not, actually. I'm looking..." he waved his hand airily as though reaching for the word. "...really rather psychological."

Neil straightened, surprised. "You're kidding me. You signed up for psychology?"

"Naturally."

Neil stared at him for several seconds. "This is because you saw some babe in the psychology queue, isn't it?"

"Not at all. What would you use philosophy for anyway? It's just playing at being a smartass."

"Last year. You saw that Ingrid girl, Dutch or something, signing for Political Science. Joined up and never spoke to her once."

"She left after the first term. Went back to...Dutchland or wherever Dutch people come from."

"Well, just don't do Geography."

"I got an A in my geography O level. I've just chosen to forget it all to concentrate on psychology."

Neil shook his head and David had to ask himself, why did I choose psychology?

Neil seemed to be in an odd mood, surprisingly pissed off at David for joining Psychology, like it was anything to do with him. Over the summer, it had felt as though Neil was never far from being irritated with him. Still, it hadn't stopped him from spending most of his time at David's house, even if they were just watching *The Six Million Dollar Man*.

David seldom visited Neil's house, despite the attraction of his sister, Rachel, who could make his insides turn to liquid with a glance. But, despite the kiss last summer, the one *she* had started by the way, both boys were much more comfortable at David's. The Kerr house was always dominated by the heavy presence of his father, whether he was there or not.

When he was there, it seemed the thing to do to talk in whispers and stay out of his way. His tread was heavy and his breathing always sounding loud, like it was hard getting his lungs to inflate against the weight of his chest.

One day in August, Neil had said his dad was an alcoholic, throwing it out there like it was nothing, not fooling anybody. David replied that he'd never seen him drunk. It's not like that, said Neil. He's just constantly half in the bag.

Then he said, he's a scary old bastard.

David asked, did he ever get, you know, violent. Neil's response took a second or two and when it came it was a cantilevered "No-o." Like it was two words. David didn't push.

Now, with Rod Stewart replacing The Who on the turntable, David pushed off.

Back in his room, he chose Soft Machine 1 from his line of albums, not their best but still a work of significance, and, with it tucked under his arm, walked to the refectory. He got talking to a large pink student about the Softs, and ended up playing poker with him and two law students. They played until almost ten, smoking and drinking Nescafe, by which time David had won more than seven pounds and the atmosphere was getting tense. The law students had brought a couple of records from their rooms, *Year of the Cat* and Chicago, for God's sake, which they swapped about on the turntable. David eventually took Chicago off mid 'If You Leave Me Now'. That didn't help the atmosphere one bit.

Walking back to his room, the main noise was the wind, which was really getting up, and the background croak of crows. He could hear students speaking in their rooms, a bit of music in there too, but nobody playing anything at volume.

The deeply strange house master, Dr Bernard, invariably known as Brainiac 5, had already had his dampening effect, he guessed.

Although, now that he was thinking about the Brainiac, he realized that he had barely seen him creeping his way around the building. Hadn't noticed him gardening in the grounds, one of the man's obsessions. Last year, if he wasn't lecturing, he seemed to be out there pretty much every day, staring at students as they came and went in that intense, unsettling way he had.

Letting himself in, David crossed to the window and stared into the blustery darkness. The grounds were dark, Perth Road a line of orange streetlamps and the little towns on the far side of the river a scattering of lights, crawling up in the hill. Sometimes those lights would be perfectly reflected in the river, but today the whole scene was in violent movement, trees being whipped around.

David pulled the ratty curtains closed and rubbed his arms. He sat, then hopped back up to lock his door. Last year, in this same wing, he seldom locked up. He harbored no real hope, but would still fantasize about girls from nearby rooms, opening his door in the early hours, smiling shyly as they came in.

This year, he was embarrassed to admit, he felt scared. He pulled off his jeans and brushed his teeth noisily at the wash basin. Then he turned on the bedside lamp and picked up the Dickens, but couldn't read. Instead, he put Paul Simon on the turntable, down low.

With 'Kodachrome' bumping nicely along in the background, David switched the lamp off, curled into a ball, and listened while the wind dropped, and the album came to its end. The building had quietened, but the crows croaked on. What were they doing out there? They should be curled up in their little crow beds.

Time passed, the wind dropped and even the crows gave it up. Now it was properly quiet, the main sound his own breathing, and still he was scared. So scared, that he slipped his hand out and turned his bedside light on. For a while he lay like that, listening, and then the thought occurred that his window wasn't locked. He frowned, thinking why would that matter? It was fully fifteen feet off the ground and, last year, he had sometimes slept with it open.

It made no sense, but the fact of the unlocked window grated at him. He swung his legs to the floor but did not stand. He wanted to lock the window, but didn't like the idea of his shadow being visible against the curtain.

Another thought then, that the bedside lamp made his room stand out like a beacon to anyone looking from outside.

He scolded himself for being a silly prick, but it did no good. He edged the curtain open, but the solid black of the grounds unnerved him. Beyond, the river was darker than black, reflecting none of the lights of the faraway town.

"Get a *grip*!"

He swallowed noisily and switched his lamp off, waiting a few seconds before cracking the curtains. He looked into the dark for a long time, fear building, along with a feeling that something had noticed him, his dread acting like a scent.

A headache was building too. He finally slid his arm out and twisted the lock, stepping back to fumble the lamp back on and climb into bed, accepting he would sleep like that. Like a baby.

He closed his eyes, but seconds later they snapped back open. He had been scared before, but now the hair rose all over his body. He pulled the covers around himself and fixed his attention, not on the window, but the door.

2016

It was after ten when Dudek got to the station. He was feeling slow from the Rioja he had finished before finally falling asleep, flicking through TV channels in the early hours, waking up still wearing the Ted Baker suit, with its snappy pin stripe. At this rate his dry-cleaning bill would be higher than his mortgage.

He told himself he would be fine once he got going, well in gear for the press conference. Looking at himself in the mirror, he wondered how much longer he could keep living like this before it showed. For the moment, he still looked something like his rep, what he heard said about him; too smooth to be a cop.

He walked into his office and there was a file, an old one, on his chair rather than his desk, something somebody wanted him to see straight off. His in-tray was full and there were other files building on his desk; a situation sliding out of control. He considered taking an hour, making sure there wasn't a ball in there waiting to drop, trouble he could no longer afford.

Nathan was in the room even before he finished hanging his coat up.

Dudek nodded to the old file, the one on his chair. "I take it Kerr has form?"

Nathan's surprise showed on his face. "How did you know that?"

Dudek waved it away, not wanting this kind of discussion again.

"Nothing much, Sir. A caution, for LSD. In 1976."

"And you found that?" Dudek could hear his own West Country accent, stronger this morning, as it was when he was annoyed, or drunk. "All we've got on and you're wasting time hunting through ancient records."

"I thought it..."

"Never mind."

He walked across the room and grabbed the file, spoke without looking up. "Get me a coffee."

He opened the file as Nathan left, the guy biting down a reply. Wanting to tell him to piss off. He scanned the pages in there, then stopped, beginning to smile.

When Nathan came back with his coffee, Dudek said, "You see who bust him?"

"The Chief."

"Mackie himself, when he was a Detective Constable."

Nathan put the cup down. "Looks like it was from last century. Typed on an antique typewriter."

"Antique?"

"Mechanical. With the little arms."

"We were still using those things ten years ago." Dudek thought about it. "Fifteen."

There were two other papers in the file. The first was a memo, again from Mackie, to an Inspector Dibben.

"The language they used in those days, Jesus." He rubbed his eyes, wishing he hadn't finished the bottle. Wondering now, if he opened a second. He sipped the coffee and felt his stomach roll slightly. Had to take a minute, pretending to read. He looked up, aware that Nathan was speaking.

"What?"

Nathan was looking at him, his expression wary. Dudek had gotten used to wary expressions over the last couple of years.

"I was just saying, something weird happened, back in the seventies."

The subject of the memo read 'Derelict Factory, Brook Street- Recent Incidents'.

It started by thanking the Chief Inspector for his interest, Dudek taking that to mean sticking his nose where it wasn't wanted, into one of Mackie's cases. The irony wasn't wasted on him.

Then it went on to say that the factory had been broken into by hippies, for the taking of hallucinogenic drugs.

"Can you believe this? He actually calls them hippies. For the taking of hallucinogenic drugs."

Mackie went on to say the factory had been derelict for years, its ownership uncertain. Drugs had certainly been used, but there was no case of possession to be made. Talking about a missing person, Angela Murray. No evidence of foul play, just a drug addict skipping out. Missing person report had been filed, but there was no reason for further investigation.

Fair enough for the seventies, thought Dudek.

Now Kerr getting a mention. The guy had been cautioned for possession of LSD, but nothing since then.

Dudek said, "He must have been in a bad way, Kerr, hanging out in some old factory. Didn't he have digs?"

Another name now, David Haddow. Haddow the victim of some rogue batch of drugs, possibly concocted by Kerr and Haddow themselves, suffering a severe reaction. Harmed himself with a knife. In a coma, unlikely to recover. Family are hoping to return him to Aberdeen as soon as possible.

Nathan pointed. "He mentions that Haddow's dad is a school headmaster."

"Letting the Chief Inspector know he comes from a good family."

Mackie now mentioning another name, Ian Minto.

Dudek turned to Nathan, his eyes narrowing. "Ian Minto. That seem familiar?"

"1976. I wasn't even born, Guv."

Dudek shot the younger man a sharp look. "Me neither."

Minto's involvement with the students wasn't certain, although it seemed likely that he had supplied them with drugs.

Dudek's eyes widened, "Wait now, a body."

"That's where it gets weird, boss."

Dudek read out loud. "The body has no connection to the drug taking, nor to the parties concerned. The cause of death has been determined as natural causes (heart attack). The time of death is uncertain, but was some weeks before the break in."

He squinted up at Nathan. "It was all happening in '76. A spike of murders and suicides."

"I got that at Uni. Theory goes it was the unseasonable hot summers and cold winters. The dead body, was that the guy…" he looked over Dudek's shoulder, "Minto, d'you think?"

"I didn't read it like that. Seems to me these kids got some homemade LSD, broke into this factory and took it. They fry their brains, and the woman, Angela Murray, goes missing. A corpse must have been found in the same building, but with no connection. A rough sleeper maybe."

"Why do you think that?"

"No mention of him being a missing person. Nobody was missing him."

"So, our shooter was into the drug scene here in the mid-seventies."

"Like half the university back then."

Dudek was becoming irritated again, Nathan wasting his time with this when he had more to do than at any time in his working life, things just waiting to go wrong. Annoyed at Nathan, at Mackie, even at the dead guy Kerr, he tossed the file down and started looking through his messages. Two regarding the Mullins case, several from journalists, one from Mackie. Even though he knew how careful you had to be with Mackie, the most important message was from France. The local police had contacted the Mullins party and they were on their way home. He showed it to Nathan.

"They'll be landing in Manchester at six. Brief one of the uniforms. Have them met and ferried up here."

"Sir."

Nathan took the file his boss was handing him, but asked, "You think this will go down as another historic spike?"

When Dudek just looked at him, he shifted uncomfortably. "I mean." He pointed at Dudek's desk. "Everything seems to be going wrong."

"I doubt that very much."

He made himself sound casual, but Nathan's question had brought something to mind. Not '76, but a time two years ago, when his life changed, and things went wrong that could never be put right.

He put his cup down, but somehow it ended up on its side, coffee swilling across the papers on his desk.

"Damn it!"

Nathan moved forward, but he waved him off. "Just get out of the way."

He dumped a wad of tissues on the spill, looking up to find Nathan staring. Waited a beat before saying. "Another coffee."

2016

Nathan thought that Dudek had smelled again of alcohol, hard to tell behind the aftershave. He still looked fit, a runner Nathan knew, always sharp in his expensive suits.

But his eyes were sometimes puffy, and it was obvious he drank, maybe heavily. There was a moment this morning when he just sat there, looking at Nathan but not seeing him, like he'd been switched off. Anybody can do that, but it had gone on for, what, ten seconds?

Dudek had a confused reputation. Some of the guys said he could make connections he had no business making, like Sherlock Holmes, but Nathan thought the real story was how he had lost it big time a couple of years back and still somehow kept his job.

The way Nathan heard it, Dudek had a child kidnapper in custody, and simply threw the rule book out the window. Marched the guy straight out the station, somehow made him spill the beans and found the boy before it was too late. What he did to him, that was where the serious speculation started. A lot of the guys took the view that, whatever it was, fucking good on him.

Dudek survived with a written warning, probably sympathy for a personal tragedy, his wife and child dying about the same time, helping him. For his part, Nathan couldn't understand why he hadn't been fired.

Nathan was in no hurry to go back in there. He called home, smiling subconsciously when little Debs picked up the phone, telling Sarah had been naughty again. Throwing food on the floor.

"She's only a baby, sweetie."

"And she said a bad word."

"Did she?" Her first word, a swearword. "Well, she is Scottish."

Then Sue was there, "How's Grumpy D then?"

Nathan looked around. "Better not call him that, when I'm calling from work."

"How's he been on the jerk off scale?"

"Give him a nine so far."

"Snarky comments about your degree?"

"I've stopped noticing. I don't think that's what it is, anyway."

"No?"

"They're common enough. It's more, this other guy he thinks should've made detective before me, didn't have one."

"He needs to get over himself."

Nathan shrugged. "The guy's been through some stuff. Losing his family like that."

"Yeah. He was busy dangling somebody off a balcony when he should have been looking after them."

Nathan looked around, wishing he'd never told Sue that particular rumor. "Wasn't proved, remember. Look, I got to go."

"Ok. Don't take any shit off him."

"See, what that proves. You've never met Dudek."

September 1976

Back home in Glasgow, Angela Murray was used to people commenting on how she held herself, often telling her, you're just like your mother. There was no doubt that was true. Her mother walked straight backed and head high, turning heads even though she was elderly, over forty now.

Still, everything about her mother's demeanor, said, I am special. Angela's had a horrible suspicion that her mother had instilled in her an insipid shadow of her own élan. And, because she was only herself, it came over as simply arrogant or stuck up; the two most common descriptions people used about her.

As a child, her mother drummed it into her; "Sit straight, walk straight, head *up!*"

She had a photograph of herself at nursery, a copy her mother made for her, one of her favorites. It wasn't a favorite of Angela's, but she would bring it out occasionally as a curio, a disturbing one.

It showed a group of laughing three-year-olds, all with that easy grace of the very young, except for Angela. Not laughing, but smiling, that girl, a rigid, hard kind of smile that sat poorly on the face of such a tiny child. It was, undoubtedly, her smile. She stood, straight backed and apart even then, head high as her Mother had told her. And told her.

Rebellion against her mother was never an option. Until the decision to go to Dundee. It had always been assumed that Angela would attend Cambridge or Oxford. Her mother talked of law, or medicine.

And the weird thing was she could clearly recall how excited she had been to get the solid A's that lined up with her offer from Cambridge. It had been *her* ambition too.

She planned a visit to the campus, made contact with the Cambridge Flute Choir, then completed her application. To the University of Dundee.

Her mother's shock when she told her of her decision, to study psychology of all things, made her queasy even now. Her mother assuming she would simply force her daughter to drop this aberrant notion. Angela wondered where she had found the will to fend off the increasingly determined onslaughts.

Now, two weeks into her course, she came back again and again to that decision. It wasn't as if she had even known the place. Two weeks and she had made no friends. Nothing unusual about that, of course. She thought about joining the tennis club, but that's as far as it went.

Iris, a large Irish girl, her neighbor in Rankine Hall, had tried more determinedly than most to persuade her out 'for a pint'. Irish Iris, as she was universally known, was tall, wide and beautiful with long auburn hair, worryingly mobile breasts and an extremely loud voice. Angela often found herself walking back to Rankine with her, Iris saying something like "Come to the pub, it'll be a giggle. What do you say?"

"It isn't my thing, thanks."

Eventually, Iris demanded, "You do take a drink now, don't you?"

"Not really."

"Jesus Christ. First time I got hammered I was thirteen."

Then, after a pause, "You have your eye on anybody?"

When Angela just looked at her, she said, "I mean a boy."

Angela had been sixteen when she developed her first and only crush. Steven was tall, blonde and slim as a rake. She would try to get near him, which was why she was there to overhear him say, "Hockeysticks? It would be like screwing an ironing board."

It wasn't a nice memory. Nor was the one of what she'd done to him.

She shook her head at Iris. "I don't have my eye on any boys, no."

Angela noticed that heads turned when Iris was around. She was *big*. She was *loud*. She was curvy in a way that made Angela feel uncomfortable. An almost aggressive curviness, she thought. But no, it was more the way she moved. Was she even aware?

She also, Angela noticed, smelled great. Whilst most students smelled of cigarettes, or patchouli, the scent coming off Iris was invariably clean and expensive. Her hair shone. Her clothes were largely standard issue occasionally matched with more unusual items. Today that was a skirt that was surely from the fifties, spoiled, in Angela's view, by her Doc Marten boots.

Nothing fashionable about her, though, too heavy, too wide. Features probably too strong. Still, she was probably the only person that Angela knew personally that she would describe as, not just attractive or pretty, but beautiful.

If Iris knew that, the only cue came from the way she *swayed*. She was noisy, even alone with Angela, but underneath... what? Something shy, or vulnerable? Angela shook the idea away. Nothing vulnerable about that oversized Irish girl, surely.

Another thing that surprised Angela about herself – she wasn't working. The winner of academic and music prizes, she prided herself on her abilities. Now her flute lay untouched in her box and, instead of studying, she walked. She hiked around the city's steep streets and old tenements of muddy stone, through wide avenues of trees and dense estates. She walked up the central hill, the Dundee Law, to see the city sprawling and crawling towards the spectacular estuary whilst dark hills rose to North and South.

She walked at night, and during the day when she should have been at lectures, but whenever she walked her feet invariably brought her down to the Tay. There was always a feeling of relief when she reached the side of the great river, a breathing out as she stared across the huge expanse of water, fading to the far horizon and the North Sea. The sound of waves, the smell, the power that lay in that water; everything about it soothed her, and let her return to the Halls.

The third week of term found her sitting in the main lecture hall, thinking about nothing. The boy, she didn't know his name but thought of him as The Record Boy, was sitting behind and a little to her right. She'd noticed him come in, dressed in denim like everybody else, and carrying a record, as usual. She saw him glance over and for a moment it seemed like he would acknowledge her but, as ever, he looked away.

The Record Boy was tall, with wavy shoulder length hair that Iris described as dark blonde, Iris saying he was good to look at, but only when he was sitting down. She didn't like the way he went about the place; her words. There was, Angela thought, something almost pretty about him.

As usual, he sat one row back from her and a few seats to the right. She wondered how that worked out, as she made a point of never choosing the same spot. She had noticed that most people did that, ending up talking to their neighbors, a practice she hoped to avoid.

But the Record Boy didn't *wait* for her. More than once she had sat down and looked around to find him already in place, one row behind and a few seats to the right, his notebook open in front of him. She tried out a few words to describe him; intense, shifty, deep, weird. But none of them were right. Something about him drew her eye again and again, but she didn't know what it was, or even if it was good or bad. The best description to suit him was one of her mother's and when she said it to Iris, she agreed straight away. There's something about him you just can't put your finger on.

2016

Dudek, looking at the notes on his desk, said, "One of these journalists has called three times. Hilda Jarvis. From *The Independent*."

"Yeah, she's downstairs, boss."

Dudek looked at Nathan, frowning. "Downstairs? Jesus Christ. Doesn't she know that we've got a press call at noon?"

"She got here a half hour ago, but it's not to do with Mullins. Said she might as well sit there as anywhere else, working on her laptop."

The thought of a journalist downstairs, trying to railroad him, irritated him, but Dudek put it away.

"Any progress getting us into Kerr's flat?"

"I've left a message on the landlord's answerphone."

She laughed, and he liked that. Knew he was almost flirting with this journalist but not caring much.

"Ever been in an editor's office?"

"The only way you'd get me in a place like that would be if someone killed the editor."

"See, there you go. Typical police. Press as the enemy."

"I wonder how we got like that."

Sparring a bit, but nothing in it. They were both smiling.

"You don't have your notebook out."

"So, we must be off the record."

"I've been stung like that before, Hilda."

"Not by me, you've not." She raised her hand, "I know. It takes time to build up that sort of trust."

Dudek liked how she looked when she moved. Liked her smile. He told himself to be careful, and the shadow of what happened two years ago, the kidnapper Hardy still on the streets because of what he did, crossed his mind again. He wondered, does she know about that?

If she'd looked into him at all, she would. Maybe she even knew about Caroline, and Shaun.

There was a knock at the door, Nathan looking in to ask if he wanted coffee, another police officer smiling a bit too wide. She told him, black please no sugar and, when he left, said, "He's tall."

"We still like a few monsters about the place. What can I do for you, Hilda?"

"The shooting yesterday."

"You not had the…"

"The party line, yes. But, come on."

"I can tell you that a single white male has died from gunshot wounds. A white female was hit by a stray pellet, but isn't critical. There's it, so far."

"Who was the guy? Do you know?"

"We think we do. Relatives haven't been contacted yet, so…" He held his hands out.

She nodded slowly, like this was pretty much what she expected. Then she said, "I understand he fired the gun six times."

Dudek shrugged, "There were six shots. Can't say yet who fired."

"What I heard, he shot himself three times. Twice after he was dead."

Dudek sat back, cautious now. "Does that seem possible to you, Ms. Jarvis?"

She sat back herself, but with the smile still in there. "I'm just telling you what's been said."

They looked at each other for a few seconds till Nathan came in, carrying two cups. She got to her feet and took one.

When Nathan left, she said, "It's been years since I was in Dundee. It's looking pretty good these days." Her tone was different, conversational.

"You reckon?"

"Don't you? The old Overgate was one of the ugliest bits of City Centre I ever saw. Looks fantastic now."

"You lived here?"

"My Dad was a journalist too, worked here for years before moving south."

Dudek sat straighter. "Not Jack Jarvis?"

"My old man."

"I know him from *The Times*, I guess. He broke that banking story."

"Yeah, that stuff really ground his gears."

"The old stagers still talk about your dad. In a good way. Had some kind of bust up with my boss, way back."

"Mackie, that the name? I remember Dad going off about it. He'll be long gone."

"He's *the* boss now."

"I thought you police retired, after a certain time on the force."

"Mackie was long term seconded to the Scottish Office. Retires next year."

"Well, he's going out with a bang."

Dudek, wary again, "This about the campus shooting or are you trying to put something else together?"

"Are you kidding? Other people are already looking at a crime wave story. Not that the spike is restricted to this area."

"That's what it's called? A spike?"

She ignored the question. "Can I ask you a few more questions about the shooting? The campus shooting, you called it."

Now the pad was coming out.

"I called it that because shots were fired. And it was on campus."

"Right. Are you looking for anybody else in connection with this shooting?"

It was so obvious and yet he hadn't been ready. He wondered how much he'd had the night before.

"We're following up certain lines of enquiry."

"That's all you're going to give me?"

He leaned forward, finding himself wanting to tell her. "To be honest, Hilda, I'm…tell you what, put the pad away."

Now he was wondering if he was still a bit drunk, not sure what was going to come out of his mouth. And there it was again, that unsettling connection, like a taste in the air. The same as when he was marching the kidnapper, Hardy, out of the station, nothing in his head but finding that boy.

She dropped her pad and spread her hands. "Off the record. When my Dad said that, he meant it. And so do I."

"Ok. To be honest, I don't know what happened. We don't have a good witness and the crime scene was a mess. I'm hoping our SoC guy can shed some light, but he's disappearing up his own behind with all we got on, same as the rest of us. Why are you here?"

The question seemed to throw her. "What?"

Dudek's turn to smile. "You're based in London, must have jumped on a plane pretty sharpish for a story that's not all that. We've got locals from the Nationals here already. Gave out a statement last night…"

"I saw you on the TV."

"You did? The point I'm making, why would anyone travel the length of the country for this?"

"I'm not in Scotland for this. But as it's going on…" she shrugged.

They looked at one another. It seemed she had her equilibrium back.

"Look, I've got a feeling about this. I'm not going to print a single word today, but I'll call you tomorrow. How would that be?"

He nodded. Then she said, "Something happens…well, I'd be delighted to hear from you."

Dudek walked her downstairs, standing close for the first time. They bumped hips rounding the corner, but she didn't mention it, talking about Dundee again.

He thought about asking her did she know anyone locally still, friends to call. It felt that it would be okay to say that, the way she kept looking at him with that smile, holding his eyes just a bit longer than you would expect. Maybe make it sound like they might see one another outside of the formal relationship.

He could see George at the desk, staring, but didn't invite an exchange of looks. She smiled one last time at the door and was gone. He turned and trotted up to his office, getting to the window in time to catch her reaching the corner, stepping out of sight.

Nathan came back into the room, looking pleased with himself, and Dudek lifted a new file out of his in-tray, handing it to him before he could say anything.

"Taxi driver reported missing by his wife. Called in a big fare, Edinburgh direction, but never came back. Maybe the big fare didn't want to pay. See what you can find out."

October 1976

Saturday afternoon, and David wandered up to Neil's room to find him looking hung over, a night out with those idiot rugby guys. David had agreed to go out with Neil and the rugby crowd only once, and their ignorance of music was spectacular. That didn't stop them pratting on about it, though.

They were into bashing each other and showing their biceps, like overgrown primary kids, unaware of how deeply uncool the whole muscle thing was. Neil had one particular rugby friend, unimaginatively nicknamed Mick Beard. David had had several thankfully short conversations with him, ending with the guy telling him he was full of shit. This after David had offered his opinion on Mick's great favorites, Hall and Oates.

So, David had spent the night playing poker with a Nigerian called Harold and an Irish guy called Coker. They had gotten through Bowie, Blue Oyster Cult, a six-pack and a quarter-ounce of hash, which they'd smoked without tobacco through Coker's bong, Coker claiming that it gave you a cleaner hit.

"Keepin' it clean, man."

Coker also claimed that penguins were cool, and only took to do with people who immediately saw the innate truth of that, claiming it was a filter to avoid spending time with assholes.

David thought it would be good to put Mick Beard and Coker in the same room, get them talking. If they could understand each other's accents, Coker would very quickly suss him out. He could not imagine Mick thinking that penguins were cool.

They gambled for hours, cross-legged on the floor of David's room, David happy to have them there despite the risk of being caught by Brainiac 5, because he wouldn't have to walk back to his room alone in the early hours.

And anyway, the Brainiac had been largely posted missing.

The later memories of the evening were hazy, but when he checked his pockets next morning, he seemed to be up by almost ten pounds. He made a mental note to watch it, not repeat the troubles of last year.

Now he looked around his friend's room, as Neil rummaged for a pair of clean jeans, and noticed a newspaper.

"What's this? Don't tell me you're going to speak to me about politics, I nearly lost consciousness last time. Having a friend who's a Conservative, it's embarrassing."

"There's a bit about crows."

David picked up the rumpled copy of *The Courier*, reading, *Crow attacks spark outrage. By Jack Jarvis*

He read aloud, "Dundee dog owners demand action after a spate of crow attacks on their pets."

"Why are you reading in an American accent?"

"For added drama. You read about Hector? Who would call a dog Hector? Here's who, Mrs. Agnes Calder. Morose old bat."

"Well, she had to fight them off her spaniel."

"With her walking stick! Brilliant!" He read aloud again. "It was like something from a horror film. Hector wasn't doing anything when suddenly they were on him. He was screaming with fear and I just waded in. If two workmen hadn't been there, I might have been a goner. We've had enough of Council excuses. It's time they got out of their offices and did something for a change!" David tapped the paper. "That's telling them, Mrs. C."

"The expert guy says keep away from trees where crows are nesting till the situation normalizes. How would you even know if there are crows nesting in a tree?"

"Because of all the crows, pecking the fuck out of your head."

"See this bit, 'Instances of crows taking lambs are not unknown, but reports of other birds being killed, including seagulls and cats, appear anomalous.'"

"I'm fairly sure a cat isn't a bird. Too furry."

David wandered to the window and watched crows circling the monkey puzzle. It had been a cold morning of hard sunshine but now the grounds were filling with mist, as they often did, and the big tree looked like it was floating in a milky sea. The river was invisible.

Neil had been rummaging in his bag and now came out with jeans that David hadn't seen since last summer. Neil had painstakingly sewn triangular patches into the bottom sections of the leg, to widen the flare. The patches were mustard velvet, from curtains that David's Mother had been throwing out but had offered to Neil. She even sat by him, helping him sew. At the time, David had been unaccountably irked.

He put a hand up. "You can't wear those."

Neil paused, looking unsure, but also slightly hurt. "Why not?"

"It's 1976. Who do you see wearing those things these days?"

"Why does that matter?"

David was briefly at a loss, not wanting to appear as though he was swayed by fashion. Finally, he said, "Those patchers were always horrible. It just took a while for folk to realize. If you wear them, I'm not walking beside you."

Neil sighed and brought out a pair of standard Levi's. As he pulled himself into them, he said, "I saw that girl you were talking about. The one that dresses like your mum. I mean like a stereotypical mum. Your ma dresses pretty cool for being somebody's mum."

"Hah! You fancy my mom!"

To David's consternation, Neil colored, and he quickly added, "So what did you think of her? I mean the lady-girl."

"She's too…" Neil made angular shapes in the air with his hands, as though trying to get to grips with a section of board.

"Would you screw her, though?"

"Sure. Would you?"

"I'd screw Brainiac 5 if he'd let me. Do you think you can get your virginity back? I think I'm just about there."

Neil, ignoring his friend's claim not to be a virgin, asked, "Know what impresses me about her, though?"

"The way she marches about like it's all about her?"

"No, that's just weird. It's that she doesn't give a shit about what people think. Wears that neat coat and everything, because it just doesn't matter to her. She doesn't want to…what's the expression?"

"Be in Dundee."

Neil blinked. "Where did that come from?"

David, having no idea where it came from, shrugged, and Neil continued. "She doesn't need to conform. And here's me uncomfortable wearing jeans that I thought were the coolest thing a year ago."

They hurried out of the room and down the wide, carpeted stairs, thinking about food and beer. David said, "I always hated those jeans. Even hated them when they were curtains."

They came to the landing and slowed. The spectacularly curvy Irish student, the one with the red hair, was leaning over the elaborate wooden balustrade, looking at the steps below. She was frowning, anxious, and didn't glance their way.

Doctor Bernard, Brainiac 5, stood on the half-landing. A beam of sunlight was slanting across the lower stairs and the man seemed mesmerized by it, or the dust motes that danced and sparkled inside it. Rowland Rankine glared down at him from his huge portrait.

David whispered, "He looks like he's stoned!"

The red haired student turned and they shared a confused look, although David struggled to keep his eyes on her face. He'd seen her around, and heard other boys commenting, but had never been this close. She turned her attention back to the Brainiac.

As far as David knew, Bernard had always been known as Brainiac 5, a relentlessly strange man, strange to talk to and strange to look at. He was short and thin, with a bald head that seemed way too large for his body, too bulbous.

David, describing him to friends, had put his hands inches out from his own head and said, "His bean is enormous. Shines it with Pledge or something."

Neil, as though in defense, "He's not completely bald."

"No, he's got the worst comb over you've ever seen, cos of the distance it has to travel to reach the other side, must be three feet long."

Now, warming to his theme, "And this scrubby little mustache and boggly eyes. He fixes you with them and walks sideways, like this, staring at you and puffing on his mustache like he's trying to inflate it.

"He goes about with his trousers tucked into these huge socks that he pulls right over his knees. Plus bicycle clips, which he never takes off."

Now the girl David thought of as Hockeysticks was climbing the stairs, slowing as she came abreast of Bernard, staring openly. Then she was past, the big redhead laughing loudly as she fell in step with her, the pair of them turning towards the corridor. Hockeysticks didn't return the laugh. Two young guys came barreling up the stairs then, laughing and pushing at each other, till they caught sight of Dr Bernard.

One said, "Whoa!" and stepped right in Brainiac's face, staring.

Neil whispered, "You think maybe he's had some kind of stroke? Some brain thing?"

"Some brain thing. You sure you're a medical student?"

The two guys were moving past Bernard, looking troubled now. Coming to the landing, one asked, "You think he's ok?"

Neil shrugged. "There was nothing like this last year. You didn't mess with him."

David thought the man's skin had an unhealthy tone to it, like wax, and he considered asking Neil what jaundice looked like, but instead found himself following the man's stare, seeing how the last, slanting ray of sun turned dust into a sparkling show. It was, he had to admit, rather beautiful.

In that moment, Brainiac blinked and straightened, looking up at the four students.

"You boys!"

They all jumped.

"What are you doing there?"

They mumbled about just going to their rooms and turned. Neil, following David whispered, "Thought we were going out?"

"We'll go in a few minutes, Jesus."

"He was right into it. Staring at a lovely little sunbeam." Neil made the peace sign. "Far out, man."

David frowned, but didn't comment.

2016

Barry Batterham from SoC was looking tired when Dudek met him the following evening, Barry sitting in Dudek's office, scowling at a sheet of paper, a box of evidence bags on the floor beside him.

"You look like you've been here all day."

"Not far from it, man. I mean Sir."

Dudek sat down opposite him, saying, that was a strange crime scene.

Barry leaned forward in his chair. "I was in London for years, John. Worked more shootings than most SOC's and, usually, it's obvious what's happened. Somebody's had enough and bam, there it is, plain as day."

Dudek let him talk, the man running through what had been in his head all day, knowing he didn't have to tell this stuff to an old hand like Dudek.

"Most crims are thick as shit. Even when they're trying to be clever, they're dumb."

Thinking the man needed to get this out, Dudek nodded. "It looks like we can't catch them, they'll tell somebody. Just to help us out."

"The crime scene…you learn to read it. See where the perp stood when he shot, where the victim was standing, how he fell." Looking up at Dudek now, "This one's fucked up."

Sounding just like Devlin, the armed response officer who looked like he might unload on a bunch of crows.

Barry laid a plan of the shooting on his desk, lines and crosses drawn on it, the positions of cars.

"See, the shooter comes from the corner of the Union, moving across the square. His first shot was here, into the cars, cartridge was found right there." Pointing with his pencil at a blue cross.

"The casualty, the student, couldn't have been hit, because the cars shield her. The one most affected is a Saab. This photo shows the spread of the shot."

"Really got that car, didn't he?"

"Most of the cartridge hit the lower part of the door, the spread blowing its windows out. Guy aimed low for shooting at a person, unless he wanted to hit their legs."

Dudek rubbed his face. "He was running. Maybe he just missed."

"Maybe so. He moves sideways two paces, and shoots again, here." Again, pointing with the pencil.

"He now has line of sight with the girl, but only a single stray pellet hits her. A few pellets, I call them pellets, but they are massive, non-standard, mix of lead and tungsten, hit the back end of this Galaxy."

Dudek took the photo.

Barry continued. "He's aiming higher now. First shot, he hit the Saab low. The Galaxy, he raises his aim. But, here's the thing. Where's the rest of it?"

"Sorry?"

"Look at the Saab. A nice spread of shot, closely bunched in the center."

Dudek was seeing what the man was talking about now. "The distance was the same?"

"Pretty much. The outer edge of the pattern on the Galaxy is clear, so, here's my question. What happened to the main bulk of the shot?"

"You're saying it hit somebody."

"It hit *something*. Something that isn't there now. Here's the next question. It hit a person, where's the blood? The size of those munitions, it would blow your arm off, if it caught your shoulder."

Dudek nodded but didn't say anything and Barry had to ask him, "You got a witness, John?"

"We got one said she saw somebody being hit. Trouble is, she's a nutcase."

"What did she see?"

"The second shot."

Barry sat up straight, this was the one he was interested in. "She said somebody got hit? Where?"

Dudek reluctantly pointed to the spot Wendy Lawrence had marked for him, immediately in front of the Galaxy.

Barry took a long breath. "You sure she's nuts?"

Then he said, "The third shot was wilder, straight into the sky. Christ knows what he thought he was shooting at. A crow maybe."

Meant as a joke, but Dudek didn't laugh. "So, no evidence that anybody got hit?"

Barry produced four evidence bags containing cloth fragments.

"This is from the second shot. Threads from what looks like tweed and silk. But no blood or anything, so it could have been a rag, a bit of cloth lying on the ground."

"A tweed rag, with silk lining."

"I'm telling you what we found."

Now he produced a close up of the interior of the Galaxy, a hole in the head rest.

"We dug a ball out of here. It had fiber on it that's being checked now, but I'll bet it was the same stuff, the tweed."

"What are you saying?"

"It couldn't have been lying on the ground."

Dudek looked away, came back. "Could it have been wrapped around the muzzle?"

Barry shook his head. "Not without it being scorched. What else did the woman, your nutcase witness, say?"

Dudek was thinking about what Wendy Lawrence had said about bulky clothes, and asked, "What if the guy was wearing a vest?"

"Unless he had proper armor, not just a vest, there'd be blood."

"Our witness said his clothes looked too large for him. I'm wondering could he have been wearing protection under there?"

Barry nodded, apparently thinking about how that could work. "You ever hear of anything like that?"

Dudek shook his head, thinking he should call Lawrence. Ask her again what she saw.

Barry was still talking, saying that this was where it gets really weird.

"The fourth shot went into the guy's mouth, same position as the third. Maybe a pace to the side."

"The same gun fired all six cartridges? We know that for sure?"

"We do, yeah. And we know the last three all hit our man."

"Who did the shooting, is the question."

"I'm getting to that. Shot four goes in his mouth, I talked to Doc Wright. Doc says, yeah, the killing shot went inside, with the mouth open. Scorching, soft tissue blown away, teeth shattered. I asked could Kerr have been able somehow to keep moving, still be alive. What he said, sometimes they say death is instantaneous when it isn't exactly. In this case, it was instantaneous. Back of his head was blown clean off."

"Ok, so Kerr fires three times then turns the gun. Commits suicide."

"Yeah. The killing shot happened right here, you could see the spray perfectly, and he falls backwards." Pointing at the map, the photos getting messier. Dudek had a sudden image of the crow, a piece of Neil Kerr's head in its beak.

"You ok, John?"

"Me? Sure."

He looked at Dudek for a long moment. "Sorry, I know you of all people need this like a hole in the head. No pun intended."

Barry had worked the cellar on the Hardy kidnap case. Now it seemed like he was working up to something.

"I never said this at the time, but whatever you did to that shitebag to find the kid. Well, that's just fine with me."

He caught the way Dudek was looking at him and put his hand up. "Sorry, Sir. Out of line. This whole thing has shaken me up. Brought me right back there, somehow."

Dudek had been about to speak but that quietened him. Somebody else feeling some kind of link with that time. But he would bet that Barry couldn't *taste* it.

Batterham pointed at another photo.

"There's this bloody handprint now. His own handprint, as it happens. In a position consistent with a guy getting up from lying down, where the killing shot occurred. There was a lot of weight on that hand."

Barry was looking at Dudek, as if expecting him to say, you're shitting me. Dudek kept his eyes on the map.

Barry said, "The next shot is back and to the left. The spray goes over the cobbles, indicative of Kerr being shot point blank in the throat." He paused. "Whilst standing."

"Or held up."

"Or held up. You notice his hand, the left one?"

"What about it?"

"The tip of the thumb was gone."

Dudek shook his head, surprised he hadn't noticed.

"Doc Wright finds the guy's thumb, what's left of it, in his throat. His left hand must've been around the muzzle when the gun went off."

"You're saying he shot himself twice? Once after he was dead? Stood up to do it?" Thinking now about what the journalist, Hilda Jarvis, had said to him earlier.

"I'm just giving you facts. The third shot is here, a couple of yards back."

"Where we found him."

"Yeah. This time the shot goes through his chest and cracks the cobbles underneath. So, he was on his feet for the first two shots, and lying down for the third."

"And that was the end."

Barry took a breath, as though he had to make himself say it. "Not quite. He racks the gun." He stopped, caught himself and started again, "The gun *gets* racked. Remember there were six shells on the ground. They only get expelled when you rack the thing, loading the next cartridge."

Dudek finished for him. "Only there was no next cartridge."

The two men were silent, Dudek thinking that if there had been more shells in the gun there would have been more shots, the body in an even worse mess.

He said, "You see where this is leading us?"

"What it looks like, the guy shot himself three times. Twice after he was dead."

The same words that Hilda Jarvis had used.

Barry waved a hand at the photographs. "Or somebody picked him up after he was dead, held the gun to his throat, and shot him. Then shot him again in the chest on the ground. You, me and your big Nathan could just about manage that, but it would be a right fucking pantomime."

When Dudek didn't speak, he finished with, "What I'm saying, there are two explanations for this, I can think of. Neither of them possible."

Dudek leaned forward. "Then there's another one out there, Barry. 'Cause the guy was shot three times. And he didn't do it himself."

Barry made a face. Dudek shook it all out of his head, for the moment trying to concentrate on the possibility of someone out there wearing combat body armor.

September 1976

Neil and David had been friends since starting school, so Neil knew a lot about his friend, including the fact that there was something different about him that he didn't want mentioned. This despite, in Neil's opinion, it being seriously cool.

Mostly it was an unconscious thing. Neil had first noticed it one day in class, the boys at this time in second year of high school. Mr. McGoldrick, their English teacher, had handed out sheets of text and David immediately started writing.

McGoldrick, a sarcastic prick of a man, came to a melodramatic stop in front of David, the only person in the room not noticing. Then, even he picked up on the silence and looked up. McGoldrick said, "You don't actually need to listen to know what to do, Haddow?"

One long, aggressive step and he whipped the page away. Then, his face changed.

David was at a loss to explain how he had known to underline all the similes in the text. He was even hazy about what a simile was. McGoldrick was furious but, Neil could see, simply didn't understand what had just happened.

After that, Neil started looking for it. It was always small things. David would walk to a telephone before it rang, and sometimes answered Neil before the question was asked. Neil learned not to play cards with him. Especially for money.

He tried talking about it, resulting in their only major falling out. Neil struggled to understand. If he had had some kind of ability; prescience, telepathy, whatever it was, he would have been delighted.

In their first year at university, though, David had become obsessed with poker, and found several serious card games. He would sometimes play until the early hours, winning steadily. The bets were small, but they mounted up and eventually the whole thing turned sour when two biology students claimed he was a cheat and punches were thrown.

Neil understood how they got there. David, despite playing a lot, wasn't *good* at poker. Neil would watch some of the things he did with bafflement. It was clear that he paid little attention to what others were doing, not applying himself to anything but improving his own hand, and that through blind luck.

But he knew what to bet.

Towards the end of last term, Neil had felt he and David were drifting apart. Neil had his first serious girlfriend, Natalie, a truly gorgeous girl from Manchester. David didn't insult her, or blank her, he just...Neil thought it over. It was like David hardly knew she existed. Over the summer Neil got the call, telling him that she was dropping out and it crossed his mind that part of her decision had to do with David, but surely nobody would drop out because their boyfriend's pal made them uncomfortable. It wasn't as if David ever *did* anything.

Neil had really liked Natalie, she made him laugh and got him randy as hell. But he didn't love her. This had been his third relationship, the most serious by far, and he'd come to the uncomfortable conclusion that either the romantic love thing was bullshit or he had something missing. He could go along with it, liking the look in Natalie's eyes when he told her he loved her. That was as far as it went.

Natalie was only part of why the boys seemed to be drifting. David's measure of someone was based firstly on, did they smoke dope. If they smoked, he might be interested in them, if not, they were straights and not to be dealt with.

Secondly, they had to be into music he thought was cool, and that was where the real trouble started. Most of David's money went on records. In his room in Rankine Hall, he had a smaller, but still impressive, collection and the most expensive hi-fi system he could afford.

David's albums were lined up in an order he clearly understood, but could not explain, even when asked. The first three albums on the left were Nick Drake's. That was easy, because they had been David's favorites for some time. Then it was John Martyn. Ok, both on Island Records. But then it was David Bowie.

He carried albums wherever we went. If somebody reacted, that was somebody he might be interested in. Sometimes, their reaction might be to ask did he like Supertramp or The Who. David would not be interested in anyone who liked Supertramp or The Who, making a special allowance only for Neil.

As for Neil's rugby friend Mick Beard, David suspected him of liking Leo Sayer. There would be no special dispensation for Mick.

2016

Dudek had known Mackie since he had come to Dundee from Somerset, nearly fifteen years, and his relationship was as easy as anybody's was with the man. He had been surprisingly supportive after the Hardy hearing, telling Dudek that, back in the day, he'd have gotten a commendation, not a written warning. And that he should have just dropped the bastard.

When Dudek said he hadn't hung him off anything, had been cleared of that, Mackie just winked.

"Should've dropped him anyway."

The man had a way of holding himself, walking right into your space, that had earned him a lot of nicknames over the years, but the one that stuck was Shrek. Arms stiffly out by his side as though he was a body builder, which he wasn't, he took slow deliberate steps, body rocking forwards with each one.

Mackie smiled almost constantly, but it didn't make him appear genial. It was unsettling. He was smiling as Dudek knocked and entered his office.

"Five minutes, Sir?"

Mackie's desk was impressively shambolic. He dropped some new papers on top of the pile and winked.

"I'll get chased about them later. I hear you broke this Mullins thing?"

Dudek sat. "You know how, it looks like somebody did it, well, they did it? I was thinking, this time it has to be different. Blindingly obvious clues all around the guy's house, and he's on holiday. But I get Peter Mullins in the interview room and he says, straight off the bat, Nicholas should never have said that about Kylie."

"Kylie Minogue?"

"Yeah. Guy's a heavy-duty Kylie fan. You remember that video, for the song 'Spinning Around'?"

"Where she wears the gold pants?"

"That's it. Nicholas tells him that wasn't Kylie's own ass. It's a body double. Won't let it go. So, he goes home, makes a garrote out of a trowel and a guitar string, kills his brother, then goes on holiday."

"He's admitted to this under caution?"

"Sir."

"What does he do for a living?"

"Social worker."

"Jesus. Copping for insanity?"

"We're having him assessed, but no. He and his brother were close. Then, bang, he hates him. I mean really, really hates him."

"Press?"

"Later today."

Mackie tutted. "Should've retired last year. Can you believe this? I'm presiding over the worst year since seventy fucking six. This shooting?"

"Shooter was a Neil Kerr. Only previous is a caution for possession, back in '76, actually."

Mackie's expression didn't change. "Local lad?"

"From your home town, originally, Aberdeen. Was at the university here. Not sure yet where he's been since, but he's not come to the notice of the Police. Came back last year. I'm meeting his landlord this afternoon."

"Who was he shooting at? Not the girl?"

"She was hit accidentally, we're sure, might end up with a little scar on her leg and that's it. The picture is confused, but we don't have a specific target at this point,"

"Shooting at someone *in* a car, maybe?"

"We just don't know."

Mackie's smile, if it was a smile, compressed as he considered this.

"Gun?"

"Illegal import, heavy-duty, with heavy-duty shells. We're having a tougher time putting together what happened to Kerr."

Mackie's expression was flat. "He shot himself."

"It's not as simple as that, boss. He was shot three times."

"You're saying *was* shot. Like someone else did it."

Mackie was smiling hard. Dudek ducked it for the moment, saying, "We'll work it out."

"You better. Saw you on the box, by the way. You pass that by comms?"

"Wasn't time, Sir. Had to be done there and then or Christ knows what they were going to make up."

"I want all press stuff through comms. Thought I'd made that clear."

"It was ten at night and they were getting pretty pissed off. It was a campus shooting."

"One guy tops himself. End of. Enough of this grandstanding shit, especially you, after Hang-the-man Hardy. Press are making it sound like he was shot after he was dead.

Shot *himself* after he was dead. You won't survive another public screw up, John."

"Sir."

Then Dudek said, "Neil Kerr. It was you who gave him his caution."

"Me? What for?"

"Possession. LSD."

"Sounds like I should have done the little bastard. Enough of this caution shit."

"There was something else going on, I mean that he was involved in. A memo from you to somebody called Stephens."

Mackie laughed. A strange bark that didn't involve the rest of his face.

"What a guy he was, always getting into it with you. Great big nose on him, purple."

"I got the memo here, you want to see it."

Mackie put his hand out, reading it without any change of expression.

"Do you remember what that was all about, Sir?"

"Funny seeing some letter you wrote, this long ago."

Mackie's eyes swept back and forth.

"Students breaking into an old factory, getting stoned. One of them disappears someplace, and an old body gets found in the search. Heart attack. Typical Stephens, trying to link it all up."

"You don't remember Kerr, then?"

"You remember everybody you ever cautioned?"

"This is a big guy. Six-four, plus."

Mackie shook his head. "Look, just get this bottomed out, fast. We want to show this is a lone nutcase that shot himself. Once. Press onto to the hurt girl yet?"

"Probably."

"They're bound to have photos of her, with that long-suffering expression. My Shotgun Hell. Let's hope she's not pretty."

"Sir."

"Know what this puts me in mind of? Moore, your old boss. That was…well, you know what it was better than anybody. All the shit I've seen on the job, that has to be the worst. Moore, Jesus. Guy like that, who would've thought it?"

Dudek knew he hadn't kept the surprise from his face, having had the same thought himself, but Mackie didn't notice. He was looking away, thinking hard. He turned back to point a blunt finger at Dudek. "That was Kylie's ass in that video. No question."

September 1976

David settled in for another hour of Psychology and there was Angela Murray beside the loud Irish redhead. Angela's hair was neat as ever, her shirt, an actual blouse, ironed. Feeling her about to turn, he focused on his notes, but knew the exact moment her eyes landed on him.

At the end of the lecture, Dr Phillips asked would anybody be interested in helping out with experiments, making a joke about not wiring anybody up to the mains. Simple tests, a whole pound on offer.

David had taken part in one last year, involving pressing buttons in response to colored lights, repeating the task wearing headphones playing white noise, which made no difference. Then the white noise was replaced by one of those K-Tel records where every bit of inspiration that might have inadvertently snuck into a chart song was wrung out; an affront to any music lover. David deliberately made mistakes in protest. Maybe it would lead to the banning of K-Tel on the grounds it turned people into morons.

Now, hoping for another opportunity to strike a blow against the homogenization of music, he joined the queue. Looking around, his eyes met Angela's, so they were looking right at each other for the first time since that first day, in the library. He quickly turned away.

2016

The old tenement seemed in good shape, its muddy stone made only slightly darker by that morning's rain. Nathan led the way to the topmost floor and paused, holding the keys the landlord had given him.

"No nameplate."

When Dudek just shrugged, he unlocked quickly and nudged the door open to see a long hallway, catching a whiff of furniture polish. They stepped inside, careful not to disturb anything.

The hall was carpeted and clean, with a long black coat hanging on a hook along with a waterproof, also in black.

Dudek. "Guy liked black."

Dudek pushed the first door on the right to show a good-sized bedroom, clean and simply furnished.

"He was neat. Neat and tidy."

They walked into the room, two large men being careful not to knock anything over. There was no art, or ornaments, apart from a nappy red velour heart, pinned to the wall by its fraying cord. Dudek stared at it for several long seconds, frowning, but didn't comment. The dresser beneath was almost bare, but Nathan pointed to a tobacco tin, Old Virginia.

"Here we go. Weed, you think?"

Dudek shook his head, nah.

Nathan picked it up and prized it open, but, infuriatingly, Dudek was right.

"Red feathers!"

Dudek looked at them, then raised his again eyes to the velour heart, and Nathan wondered what was going through his head. He waited, but if his boss had any thoughts, he wasn't sharing.

In the kitchen everything was exceptionally clean. The fridge held vegetables and there was a bowl full of fruit. One bottle of Malbec.

"Took care of himself." Said Dudek, "Expensive tastes."

The next room was the living room, which held a Bose music system, a large television and two leather couches. Dudek walked to a shelfing unit to look at a line of vinyl records.

"Ever heard of this guy? Nick Drake?" He flicked the first few albums. "John Martyn?"

Nathan shook his head, bending to look at a bookcase.

"Some of the titles here. *The Necronomicon. Magickal Attack. A History of Celtic Faeries.*"

Dudek joined him. "All by mainstream publishers. You can probably buy them from Amazon."

He looked around the room again.

"This could be anybody's house. Apart from a few books that are a bit on the odd side, and everybody has some odd to them."

"I'd have a place something like this, if I wasn't married. Minimalist."

Dudek turned. "Really?"

"It's women that like stuff. And kids, Jesus, the crap that comes with them."

Dudek shook his head. "You must've married young."

"Sue was my girlfriend at school. When she fell pregnant with Debbie, we just got hitched."

Dudek came back to the line of records. "These don't fit."

Nathan, beginning to understand how Dudek got his rep and wanting to understand how he did it, asked, "How so?"

"It's like they're..." He hesitated. "...not his."

Nathan thought hard, but couldn't see where he had got that from. Finally, he said, "They're just records."

Dudek turned away, seemingly dismissing them. But then he said, "There's nothing to play them on."

Nathan looked around, surprised to find that was true. No turntable. He remembered what Barry had said. If you're smart, you'll watch and learn, Nathan. You landed lucky with John D. Mostly he felt he'd landed anything but lucky, saddled with an unreliable and unpredictable boss. Damaged goods.

There was one other item of furniture, a desk. Dudek slid open the top drawer and leafed through papers.

"He wasn't poor, our boy."

"Yeah?"

Dudek sat down, reading.

"Seems he had a good-sized building firm, right down south. Brighton. Sold out a couple of years back."

He turned to Nathan, frowning. "Think about that. A successful businessman, living about as far away from Dundee as you can get without going abroad. Sells up. Comes here. Then…"

He left the sentence unfinished and stood. The last room was another bedroom, but it didn't have a bed in it. The walls were covered in building drawings and photographs. A rifle on one wall, with a telescopic sight.

The detectives walked into the center of the room, not touching anything. Nathan pointed.

"Scuba gear, look."

Dudek squinted at the rifle.

"Ruger, a hunting rifle. You think he was a sports marksman? A hunter maybe, you see him shooting deer?"

He was looking right at Nathan, seemingly wanting to hear what he thought. Nathan found he wanted to impress the guy, show he could make connections too.

"We've not seen any clothes that would fit that. Doesn't strike me as the outdoors type. No gun license."

Dudek seemed satisfied. "What does this place, this room feel like to you?"

"An operations room."

"Right."

"You think we should get out of here? Call in Counter Terrorism?"

Dudek looked around, thinking.

"If he has C4, something like that, where would it be?"

"The fridge."

"Right. It wasn't there."

Nathan stood in the middle of the room, looking at a large architect's drawing tacked to the wall, an industrial building, but old. Beside it was a map of Dundee, marked with lines, radiating from a central red dot, a hub North-West of the city center, not far from where the man shot himself. Each line ended in a cross, and beside each cross, a brown envelope had been pinned.

Nathan took another step closer, aware of Dudek on his shoulder. He placed his finger on the red dot. "This seems like the center of whatever he was looking at. All those lines coming out of it. Likes spokes."

Dudek nodded. "You know where that is. The site of the old building they're redeveloping, where all the road works are. The Coffin Mill? No, the other one, the Tombstone Mill."

"The factory from Mackie's memo."

Dudek's eyes widened. "Shit."

Then he said, "We're not dealing with a terrorist, are we?"

"No."

Nathan followed a line with his finger, tracing it from the central red dot to a cross.

"Student's Union, boss."

Dudek lifted an envelope that was pinned to the wall beside the Union, revealing a photograph. It seemed that the only function of the envelope was to act like a flap, covering the image.

Nathan said, "Just a photo of the Union. Looks like it was taken in the dark, some fancy film or something."

Dudek didn't look happy. "What does it *show*, though?"

"The building. That's all I can see."

Dudek stepped away, letting the envelope drop back over the image and massaging his temple, like something in there hurt. "Let's see the others first."

All the photographs were of places in Dundee. One, beside a cross marking a site in Perth Road, was of a once grand old house with a white pillared portico, now boarded up. Beside it was another photo, this time of a monkey puzzle tree.

The images had all been taken in darkness, none having any detail that struck Nathan as important, although Dudek clearly thought them significant. The man looked anxious, even unwell. Nathan had caught the smell when they were leaning over together, wondered now if he maybe kept a bottle in his desk.

Dudek rubbed his face hard, sounding frustrated. "What are we looking at here?"

"Just sites around Dundee."

"In different seasons, but always at night. So, he's been doing this, whatever it is, for at least a year. Maybe the student, Morag, saw him take that exact one of the Union. What connects them, though?"

It felt like the man really wanted to hear what Nathan thought. Nathan put his finger again on the central hub, marked in red. "The Tombstone Mill. All the lines converge there."

Dudek stepped away, looking gray.

"Ok. Check these places out as soon as. Confirm that's where the photos were taken."

He pointed to the two envelopes, covering photographs at the Perth Road site. "Starting here. The derelict mansion."

As they walked down the stairs, Dudek suddenly stalled. "What were the envelopes for, though? Why cover the photographs up?"

Nathan shrugged. "So nobody could see them."

"There was a hunting rifle, right there on the wall."

"Maybe he just didn't like looking at them."

Dudek thought about that. "I didn't like looking at them either."

October 1976

Sunday morning was sunny and barely cold, even before eight, when Neil jogged from the sleeping Halls, nursing a slight hangover. He returned just after nine, steam rising from his shoulders, and it seemed the building had hardly stirred.

A lot of people in there would be struggling with hangovers of their own, he knew. For many of them it would turn into a lifelong routine.

Neil was fifteen before he realized his father was an alcoholic. The thing was, the guy never seemed drunk. He just got slower, drinking steadily in front of the Rockford Files or the Waltons, this despite his unexplained hatred of John-boy, till he fell asleep.

Neil's earliest solid memory was of the front door opening and this titanic man, darkly uniformed, filling the doorway. In this early recollection, his father was bursting out of his shirt collar, like he would be years later. Neil could see from photographs that wasn't so. They showed a man who was powerfully athletic. In Neil's memory, he was round. Not soft, though, hard, his stomach taut like a drum. The memory was branded in by fear. He turned to run, his mother shouting, her voice reedy. "It's just Daddy, Neelie Pie!"

Then he was in the air, held so his hair touched the ceiling and he was looking down in terror at the massive, grinning face of his father.

There were other memories that blended into a feeling of enormous mass and noisy breathing, a brooding presence to be tiptoed round. As for the smell, it was a long time before he learned that it belonged to whisky.

School was an escape and Neil liked it from the start. He would show his mother his results and she would hug him and tell him how proud she was, that when his father came home, they might show him too.

Sometimes that happened. Sometimes his father would clap him between the shoulder blades with a hand the size of his whole back. More often, his mother would scuttle to get food on the table and Neil would get himself quietly upstairs, taking Rachel with him.

That was his normal. Even now, he could not find it in himself to call it strange.

He showered and settled down with a text book, Bohemian Rhapsody low in the background. Roxy Music had replaced Queen before David appeared, wearing the same clothes as the previous evening. Even his face looked rumpled.

"Need beer."

"You look like you need a wash."

"It's a beer emergency."

"What about breakfast?"

"Crisps can be bought in beer places. Laing's."

Neil sighed. "You're going to be flat broke by January."

"Played cards till late. Have money."

"For beer?"

David nodded. "Beer."

David said almost nothing else until they were sitting in Laing's with pints of lager before them. He took a long swallow, then said, "You know. Beer is often a great disappointment."

Neil threw his hands up. "See you!"

"What?"

"I've no rugby today and I was about to get myself a massive fry up. Maybe go to the movies."

"What's on?"

"Too late, I don't like the movies when I've got a drink on me."

David rolled his eyes at this, but stayed quiet. Sipped his beer.

"Who were you playing cards with?"

"The guy with the Honda 750."

"You're going to end up in trouble again."

David had taken another long swallow of his lager. "That's better. You've just got to stay with it, when it comes to drinking beer. Be dogged. Determined."

"I scored last night. That boy with the weird nose had some Lebanese."

"You should've said before we came out!"

"You said it was a beer emergency."

"Well, that's true. And would you look at that? I've finished my beer."

"And you'd like another."

"I think that would be the wise choice. Then we can repair to the smoking room and do something about that impudent Lebanese."

After their second beer, they had a third. When they left, David said, "I'm sloshed, you know."

"Yeah, I do know."

"Three pints and I'm hardly even walking straight, look!"

"Your mum would be proud. I think that's what happens when you have beer for breakfast."

David slapped his forehead. "We forgot the crisps!" Now he looked into the cold blue sky. "Hey, look at that. It's like high summer."

"Yeah, let's not spend all day inside eh?"

"I was hoping we were going to smoke some dope."

"Let's go to Brainiac's hidey hole."

"Perfect!"

The previous year they had noticed Brainiac 5 crossing from the campus onto the grass opposite and watched him disappear. Investigating, they found steps leading down through thick bushes to a secluded space overlooking railway sidings and the river, just enough for two benches. The Brainiac was sitting, eating what looked like a cabbage sandwich.

He frowned. "What are you doing here?"

"Just messing about."

"Messing about is your specialty, Mr. Haddow. Are you following me?"

"No!"

"Well, how did you come upon this spot then?"

"It's not a secret, is it?"

Brainiac was glaring at them, his jaws working noisily.

Neil. "We wondered what was here, that's all. We'll leave you to it."

"Do that. This spot is quiet, yet it's just opposite the University." He pointed a warning finger. "I would be furious if it became filled with milling students."

Now, walking down the steps, David said, "Can you believe he thought that, if students found out about this place, we'd all be crammed in here."

"Well, it's a fine thing for a student to have. His own bench."

"And bushes. Students like a good solid bush."

"It's a wonder we can squeeze in."

As expected, they were alone. The sun was very nearly warm on their faces as they sat on the bench while Neil rolled a joint. For a while they smoked, neither boy speaking as they watched the river, a glistening metallic blue today. Then David said, "Good stuff, man. Really good."

"You know, you only call me 'man' when you're smoking a j."

"So what?"

"So, that proves you're an asshole."

David doubled over, giggling, joined quickly by Neil. The laughing jag lasted for several minutes, with David several times managing to say no more than, "You're a..." before doubling back over.

Suddenly, as though a switch had been flicked, David straightened and sobered. He flicked the remains of their second joint far into the bushes below. "The dope!"

"What?"

"Dump it."

Neil's expression changed, and he dug the little foil lump out of his pocket, throwing it well down into the bushes.

The boys looked at each other as seconds ticked by. A minute. Two. Finally, exasperated, Neil threw his hands in the air. "That cost me eight pounds!"

The voice, when it came, came from above.

"Alright boys, what's going on here?"

They looked up, but a uniformed policeman was already at the foot of the steps, casting around him. Behind him came the owner of the voice, in a gray Mackintosh. Neil felt a jolt of fear, recognizing him.

The man pointed, "I know you two, don't I? Came across you, where was it, outside the Howff? We bust ten junkies that day. You were lucky, though, eh? Either not scored yet or..." He left the sentence unfinished.

David and Neil glanced at each other. The man sniffed the air.

"That's pungent, lads. Don't think you're going to be so fuckin' lucky today. Remind me, what's your names?"

As the boys mumbled their names, both policemen were searching the area. The uniform said, "Can't see anything, Mac. Search them?"

The other man had walked right up to the boys. He was shorter than David, but there was something imposing about him, the way his chin jutted out at you. He moved in front of Neil, who stood docile, not giving him an excuse. The boys remembered that day, how he clubbed a little hippy guy with his fist, just for speaking when he hadn't been spoken to.

And this place was a lot less public than the Howff bar.

"Empty your pockets."

Once the contents of their pockets were spread on the bench, the uniform frisked them, being none too gentle about it.

"Nothing."

Mackie picked up Neil's packet of Rizlas, the cover ripped to make roaches for joints. He flicked the torn edge back and forward with his thumb.

"Reminds me of that day." He fixed them with his mean, piggy eyes. "I can understand that once. Everybody gets lucky. But this place was stinking of dope when we got here. You never had a chance to throw anything away. So, where is it?"

David replied, "Really, Sergeant. We don't have any."

"Detective constable, actually. Mackie, in case you've forgotten."

Mackie hit David in the stomach, making him double over, gasping for breath.

He turned to Neil. "Thinking of doing something about that, big fella? Go on, take a pop. We won't do you for it, will we Alex?"

The other policeman smiled. "Nah, we're all men here. Let's see what you've got."

Neil stood frozen, his face tight. David caught his eye and shook his head.

Mackie said, "Something is going on with you two. And you know what? You'll do something stupid and we'll meet again. Haddow and Kerr." He tapped his temple with a blunt finger. "You're filed away."

Once he had left, David slumped on the bench, getting his breath back. "Let's never meet that guy again."

2016

Nathan pulled off the road in front a pair of tall cast iron gates, chained and locked. An ornate shield carved into the stone post, weathered but still clear, told him this was Rankine Hall.

There were no pedestrians in sight, the only noise being crows and the occasional passing car. Nathan walked along the high wall to a side street, eventually doubling back down a service lane running along the rear. The wall on this side was lower, hardly above his head.

With nobody in sight, he clambered over, dropping into an overgrown border. He stood, brushing dust from himself, but was brought to a halt by his first sight of the house.

Rankine Hall was huge, a bona fide mansion, now falling into decay, its extravagant peaked roof sagging badly, and its many windows boarded. The sky teemed with noisy crows and, as Nathan watched, one flapped into a gap in the slates.

He walked through thigh-high grass and nettles, passing the house to come level with a tree, surely the monkey-puzzle from Kerr's photograph. Here too was the white pillared portico. So, job done; this was the house in the photograph.

Ignoring the crows, Nathan walked towards the portico, finding the front door secured by a bolt and padlock. The padlock, heavy duty as it was, lay open.

Nathan knew he could walk away now, but instead slid the bolt free, letting the door creak open to show a large, dark space, smelling strongly of damp. Slipping a pencil flashlight from his pocket he stepped inside.

The hallway was huge, like everything else, deeply cold, and, if a place could be said to be darker than it had any business being, this was it. The floor, pink marble, was under a lot of dust, but heavily tracked by footsteps. He walked on, until his tiny light found a wide stairway. The footprints led there, going to and fro. Shivering, he played his beam, picking out an incongruous line of dusty plastic domes that, after a moment's thought, he recognized as old-style telephone booths.

There was no reason to check this place out further, he told himself. Whoever had made these tracks, it wasn't Kerr. They were way too small. Still, he picked his way to a side door, which he opened. He hadn't known that he had been creeping until the sound of the hinges made him dip, like he was ducking a blow. The creak reverberated in the silence, so like an old school horror it was very nearly comical. But Nathan didn't laugh, instead he froze, breath pluming.

He had to admit it to himself now, because it was obvious; he was scared. Dry mouth, check. Goosebumps, heart racing; check. Hair now rising on his scalp. He had been apprehensive since the first moment he set eyes on the place and, even though he had no need to enter it, he'd done so as a sort of dare to himself.

A detective in a creepy old house and he might as well be ten years old.

After several seconds of hearing only his own booming heart, he looked into the room, seeing narrow couches facing an ancient TV set, other utilitarian furniture at odds with the grandness of the place.

He backed up, but didn't close the door, not wanting to repeat that horrible creak, and walked quietly to the stairs, finding his light reflected off a dusty Perspex sheet, screwed to the wall on landing, covering some kind of painting.

Nathan wondered if his battery was giving out. The beam, pathetic to begin with, was struggling in all this darkness. It occurred to him then that only those things directly in its shaky line had any light on them at all. That he himself stood in total darkness and, behind him, it was absolute. The front door was almost closed, showing only a fuzzy line of sunlight.

He took a breath, deliberately recovering himself, then put his foot on the first step in the same moment that, high above, a heavy thump broke the silence. His heart speeded instantly, so fast now. He listened, playing the tiny beam upwards. Another bump, deep and dull and surely nearer, followed by a long, rattling rustle. He opened his mouth to call out, Police! Who's there?

He didn't call. Instead, he backed up, keeping the beam on the stairs. A series of rapid thumps now, closer still, and his light suddenly caught flickering movement, slick and shiny. He heard himself gasp out loud as his beam found a crow on the half landing, head cocked, looking at him.

He and the crow stared at each other for a few breathless seconds, before another bump, much heavier than any bird could make, made the beam jump and jitter. It was close now, maybe on the stairs above the landing, and Nathan backed up fast, finally giving in and turning to full-out run. He burst through the door and skittered into the sunshine before turning to look. See if anything followed.

Even with the door wide, it was so dark in there he could barely see the first few feet. He waited, angry at himself, embarrassed and feeling ridiculous. His heart, though, still boomed, high and painful in his throat.

He gave it another minute, thinking again about calling out, Police, but even in the sun he couldn't bring himself to. Instead, he stalked off, giving the house a wide berth as he retraced his steps.

At the wall, he shaded his eyes to look at Rankine Hall again. An overgrown Addams family house, boarded, rotten and surrounded by crows. As he watched, a crow flapped lazily out of a hole in the roof and perched on the gutter. Maybe the same one, because it seemed to be looking at him.

October 1976

David pulled his Afghan coat tighter as he crossed the dark and windy parking lot. This was the sort of cold where David's Gran would say, with some relish, "It would freeze the face off you."

A crow landed noisily on the roof of a nearby Ford Anglia and he edged away, hurrying towards the psychology block, an ugly cube of glass and concrete. Inside, he could see rooms harshly lit, students hunched over desks.

People were already in the hall when he entered, three from his psychology class and two guys with trimmed beards. Of the three from his group, two stood, heads together, sniggering. The third was Angela Murray, and she stood well apart, wearing an actual raincoat, belted tight around her tiny waist. The other two, he knew now, had been sniggering about her.

One of them, a boy who always looked as though he had been recently electrocuted, nodded to David and raised his eyebrows into his crazy hair. An invitation to join him and his dishwater companion. David felt a vague irritation at them, for no reason he could pin down, so just nodded and stayed where he was.

A young man in lab coat and trainers, a postgrad surely, hurried down the stairs, stopping to look around with a distinctly unimpressed expression.

"You'll be our volunteers then? Amazing what the offer of cash will do."

He raised his clipboard and started calling out names, his voice pointedly bored. David was first, and he answered 'here', as did both the bearded students. When it came to the electrocuted boy, who turned out to be called Keith Chesterman, he raised his hand.

It was clear the postgrad had seen him, he was three feet away, but he called again, putting some real into it. Chesterman went red, and said, "Here."

After he called Angela Murray, he waited, pen hovering. David looked at her, but she just stood there. The postgrad did the same trick, calling her name louder and with annoyance. Angela, the only female in the hallway, remained silent.

Now the man looked up, straight at her, and she just looked back, no expression on her face at all. He blew his cheeks out with exasperation and pointed his pen at her. "*Angela Murray?*"

She continued to look at him, her expression flat and now it was he who was going red. Finally, in an absolute matter of fact tone, she said, "Don't be rude."

The man was stunned. "Don't *what?*"

Again, she simply didn't answer. He closed his eyes, making a big deal out of showing he was calming himself. Then he opened them and asked, "Are you Angela Murray?"

The habitual, hard smile appeared. "Yes, I am."

"Right!" He slapped the pen into the clipboard and turned, shaking his head. "Follow me."

The other four fell into line, ascending the stairs, and David found himself eye to eye with Angela. They stared at each other for a few beats, then she was past him, climbing the stairs to a long, narrow room that smelled of pine cleaner. On one side, windows looked onto the brightly lit Union and darker parking lot. The opposite wall held a long work bench, separated by room dividers into six simple booths.

In each booth sat a chair facing a console similar to the one David had used before; a wooden box with colored buttons. The postgrad said, "This is a very simple test. You will sit in a booth. You will not be able to see each other. Do *not* speak during the test."

He pointed to one of the consuls. "Gather around."

Once they had bunched up, David found he was acutely aware of Angela, inches to his right.

"You can see there are four colored buttons; red, blue, green and yellow. You will hear a tone like this, Jerry?"

From inside a small cubicle, there was a loud beep.

"Each time you hear a beep, press a button."

Chesterman leaned closer. "How do we know which one to press?"

"Your choice. Choose at random, but press once only."

Angela asked, "What is this for?"

"We are doing a series of experiments but need a control, to show the range of natural coincidence arising from random choices. We will be comparing how frequently you choose the same color as the master, with how often mathematical probability suggests you will.

"But all you need to know is; you hear a beep, you press a button. Every ten seconds. Do not choose the same color every time. Do not press the button more than once. Are we clear?"

David asked, "How long will this take?"

"As long as it takes to make 250 choices. We are paying you, remember."

Angela turned to David. "Forty-two minutes."

The postgrad frowned and pointed at a seat, "Sit here Miss Murray, next Mr. Chesterman, Mr. Haddow, Mr. Dobson..."

Sitting in the booth, David examined the consul. It was a small wooden box, with buttons painted with what looked like nail varnish. Wires coiled from the side and the whole thing had a distinctly homemade look to it. David wondered if Chesterman got his electrocuted look from pressing buttons in this place.

A minute later the postgrad said, "Ok, we're going to check first that button pressing is within your capabilities. When you hear a beep, press your red button."

Beep

David pressed the red, feeling it clunk under his finger, hearing others doing the same. A short tab of paper appeared out of the rear of the consul, and he realized there was a roll of tape inside there. When a button was pressed it was stamped and rolled on an inch.

"Good. Now green. Now blue. Now yellow." David could see a few inches of tape now, colored circles marked on it.

"Ok. Let's begin. The next beep will be your cue to choose a color at random. Choose whenever you hear a beep.

There will be a beep every ten seconds. 250 in all. Any questions?"

At first, David put some thought into choosing, but soon let his mind drift. The tape with the colored dots grew longer, curling beneath the bench.

Then there was a pause, and the postgrad said, "That's it. Sign on the dotted line for your pound."

Angela was first to sign, and the man made a production of handing her a crumpled note. She took it and left, not glancing David's way.

2016

Nathan waited for Wendy Lawrence to pick up her phone, but it was a man who answered, his voice strained.

"Mr. Lawrence?"

"Who is this?"

"Detective Constable Findlay."

"Your colleagues are already here." The man sounded confused. "Do you want to speak to them?"

"Please."

A woman's voice now. "Hello, Constable Karen Barclay. Sorry, you are?"

"DC Nathan Findlay. Based in Dundee."

"Oh, right. I left a message for DCI Dudek. About the incident a couple of days ago?"

"He's my boss. Sorry, has something happened? I was hoping to speak to Mrs. Lawrence."

Another brief pause before she spoke again, all business. "Thanks for that. Can I call you back in just a moment or two?"

"Yeah, no problem."

Nathan broke the connection, thinking something had happened, Karen not wanting to spell it out on the phone. He tapped his pencil on the desk, a worm of anxiety in his stomach, the one he had since working with Dudek.

The call came through minutes later, the woman sounding slightly out of breath on her cell phone. Like maybe she had hurried away from the house.

"Nathan?"

"Karen? What's happened?"

"I'm afraid Mrs. Lawrence is dead. Threw herself in front of the Edinburgh train."

"Shit. When was this?"

"This morning."

"Sorry to hear that. She seemed pretty upset when we spoke to her."

"Yeah. Mr. Lawrence said that the shooting shook her up pretty badly. She couldn't sleep. Was having nightmares. And nosebleeds."

"She didn't seem exactly stable when we spoke to her."

"More than just upset?"

"To be honest, she seemed like a nutjob."

Karen made a noise, sounding none too pleased.

Nathan said, "Sorry, but you did ask."

"It's just that it doesn't gel with what I've got on her."

"How do you mean?"

"Well, she was unusual, but a pillar of the community type. Local Councilor. Gave it up to concentrate on retraining for a new career."

"Why she was at the university."

"That's it. My boss knew her, actually. Said she looked like a flake, but was solid. Her husband said she saw somebody being shot."

"Maybe it was just too much for her."

"I doubt that, she was a theatre nurse, going back, a tough cookie, and smart. Only properly odd thing was that she was a medium, you know, one of these people help you speak to your dead dad."

"Maybe she was unravelling, and the shooting pushed her over."

"I've got to tell you, Mr. Lawrence might get to looking for someone to blame. Strikes me as that kind. Just a warning."

Nathan put the phone down with the feeling that he was somehow in trouble.

2016

Dudek answered the phone and said, "Dudek."

She said, "You didn't phone."

He felt his heart pick up, but his voice sounded fine when he told her, "I've been sort of busy." Thinking, does this sound like a police officer speaking to a journalist?

"I didn't go to print."

"You didn't have anything to print."

She didn't answer straight away, and he asked where she was. She told him she was in her hotel room and he looked at his watch to see it was still early, so maybe she was still in bed. He pictured her there.

He asked. "You want a coffee? Breakfast?"

"Give me thirty minutes. Where?"

He was already in the café when she arrived, drinking coffee. She walked straight to where he was sitting, casual today in jeans and a tan leather jacket. The café was long and narrow with booths opposite the counter but the entire front made of glass, so it felt lightsome.

When she slid opposite him, he asked, "Black coffee, no sugar, right?"

She said, no, she wanted a Ribena. The sweet blackcurrant drink.

He laughed, right out loud, and said, "Ribena? Seriously?"

Once it was in front of her, she took a long sip. "Do you remember when you were first making your own money, getting a bit of independence?"

He put his mind back, got there and nodded.

She leaned towards him. "When I was first working, I used to go to a café every day, feeling all sophisticated."

He grinned, seeing what was coming. She said, "I'd go in and order a Ribena. Sit there with my big hair and drink it. You do anything like that?"

"Used to go to The Mixed Grill, back where I come from. Went in there once a week and had liver and onions. Spending my own money."

"You were striking out on your own and eating liver?"

"You were drinking Ribena."

He thought she might say something like, touché, or you got me there. Instead she frowned, and he could picture her trying to imagine him, the young Dudek.

"What age were you?" she asked. "When all this liver eating was happening."

"Seventeen."

"Twenty-one years ago."

"You know my age?"

When she shrugged he thought, if she knows my age, she'll know about Jason Hardy, still out there because of me. Also Caroline and Shaun. Not out there, because of me. The thought of what happened with DCI Moore, his one-time boss, crossed his mind again. Did she know about that too?

He put it away. "So, how old are you?"

"Guess."

"We both know a man can't guess a woman's age. You got to go five, six years below what you think. More for an old dame."

"Dame? That's a word you use? Tell you what, get as close as you can. No bullshit."

He looked at her closely. "Ok. I'd say…twelve."

"Come on, you can do it."

He took a longer moment. "When I first saw you, I thought you were around twenty-eight, maybe thirty."

"And now?"

"I think you're older. Maybe thirty-four."

"I'm thirty-three."

"Why are you here?"

She had been sitting forward, now she sat back. "I was in Edinburgh doing research for a book, and the shooting happened."

"You get a lot of freedom."

"I'm on kind of a sabbatical."

"So, not working for *The Independent*?"

"They take my articles. I heard about the shooting and…I mentioned my Dad?"

When Dudek nodded, she said, "All the stories he covered, you'd never be able to count them. What got him going, though, was big business. Dundee, he outgrew the place."

Outgrew the place. Speaking that way to someone who had chosen to make his life here. But she was still talking about her father, the great journalist.

"He broke some of the world's biggest business stories. But there was one, he told me it was the biggest thing he never did. It didn't fit his usual line, more of a world of weird story.

See, I'm sitting here wondering do you know exactly what I'm talking about, letting me ramble."

"I don't know what you're talking about, no."

She looked at him, not smiling, trying to decide, it looked like.

"How's this, I'll give you some names. You tell me, do you recognize them."

He shrugged. She was different now, an edge to her. Still, he liked the way she was going about this, moving him around to something.

"Angela Murray."

It took him a few seconds to get to it. A memo in an old file. He shook his head, no.

"Neil Kerr."

The name hadn't been released yet, but he guessed she'd heard. The way she sprang it on him, though, no tone in her voice at all, he found himself sitting back in the little booth, thinking who was this woman, and what was her angle?

"How did you find out?"

"I suspected, what with the history to this. You just confirmed it."

"I've got to watch you, haven't I?"

"You need to trust me. David Haddow."

This time he didn't answer. She stared at him and he found himself thinking she would make a good detective, say something, just throw it at someone and watch how they reacted. Whichever way, it told you something.

"I'll take that as a yes. Ian Minto."

He frowned. "That one rings a bell. I can't quite get to it."

"Simon Bernard."

"Nope."

"Five people." She counted them on her fingers. "Murray, Kerr, Haddow, Minto and Bernard. The last two are Doctors."

"If you say so."

She sat back, but her expression said she was sizing him up. "My bet, you're good at finding a liar out, same as me, but not so good on the other side. I mean lying, keeping stuff back. What I'm thinking, you know Haddow and Murray, the names at least. You don't know Bernard and that means you don't know about what happened in the seventies. You aren't part of it. But I'm not all the way sure, you might be much better at this than I am."

She sipped her Ribena.

He said, "Part of it? I'm not sure what *it* is, but I'm guessing some kind of cover up?"

She didn't answer.

"From before either of us were born."

Again, she didn't say anything. He said, "Your dad, the way you talk about him, it's the past tense."

She nodded, her eyes on his.

"I'm guessing he died recently, but not in the past few weeks. In the last year."

"It was January. Why do you say that?"

He opened his mouth to answer, closed it again.

She frowned, looking hard at him. "What you are thinking, people sometimes do something for their loved ones. Not immediately after the death, but months later. You're thinking that I'm here to try to finish my dad's great unsolved case."

He said, "Hilda."

Now it was her turn to look surprised and all he did was say her name. She swallowed, and he saw her throat move like it was tight suddenly.

"Hilda. You're asking me to trust you but you're playing with me. You've got something to tell, something serious. Just say it. Maybe it's you who has to trust me."

She looked away for a moment, then brought her handbag onto the table, took an A4 envelope out and put it on the table. "Have a look at these. Don't worry, it's just press clippings, my dad doing his stuff. Read it and get back to me. I'm staying at the Craig Hotel."

He took the envelope as she slid from the booth, pulling her bag onto her shoulder.

"Was I right?"

He thought about frowning, asking right about what?

"You were right. I saw Angela Murray's name on a file note yesterday. Haddow's too. I can't remember who Ian Minto was."

"You'll go like this." She hit her head with the heel of her hand and gave a Homer "Doh". But didn't smile.

She stepped away, then turned, "Just one more thing."

He actually laughed, this little blonde woman doing a pretty good Peter Falk, getting the voice and the way Columbo used to look, turning to deliver his killer question.

"Know what I'd do, if I was you?"

A few things went through his head, none of them to do with the case.

She answered her own question. "I'd find somebody that knew Kerr in the seventies."

When she had gone, he thought about her saying, I'm staying at the Craig Hotel. Something she didn't need to tell him.

Iris

Iris Colhoun, aka Irish Iris but, long before that, aka Cheesy Biscuits, only discovered she was poor when she started school. Her view of poverty was the Little Match Girl, or Jack, selling his cow to save his mother from starving. Finding out she herself was poor, and that it was a shameful thing, that she was a bum and a gypsy, was a painful lesson. It made her early school days a kind of torture.

On that first school day she was more excited than anything else. At five, she was only slightly taller than average, copper haired and slab cheeked. Her clothes were from the Salvation Army, but not far from new.

Unfortunately for Iris, the family home, a broken-down house in a saggy line of one-time farm cottages, was close to the school, easily visible from the corner of the playground. It was properly called Back Street but was known locally as Minger's Row.

In 1963, when Iris started at St Peter and Paul's, Back Street sat empty and awaiting demolition. Except for Number 3, which somehow remained home to the Colhoun family.

That first day, Iris waved goodbye at her front door, her big, blousy mother standing in a threadbare robe and holding baby Edwin. Iris, bright eyed and with electricity running through her legs, shouldered her brother's old satchel and joined a mixed group of children and parents in the street. She had watched similar processions since the Colhoun family moved to Back Street, itching to be one of those children.

She turned and waved again to her mom, grinning hugely. Her mom's answering smile was less wide. She seldom smiled out of doors on account of the state of her teeth. Iris walked quickly, knowing her mother would watch all the way. She was singing 'Run Rabbit Run' under her breath, the same few lines over and over. Years later, she would wonder why that song. Maybe her mother had been singing it. She only knew that she could never hear it again without feeling nauseated and panicky.

Iris smiled at the other pupils, a smile that said, I'm one of you now! Nobody smiled back, but Iris remained unfazed, unaware of the nudges and whispers. She was, after all, only just five.

At the gate, she turned a last time and stood on her tiptoes to wave, beaming her excitement across the hundred yards to her mom.

A confusion of teachers and children whirled around her. The ringing that Iris had heard so many times turned out to be an actual hand-held bell, rang with gusto by a tall man wearing black robes. At this point of high excitement, she had not yet learned that she smelled of cheesy biscuits. That came soon enough, as they were being ushered into lines, hand in hand and two by two, in front of Miss Entwistle, who would be her teacher for the next two years. She was stung when a girl, Helen Mulreany, refused to hold her hand. Miss Entwistle demanded to know why, and Mulreany shouted, "She smells like cheesy biscuits!"

Everybody was laughing. In Iris' memory of the day, Miss Entwistle was laughing too. Much later, in her late teens and only months before she died, she would wonder about that. Was that memory wrong? Her other recollections of Miss Entwistle were of a stern but kind woman.

Sometimes, it felt to Iris that her life was spent hiding from the memory of cruel laughter and the feeling that her face was burning, skin shriveling away from the overheated blood in her cheeks. Even the tears on her cheeks were scalding.

The little girl, Iris, only minutes from the comfort of home, was in shock. She wanted to run, actually twisted to go, but Miss Entwistle caught her, brought her to the front of the queue and held her now sweaty hand herself. She dropped her head in shame as class 1E filed into the building, and kept it that way for the best part of a decade.

The sound of children's laughter held no joy for Iris Colhoun. Ever. The shame of being herself became the uniform she wore in primary school.

So, Cheesy Biscuits became her name. Even though she washed from head to toe every morning, standing in the kitchen in a plastic basin of water heated by the electric kettle. Sponging herself obsessively with coal tar soap. Later, Imperial Leather replaced the coal tar and, by the time she met Angela Murray, it was Clairol and Camay. Her mother would say, "You'll be washing yourself away, Iris Colhoun."

It made no difference. Helen Mulreany, her tormentor in chief in the first few years of school, would call out when she saw her in the playground, "Run, here comes Cheesy Biscuits!" And they would run from her, squealing. Holding their noses.

Back home, her mother finally refused to continue sniffing her to check for odors, saying, "You're letting them knock you bonkers. For the last time, you smell lovely."

Another mystery, looking back through the lens of years, was why the family were poor in the first place. Iris' Father was normally in work, mostly as a butcher, working in a shop in town. Not a high payer, but so many families had no work at all, and there were only three children, Iris, her older brother Jake and little Ed. Surrounded as they were by large Catholic families and men out of work, there was no obvious reason for the Colhoun family's poverty. Jake, years later, claimed their father was a boozer and a mad punter, spending all they had in the bookies.

That didn't work for Iris. Her father, a bulky man with a shock of red hair, would come home smelling of drink on a Friday and Saturday but, during the week, he would watch television like everybody else.

They didn't stay poor either. They moved out of Minger's Row when Iris was eight, into a Council house with running hot water, a bath, and an inside toilet. It kept getting better, financially, for the Colhouns. From someplace, her father and a friend borrowed money and set up their own butcher shop. Two years after moving into the Council house they moved again, this time to a three-bed semi. Her father drove a fairly new Rover and her mother got her teeth fixed, and took to wearing clothes from Marks and Spencer.

Although primary schooldays were unhappy times for Iris Colhoun, there were compensations. She found that, if she listened to her teacher, she normally understood and, more times than not, would remember. If she tried hard – she tried hard – her marks were consistently high. She kept her head down, and was never once invited to a classmate's birthday party.

In Iris's dreams, Helen Mulreany would turn to her one day and ask for help with long division, or pronouns, and Iris would frown in concentration before giving the answer. Helen would look at her, nodding and re-evaluating.

That didn't happen. In her last year of Primary, Iris took a growth spurt that put her a full head above most of her classmates. She hated it, hated standing out, and would walk with her head bowed, the desire to be *less* vying with the habitual shame of being herself. She left St. Peter and Paul's for the last time and sobbed at the gates, unsure what she was crying for. Maybe the loss of all the hopes that her five-year-old self had brought to the place.

She arrived at High School fully 5-10 and wearing a brassiere. Her hair was cut just below her jaw line and she walked slightly stooped, with books pressed against her embarrassing breasts. She smelled of Mum deodorant and Sunsilk shampoo. Her uniform was new, and her jacket a 'dress' blazer, which she thought of as smarter than the wool kind. Her skirt was regulation mid-thigh and she was wearing new shoes, with no heel.

Children were milling all around in the school ground, which was on a much larger scale than St Peter and Paul's, thousands of them, it felt like. Iris kept moving, trying to avoid attention, but had to join a line not unlike the one at the start of Primary.

She found herself next to a small girl with silky black hair, cut even shorter than her own. She had already noted where Helen Mulreany stood, thankfully in another queue, looking nervous and slightly bewildered.

The girl with the short black hair said, "You're a big girl, yourself."

Iris coughed on a response and the girl said, "I mean you're tall, not like you're fat."

Iris grunted, and the girl went on quickly. "I'd love to be tall. I've been eating bananas all summer to bring on the growth. Bananas are marvelous great fruits for bringing on the growth but it's hardly working at all. I'd give it up, cause I'm sick of them, but I'm thinking if it wasn't for the bananas I wouldn't have grown an inch.

"I mean, if this is the state of me *on* the bananas, what would I be like without them? What do you eat, because I'm eating it too?" Iris was having trouble keeping up, the girl was speaking so quickly.

"Chicken, I suppose and..."

"Right, I'm getting my Ma down to Colhoun's and I'm not eatin' any more of them shitty bananas. Beatles or the Stones?"

"What? Oh, the Beatles."

"Me too! I can't stand the way that Jagger fella jumps about like a skinny monkey and goes all poochy lipped." The girl winged out her elbows and hopped. "I'm Pauline Clover, by the way, call me Paulie. Have you got a *bra?*"

Paulie bent close to peer under the book Iris was holding, having to move around to get a better view. "Christ Almighty, those are great big boobs you have on you. I'm definitely on the chicken tonight. What are you lookin at, spotty?"

This to a boy in front who had turned to stare, drawn, no doubt, by the talk of great big boobs. He confirmed this immediately, with, "I was just wonderin about the boobs."

"Well, piss off, you little pervert. They're not for the likes of you."

The boy stared for a moment at the books Iris clutched at her chest before shrugging and turning back.

"Typical men. Always ogling up your bosoms. Well, once I get them. What's your name?"

"Iris Colhoun."

"Hah, like the butcher!"

"Yeah, that's my Dad."

"It's *never*! John, Paul, George or Ringo?"

Iris, beginning to get used to the random leaps of subject, said, "George."

Paulie, wide eyed, put her hand on Iris's arm. "No! That's great!"

"You like George too?"

"No, I'm mad for that Paul. I like his eyes. But this way we won't fall out."

"What, when we get off with them?"

"Yeah. You can have George, I'm having that Paul. Do you think Paul is tall?"

"It's hard to say." Then she asked, "Are you one of Helen's friends?"

"Helen O'Shaughnessy?"

Iris shook her head and tried to keep the shake out of her voice. "Helen Mulreany."

"Yeah, she's a great friend of mine."

"Oh."

Paulie was looking at her closely now. For the first time she was quiet for more than a few seconds. Then she said, "This Mulreany. She's not a pal of yours?"

Iris shook her head, no.

"Is she about here, at all?"

"Down there in the next line."

"What, the girl with the head on her like a pineapple?"

"No, in front of her. Black hair. I thought she was a friend of yours?"

Paulie waved it away, "Nah. Never met her." She stared at Mulreany for a few seconds. It seemed a few seconds was all she could go without speaking.

"Looks like a little prick."

Then she said, "And her boobs are of little consequence."

The boy in front turned again. "Whose boobs are of little consequence?"

"Her across there in front of the girl with the head like a pineapple."

The boy craned, then shrugged again before turning, telling them he was only twelve, so didn't know much about boobs yet.

"Watch now, your man is coming out with a clipboard. Oh, shit. I think we have a feckin' Nun!"

Moments later they were moving, walking abreast of the next file. As they came close to a tall skinny girl, she smiled at Paulie. "Hi Maddie."

"I thought you were called Paulie?" asked Iris.

"I am too, but Maddie was my nickname in Primary. Cause I'm a bit mad. I don't mind it really, but I'm hopin' to leave it behind now. What about you?"

"What about me?"

"You have a nickname?"

Iris shook her head, no.

"Ah, you do now. I can see it on your chops. Come on, what was it?"

Then she said, "I could ask the Mulreany girl."

It took a few moments, Paulie staring at Iris as they walked, before she whispered it to her. And, seeing how things were with the smaller girl, added, "Please don't shout it out."

"How did you come by that? Did you...it was something nasty, eh?"

Iris nodded her head.

"That Mulreany call you it?"

She nodded again.

"Why did you not beat the shite out of her?"

Iris looked shocked and Paulie went on. "You're the size of feckin'..." she waved her arms about, "some enormous great feckin', what's the name of that guy? The hairy fella, on the Empire State."

"King Kong?"

"Listen, next time she says anything like that. You just tell me. I'll get you to kick her behind into next week."

Over the next few weeks, it became obvious to Iris that she had a friend. Her first, who wasn't a relative. It became completely clear when Paulie said, "Look, enough of this keeping me at arm's length shit. I've decided I'm going to be your friend. Whether you like it or not."

And, years later, on a drunken night out before Iris went to Dundee and Paulie to drama school, Paulie admitted. "On that first day. I followed you, you know."

"What are you gabbin' about now?"

"At school. I saw you and I just thought, Jeez-oh, would you look at *her*! Actually, no." She shook her head. "It was before then. I saw you down town a few times over the summer. First time it was like I got an electric shock. And that was when I thought, would you *look* at her."

Iris was laughing, but her eyes were wide and amazed. "What, a great huge beast?"

"I think it was love at first sight. I thought you were absolutely feckin' gorgeous, with the hair and the legs. That first day, you were a woman amongst children."

Iris giggled and looked around the pub before asking, "Did you want to *screw* me?"

"Don't sound so shocked! I wasn't thinking about screwing at all in those days. But I think I've always wanted to screw you."

"You know the trouble with you? You're so feckin' full of shit, I never know when you're *not* talkin' shit."

"Well, I'm not talking shit and before you say it, I'm hardly drunk at all. I've always had a crush on you."

She dropped her eyes, raised them again. "Remember those Valentines? Your first two."

Iris blinked. In February of 1970 she was shocked when a card arrived at her house. It was horribly mushy and inside, scrawled in block capitals, "YOU ARE MY SECRET LOVE."

The following year she received a similarly mushy card, with exactly the same message. Word for word. She recalled showing them to Paulie, the two girls giggling in her bedroom.

Now she said, "Nah. You're so full of shit." But she was bent over the table, clutching her friend's hands. Tight.

"I know what was with the card. You never even told me there was anything in there."

No more than a whisper. "What, then?"

"Red feathers."

It took Iris a few seconds to process this. To be able to say. "I always wanted to ask, why red feathers?"

Paulie colored. "I was at a fun fair with my Ma and I saw this thing, this stupid, cheap fuckin' red heart made of fake velvet. It had feathers all around and *I love you*, on. I had this crazy mad thought. If I win it, I'll give it to you. And you'd love me back."

"Paulie!"

"I know! It was on a shooting stall and I tried about ten times to knock these fuckin' cans down. I was near crying and the stall guy finally just gave up and handed one over. I think I was scarin' him."

Iris sat back. Took a swallow of her lager. "Why didn't you tell me?"

"We were best pals. Goin out with our lads. I didn't want to chase you away. And I was scared."

"Do you think you're gay then?"

"I don't think I'm out and out. I like boys. But I've never felt for anybody like I felt...like I feel for you."

Iris was still clutching her friend's hands, staring at her. "Wow, Paulie. Eff sakes. I don't know what to do with this. You're going to London at the end of the week. I'm going to Scotland."

"Well, maybe you can just think about it. When we're apart."

"Paulie, are you going to cry?"

"No, I'm just wellin' up. With the emotion."

Suddenly Iris bent over and kissed Paulie on the mouth. In the middle of the crowded pub. Somebody, a man, said "Whoa!" A woman said, "Would you look at that!"

Iris sat back and smiled her huge smile. "Let's go back to your place."

2016

Dudek hadn't been to their grave in months and felt guilty, walking into the cemetery with flowers bought at Tesco. In the back of his mind was Hilda Jarvis and that made it worse, like he was being unfaithful.

He walked slowly through the huge graveyard, having to search for landmarks, thinking it wasn't good, not being certain of the way to your wife's grave. Your wife and son's.

Still, here it was. He knew that Caroline's mother, Kate, got comfort from coming here and struggled to understand. His view was that this sad little corner of the world had nothing to do with Caroline, or Shaun. It made him feel cheated and angry, more often than not.

And how many times could you say you were sorry? He could say that just as well staring into the last glass of the night, hoping it might be the one that would let him sleep.

The only time he'd come with Kate it had been worse, Kate telling her daughter straight off, look who's here!

Chattering away as though Caroline was right there in front of them, expecting Dudek to do the same. The thought in Dudek's head; Caroline and Shaun just lying there in the ground waiting for visitors. Was that what Kate really believed?

He stood in front of the stone and held out the flowers, like he was showing, then got on with the business of changing them for the sorry looking bunch in the jar. He was surprised that Kate hadn't kept the flowers fresh, it being her thing.

Nathan came into his mind then, how he would smile down the phone if he called his Susan, dropping his head as though that made it private. Telling her he loved her, not even thinking about it.

He tried to make a connection now, talking out loud, telling Caroline about the job, what was happening. Too many murders this year, something nasty in the air.

Then he had to say, "I suppose you know about this journalist, Hilda Jarvis?"

It stopped him. He had only met the woman twice. Some minor flirting and now he was talking to his dead wife about her.

When Hilda left the café, Dudek had opened the envelope, finding photocopied press cuttings.

The first one was headlined, 'Drugs Student Missing'. The page number wasn't shown, but it hadn't made front page. Two students had been picked up in the early hours of Wednesday morning, suffering the after effects of a drugs binge, both in a critical condition. Police yet to issue a statement, but sources suggest this is part of a growing drugs problem.

The missing girl, Angela Murray, 18, of Rankine Halls of Residence is believed to have taken the same drugs and anyone knowing her whereabouts should contact the Police.

The second clipping was two days later and front page. Student Drug Mystery- Body Found.

This time 'by Jack Jarvis' was written under the headline. A body had been found in a disused factory, but not the missing girl. Police had intensified their search and were appealing for witnesses. The tone different now, concerned. Maybe thinking of her as a person and not a drug addict.

A photograph of her. Pretty enough in a formal way, Dudek thought, with that oddly tight smile. Her mother had come from Glasgow to aid the search.

The other two boys were named. Neil Kerr, medical student. Described as having an outstanding academic career and a star of the University Rugby Team. Out of danger but permanent brain damage not ruled out. His Father, Chief Superintendent Kerr, has rushed from Aberdeen to be at his son's side.

The other boy, David Haddow was in a coma. Hospital sources tight lipped.

A manager of Tayside Transport described how he was on his way to work in the early hours when he stopped his car, seeing a man struggling to carry another across Lochee Road.

"I was shocked at the state of him. He was soaked, like he'd fallen in water, and couldn't make out what I was saying, or even where I was. I thought the other guy might be dead. Then I saw the blood."

Dudek sat back, wondering what could have happened to get the guy drenched there. Maybe there had been a fountain, back then. The blood? Dudek recalled one of the boys had cut themselves.

Reading on, the Police thought they had broken into The Tombstone Mill to take drugs. A well-known eyesore, long overdue for demolition.

Dudek thought again, why would anyone do that? These people were students, with accommodation.

Now some detail on the body, found by Police in a remote part of the factory, unconnected with the students. Cause of death thought to be natural causes and time of death put at several weeks or even months ago. The identity of the deceased not yet known.

Dudek picked up the last page. This one was from the following Monday.

Identity of Mill Body. Dudek guessed it would be one of the other names that Hilda had given him, maybe Ian Minto, the one he should remember, would hit his head, 'Doh'.

The body wasn't Minto. It had been formally identified as Doctor Simon Bernard, Political History lecturer and warden of Rankine Halls of Residence.

Dudek pursed his lips. Not some rough sleeper then. And, despite what Mackie said in that long-ago memo, a clear connection with the students. Plain as you like.

There followed some conjecture about what an academic had been doing in an abandoned factory and infamous drug den. The picture the journalist painted was of a very weird and solitary man, becoming weirder. Missing lectures and becoming a virtual recluse, before disappearing altogether.

Kerr was receiving ongoing medical treatment. Haddow still in a coma, and no sign of Murray.

Dudek shook his head, wondering about Mackie, thinking there was no way he would forget Kerr, and no way he would have missed the link with Bernard.

He picked up the final press clipping, this from the following Wednesday, and read, Grisly Death of Council Official. Then there it was, Ian Minto. He didn't hit his head, but only because she'd said he would.

Now, at his wife and son's grave he looked up, hearing someone nearby and Caroline's mother was coming across the scrubby grass towards him. She seemed properly happy to find him there.

"Hello stranger!"

She hugged him, and he hugged back, catching her familiar hair-spray odor.

For want of something to say, he told her, "I brought some flowers."

She frowned at the dead bouquet he had put to one side. "Flowers don't seem to last just now. I was telling Caroline."

He managed a smile. "I was telling her a thing or two myself."

She looked back at him, that sidelong look he had all but forgotten, and he suddenly wished he hadn't come. Knowing she was going to drag it all up again, because she couldn't help herself.

She put her hand on his arm, no surprise that she was getting right to it. "Do you talk to her about what happened, John?"

When he didn't answer, she squeezed harder. "You should. It's important. She isn't sick now."

Dudek found his throat was almost too tight to speak. "I know she's not sick."

"It wasn't her fault."

"Nobody's blaming her, least of all me."

Kate threw her hands up. "We all knew about baby blues, everybody does. But, postpartum psychosis, I'd never even *heard* of it."

"It was terrible, what happened to her."

"Caroline was the last person in the world to have delusions. It was the *sickness*, John."

"I know."

Dudek knew what she was going to say next, almost word for word.

"I've joined an online support group. Did you know that most new mothers who commit suicide have it? Postpartum psychosis? PPP."

Dudek nodded, knowing she wouldn't halt, no matter what. Had to get it out there again and again.

"Most mothers who kill their babies too."

The woman's face twitched and crumbled, her eyes tearing up.

"And you were so distracted. Saving that other boy."

Dudek accepted it because it was true. He hadn't seen how sick Caroline was. Desperately trying to save the kidnapped kid instead of looking after his own.

"All that crazy stuff in her head, about little Shaun."

"Don't keep doing this to yourself, Kate. You've got to move on."

"I'll never move on." That sideways look again. "I tried to call you, that morning."

"I know!"

She was dissolving. Dudek pulled her to him. At first, she resisted, angry, like she wanted to hit out, then she fell against him.

"I tried and tried. But I couldn't get through."

He pressed his lips together, willing her to shut up.

"Why didn't you see it, John? That's what I don't understand. To hear Caroline talk, you could figure anything out. But you didn't see what was right there under your nose."

Later that night, he dialed her number and when she answered she sounded like maybe she had been sleeping. He started to think about her in bed but made himself say, "It's Dudek. Who is still alive? I mean from those students."

"You want to speak to David Haddow."

"I knew you'd know. But how do you know?"

"I'll tell you next time you call. Some of us sleep at these sorts of times."

"Sorry."

He listened to rustling, her moving around in bed. "You want his address?"

2016

The police phoned at about ten-thirty and David Haddow picked up straight away.

"Sorry to trouble you Mr. Haddow. This is Nathan Findlay of Tayside Police."

"About the shooting."

"That's right."

The silence spun out and the police officer hurried to fill it.

"I understand you and Mr. Kerr were close friends."

Haddow waited to hear what was next.

"We're trying to piece together what happened and I need to talk to someone who was at university with Neil."

"Will the Inspector be there?"

"The inspector?"

"Dudek."

"No, only me, I'm afraid."

"No."

"Sorry?"

"I only speak to principals."

"Chief Inspector Dudek is really very busy. This is an inquiry into-"

"Spare me the lecture, and any threats you might be considering. If Dudek comes, I will meet. If not, my lawyers will prevent you harassing me."

Findlay digested this.

"You are being extremely difficult, Mr. Haddow."

"You can leave a message to say when Dudek will be here. I have no appointments."

Haddow broke the connection and then stood very still, for a very long time.

October 1976

David and Angela left the lecture hall, side by side but not talking, even when David held the door for her. Outside, she picked up the pace, eyes fixed ahead, like she was annoyed with him. She obviously didn't intend to speak. Well, he wouldn't speak either, see how she liked that.

They crossed in front of the Union, angling towards the psychology block. David pulled his Afghan tighter and asked, "What d'you think this is about?"

She shook her head, not slowing, but he could tell she had something in mind.

"I don't know, but Dr Phillips didn't seem very pleased."

"No."

David was feeling nervous, thinking about the funny things that sometimes happened, where he knew stuff he had no business knowing, never recognizing it until later. And it was plain weird, that thing Angela did, sitting near him all the time. How and why did she do that? Either way, he was regretting the experiment.

Phillips had asked them to stay behind, telling them they were wanted back at the lab, something to do with last week's experiment, but not giving anything else away. Not happy about it, though.

The postgrad was waiting, standing behind the glass door with his arms folded. He fixed them with a hard look, first David, then Angela, taking his time, then turned on his heel and they had to follow him to the same room as before.

David was nervous, feeling exposed, but the guy seemed in no hurry. He looked from one to the other. "You think it's ok to mess with experiments? Important work that people have spent a lot of time over. I mean a *lot* of time."

The silence stretched out, till he said, "You're not even asking what you did."

David. "You think we messed with the experiment?"

"What do you think?"

Angela surprised David, saying exactly what had been in his mind. "We got them right, didn't we? Chose the same colors as the master."

The man lifted his eyebrows. "God, no. You didn't even get a high ratio of right answers."

He motioned with his finger then, imperious, bringing them to a table holding three long strips of tape, marked with colored dots. David's name was written on the right-hand tape, Angela's in the middle. The left one was marked 'master'.

David leaned over. "What are we looking at?"

"Each dot represents the button you pressed."

"So what? Neither is remotely like the master."

Beside him, Angela said, "Oh."

"You both start off random, no pattern that I can see. Till dot number forty-three."

"What?" But he could see it now.

"At first it's not obvious. You and Miss Murray choose the same color four times out of the next set of ten. Then six out of the next set. Then, for the entire rest of the sequence you choose the same color as each other."

The postgrad used his finger to tap David's tape. "Every. Single. Time."

David could feel his face burning, and didn't look up.

The graduate leaned in. "Did you agree a signal, like coughing? I remember one of you coughing."

"That was the electrocuted guy."

"What are you talking about, electrocuted guy?"

"Chesterman." David waved his hand above his head.

The postgrad sighed. "Come on, give. What did you do?"

When neither of them answered, he put his hand out, palm upwards.

"What?"

"I want those pounds back."

"You're kidding, right?"

They walked out of the building in silence and stood awkwardly in front of the building before Angela said, "I'll pay you back tomorrow."

He watched her turn and walk a few rapid steps before calling, "Wait."

She turned. "What?"

He could feel himself color, the way she was looking at him, waiting for his reason for stopping her.

"You want to get a coffee?"

She patted her pockets but surprised him with a proper smile, one that changed her face.

He shrugged. "I could buy you a coffee. Maybe even a Paris bun."

She dropped her head, came up again and nodded and, after a brief dither, they turned towards the city centre.

"What's a Paris bun?"

"Like a rock bun with anemia."

"Sounds good."

"And sugar lumps instead of currants."

"Sounds Dundonian. You're from up North?"

"Aberdeen. You're West Coast?"

"Glasgow."

"But posh Glasgow."

She nodded, not denying it.

"How long you got? There's a café I found in the city center."

"I've no more classes this afternoon." She lied.

"Me too." He lied.

They walked past the craft shops and University Bookshop in silence, till she asked, "Why do you always carry a record with you?"

He glanced at the album under his arm. Supersister today.

"I'm into music. You into music?"

She paused before shaking her head. "No."

"Oh."

Then, "I quite like The Carpenters."

"Oh. Ok."

For a few seconds, they walked without speaking. But there was something about how she had answered the question about music, that pause before she said no. He asked, "D'you play? An instrument or something?"

She walked briskly along. Straight back. Long jaw. Eyes front. She turned that smile that wasn't really a smile on him. "I used to. What about you?"

"I play a bit of guitar."

"What bit?"

"The back. Put it over my knee and bash it with a stick."

He could swear she almost laughed at that, but, once more in silence, they crossed into a wide paved area, where an old steepled church rose opposite a concrete shopping complex.

David took them into a glass fronted café, long and narrow with Formica tables and booths. She slid into one of the bench seats, looked around and smiled. "I like this place. I don't know why, exactly."

"I like the cups."

"The cups?"

"You get those thick glass things."

"Perspex?"

He nodded. "Probably."

Once they were drinking their coffees, and with oversized buns before them, she said, "So, what do you think happened? With the tapes."

He looked at his thick Perspex cup, and shrugged.

She asked, "Anything like that ever happen to you before?"

Again, the shrug. "You?"

She seemed to be coming to a decision. "To be honest, yes. Only with my mother, though. We could play this trick where I could guess what she had in a box. You know, pins, a bottle of perfume."

"What, every time?"

"Most of the time."

"This something you would show to people?"

She shook her head. "Mother was worried about what people would think."

"Did it only work the one way? She couldn't guess?"

Another shake of her head. David noticed that her eyes were green. Asked himself, have I ever seen anyone with actual, proper green eyes before? She was speaking, saying it was only her that could guess, and they never could work out if the trick was her seeing or her mother showing.

"You mean I'm the only person knows about this?"

She smiled, and he found himself smiling back. "You're the only one."

He put his hand into his pocket, encountered his Zippo.

"What do I have in my hand then?"

"A cigarette lighter."

"Wow."

She laughed, another change in her that surprised him. "Well, you're going to have a lighter in your pocket, aren't you?"

"How do you know I even smoke?"

"You smell of smoke. Quite strongly."

"Oh, ok."

In his other pocket was a badge, which he knew was a Fabulous Furry Freak Brothers badge that Neil's sister, Rachel, had made for him, drawing it herself.

"What now?"

"A pen?"

"Try again."

"Cigarettes"

"Well done."

"Still, it might be a guess."

"But there was the experiment. That prat found a genuine psychological phenomenon and was too dim to see it."

She picked up the Paris Bun, a yellow mound studded with lumps of sugar, and bit into it, then smiled in surprise.

He smiled right back, finding that he was feeling pretty good about sitting across from her. He bit his own bun, spraying crumbs when he spoke.

"I've got an album by Genesis you might like, *Nursery Cryme*."

She shook her head, but kept the smile. "Why would I like that?"

"It's got some mean flute music on it. Maybe you could learn to play it."

David was bending, concentrating on his bun, so missed her change of expression.

2016

Stirling house was screened from the road by a long, dark line of conifers, overhanging the stone wall. The road itself was single track, surprisingly remote although it was only a few miles from the village of Crammond and the Forth Bridge. There was only a single other car in sight. A blue Fiat, stopped in a distant passing place. It briefly occurred to Nathan that it was an offence to park there, but that was no longer his concern.

The entrance was certainly grand, but the conifers were badly overgrown and the ornate gates rusty. Nathan got out and pushed them open, wincing at the grind of metal against metal before hopping back into the driver's seat, easing the Ford forward. Dudek wrinkled his nose against the damp green smell.

"These get any thicker, we'll need headlights."

He had surprised Nathan, seeming relaxed about Haddow's insistence on seeing him. No, not relaxed, more curious, maybe wanting to see Haddow for himself now.

The driveway opened out in front of the house, this so large that Nathan whistled. Dudek peered up, into the sky. "That's a lot of crows up there."

They stopped beside a stone fountain, heavy with algae and weeds. The only other car was a rotting Jaguar, and the surrounding area seemed meadow like, with high grass and nettles. It took Nathan a moment to realize what it reminded him of – Rankine Hall.

Climbing out of the car, Dudek said, "He's watching us."

Nathan followed his gaze, but couldn't see a thing behind the heavily curtained windows. He trailed his boss to the imposing front door, watching him pause before pressing a porcelain button. Deep inside, someone shouted something.

Dudek frowned at Nathan, and leaned closer. "What?"

"It isn't locked."

They shared a long look, before Dudek pushed the door open. Nathan found himself looking into a gloomy hallway, smelling airless and dusty. Haddow was standing some way back, in shadow, but was still a shock to look at. Nathan could see there was something wrong, a disability of some kind, but then the hall light came on and it was the man's skin he focused on. It was a strange tan color, as if he had overdone the spray and UV light.

His clothes were almost deliberately bizarre. A lightly built man, he was wearing oversized pajama pants, cotton paisley, green wellingtons and a formal shirt, billowing over his thighs.

Dudek thanked him for seeing them, but Haddow just stared at him, not even glancing at Nathan. Dudek had to speak again, sounding more uncomfortable than Nathan had ever heard him, introducing them both.

The man had to shift his whole body to look at Nathan, and his left arm swayed dangerously in its cuff, palm turned outwards, swinging as if there was nothing much holding it on.

Haddow stared at him for an unpleasant moment. "You didn't sound so tall over the phone."

Something wrong in his voice too, the scratchy thing that Nathan had noticed before more evident. Haddow returned his gaze to Dudek, which was a relief. Nathan glanced at his boss, seeing him standing there, saying nothing as the seconds spun out.

After a much longer pause than seemed right, Haddow turned, his left leg needing effort from his whole body to get it pointing in the right direction. For a second, Nathan thought he was going to topple over, but didn't even start to move.

He did not want to touch the man.

Haddow got into his stride, moving with long steps of his right leg, his left foot dragging, and they followed down the gloomy hall, in the powerful wake of his cologne.

1976

David sometimes wondered why Neil felt he had to work so hard at the laid-back image that was so different to who he really was. The guy had an infuriatingly good memory and David sometimes found himself sulking because, if he was honest, Neil made him feel less than bright.

But he knew his friend had to work at it. How often had David come to his room, interrupted him studying? Neil with some music on, 'Baby I Love Your Way' or something, pretending he'd been chilling, the book he had just been studying shoved under the bed.

At school it had been the same. Neil saying he really needed to start revising for the exams. Like there was ever a time when he *wasn't* revising.

David could see the determination, the disappointment if ever his friend fell below his own crazy standards and wondered would it always be that way. Neil a surgeon, pretending he just happened to know how to do a triple bypass, with pike. Maybe once his dad's fat heart finally gave it up, Neil would also give up the pretense. Did he do it to try to impress the old man? Who never seemed impressed with anything.

It was the same with rugby. David knew that his friend trained hard, running early mornings, like it was a guilty secret. He had gone to support the University rugby club only a couple of times but watching sport bored him mindless. He liked playing tennis, but watching? Nah.

Still, there was something about watching Neil play rugby, like seeing something being unleashed. Neil, for reasons that were unclear, didn't seem to like being big, never acted tough, but on the rugby field that was set aside, as if that was the only place where a submerged part of himself could make itself known. On the rugby field, he was a brute. A warrior.

And he was *fast*.

Seeing him on the rugby field, even David could understand why people called him electric. Mostly, those great lumps would lumber three steps before another great lump grabbed them, and they would fall grunting to the mud. Brilliant.

When Neil got the ball, he could suddenly be flying, defenders flapping the air where he used to be. If someone got in a tackle, they might bring him down, but often it looked like Neil was made out of different stuff. He would crash straight through.

The coach had once told David that his friend was destined for great things. David was inclined to agree, but didn't think it had anything to do with rugby.

2016

Like the hallway, the kitchen blinds were down, the only light being electric. Haddow had a pot of coffee ready, and now he poured it in the vicinity of three cups, apparently not noticing how little was going in.

Dudek watched brown liquid run across to where he was sitting and glanced at Nathan, jerking his head towards the washbasin. Then he watched Haddow, wondering what he would make of the big policeman bustling about his kitchen, bending to clean the spill, and the answer seemed to be, not a thing. The man's eyes were fixed on Dudek..

Dudek, a man used to intimidating others, had to look away from that unwavering stare, sipping his coffee, surprised to find it was excellent. There was also a plate of Wagon Wheels and Breakaway biscuits, his favorites, but he didn't touch them. Haddow had an odor, underneath the overpowering cologne, that reminded him of old mushrooms.

He looked up. "This must be terrible for you. You were close friends, weren't you?"

Haddow nodded.

"We're trying to figure out why Neil did what he did."

When Haddow nodded again, Dudek thought, fuck it, and got straight to the point, "What happened in the seventies?"

"You mean the Tombstone Mill."

"Yes. The night when you and Kerr broke in."

"My memory of that night is not good."

"Anything would be a help."

It was making Dudek more and more uncomfortable, the way the man, sitting in his comedy get-up, was staring, barely speaking. He didn't like meeting his eyes, which were oddly filmed, and could feel the beginnings of a headache. More than anything, he simply wanted out of there.

"Give us some background, at least. The Police thought that you had broken in to take drugs. Don't worry about drugs offences, we just have to work out why Kerr did what he did."

"We went to take LSD."

Dudek instantly thought, no. No, you didn't. His eye was drawn to a hole at the side of Haddow's neck, mostly hidden by the shirt collar. Maybe from some long-ago surgery, but you could fit a finger in there.

Nathan asked, "Why the mill, though?"

The man answered Nathan, but didn't take his eyes off Dudek.

"Bravado."

"There has to be a connection with what Kerr did last week, though."

Dudek was finding it difficult to keep his train of thought. He could feel the headache building behind his eyes, told himself that he wouldn't drink anything tonight. Haddow blinked then, and Dudek thought that he hadn't seen him blink up to that point, was almost sure of it. The man was back to being silent, so he changed tack. "Tell me about Angela Murray."

"My girlfriend, a long time ago."

Some new information, at last.

"When was the last time you saw her?"

"That night."

"When she went missing?"

"Yes. She's hiding."

"Hiding? Why do you say that?"

"Missing, then."

"You must have been worried. Your girlfriend going missing."

"I was in hospital."

"Did you try to find her? After you came out."

"I tried very hard."

"In what way?"

It seemed, though, that Haddow had no more to say on the subject of Angela Murray.

Nathan spoke again and Dudek felt himself jerk with surprise, as though he had forgotten he was there. He was feeling slightly dizzy, could feel clammy sweat running down his sides.

"How did you know Ian Minto?"

Still, Haddow wouldn't turn his gaze from Dudek. "The archivist? I didn't know him well."

Dudek, pulling his concentration together with an effort, picked it up. "Still, how would you meet a person like that?"

"He was a guest lecturer. An authority on Dundee's history."

"I can't get to what happened, in my own mind. Five people, dead or damaged from one night."

Haddow didn't respond, so Dudek continued, "And now, one of those five returns, and shoots the place up."

Haddow said, "Neil and I were on a normal track, before. We thought we were."

"That night changed the course of your lives?"

Haddow nodded, a slow movement that didn't break his eye contact.

"He ever mention it to you? I mean later."

"There was no later, for me and Neil."

Nathan asked, "When was the last time you were in Dundee, Mr. Haddow?"

"I've never been back. I never leave this house."

"Dr Bernard. Did you know him?"

Instead of answering, Haddow stood, getting himself upright in stages.

Haddow was leading the way back to the front door when Dudek stopped, Haddow having to turn around to see him standing at an open doorway.

Dudek said, "I've never seen so many books outside a library."

"It is a library."

"I mean a public library. It's like something out of a movie set, from the forties maybe." He pointed at the walnut gramophone and the shelves of vinyl above it.

"You like big band music?"

"Yes."

Haddow turned again, sawed his way towards the front door, but stopped well shy of it. He indicated with his hand. "Close it behind you."

Dudek said, very quietly. "You haven't told us anything."

Then, after a pause. "We've come all this way, Mr. Haddow. A man has died and you dodge our questions. Now you just stand up, and walk us to the door? You think that's how this works?"

"We had come to the end of the conversation."

Dudek walked to the door and opened it. Then he pointed at the double garage. "Is there a car in there?"

"No."

"Where were you three nights ago? Between five and midnight."

"Are you honestly suggesting I had something to do with Neil's death?"

"Where were you?"

"Here. I never go out."

"Alone?"

"Of course. Am I suspected of something?"

"You're not suspected of anything. But something happened back then, and I can't believe it has nothing to do with Neil Kerr's death. I have other lines of enquiry, but I can tell you right now we will speak again, because you were the only person who was actually there."

Haddow didn't reply. Instead, he turned and dragged his leg back into the darkness of the house.

In the car, Dudek took a few deep breaths, getting himself together. "He's not telling, is he?"

Nathan shook his head. "If that's how that night left him, though, no wonder he can't talk about it. What a mess."

"I don't think that's from then. Not all of it."

Nathan frowned, but didn't ask how he could know that. "He's the weirdest person I've seen in my whole life. Never been so happy to get out of a place."

He shook his shoulders in an exaggerated shiver.

Dudek said, "He didn't contradict me, when I said five people, all connected."

Nathan frowned and Dudek watched him going over the conversation in his mind, trying to think what it meant. Haddow, Kerr, Murray and Minto made four.

Nathan smiled. "You're sneaky, boss. That means that there's a connection with the corpse found in the mill. Bernard."

"Or he just didn't notice."

Dudek felt himself relax when Nathan got them back onto the road, putting distance between him and the house.

Nathan glanced across and asked, "Weren't you weirded out, Sir? The way he was staring at you?"

Dudek rubbed his temples. "Damn right. I was..."

"You see the hole in his neck? Gross." Then, looking around again, "You ok, boss?"

"My head is splitting, to be honest."

What Dudek didn't tell his Constable, there had been this feeling, this taste in the air that he associated with Jason Hardy. And, now that he was admitting it, with his old boss, DCI Moore, just like Mackie had said. Too many threads, connected by nothing more than a feeling.

2016

Nathan was concentrating on driving, Dudek sitting silent beside him. He had tried a couple of times to engage, but Dudek just grunted in response. Irritated, Nathan, finally decided to say something.

"You sleep ok last night, Sir? Only you look a bit tired out."

Dudek puffed out a tiny laugh and for a few seconds it seemed that he was going to snap.

Instead, he said, "I've not slept too good since this thing started."

A pause. Nathan had to ask, "No?"

"It's a bit too much like something that happened, before."

Nathan thought, oh shit, he's going to talk about his wife killing herself and his kid. Not wanting to hear it.

Dudek said, "I mean, the thing with the Saint."

Nathan was baffled. "The Saint?"

"Shook me up at the time, and this...well, you can see the comparisons."

"I thought The Saint was the nickname of a retired copper."

Dudek turned in his seat, giving Nathan his full attention.

"Come on. You must have heard about this. It was before you joined but, Christ, it was national news."

"Sorry."

"Roger Moore. You aren't going to tell me..."

"Roger Moore! The ex-copper who killed his family?"

Dudek sounded exasperated. "Yes. Roger Moore. The Saint."

"I was a school kid. All I know is the guy went at his family with a machete."

"It was a hatchet. Like for chopping kindling."

For a while they were silent again.

Nathan asked, "So Roger Moore was The Saint?"

Dudek tapped his head with the heel of his hand. "I'm going to tell people about this conversation. Roger Moore. Same name as the actor."

"Right, the old guy who used to play James Bond."

"Before Bond, he was The Saint."

Dudek was watching Nathan frown as he thought this over, and stopped him as he opened his mouth to speak.

"You're too young to remember the television series, aren't you?"

"It's beginning to sound like it."

"Roger Moore, the actor I mean, used to be best known for playing The Saint. Val Kilmer played him in a film, but that stunk."

"I get it now. That's why Moore got tagged with The Saint."

He glanced at his boss, could see him going back in his memory.

"Except it wasn't just that. I'm not saying he was a saint or anything, but he was a good guy. Straight arrow. Got to be chief inspector, at this point he's early thirties, going places."

Nathan thought, just like you before you lost the plot. A man once tipped for the top.

Dudek said, "He gave it all up, so he could have a proper home life, spend time with his wife and kids. He loved them to bits."

For a while they drove in silence and Nathan thought that Dudek was finished talking, but a few minutes later he picked it up again.

"He trained me, Moore. Those days we didn't talk in terms of mentors, but I guess that's what he was. He was the sort of guy... This was a time when most of the guys just did whatever secured the conviction.

"Moore didn't go for that. One day I saw him and Mackie going at it..." He shook his head.

"So, what did he do, when he left?"

"Private investigator. It was working out, so it seemed."

"Were you involved in the investigation?"

Dudek turned all the way around to look at him again. "You really haven't heard any of this?"

Nathan made a face, shrugged.

"I must have been the same age as you are now. I'm getting in my car and the call comes through, officer requires assistance, just streets away. A minute later, I'm running up to the front door of this house and I can hear a serious fight going on, you know what that sounds like? Thumping around, really heavy?"

Nathan nodded, putting himself there.

"I run inside and here's Bryan Colvey. Before your time, but Bryan was a hard bastard. There's blood everywhere and Bryan is wrestling this guy on the floor and I'm just standing there 'cos the guy on the floor is the Saint and he only has one hand. There's blood like you wouldn't believe. His hand is cut off, his head is mashed in, and he's wrestling Colvey and Colvey isn't winning."

Nathan risked a glance at his boss, trying to see how he was handling this, because his voice didn't sound too steady. Dudek stared out the side of the car.

"We held Moore down for maybe five minutes till more help came, but it was tough. I was soaked in blood, Colvey was soaked in blood, the floor was soaked in blood."

"He lived though?"

"It was touch and go. But here's the thing. We found out later that he'd come home from shopping. Bought a *Guardian*, two liters of semi-skimmed, and croissants. Puts the milk in the fridge then opens *The Guardian* on the kitchen worktop. Got to page five, before he decides to get the hatchet from the shed, and take after his wife and kids. Chased them down one by one. The guy who gave up his career for his family."

"Jesus."

"Then he started on himself. Chopped his hand off, for starters. That's what saved him, I reckon. He was right handed, and that was the one he cut off. Had to hit it three, four times to do the job or maybe they could have stitched it back on for him."

"You think maybe that was, you know, the hand he'd killed his family with? First thing he does is to chop the damn thing off."

"Actually, I think just that. He mashed his wrist up, chopping lumps out of the top banister doing it, and his hand tumbled down the stairs. I could see it during the wrestling match. Then he whacks himself right in the nut. Can you imagine doing that?"

Nathan thought about Susan and the girls. Debs and little Sarah. Threw that thought as far away as he could. "I can't imagine doing any of it."

"Standing at the top of the stairs and he just pointed the blade at himself and whack! Right here."

Dudek pointed to a spot just above his right eyebrow.

"The axe fell downstairs. He shouldn't have been conscious, but he was, and he walked down to get it. Colvey kicks the door in, but he can't overpower him. Both of us together could hardly hold him. He wanted that axe. You see what I'm saying?"

Nathan didn't want to see the connection, but had to say, "You mean it's like Kerr with the shotgun. Shooting himself after he's dead."

He winced as that came out of his mouth, knowing the boss didn't want it referred to like that. The guys at the station making a joke out of it.

Dudek didn't answer at first, then he said, "See, I wonder now, what would have happened if we hadn't stopped him. Would he have just kept hitting himself with the axe, even after he was dead."

Nathan blew out a long breath, thinking that Dudek was losing it again.

November 1976

It was just after six. Neil and David were in a pub in the Hilltown, well away from the campus, one of the Linoleum and nicotine variety that Neil liked so much. It was smoky and narrow and surprisingly busy; the clientele mainly working men or old timers.

David bought two pints as Neil found vacant seats near a very small old man drinking on his own, neat whisky sitting on the table before him. Neil nodded amiably as he sat, but the man didn't smile back. He stared at Neil with watery eyes, his lower jaw trembling steadily.

Neil shifted a few inches and took his pint from David, who sat down opposite. He glanced back, to find the man still glaring at him. He smiled again. "Alright, Mister?"

It seemed the man would not reply. Then he did. "You a teuchter?"

A derogatory term, meaning a country lad. Almost spitting the word out.

"Aberdeen."

"Sound like a teuchter."

Neil looked across at David who was grinning widely, clearly enjoying the exchange.

The old man was speaking again. "Think you're tough, do you?"

Neil put his hands up. "Not me, no."

"I could have yer nose in my pocket. In a second." Still glaring, he made a noise through his dentures, somewhere between a hiss and a cutting noise, and moved suddenly, whipping his hand to his jacket pocket.

Neil blinked at the man, who repeated the motion and the noise. He glanced back at David, who remained delighted.

"I'll split your chimp."

Neil looked at this guy, a foot shorter and sixty years older, and eventually had to ask. "My chimp?"

"Split yer chimp for ye. Ye big teuchter. Slit it open." He rolled his purple red tongue against his dentures, as though savoring something. Then he said, "Would you like that?"

"Not really. I like my chimp just the way it is, thanks."

"Crackin' wise are ye?" he moved his hand again to his pocket, making the hissing noise and Neil felt suddenly that something very wrong was happening, the hair prickling on the back of his neck. He was thinking, maybe this guy is ancient, but he might have a knife, and his movements are quick. He glanced again at David, who had stopped smiling, maybe feeling the wrongness of it too.

The old man put a shaky hand out to his glass. He pointed at David, staring at him across the table. "I'm with the craws."

Then he lifted the glass, to David again, and spoke loudly, like a toast. It sounded like, "The crater."

He downed the whisky and shuffled out from behind the table, struggling to his feet and a stick that Neil had not noticed, before limping to the exit.

Neil leaned over to whisper. "That guy's bonkers. What was that he said at the end?"

"It was a toast."

"Yeah, but was it to the creator, the creature or an actual crater?"

"Dunno, but he didn't like you one bit."

"No, he didn't."

David picked his beer up, smiling again. "He thought I was great, though."

"Yeah, but as he said himself, he's with the crows."

The boys clinked glasses, and drank.

2016

Nathan drove across the Forth Bridge, the second time in two days, as Stirling House and its spectacularly weird owner David Haddow were only a few miles further on. Today, though, he swung towards the hotel that rose above the slip road, eased into the parking lot and there was the taxi, a green Passat, a 'Police Aware' sticker on the window.

He had hoped to meet a local plod, but there was nobody. The parking lot wasn't full, with only the Passat at this side, overlooking the river. The car was parked diagonally across two spaces, its front wheel dangerously close to the crumbling edge and the steep slope beyond.

Nathan put on gloves and pressed unlock on the spare key. No clunk, no indicator flash. Walking closer, he saw it was already unlocked, and opened the door, immediately hit by the odor of cologne and stale smoke, despite the 'No Smoking' sign on the dash.

The keys were in the ignition, in the on position. Nathan reached and turned it off and then on, but nothing happened, the battery dead. There was an almost full cup of milky coffee in the cup holder, most of a bar of chocolate beside it. He opened the ashtray and there were some butts in there. He would have to ask, see if the guy was a smoker, check did he take milk in his coffee. There was a semicircle of scummy brown showing on the rim of the cup, a lip print. The car seemed otherwise clean. The usual documents were there, the Taxi license on display.

He touched the handbrake and, realizing it wasn't on, pulled it quickly up, worried about the incline inches from the front wheels. Then he thought to check and saw it was in gear – third. This car had been left with the key in the ignition, in third gear, lights on, but handbrake off. What did that tell you?

Nathan checked the boot, relieved to find it free of dead taxi drivers, then he came back to the cab. There were strands of thread on the passenger seat, a few longish blonde hairs on the back seat.

But then, it was a taxi. He dialed a number on his cell phone, wondering would he have trouble persuading somebody to pick the car up and take it to the pound.

He finished the phone call, irritated, knowing now he would have to hang around for over an hour before the Passat could be picked up. Looking towards the bridge, he saw he could walk straight onto it from here, the walkway that ran its entire length.

With time to kill, he trotted down the steps and strolled onto the bridge. As he walked further out, he was surprised to find that, when cars went past, the structure bounced under their weight. He hadn't realized it was so flexible, nor that it was so high above the gray, choppy water.

He walked for about ten minutes, thinking about the taxi driver, buying chocolate and coffee, probably for the return trip to Dundee. But he didn't drink his coffee. He didn't make the trip. Instead, he drove into the parking lot, rolled to a stop in third and stepped straight out, walking away without locking the door or pulling the brake.

Where did he go? Nathan stared down at the water, feeling the bridge bounce as a truck sped by.

November 1976

David felt only slightly uncomfortable turning up at the court wearing jeans he had cut off above the knee, topped with a yellow tee. Angela had given him her spare racket and he was swinging it manfully, easing his shoulder.

He had played intermittently throughout the summer and was feeling pretty good about this. It was Saturday, a dry, bright and unseasonably warm day and Angela had turned up in proper tennis whites, no surprise there, the look of it suiting her angular frame. David found himself staring at her legs and made himself look away. He just wasn't used to seeing so much thigh.

He expected to beat Angela, who was a girl, but thought she might give him a game. She hit a few practice serves, and he had to admit they came over pretty fast, deciding to revise his plan of being showily generous, taking it easy on her.

Two sets later, having won only a single game, he was feeling pretty demoralized. Angela shook his hand over the net and said, "You know why you scored so few points?"

"Because I'm shit?"

"Because you stopped dead every time you hit the ball."

He shrugged. "I wanted to see what would happen."

"I noticed. I just hit it to where you weren't."

"Hardly sporting, that."

"And you set yourself wrong to play your backhand."

"I don't like backhand."

"Well, obviously. All I had to do was target your backhand and I won the point. Can I show you?"

Without asking, she came around his side and started talking about how he should stand, and hold his racket. David came close to being annoyed, but found that he couldn't muster it up. For a start, when she bent forward, he could see her bra.

"Are you listening to me?"

"Sorry, yes."

She made a noise, impatient but amused, and was suddenly behind him, twisting the racket in his hand and showing him how to stand. She smelled of soap and clean sweat.

"You want me to hit a few to your backhand?"

They played into the afternoon and David surprised himself by not getting bored, or annoyed. It seemed that she really knew what she was talking about and wanted him to improve his backhand. Sometimes her tone got sharp, and again he surprised himself. Instead of telling her to piss off, he took it, even when she all but shouted, "No, no! You're doing it again. Right leg planted first, then hit!"

By the end of the session, he was hitting proper backhand shots. Mostly they hit the net, but some fired over, bending to the line with a satisfying top-spin dip. Angela's patience seemed to be wearing thin when he said, "Fancy some tea? I'm starving."

"When you say tea?"

"Sorry, forgot you were so posh. I mean dinner, or supper. The evening meal."

"Are you offering to buy me dinner?"

That hadn't been in his mind at all. He had been thinking they could go and buy chips, eat them in his room, where a bottle of ketchup stood ready. But she was smiling at him and he found himself saying yes, thinking he had better get a few hands of poker in before next week.

Angela, now with her jacket over her shoulder, fell in beside him and he fancied he could feel the heat from her bare arm radiating against his own. She looked up at the trees. "Is Dundee always like this? I mean all those crows?"

David looked up, as usual feeling slightly uneasy when he looked straight at them, as though they were aware that they were being studied.

"Not really. The local paper says it's to do with the hot summer."

"Did you see the sign on the notice board at Rankine Hall?"

"The one about tickets for Steve Winwood? That would be so cool."

"I'm guessing he's a pop star. You winced, ha-ha! I mean the one about meningitis."

"Neil thinks it's to stop students screwing."

As soon as the word was out of his mouth, David felt himself redden, but Angela didn't seem to notice.

"I'm not so sure. Four students are very ill, one has died. All they are asking is that people observe good standards of hygiene."

"Isn't there something about avoiding kissing multiple partners?"

"I don't suppose I'll have much trouble with that."

David glanced at her again. She was looking ahead, frowning. She slowed and put her hand on his arm. "What's he doing?"

In the square in front of the Union, a middle-aged man wearing a car coat was holding a clipboard and looking around him. There was nothing strange about the sight, apart from the way he was moving, a clumsiness in his movements apparent even at a distance.

"I know him, he was, what do you call it? A guest lecturer." David thought, "He's the city archivist. You could ask him anything about Dundee history and he knew it. Did you know there's an underground river somewhere around here?"

"Maybe he's looking for it. That's a map he's got."

Coming abreast of the man now, David could see that he had what looked like a very old map indeed. Above them, the crows suddenly took flight with an explosion of flapping and cawing, and the man ducked. So did David and Angela but, unlike the archivist, they straightened immediately. He looked up with something like fear on his face then, noticing them for the first time, turned away, seemingly embarrassed.

David whispered to Angela, "I think he's Brainiac 5's hairier brother. His name is Mooney. No, Minto."

Minto wrote on his clipboard and walked off in the direction of West Port, but David noticed how he kept looking up at the sky.

2016

Nathan was walking past the canteen when Mike Piper, from car crimes, caught up with him.

"Heard you and Dudek were at Crammond."

Piper was small and seemed to be constantly moving. Nathan felt awkward speaking to him, knowing that he had been favorite for the CID post that Nathan got. The guy Dudek had wanted.

He told him, yeah, they'd been visiting an old friend of the university shooter.

"Haddow, right? I've got a coincidence for you. You remember Micky Waters?"

"Give me a break." Nathan was smiling along with Piper now. "You and I busted him for boosting that Lexus."

"Guy always let his heart rule his head. Could never resist a quality car. I've just charged him with stealing this

Mercedes soft top, 1969. A real classic, we got it at the pound, you want to take a look."

"What's the coincidence?"

"We got a call from his wife Doreen, you remember her?"

"Large woman? Shouts instead of talking."

"That's her. She calls us up." Piper held an imaginary phone to his ear, broadened his accent and increased volume, "You know what that little bastard has done now? He's stole this fuckin' Mercedes and he's refusing to sell it."

"She called to tell you Mick had stolen a car?"

"She was totally ranting. He'd taken the railings from the front of the house, put boards over her garden, so he could park the car."

"In the garden?"

"Worried somebody would steal it. She said she'd planted roses, Princess Diana's mind, none of your shite, and that little bastard had moved them around the back, hadn't replanted them or nothing. Wanted us to lift him."

"So, you did?"

"Course. Here's this beautiful Mercedes, champagne, soft top, sitting on boards, right in the middle of the garden."

"Why'd he try to keep it?"

"It's a beauty. We stood around it and agreed it was a piece of class. Claims he bought it proper, the papers will come through any time. But here's the thing. It hasn't been taxed for about twenty years, and the last recorded owner was a guy called Sir Fraser Canfield, of Crammond."

"Stirling House?"

"Where you were, right?"

"Yeah."

"The thing that's got us, nobody seems to own the car. Somebody has to own it before it can get stolen"

"How do you mean?"

"Canfield died with no family and his estate was bought up, lock, stock and barrel by your man Haddow. Haddow wants nothing to do with the Mercedes."

"Where's Micky?"

"Interview 2. I've just finished trying to talk him into admitting he boosted the car but he's more interested in Doreen. It got sort of out of hand."

"He knows it was her who turned him in?"

"She was there. Things she was saying to him! Said she was going to slit his throat for damaging her Princess Diana's, meant it too. There was just me and Ted and the two of us were struggling to pin Doreen. Had to taser her and the neighbors all out saying how we were a disgrace. Embarrassin' man."

"Think I could speak to him?"

Piper shrugged. "I'm about to let him out anyway. Got better things to do than arrest people for boosting cars that nobody owns."

"Prints?"

"He'd cleaned it before we got there."

"To remove prints?"

"Think he was just cleaning it, man."

Nathan pushed the door open and Micky looked up, frowning, then he smiled.

"Constable Findlay, right? You CID now?"

"Yeah. I was speaking to Mike Piper. About this Mercedes."

"Bought it fair and square, man. You interviewing me? No tape nor nothing?"

"Just a chat. You see on the TV, the shooting at the university?"

"Heard it was a hit. Drugs money."

"Yeah?"

Micky looked away. "Was what I heard."

"Where?"

"Can't tell you that, pal."

"See here's the thing. The car's connected."

Nathan saw Micky's face go blank, and added, "I mean to the murder."

Micky's face stayed blank, the man being careful, thinking hard.

Nathan sat back. "I don't give a monkey's about the car. But I want to know where you got it."

"I told your pal-"

"The car's being dusted. We get a match on the guy did the hit, we have your statement that you bought the car the day *before* the shooting. Puts you and the shooter in the car on the day of the murder. And that makes you...well you can finish it off."

Nathan was in pure blue sky, making it up, but he could see Micky was struggling to be cool.

"You're trying to scare me. Get me to say something stupid."

"We're reviewing CCTV right now, see if we can spot the Mercedes. You know how that works now, don't you?"

"ANPR, sure. I seen on TV how it could check number plates going past a camera. Don't think you could do it reviewing CCTV."

"Only problem is the hassle factor. We wouldn't do it for a stolen car, but we'll do it for a murder. If the thing was moving about on that day, we'll tag it for sure."

Micky dropped his eyes and Nathan leaned in. "Sure you want to put yourself in the car the night of the shooting?"

He rubbed his head with both hands. Coming to a decision.

"Shit. I knew this was dumb, but you seen the car, right?"

"A classic."

"A fuckin' classic."

"Seriously. I don't care about the Mercedes. Maybe you'll end up keeping it. Keep telling everybody else you bought it. But tell me where you really got it."

Nathan called Dudek on his cell phone, Dudek answering on the first ring, as though he had been holding the phone.

"I've got a link between Haddow and the campus, on the night of the shooting. Only it doesn't make sense."

"Well, we don't want any sense creeping in at this stage. What have you got?"

"A car."

Nathan paused, expecting him to say, "A car?" but this was Dudek and he didn't say anything, so Nathan had to say "An old Mercedes. It was owned by the guy who had Stirling House before Haddow. When he died, Haddow took on the whole estate and the Mercedes disappeared. Now it turns up, boosted from Brook Street."

"Five minutes' walk from the Union."

"Piper figures it's Haddow's car, but he wants no part of it."

Nathan could feel Dudek thinking, finally asking, "Brook Street to the Union. You see Haddow walking that?"

"He could hardly get to the end of his hall."

"This car, could it be automatic? Power steering?"

"It's a 1969 SE."

"Ok, you'd have to *drive* the thing. You think there might be somebody else involved? A driver?"

"Could be. Maybe the guy who Kerr shot."

Dudek was quiet for a moment, then asked, "Anything on Angela Murray yet?"

"Her mother's still alive, in Glasgow."

"Go see her. Mullins is sorted, all Peter wants to talk about is how that's definitely Kylie's ass and that he hates his brother, even though he's already killed him. But I can't leave anything to chance."

Nathan signed off and started dialing Mrs. Murray's number. Then his phone rang, right there in his hand.

Dudek said, "Good work, by the way."

November 1976

"What do you mean, pizza and chips?"

They had changed out of their tennis clothes and were walking into town in failing light and sharpening wind. David had been feeling good about the idea of taking her out for a meal. Like a proper date. But she had asked the question with real sharpness and he felt on the back foot, like his suggestion was somehow foolish.

"I mean the chip shop does pizza. Not just fish and chips."

"But, deep fried?"

"Well…yeah." Meaning, of course.

"You think pizza is supposed to be deep fried?"

He looked at her, for the first time annoyed by her poshness and all that it assumed.

"What's wrong with that?"

"Have you had proper pizza? Cooked in a pizza oven?"

"Yeah, I've had proper pizza. Cooked in a pizza *fryer*."

She gave him with a flat look he didn't much like, then laughed and surprised him, linking her arm into his.

"Let's go to an Italian restaurant. You'll love it and I'll buy the drinks."

He found he had to smile back, happy just to have her linked into his arm. They passed a group of students and David couldn't help but notice the looks they got.

Angela was dressed in a pencil slim wool coat over a dark blue skirt that stopped just below her knee, and what he suspected might be court shoes. People would naturally wonder what such a cool guy, wearing an Afghan, was doing with a girl like that. He'd have to talk to her about it. But not yet.

They passed the fish and chip shop and kept going, despite the fabulous smell. He had expected that she would relent once she caught a snootful of it, but no. She was leading, he realized, steering him towards someplace she already knew, an Italian restaurant, it turned out.

Inside, it was dimly lit, and they were shown to a small table with a candle, which the waiter made quite a display of lighting. Angela seemed pleased, almost excited, and he couldn't help but pick up on it, despite his concern about the prices. This place felt pricey.

"This is nice." She whispered, leaning over and smiling.

He smiled back and agreed, coming close to forgetting the impact on his finances.

The pizza, when it came, was a shock. It was very flat but surprisingly tasty. Almost as good as if it had been properly fried.

Near the end of the bottle of wine, Angela said, "When I told Irish Iris that I…"

"Irish Iris?"

"I suppose you'd say she was my friend."

"Hang on, she's called Irish Iris and you suppose I'd say…"

"Let me start again. When I told my friend I was going out with you, she said you looked like a stoner. You know what that is?"

"Let me guess. Somebody who smokes a lot of dope?"

"She said she couldn't see me with you."

"I wouldn't say I was a stoner."

"But you smoke dope, right?"

"Everybody smokes dope. Just about."

"I don't."

She sipped her wine, "I don't normally drink either."

"Irish Iris. She the big red-haired girl?"

Angela nodded.

"I bet she smokes. I mean dope."

Angela nodded.

"So, why does she think…nah, I don't get it."

"She wasn't saying you were the weird one."

He thought about it. "How come you only suppose she's your friend?"

"I don't have friends. I'm sure it's obvious that I don't have an easy way with the world. But Iris does, and, for some reason, she likes me."

David thought, this is where I say something nice, like there being every reason to like her. But she was talking again, and the moment passed.

"Your friend is the tall chap."

He nodded. "Neil. I never heard anybody call him a chap before."

"I think Iris likes him."

David rolled his eyes. "It makes you sick."

2016

Mrs. Murray's apartment was on the ground floor of a red sandstone tenement, a different class to those Nathan was familiar with. The windows were tall, the front door positively grand, with engraved brass name plates.

Nathan pressed the button on the door entry, and a woman's voice, imperious even through the intercom, asked who was there.

"Nathan Findlay, Mrs. Murray. From…"

"My apartment is on the left."

The lock clicked, and Nathan pushed into in a tiled hallway. It smelled, not of Jeyes fluid, but of the sort of perfume he associated with old ladies. There were large pot plants, bay trees, at either side of Mrs. Murray's apartment.

The door was opened by an elderly, midsized woman with hair puffed into a cloud, wearing a lilac twin set. She stood with an exceptionally straight back, her long chin pointed up at him.

"Detective Constable Findlay?" Putting an emphasis on the Constable. Sighing, she beckoned him inside and sat him down in a room, insisting on making tea, moving with a clear discomfort in her hips and an air of martyrdom.

The furniture was expensive, polished walnut and old leather, framed photographs on the sideboard, some of which he recognized as Angela. Here was one, a dark-haired girl, smiling in her school uniform, holding some sort of scroll. Another on a tennis court being handed a cup by a grinning man; in the background, looking severe, a younger version of the woman now making him censorious tea. Yet another showed Angela focusing hard as she played a flute.

In pride of place wasn't a photograph of Angela, but of a younger Mrs. Murray, shaking hands with Margaret Thatcher. The two women's hair styles were identical.

She returned, pushing a trolley and breathing, in Nathan's opinion, a lot more heavily than she needed to, a hefty dose of theatrics in there. He accepted a cup and went through the questions from his note book, asking what she knew about the night of her daughter's disappearance and the events leading up to it.

She answered, but her answers were clipped, with a barely covered irritation. Nathan was asking about Angela's relationships, when she interrupted.

"Oh, for goodness sake! After all this time!"

"Sorry?"

"You weren't exactly interested forty years ago, when you could have been of some use. Quite the reverse."

He took a breath to answer but she didn't give him the chance. "This isn't about Angela at all is it? It's about that beastly Kerr."

"Well…"

"I wasn't sad to hear what had happened. Whatever occurred, he had a part to play in it, alongside his accomplice, Haddow."

She was sitting, if anything, even straighter. She said, "He was a policeman's son."

"Sorry?"

"Kerr. The son of some fat provincial policeman. Had the temerity to call me, after what his brute of a son had done to my daughter."

"I'm sorry, what did Neil Kerr do, Mrs. Murray?"

"He ruined her. Along with that ghastly Haddow."

It occurred to Nathan that this might be the only time he'd ever heard somebody say ghastly in real life. And beastly. "In what way…"

"*Must* you be so dense? She had everything. Threw it in my face. Went off to that damned place and took up with scum."

"I'm sorry. I'm sure this is bringing a lot of stuff back for you."

The woman gave a silent laugh, the sharp edge of its bitterness surprising Nathan.

"I expected even you would know better. You can't bring it *back* because it's never gone. When your own daughter disappears…" She pulled herself into her own pursed face

"You go through many things, but you are unable to grieve because you don't know if she's dead or alive. It's worse than a death, because on the days when I believe she is alive I feel such anger at her."

She looked at him for several seconds before speaking again.

"I employed my own investigator, because your colleagues appeared willfully incompetent. He was blocked by an odious man called Mackie but, in the end, he believed she drowned that night."

"Drowned?"

She looked at him for a long moment before saying. "In the water."

He felt stupid but had to ask, "What water?"

She sighed theatrically. "I see nothing has changed. Did you not make even the most rudimentary enquiries before coming to speak to me? Was that not your clear duty?"

She waved her hand in front of her face, "No matter. I refer, of course, to the river that runs below the mill."

Nathan made a note in his book, his cheeks burning.

"Can you give me his name?"

"He passed away, years ago."

Then she said, "That other detective, the one who came much later. I always thought that if anyone was going to find out what happened, he would. He, at least, inspired confidence."

Again, he had to ask. "What other detective?"

This time, after shaking her head for several seconds, she asked, with real venom, "What is the point of you?"

"Mrs. Murray, we're trying to shed light on things that happened before I was born."

"What does it take to join the Police? Is it enough that you're oversized?"

"Personally, I've got a law degree."

The way she looked at him, he cursed himself. Something like triumph in there.

"They must hand them out like sweets these days."

"Please, Mrs. Murray. The other detective?"

She shook her head. "Another Private Investigator. A Mr. Moore."

Nathan told himself to be cool, but imagined that his face paled, slightly. If so, she didn't notice.

"He asked me to call him Roger. I didn't, of course, but I did see the funny side. A private investigator called Roger Moore. Like *The Saint*, which might have been before your time."

"He came here?"

"Possibly four times over the period of a year."

"Sorry, I'm not getting this, Mrs. Murray. Did you employ him?"

"Certainly not."

"Well, who did?"

"He wouldn't say. But he was very upbeat the last time I saw him, told me he was close. Then, he simply disappeared. I still have his business card."

"When was that, the last time you saw him?"

"1990. No '91, I'm almost sure. It must have been summertime. Do you want to see her bedroom?"

There was nothing to mark the room as a teenager's. On the wall were framed photographs, landscapes mainly. There was a neat bed and dressing table, a wardrobe, which Mrs. Murray opened. Nathan wasn't sure what teenagers were wearing in the 70's, but he was certain he wasn't looking at it.

There was also a music stand, with a shining flute and sheet music, open and waiting.

Nathan came back to the pictures on the walls, wondering if they had anything to do with Angela, or if everything in here was to do with the woman at his elbow.

"She likes landscapes."

"That one was taken on holiday in Arran. That's Tyree. This one Scriven. She loved the islands."

It was only later, when he replayed it in his head, that he realized she talked about her daughter in the past tense.

Dudek's expression didn't change when Nathan gave him Moore's business card, but he looked at it without speaking as Nathan told him what Angela's mother had said. How Moore had been tracking Angela for over a year.

"When was it that he lost it, boss?"

Dudek looked up, narrowing his eyes. "It must have been…'91. July or maybe June."

"Last time he saw Mrs. Murray, must have been just before that."

"What are you saying?"

"Nothing. Mrs. M gave me that card less than two hours ago and now I'm giving it to you."

"Who was paying?"

"Moore wouldn't say. Did the Police look into his cases?"

"Somebody did. Mackie, in fact. I remember him saying there wasn't enough coming in to keep the house going. The business was failing. Yet he was driving about in a brand-new Honda."

"Any of that be on file?"

Dudek shook his head. "It wasn't like there was a mystery."

They were quiet for a while, till Nathan said, "I know why they were soaked through, that night. Kerr and Haddow."

Dudek gave him that flat look he had. "Are you thinking about telling me?"

Nathan swallowed his annoyance, avoided telling Dudek he'd had it with his shit.

"There's a river under the Tombstone Mill. Mackie told Mrs. Murray that Angela probably drowned in it that night, was washed out to sea."

Dudek nodded, lost in thought. "Mackie."

"Moore thought differently. He believed he was close to finding her."

Nathan waited, letting Dudek finger the business card before he asked, "Where's Moore now?"

November 1976

Later, Angela would look back and know that David had expected to walk her back to Rankine Hall, probably a chaste kiss goodnight. Based on assumptions that she supposed were understandable, he believed she was a virgin.

She wasn't a virgin and, when he asked her how many sexual partners she'd had, both of them lying in bed at this point, he pulled away when she told him it was three to his two, even looked like he might sulk.

Two weeks later, and she reflected that she'd had more sex with David than with her other partners put together. And, this time around, she was enjoying it.

Of those three, only one could be properly described as a partner, a boy she had gone to bed with on more than one occasion. Six, to be exact. It had been tense, and messy.

With David, she could barely wait to finish class, so she could get him back to his room and screw – his word, not hers – him senseless. Sometimes she didn't wait.

She had always thought of her body as too hard to be of much interest, sexually. Her breasts were small, dominated by nipples that her ex had described as bee stings. She responded by describing his penis as a wet sock, which ended things between them.

David was fascinated by her breasts. Captivated. With him, she could lie naked after sex, feeling soaked and satiated and watch his eyes come back again and again to the mounds on her chest.

That first night, after pizza and wine, they had wandered arm in arm, aimless through the night, only vaguely towards Rankine Hall. She remembered the ratty smell of the Afghan coat, thinking even then that he would have to get rid of it, how he tensed every time a crow cawed, probably not even knowing he was doing it.

They kissed for the first time at the foot of the sweeping stone staircase of the museum. She pressed herself into him and felt him stiffen, pressed harder before breaking off and pulling him onwards.

They wandered up Lochee Road, parkland rising to their right and old industrial buildings to their left. There were few pedestrians about, but a car would swish past them every minute or so. It turned out that David did not know this area at all. She told him about her walks and he said you had to watch it, some of the locals don't like students.

She laughed at that, and, a second later, he joined in.

She told him, "Iris went to a party once and ended up lost, quite drunk of course. She had to walk past a group of young girls, who were drinking vodka and screaming at each other. So she made her hands into claws, and walked past with them up in front of her."

"Did they leave her alone?"

"Wouldn't you? What do you think about Iris and Neil?"

David shook his head. "I've never seen him with a fatty."

"She's not fat! Don't you think she's beautiful?"

He seemed surprised by the question. "Not really. Anyway, there are lots of girls after the big fella."

"He doesn't have your looks, don't worry."

He glanced at her, apparently trying to see if this was a joke.

They walked on, thinking to take a left but ignoring a series of cobbled alleys, crooked and dark, reminders of a past Dundee, finally turning down a wider street. On their right was a line of tenements, with pubs and shops. To the left was some scrub ground and, beyond that, a huge, derelict building; one of the old stone jute mills that once dominated Dundee.

Beyond that, another factory loomed, dwarfing the first.

Angela thought that this must be the largest mill she had seen, and the ugliest. The windows were black rectangles along the walls, ten feet tall or more. In the darkness above, crows wheeled and cawed.

They came to a stop, still thirty yards back, and even here she could catch the thick smell of damp stone. Angela noticed something messy lying in the gutter; a pigeon, dead and torn up.

David grimaced. "I wonder why they don't pull that thing down."

She opened her mouth to say it seemed to gather shadows around itself, but that seemed melodramatic, so she nodded, wondering why they were still standing there, looking at it, instead of hurrying past.

He looked around. "I know where we are now. The smaller factory is the Coffin Mill."

"That's its actual name?"

"Yeah, and the really nasty one is the Tombstone Mill. Blackness Works is around here somewhere too. Seriously. If we keep going, we come to the Union in about ten minutes."

They started moving again, silently agreeing to pick up the pace. If the man in the car hadn't chosen that moment to pour tea from his flask, she wouldn't have noticed him at all. As it was, she nudged David and whispered, "Isn't that the chap we saw earlier?"

David frowned and nodded. "Yeah. Doctor Minto, the archivist."

"What do you think he's doing?"

They were walking past him now, so David dropped his voice.

"Looks like he's watching the Tombstone Mill."

2016

They were silent as they walked into the country house that acted as a reception for the hospital, but Nathan could feel Dudek's tension. In the hallway, an elderly man wearing a bath robe sidled quietly up, taking him by the arm. He leaned in, confidential.

"I want home to my own bed."

A nurse took them through a locked door into a long corridor, then up to an orderly in a glass cubicle.

"George, this is the policemen."

George came forward, hand out and smiling.

"Chief Inspector Dudek is it? And Detective Findlay? Roger has agreed to meet, but we'll have to play it carefully. If he becomes distressed..."

"I understand. Is he still on suicide watch?"

"He'll always be on suicide watch."

Minutes later, they were sitting on foam chairs in what looked like a brightly colored sitting room. Dudek was on the edge of his seat, Nathan noticed, not his usual relaxed pose. The door opened, and George came in, with Moore.

Nathan wasn't sure what he had been expecting. Moore was tall, white haired and cadaverously thin. He might have once been handsome, were it not for the large dent above his right eye. The eye itself was pale and dead. There was nothing dead about the eye that glanced briefly at Nathan before fixing on Dudek.

Moore walked straight backed to the vacant sofa. When he sat down, he folded his left hand over his empty sleeve.

Dudek spoke first. "Roger, this is Nathan Findlay."

Nathan nodded, but Moore just looked at him before turning back.

Dudek smiled. "You're looking well, Roger."

Moore took his time answering. "Better than the last time you saw me, I suppose."

Then, getting right to it, "What's happened?"

Dudek didn't seem surprised. "You know the name Neil Kerr?"

Moore nodded. "What's happened to him?"

"I didn't say anything happened to him."

"That the way you want to play, John? Think you're holding cards here?"

It was Dudek's turn to pause. "Sorry, Rod. Kerr's dead." He looked at George and shrugged.

"Kill himself?"

"Why do you say that? He suicide material?"

"He was in the way of a suicide, more like."

Dudek let that go for now, with Moore talking again.

"You made the connection with the seventies yet?"

"Yes, but we don't know a lot about what happened, back then."

"What do you know?"

Dudek set it out for him, what little he knew, and Nathan noticed Moore nodding at the names, like he was ticking them off. There was an intensity about him now, the way he was leaning forward.

Dudek finished with, "Then Nathan speaks to Mrs. Murray, and we get to you."

Moore drew back, and dropped his eyes.

"How did you get involved in this, Rod? Who employed you?"

Moore's expression darkened, shaking his head at the question, and Dudek asked, "What am I looking at here?"

"The question is too big."

Dudek seemed stalled for a moment, so Nathan asked, "Did you find her?"

Moore stiffened, and George moved uncomfortably beside him. For a few seconds it seemed he might not answer.

Finally, he spoke to the floor.

"I found her."

"Where?"

"I can't say."

George put his hand up, "This is proving too upsetting for Roger. I'm going to have to call a halt."

Moore moved in his chair and looked at the orderly, saying his name. Said it again, stopping the man just like that. Then he turned back to Dudek.

"Keep going."

"Ok. I'm seeing a pattern, not one I want to admit to, but it's there. Something happened in the seventies, involving the students, and Minto, the archivist. Whatever it was, it destroyed them all."

Moore frowned. "All?"

"Murray disappears. Minto commits suicide in a way that will keep him in the police black museum forever. Decades later, Kerr kills himself in a way that defies belief."

"Your beliefs are going to change, John."

"Maybe they already have. Because, there was another incident, wasn't there?"

Moore looked away and Dudek added, "There's what happened to you."

Nathan leaned forward again, looking to Dudek who gave the smallest of nods.

"How soon after you found Murray did you have your breakdown?"

Moore took a deep breath and closed his eyes. When he opened them, they were shining.

"Breakdown? Call it that, if it helps you. Found her on a Tuesday. Killed my family on Wednesday."

Dudek said, "Just to be clear, were the two things connected?"

"Of course."

For several seconds nobody said anything. Then Dudek asked, "What are you telling us?"

"Be careful, John. You're into something that nothing in your life could prepare you for. Did you and Caroline have children?"

"Caroline passed away."

Moore opened his mouth to speak, then paused, looking closely at Dudek. "You have a child though?"

"Had."

Something passed behind the man's eyes. Something close to eagerness. Nathan noticed that as he moved forward, Dudek sat back.

"How did he die?"

Dudek's expression didn't change. Nathan was willing him not to tell, and George was shaking his head.

"They both drowned."

The Saint seemed to take a while, processing this. Then, "You continue with this, that will turn out to be a blessing."

He looked at Nathan. "You're married, I see. Kids?"

When Nathan nodded, the man whispered, "Still time to get out."

Then, in a more normal voice, "You haven't mentioned Bernard."

"The body in the Mill?"

Moore nodded. "The only criminal thing in his past was that he was criminally dull. Did you read the file?"

"There's not much in there."

"Funny that."

"What? You think someone disappeared stuff?"

Moore shrugged, "Was the autopsy report in there, at least?"

"No."

"I spoke to old Willie Martin, the coroner. Speak to Willie, if he's still around. If not, try Charlie Rose, his assistant. The point is the body had been hit with a machete or something weeks *after* he had died. This is news to you?"

"I didn't know anything about a machete."

"Did you know that Kerr made a report about somebody accosting students. Maybe something occult."

"I didn't know that, no."

"It was dismissed as crazy."

"Who by?"

"You can guess that one. Next thing he breaks into a disused factory."

"The Tombstone Mill."

"Yeah. They go right under the building to where the Scourin Burn is. I never got anywhere near understanding what happened, but..."

Moore turned to George now.

"Want to know what happened to Minto, Georgie?"

George just looked at him.

"The only heating in his bedroom was a two-bar electric heater, you know the kind of thing? Curved steel body to reflect the heat from the elements."

George nodded. "Got one in the staff room."

"'Course you do. Minto turned it on, both bars, picked it up and...that's about it really. Sat in his armchair and hugged it. He was wearing a gray tank top. All gone at the front, but the back was intact. His specs had melted. House was mainly ok, but he wasn't."

He looked at Nathan, "You've seen the photos?"

"My first week on the job."

"What went through your mind?"

"I thought, how could somebody *do* that? Actually, physically do it."

Moore was suddenly intense, leaning forward like he had been building up to this. "There's an answer to that. I found it. You will too, if you keep going with this."

Nathan and Dudek looked at each other for a long moment and Dudek asked, "So, what don't I know about what happened?"

"You don't know anything about what happened. All that violence, murders and people dying of an inexplicable disease. Kerr thought it was caused by an occult presence."

"An occult presence." Dudek repeated the phrase, his voice flat.

"You think occult is a good word? How about vampire." Moore seemed to be enjoying himself, suddenly.

"They thought they were dealing with a vampire?"

"Not the toothy kind, but something like that, yeah. And they had a meeting with a witch, a real live one, not long before they broke into the factory."

Dudek rubbed his hands over his face, looking tired.

"Tell me about when you met Kerr."

"I met him twice, in Brighton. Asked him about Angela, what happened back then. He told me something that led me to her. Accidentally."

"What was that?"

"She wanted to live on an island."

Nathan blinked, thinking about the photographs in the room in Glasgow. Arran, Scriven.

Moore stood suddenly, stepping away, towards the door. "I think we're done."

Then, he turned "Your son."

"What about him?"

"Caroline drowned him, didn't she? Before she drowned herself."

When Dudek didn't answer, Moore turned away again. This time, he didn't look back.

2016

Nathan parked in the street and pretended not to notice the old man, Charles Rose, watching from behind his curtains. He walked up the steps, pressed the entry button and the voice came through immediately.

"Hello."

"Mr. Rose, its Nathan-"

The buzzer sounded, cutting him off.

Rose was on the first floor, opening the door as Nathan came up, waving a veiny hand to usher him inside. Nathan stepped into the smell of years of tobacco smoke. The house hadn't been decorated for many years and Nathan's guess was that, when it had, Rose hadn't been involved. The living room, however, had large comfortable sofas and an impressive widescreen.

"Nice TV."

"It's got surround sound, see the speakers, in the corners?"

"Must sound good."

"Should do, the amount it cost. You stop noticing, though. Might as well have the old Phillips back. Have a seat. Coffee?"

"Thanks, black, no sugar."

While Rose was gone, Nathan glanced at his video collection, noticing a lot of old stuff, Arnold and Sly in there, Bruce Willis. Rose bustled back, with the cups.

"How can I help? Something to do with an autopsy?"

"Yes. I tried your old boss, first. Dr Martin. I suppose you know he passed."

"Old Willie. A true gentleman."

"It's about a case you both worked on. Simon Bernard."

Rose grimaced, showing yellowed teeth, and shook a cigarette loose. Nathan shook his head when he offered him one.

"I knew it. Been waiting for, what, near on forty years."

"It wasn't exactly…"

"We didn't make a habit of it!"

Nathan was surprised by the vehemence, but this is how things often went. People assuming you knew something, telling it to you. "I'm sure you didn't."

"Willie was the most professional guy I ever worked with. Last man in the world to falsify a certificate."

Nathan kept his expression neutral.

"What do you remember about the autopsy? You don't mind me taking notes?"

"I remember it better than any other I did, that's for sure. Right from the start, I knew something weird was happening. Right from when the guys brought the body in."

"Because it was a murder?"

"Don't be stupid. I did a dozen murders. You know in a job like that, you get a certain sense of humor? Same as Police, I guess, you got to laugh, haven't you?"

Nathan nodded, and Rose asked, "You have a laugh, do you? A laugh?"

The man was nodding, strangely expectant, and Nathan found himself smiling and nodding. Rose made his hands into skinny fists and pretended to do a little one, two three, with accompanying sound effects, "Pah, Pah, Pah-ow."

Then he was back to nodding, saying "Eh? Eh?"

Nathan tried not to laugh, but it came out anyway and he thought, I've cocked it up. But no, Rose was laughing along with him. Like they were sharing a joke. The guy took a shaky drink of coffee, spilling some.

"The autopsy?"

"Yeah. Colin Furness, one of the guys who brought it in, was a real joker. When I saw it was Colin, I called something out, can't remember what now.

"Normally he'd send it straight back, but this time he didn't crack a light, just kept rolling the trolley. Other guy the same. I wondered had they had a fight or something, but when I signed the paper, I caught his eye.

"He couldn't wait to get out of there. Then this policeman came in and has a quiet word with Willie. I don't know what was said but I could see Willie was worried."

"Policeman?"

"Mackie. Upset old Willie and then pissed off, saying he'd be back."

Rose had been smoking steadily as he spoke and now he stopped for a particularly deep draw and a swallow of his coffee, like he was swallowing smoke.

"We unzip the bag and I see that the body is male, his head damn near hacked off. Not much holding it on."

"Sounds nasty."

"Nasty?" Rose seemed lost for a moment in his memories. "Nasty."

"Mr. Rose?"

The man recollected himself. "It was beyond nasty, son. I couldn't even touch it, made an excuse and scarpered. Ten minutes later Willie comes looking for me. Says he needs me to assist. But that wasn't it. He was *scared*."

"What of?"

The man wasn't listening. He was talking. "Willie Martin scared! Tried to hide it, but I knew. So, I follow him and fuck me if I'm not scared, even to go back into the room."

"What was scary?"

"I don't know. Little scrawny guy with his head nearly off. Willie hadn't touched him."

He took another gulp of coffee, not noticing some spilling down the front of his shirt. It wasn't only his hands that were trembling.

"Willie points out the main wound, saying how it was caused by a long blade, cutting downwards, almost severing his neck. Must have taken some strength. But the main thing, there was no blood. The cut was dry, like old meat. See, what I'm saying? The guy died before that cut had been made. Long before."

Nathan stayed quiet, letting the man talk. It seemed, now he was going, he wanted to tell it.

"Willie took a fold of skin and I felt my hair rise right up, seeing him touch it. He says look at this, the skin is dried too. I can't tell when this person died, Charlie. I mean what *week* he died.

"I say, well, there's no smell. But there was. It was like a damp cellar. What I had meant, there was no decomposition. The body wasn't rotting."

"How do you mean?"

"Just that. Like it had been mummified, except mummies have their internals removed, veins filled with chemical.

"Willie took some threads from the cut across his neck and matched them up with the guy's shirt. Then we laid the shirt out, happier messing about with that than touching him, you see, and you could see how the slash matched the neck wound. Threads had been forced into the wound, but they were dry too.

"Willie made the Y-incision and opened the guys thorax and abdomen."

Rose gulped more coffee and Nathan caught the whisky on his breath when he spoke, Rose beginning to show signs that he had been drinking steadily, his coffee not just coffee.

"Another surprise. His stomach and intestine had atrophied, like they'd been empty for a while. I'd never heard Willie Martin swear before that day, but he says what the fuck is this now. The guy's guts were collapsed, crispy."

"Is that what killed him?"

"That's what I said! Did this guy starve, some disease of the intestines? Willie mutters away, didn't know what he was looking at, see? There were no signs of starvation."

Coffee cup empty, Rose hung his head.

"What happened then?"

"Mackie came back. Willie showed him what he's found, and they talk about the cuts."

"More than one?"

"Yeah. The first one, the one that nearly took its head off, was the largest."

"They were in a sequence?"

"The first one was like I say. The next one was on its, his, back, but with part of the cut across his head."

"I'm not with you."

"Somebody had nearly whacked its head off. Then cut the body from the rear, striking both the head, which must have flopped over the back, and the dorsal region of the back. Imagine that, for a minute."

Nathan was thinking about standing beside Neil Kerr's body. He pulled himself back into the room to ask, "What did you make of that?"

"Not a fucking thing. There were other cuts, on the inside of the fingers and the palms of the hands."

"Like he gripped the blade?"

Rose nodded. Nathan shifted in his seat, aware that it had been a long time since he had written anything.

"So, the certificate?"

"Mackie asked about time of death, but Willie couldn't give him anything. Willie asks what the hell is going on, getting angry, and Mackie gets angry too and shouts how the fuck should he know, that was what we were for.

"Willie asks, when was he seen last, and Mackie says three weeks. Willie says, okay then, three weeks after he died, he had a fight with a huge guy with a sword, and Mackie says very fucking funny.

"Willie calms down and tells him that he doesn't have a clue, can't tell what killed him. Mackie says, how about natural causes, three weeks ago?

"That's about it. Willie wrote him up as a heart attack. Me, I didn't last six more months in the mortuary."

Rose sat back and closed his eyes. "What now?"

"We're still investigating."

His eyes flew open. "Wait now, what are you investigating? Not the falsification?"

"No. Don't worry about that."

Rose was sitting forward, almost toppling from the couch. "What then?"

"Something that might be linked. That's all I can tell you, for now,"

Rose's skinny chest rose and fell, worryingly fast. "How could something be *linked*?"

"I can't go into details. If you can think of anything else, here's my card. You've been very helpful, Mr. Rose."

At the door, Rose stopped him, clutching onto his arm, quite obviously drunk now.

"I keep thinking about that body, in its coffin. Can't help thinking it'll be exactly the same as when we put it in there."

November 1976

Iris, walking beside her, said, "It suits you."

"What does?"

"Being in love. I was never sure about the way you walk, but now when I look it looks great."

She bounced, enthusiastically. "Springy."

"I'm not in love."

"Right."

"Really."

"Good. Because he doesn't fit you at all. I mean he fits you better now you've made him get rid of that awful old beast of a thing, got him to wear an actual coat."

"Can you believe he sold his Afghan for more than he bought that nice duffel coat?"

"I can't believe he sold it, full stop. That means somebody bought it."

They were walking past a stretch of grass and Angela suddenly stopped dead, staring. "Look at that crow."

They watched the crow hopping across the grass, something in its chunky beak.

Iris made a face, "That's not another bird is it?"

"A sparrow."

As they watched, one of the sparrow's wings fluttered, making a dusty noise as its feathers scraped the larger bird's beak.

"Have you noticed how few birds there are? Apart from crows."

Iris, linked her arm, pulling Angela on.

At Rankine Hall, Iris followed Angela, uninvited, into her room and threw herself across the bed, bouncing noisily a few times. "Yours is even worse than mine."

Angela, trying not to feel put out, sat primly on the chair as Iris looked around.

"This place probably had more character before you moved in. Don't you want a poster?"

"No."

Iris picked up the only photograph in the room, a framed landscape. "What's this?"

"Arran. That's where I'll live, eventually. Not Arran, necessarily, but an island. The Hebrides."

"What's so great about an island?"

"Being near the sea. Maybe that's why I came to Dundee."

"Hah. This fuckin' room doesn't even look out over the river. What's this then?"

Iris was picking things up, putting them down, and now she opened a long black box. "A flute! You play?"

Angela did her version of a shrug. "Not really."

"Give us a tune."

"No."

"What else are we doing? Put it together and give us 'Living In The Past'."

"What's that?"

"Never mind." Iris pulled sections of flute out. "How does this thing go together?"

"Stop that! What do you think you're doing?"

Iris jerked in surprise and a look of something close to dismay crossed her face. Angela had expected...she hadn't really expected anything. She simply wanted Iris to stop. What she didn't expect was for Iris's face to crumple and for her to start crying.

Iris fumbled, trying to put the parts back and, when that wasn't straightforward, dropped them on the bed and turned to run. All the while she was crying and saying 'Sorry, sorry."

She was halfway to the door, head down, when Angela got in front of her, putting her hands on the bigger girl's arms.

"Don't go."

Iris looked at her and she added. "I don't want you to go."

Somehow, they ended up sitting on the bed with Iris in Angela's arms, her sobs subsiding. She said, "See, now you know. I'm full of shit."

Angela was thinking how small she felt, how large Iris was when you put your arms around her. Her breasts against her stomach.

"Full of shit, how?"

She sat up and Angela looked around for a tissue, but Iris was already cleaning the mascara from her face with her sleeve.

"I act like I'm so tough. Say anything to anybody. Truth is, this is what I am."

They were side by side on the bed, effectively looking into each other's eyes from a distance of inches. Angela thought again about how beautiful Iris was, how beautiful her eyes were. She shifted back and, after a moment, Iris did the same.

"Tell you what. Take the flute back to your room and work out how to put it together. Get a tune out of it."

It seemed the armor was back on.

"What a girl you are! Trying to get rid of me. Well, I've made up my mind that I'm going to be your friend, whether you want it or not. You don't have a say in it."

Angela surprised herself by laughing and Iris bounced off the bed, holding out the box. "Come on, let's hear you. I bet you're brilliant, aren't you?"

Angela took the box and looked at it. "Maybe one day. Tell you what, let's go for a drink."

"Really? You'll come to the pub?"

"Just for one."

"Don't think this means I'm not going to pester the life out of you till you play me something on that flute."

Angela was shaking her head and smiling. "You're the only person in the world who would say something like that. I'm going to be your friend whether you want it or not."

Iris looked like she was going to disagree, then said, "Pub. Come on."

Then she asked, "You want to bring Mr. Beaujangles?"

2016

Mackie held the smile in place for several seconds, the one that seemed pushed out from his face by his chin. His eyes weren't smiling, though, and they were on Nathan. Dudek sat to one side.

"You interviewed Charlie Rose?"

The way he said it, it sounded like the stupidest thing Nathan could possibly have done. Knowing it sounded childlike, Nathan asked, "Was that not okay?"

"So long as you don't believe anything he said. Did he tell you about his departure from the place?"

Again, the smile, the jutting chin. The mean little eyes. "No."

"Doc. Martin fired him."

"He fired him?"

"Never told you that did he? Course not. Rose is an alky. Willie tried to help him, but he started thinking the cadavers were moving. You know he had to be sent away for a spell?"

Sent away. Nathan knew that meant a mental hospital. "No, Sir."

Mackie turned to Dudek.

"And as for you, all we've got on and you're dicking about with something from the fuckin' seventies."

"I need to figure out-"

Mackie cut him off. "Nothing. I'm telling you to drop this line of enquiry. Do you understand?"

Dudek nodded.

As they walked along the corridor, Nathan thought about telling Dudek he had tracked down Kerr's sister, Rachel, but decided to keep quiet. Then he thought, hell with it.

"Want to hear about Kerr's sister? What she had to say?"

"Was it useful?"

"His Dad was Chief Super in Aberdeen, back when it all kicked off. Dead now. Sister said he never really recovered after Neil came back. His golden boy a basket case."

"She shed any light on what happened?"

"Neil wouldn't talk about it. Spent a year recovering, then moved to the South coast. About the only thing he said to her, promise me you'll never go near Dundee."

"What about more recently?"

"She didn't even know he was back in Scotland. You could see that really hurt her."

"What about Haddow?"

"Cut himself off, same as Neil. Not just him, either."

"How's that?"

"Rachel knew Haddow's parents, real active community types. A lot of fun, she called them. But, as soon as he gets home from hospital, they immediately change, go reclusive."

"Is she ok?"

"Teacher, married, with a child. Really wanted me to know that she was fine, and that she didn't drink."

Dudek shrugged.

"Well...write it up, file it, forget it. We've got our orders."

December 1976

David was talking about some gig, as though he expected her to be interested. Then he suddenly cut across the road to a Spar shop, mumbling about being peckish.

She had to catch him up. "You're always peckish."

Even though the light was fading and there was a splatter of freezing water in the wind, she waited outside for him. He reappeared beside her, peeling the wrapper off a Lyon's Golden Syrup Cake as they walked, back to talking about the gig.

"So, then, suddenly there was this commotion, some idiot punching some other idiot at the back of the hall and the singer..." he broke off to take a bite out of the cake and continued, telling how the singer stopped the music and said anyone into that negative shit shouldn't come to a Medicine Head gig. People clapping and saying right on man.

All the time he was telling the story, he had been taking large bites, spraying cake crumbs.

"You're going to eat that whole thing, like it's a bar of chocolate?"

His voice, muffled with cake, "Sorry! Here…"

"No thanks. What I mean is, this is your idea of a snack to eat walking up the road?"

David frowned at her, holding the cake up. "You never had one of these?"

"Mommy used to buy them. She'd make one last a whole week."

David seemed genuinely surprised. "How did she do that?"

"Cut it into slices. That's quite common with cake."

"Neil eats one of these with an entire can of creamed rice on top. That really is being a pig."

They continued towards the town center, passing a group of students, walking the other way, who turned, their expressions curious.

"Do you know what people call us? Iris told me, thinking it was hilarious. The Odd Couple."

David smiled, and Angela had to ask, did he like that? Being called The Odd Couple.

"Sure. Only one of us is odd, though."

They were coming into the Overgate, and a noise they had heard in the distance was making itself known – many voices, shouting. Another voice raised above, someone speaking loudly into a megaphone, forming a call and response.

First the woman, loud and strident through the horn, and then a large crowd shouting in reply. The words were still unintelligible.

Angela frowned. "What's that?"

They rounded a corner and could see the crowd now, men and women marching, taking up the width of the street so cars had to come to a halt.

David pointed. "It's a trade Union thing. That's a TUC banner."

A single man strode ahead, with his head high and shoulders back. Behind him, a woman was walking backwards and chanting into her bullhorn, the crowd responding.

"Look, people are clapping them."

And they were. Some people on the edges of the pavements were shouting encouragement, the marchers smiling and waving back, men and women with office clothes under heavy coats. The Police were there too, but relaxed, smiling.

Now the first marchers were coming abreast of them and Angela could hear the woman chant. "What do we want?"

The answer, three hundred voices in full throat, "Four percent!"

"When do we want it?"

"Now!"

"What do we want?"

And so, it continued. Then a loud engine noise as a car suddenly appeared opposite them, moving fast. Angela could hardly see it through the crowd but heard it rev before it shrieked to a halt, horn blaring.

Then a man, shouting. "Away you set o' lazy bastards."

Neither of them saw what happened next, but suddenly the marchers surged, some breaking into a run. Voices were raised in angry shouts and people were running in every direction, like a switch had been thrown. The woman at the front was shouting for calm.

But calm was gone. A man in a smart coat came running out of the crowd and kicked a parked car. Somewhere nearby, glass smashed, someone screamed. A middle-aged woman jumped up into an ornate planter and started kicking the flowers. The car opposite was ringed with angry men and women now, who were rocking it on its springs, breaking the windows and dragging the driver out. Then the Police were charging, striking out randomly with their batons. People were screaming, and a policeman lurched in front of them and swiped at David with his baton, but the planter woman leaped on him and they fell to the ground. Other people were immediately there, kicking the pair indiscriminately as they wrestled on the cobbles.

David made to run, turning at the last moment to put his arm around Angela, hurry her out of there. Angela, out of breath, said, "What happened? Everything was fine and then..."

She ran out of words, glancing back as they turned the corner of the Angus Hotel. The skirmishing seemed to be dying out already. Other people hurried past, just getting away. One of them wore a police uniform.

A couple of hundred yards away, everything was normal, and it was hard to believe anything had happened at all.

2016

Hilda Jarvis wasn't at the press conference and Dudek was surprised at how disappointed he was, having to make a conscious effort to concentrate. Maybe she had gone back to London.

As soon as it finished, he went upstairs, closing the door of his office before dialing her number, holding her card even though he had the number in his head.

"Hello."

"You weren't at the conference."

"No."

"Are you working this story, or aren't you?"

"Have you been to see David Haddow?"

Whilst he was wondering if he should tell her, she said, "Do you want to meet?"

"Where are you?"

"My hotel."

He was about to ask where she wanted to meet, when she added, "Room 11."

She answered the door wearing jeans and a t-shirt, nothing on her feet, stepping aside to let him into the room. A largeish room, a suite with chairs and a couch clustered around a low table, and a double bed. The room was messy with documents, a Nikon on the bed with a long lens beside it.

He made a show of looking around. "You must run up some expenses tab."

"I'm not on expenses."

"I go somewhere, I'm not on expenses, I stay in a Travelodge."

She asked him did he want coffee and, when he shook his head, sat on the couch. He got the feeling she was waiting to see what he did next, where he would sit. He took the chair opposite her.

He said, "I've been checking up on you."

She smiled. "Of course you have. And?"

"This isn't your thing at all, is it? You're an economist."

She leaned forwards and he had to make his eyes stay on her face.

"I'm a journalist."

"And an author."

"You read one of my books?"

"Like I would understand it. Right now, I'm wondering what a high flyer like you is doing here."

"Did you run a search on my name and David Haddow, try to connect us?"

"Yes."

She smiled, apparently pleased. "Well done."

"You're going to patronize me now? The dumb cop."

She shook her head. "Not me. But didn't that tell you, I mean why I'm here?"

She was still smiling and he had to smile back, taking her face in, no makeup today, like he was memorizing it. They sat like that for a few seconds, just looking at each other, and he had to say something else.

"Made a bit of a crusade out of Haddow, haven't you?"

"What you don't know, I was offered a job with *The New York Times*. My dream job. I don't know what he did, but they suddenly dropped me."

"He can do that?"

"You look him up, he doesn't make the UK hundred richest list. Truth is, he's probably in the top twenty."

"How come I've never heard of him?"

"You can hardly find anything about him. But keep digging…" She shrugged, looked to the side and, for the first time, he noticed a scratch, high on her left temple, just at the hairline. It looked painful. He wondered if her hair was different today, pulled across to hide the cut.

He said, "So, he's a successful businessman. So what?"

"Nobody can be as successful as him and be straight. You know about the dot com thing?"

"The shares went up and up, then crashed."

"When lots of people got burned, he made millions. Seemed to know exactly when to offload. That's what he does all the time. Every time."

"He's smart."

"Nobody's that smart."

"He's been investigated?"

"More than once. You heard the name Petrel Canadia?"

"Pharmaceuticals company, isn't it?"

"It was. Haddow got a controlling interest last year and did his usual thing. Made a fortune and left it dead in the water."

"You're angry."

"The guy is malignant. People lose livelihoods, pensions, their life's work. Haddow walks away with the money."

There were other scratches, on the backs of her hands.

"Haddow is the biggest corruption story of the last two decades. Up there with ENRON."

"And you want to nail him. You ever met him?"

"He's a total recluse. No photos. Never gives interviews, does all his business at home. I've only spoken to three people who have ever met him. One of them's his lawyer, another is his broker. Neither of them would give anything up, his puppies."

"You want me to ask who's the third. So, you can tell me it's me."

She laughed out loud at that. "You live up to your rep, you know. What does he look like? The only photo I ever got of him was from the early eighties. At his wedding."

Dudek thought about it, should he tell her, then shrugged and said, "Average height." Then he stopped, frowning. "You don't know about his disability."

She looked up, surprised, "He's disabled? In what way?"

"His left side. Drags his left leg, has to really swing his body to get it moving. His left arm just dangles in his sleeve."

He saw her take that in, having to make changes to her mental picture of the man, asked her, "He's married, then?"

She didn't answer that question straight away, telling Dudek, "He was badly hurt in the seventies, in a coma for over a year. People don't normally come out after that, but he did. Had to stay in hospital for months, but I had no idea he was disabled. When he did go home, staying with his parents, one of the nurses went too, to look after him. His father died a few years later, his mother just after. He married the nurse."

"The way his house looked, this massive mausoleum of a place, I didn't think anybody lived with him. The whole place is under an inch of dust."

"He's had his share of tragedy. His wife died too. That must have been tough, his wife and parents dying within a few years of him coming out of hospital. So, the place is a dump?"

"See, now, you're going to use that. Get me into trouble."

She shook her head. "I'm just fascinated to actually get something personal about him. What else?"

"He made coffee. Put biscuits out, Breakaways and Wagon Wheels. Which happen to be Nathan and my favorites."

"Your favorite biscuit? You think he checked up on you?"

"You're kidding, right? You think he had us looked into, find out what biscuits we like?"

Dudek was smiling, but couldn't help remembering how weird he felt, sitting there with Haddow's eyes on him.

She said, "Anyway, soon as he got out of hospital, he started playing the stock market, small time at first. But the guy could do no wrong, getting inside information from who knows where. Within five years he's a big player. And a recluse.

"Same with his parents and wifie. From the second he comes home, they're like different people. Hermits. Give up work and everything."

The same story Kerr's sister gave Nathan.

"What did you do to your head?"

"The way you ask, you sound like a police officer."

"You mean, like I suspect you of something."

"More like you have a right to know, trying to wrong foot me."

He found he was sitting forward, made himself sit back. "It looks sore."

She put her hand up and touched it, moving her hair to do it and he saw that it was worse than he had thought, about two inches long, crusted blood in her hair. She winced.

"Would you believe me, if I told you I was attacked by a crow?"

"Were you?"

"A bunch of them, actually. You ever heard of that?"

"Not until recently. Were you near tall trees?"

"Yeah."

"They thought you were after their chicks."

"I'm not sure that's what they thought but, after this, I'm staying in London."

"That would be a pity."

She raised her eyebrows, like saying, really?

He looked again around the room, stalling when he came back to the camera, the one with the long lens.

"Oh, right."

"What?"

"You were taking photos of Haddow's place."

She sat back. "What was it you said to me, I've got to watch you?"

"Well, what did you think? I mean of the house?"

"It once belonged to Fraser Canfield, the financier. You must have heard of him."

Dudek, having heard of Canfield days earlier, nodded. "Sure."

"Guy had everything, even an actual home cinema, but no family. Haddow buys the lot when he dies, furniture and all. Looks to me like he's done nothing since. The gardens were supposed to be something."

"You see anything at the windows? I take it you climbed over the wall."

"I set up camp in the trees. Didn't see a thing. Curtains closed. Nobody coming. Nobody going."

"Then the crows had a go at you."

"Uh-huh. Am I glad I wasn't with anybody else, something like that would be pretty hard to live down. I was squealing and waving my arms around." She put her foot out towards him, pointing the toes. "See my ankle?"

He saw his hand coming up and cupping her foot, the other hand going to her ankle, which might be swollen.

He looked up at her. "It doesn't look too bad."

"You a Doctor?"

"I trained as a paramedic."

That stopped her, "Really?"

"I just made it up." He looked down at her foot, right there in his hand, and told her, "You know, now I've got hold of your foot, I don't know quite what to do with it."

"No?"

"It seems rude to just drop it."

She folded her leg back, bringing the foot away from him but gave him her smile.

It was when he was walking back to his car that he noticed the rental Fiat 500, blue. He stopped, remembering a similar Fiat, tucked away near the gates of Stirling House. Thought to wonder if she was checking on him as well as Haddow.

December 1976

Iris, it turned out, could down a pint in one. So could David, but it was a messy business, and he looked like he might be sick afterwards. Iris had simply opened her mouth and poured it in.

Neil asked her, "You play rugby?"

"I did at school. Once. It seemed to involve a lot of boys trying to grab my boobs."

"That's the general point of the game, right enough."

Angela said, "I can't see the point of *this* game. Forcing yourself to drink an entire pint. You would never drink an entire pint of milk. Look at the state of him."

David was indeed very pale.

The pub was called Wullie Frew's, an ancient stone building in Hawkhill, and it smelled strongly of beer and cigarettes, old and new. The walls might have started out as any color but now deepest nicotine. The floor was deeply worn linoleum, and the furniture dark wood. It was packed.

Neil had been the first to sink his pint in one. Angela wasn't sure if he had been showing off, or just thirsty, but Iris brightened, said something like "Wah-hoo!" and sunk hers even faster, earning a wide-eyed look from Neil.

David had refused point blank to order a sherry and so Angela sat nursing a vodka and pineapple juice, which she had no intention of drinking.

Neil said, "My round. Same?"

Angela shook her head, "I'm fine, thanks."

Neil disappeared into the incredible press of bodies and Angela turned to see Iris rubbing David's back and smiling widely. As if his illness pleased her.

"Not going to spew now, are you?"

David shook her head but didn't look too certain, so Iris put an empty glass in front of him and turned to beam at Angela. She was wearing something that Angela would have described as a frock; patterned, flared at the skirt, like something from the 50's, but once more worn with boots.

David blinked at Iris. "Music. You into?"

"I can never think when I'm asked. I like Joni Mitchell. You like Joni?"

David made a visible attempt to focus. "Early stuff." An unpleasant belch. "Groundbreaking."

Iris pointed at one of the badges on David's lapel, a drawing of a cowboy of some sort. "Freak brothers. Nice one."

For Angela, it was as though there a secret language being spoken, excluding her, David still talking, no surprise, about music.

Iris, as Neil put three pints on the table, asked, "D'you play?"

David shrugged, "I play a little guitar."

Neil, sitting down. "Yeah, like I sing."

Iris said, "Really? You a singer?"

"I'll maybe sing to you tonight."

Then he looked unaccountably flustered for a moment. David, not noticing, said, "Don't let him. He's shite."

Iris said, "I won a singing contest when I was twelve. Had to sing 'Que Sera Sera'."

Angela brightened, pleased to know at least something. "Doris Day?"

"Yeah. I hate that song. Hate Doris Day more, though."

Angela sat back in surprise. David turned to Neil, with the air of a man making a point.

"See, this is the first glimmer of interest she's shown in music, and it's because she can't understand why anybody would dislike Doris Day."

Neil, new to his friend having any sort of relationship with a female, smiled uncertainly, but Angela just poked David in the ribs. Hard enough to cause him to yelp.

She looked around "Where's the ladies?"

Neil said, "See, I told you we shouldn't have come here. One of the girls was bound to want to go."

Angela frowned at Iris. "Are the toilets so dreadful?"

"There's only one."

"That's surely not a problem. There's not many females in here."

"One toilet. In the whole place."

When Angela showed no sign of understanding, she clarified, "There's a cubicle inside the gents. One of the boys has to stop guys going in, till it empties, but there can be a tussle sometimes."

Angela sat with her straight back and tight smile and her untouched vodka. "I see the attraction of a pub now. I never really understood it before."

After a short discussion, they decided to try another place further up Hawkhill. Not a student haunt at all – The Campbelltown.

It wasn't yet dark outside, but it was cold. As they neared the old bar, they were brought to a halt by a scream, loud, piercing and very nearby. Neil involuntarily ducked, and Iris dropped beside him, grabbing his jacket.

David shouted, "Was that a kid?"

When the sound came again, it came from above, a second before a struggling screaming bundle of black and white fell from the sky. A gull, fighting with two crows in a violent confusion of feathers hit the road with an audible thud. It was the seagull that was screaming, trying to get away.

Neil took two paces, looking like he would go towards them, but Iris pulled him back and the gull flapped itself into the sky, feathers flying and crows chasing.

For several seconds they stood looking at each other, wide eyed. Iris stepped away.

Angela pulled David close. "I had no idea a gull could sound like that. Let's just go home."

David hugged her back. "Nuh-uh. We definitely need a drink after that."

This pub was long and quiet. Most of the clientele were elderly, in their thirties or even older. They looked openly at them, disapproving, not bothering to hide it, before turning away.

One man, skinny, cigarette in mouth, hair shiny with Brylcream, said, "Take the ladies to the snug, boys."

Angela said, "What's a snug? It sounds lovely."

The man turned all the way round on his stool to frown at Angela, glanced at the boys, and came to a dead stop on Iris. Angela could see his struggle as he tried to keep his eyes from roving. The 50's frock, if anything, accentuated her curves. Finally, he said, "You're…tall, for a girl."

Another man, smaller and much older, offered, "They'll be Yanks, her and the big boy. Saw enough o' them in the war."

Neil smiled at that, deliberately broadening his accent. "You're miles off, mister."

The man's eyes flew open. "Christ, he's Aberdeen! Lock the till." There was a laugh at that, and he came back Iris. "You're never from Aberdeen."

Iris smiled and, whatever she said, she was the only one who understood it.

"Irish, Aberdeen, a posh girl from…what, Edinburgh?" Sounding like Embra.

"Glasgow."

"Right, posh though. And some other boy."

The some other boy opened his mouth, then shut it again.

Neil ordered drinks, this time there was a sherry for Angela, and the first man spoke again to Iris. "What are you, then? Six-three?"

"Nowhere near. I'm six-one."

The second man piped up, "Big Eddie is six-one. So, he says."

Another man, heavy set, in an old twill jacket said, "Well, I am."

"You're never as tall as this Irish lass."

"I am, if she's six-one."

Nothing would do but Eddie and Iris lined up back to back. She was clearly about an inch taller.

There followed a heated conversation between Eddie and the other patrons, where he finally refused to be measured, claiming that a heavy guy like him would shrink more during the day. It was basic geometry.

"Measure me in the morning, I'll still be six-one."

"It's the weight o' being so dopey that's dragging him down."

Banishment to the snug seemed forgotten, and, after a while, the locals seemed to forget they were even there. As they reached the end of their drinks, the first man to speak spoke in a loud voice. "Fuckin' crows, though eh?"

"Women in the bar, now, Shug. Mind the language."

"Ach they'll live. But them crows. When I worked with the pest control…"

"Here we go."

"We tried to cull them once, years back. They're clever, though. Walk up to a tree with a crow in it, holding a broom handle, it would just look at ye."

"What else would it do?"

"Walk up with a shotgun, it would fly off."

"Aye, they're not stupid."

"But here's the thing. They only flew if the gun was loaded."

"They're not stupid. But you are."

The man shook his head, unwilling to take part in the banter. His last word on the subject, "Fuckin' crows."

2016

Nathan looked at the display on his cell phone, but it was a private number.

"Hello."

"Inspector Findlay?"

"Detective Constable. Who's that?"

"Mister Charles Rose."

Nathan felt his heart sink. "What can I do for you?"

"You said, if there was something else."

Nathan could hear him breathing against the receiver. "I'm drunk."

"Well that's good news certainly…"

"No, listen." Raising his voice now, the man losing it for just a second. "*Listen to me.*" A pause, then quieter, "There's something I need to say."

Nathan sighed. "Go on."

"I've never told anybody this. We couldn't wait to get it in the drawer, out of our sight. Did I tell you about its eyes?"

Nathan realized the man meant Bernard's body. "No."

"They were shut."

"Ok."

"But. When we opened the drawer again, they were open."

"Is there a scientific…"

"Never mind that shit. It *looked* at me."

"The eyes moved?"

"It *saw* me, man."

Nathan rolled his eyes. "Thanks for.…"

"I was at the grave today."

Nathan paused. "You visit his grave?"

"I've only been the once, this whole time."

"How do you know where he was buried?"

"Went to his funeral."

"Why?"

"I wondered, would anything happen?"

"What sort of thing?"

"Never seen a horror movie, man? Anyway. Nothing happened. I watched them plant him, then came away."

"So, no boiling holy water?"

"The nightmares have gotten worse, since you came. Not just when I'm asleep. So, I went back."

"What did you think you'd see?"

There were tears in his voice now. A drunk crying down the telephone. "You seen that film, *Kill Bill?*"

Nathan took a moment, trying to see where this was going.

"Yeah."

"You know the bit, Uma is in the grave, punches through the coffin. Climbs out."

"Yeah."

"Could never happen. You put The Rock down there, give him a hammer and a spade, it couldn't be done."

"Thought the same myself."

"Even if you could make a hole in the coffin, a ton of earth falls on you. You couldn't move an inch."

"Seems right."

"But what if that didn't matter?"

"What are you saying?"

"I dream about him, worming his way up, inch by inch. Decades of it."

"You need to sleep it off, Mr. Rose."

"Go and see it."

"What?"

"Go and look at the grave."

December 1976

It was Iris' idea to go to end of term disco and David wasn't keen. He warned them, "They play anything at these things."

"It's the Christmas disco! This isn't musical appreciation. It's dancing."

"They'll play Brotherhood of Man."

"Not at the Union. And, if they do, we'll come back here and play you back to back Nick Drake. I'll read the New Musical Express, out loud."

They were sitting in Iris' room, David and Angela on the bed while the others two sat on the floor. Iris, as she often did, changed her own subject, a detour to Neil's feet.

"Look at those things. They don't look so bad when they're walking down the street but, God, you could have a fine Christmas dinner on one of them. You have trouble getting shoes to fit?"

David, knowing that Neil was self-conscious about his size 13's, cringed, but Neil surprised him, laughing.

"I don't suppose you're easy knocked over, either. You must have the same trouble."

Iris clicked her Doc Marten's together. "I just buy mens'." She frowned, "Not so good if I want nice shoes, mind."

Yet again, she was wearing a strange amalgam from the 40's, a dress topped by a heavy wool jumper, striped. "What about this disco? Come on, we're all going home, day after tomorrow."

Neil surprised David again by saying, it would be a giggle. He turned to Angela, knowing that she ought, by any sane measure, say, no way.

Angela said, "I suppose it might be fun."

And it was. David was picky about what he would dance to, but nobody else was. He tried to intervene when the others started dancing to Abba, 'Dancing Queen' for God's sake, warning there was no way back, once you'd gone down that route.

Angela's version of dressing down was to wear black slacks and a cream blouse. David and Angela were dancing to 'Suffragette City' when he became aware that people were standing back, clapping and for a moment he thought that they were clapping him. Then he turned around, and the crashing and bouncing he had been dimly aware of became clear.

He and Angela drew back and clapped with all the rest. It wasn't that Neil and Iris were brilliant dancers – they weren't – but the sheer scale of their hopping and whirling was a spectacle.

They were, of course, unaware they were being watched, so caught up were they with trying to match each other. Someone close to David shouted, "Look at them two go!"

It struck David that, sweaty and red faced as he was, this might be the happiest he had ever seen Neil.

When it came to the pause before 'Wham! Bam! Thank You Ma'am', they crouched low and then released into a massive leap, and when they landed the dance floor *bounced*.

Then everyone was on the floor again and a punk – David had to tell Angela what that was – thought it was a good idea to run and bounce himself off Neil, who, luckily, thought that was a good idea too. As though that were a trigger, everyone seemed to go a bit mad, bouncing off each other. David grabbed hold of Angela, thinking maybe to protect her, but she squirmed away, properly giggling. He watched in astonishment as she threw herself at Iris, almost knocking her over, and then at a hippy guy, whom she did knock over.

The DJ played his only two Sex Pistols songs back to back, followed by more Abba, which might have slowed the pace, were it not for Iris.

On the way back up Perth Road, David, still buzzing from the dance, insisted on carrying Angela on his back. Neil sprinted past, a screaming Iris on his back.

Angela said, "I wouldn't have thought that was possible. Catch him then!"

Back in David's room, he dropped the needle onto JJ Cale's *Troubadour*, volume low, thinking it was time to mellow out. He caught Neil's eye and winked, Neil swigging lager to hide his smile.

They talked a bit of films, *Taxi Driver* and *Carrie*, slowing down. Neil was sitting on the horrible chair with Iris on the floor by his feet. David could see that her back was touching his legs, nothing serious, but there was contact.

Neil bent over to put his can down, and he and Iris looked at each other, smiling, before he sat back. Iris picked up one of David's newspapers. "Do you only have music stuff?"

David shrugged, "I got a Socialist Worker here someplace."

"Cool. I've volunteered to do a stint at the Nethergate, selling *The Worker*."

David, regretting his mention of the paper, looked hard at Neil, willing him not to say it.

Neil picked up his lager, grinning. "Socialist Loafer more like."

David laughed loudly. "That was pure mental tonight when you two were dancing. Wasn't it, Angela?"

But Iris had turned and was staring at Neil, her own can paused. When she spoke, her voice was flat. "How do you mean?"

"I don't know why everybody assumes because you're a student you're automatically left-wing. Socialism is crap. So-called poor people, doing damn all and riding on the back of those who actually work."

Iris shifted away from Neil, but kept staring at him. "What do you know about being poor?"

"Ok, my family never really struggled. But that's because my Dad, whatever else I might say about him, worked. Unlike some."

Iris looked at him, searching his face. "Fuck you, Neil."

After the girls had gone, Angela following Iris with a helpless expression, David turned to his friend.

"Real smooth-talking bastard, aren't you?"

Neil shrugged but looked abashed. Opened his mouth to say something, then sighed and drank some lager.

2016

Dudek walked away from the car, noticing some activity in front of the station, two young guys being taken out of a police van. They were causing a commotion, one of them struggling and shouting, cuffs coming out as the situation threatened to turn.

Mike Piper and a uniformed cop were standing beside another car, watching, two ancient and tiny women beside them. The women were wearing long coats and sensible shoes, handbags clutched before them. Coming closer, Dudek realized that the young guys were shouting *at* the women.

These guys were dressed in black, hoodies over baseball caps, tats, being hauled away as Dudek came level with Piper, thinking he was probably waiting till the men got processed before taking the oldies in.

"What's going on, Mike?"

A look passed between Piper and his colleague, but he answered only, "Bit of a shunt, Sir."

The nearest lady's spectacles were cracked and squint on her face. The other must have been under five feet tall.

Then the other traffic cop, reacting to a signal from the desk sergeant, thanked Piper, and walked the women to the station, gentle about it.

Piper touched a scratch on his face, checked for blood. "Sometimes you think you've seen everything. Jesus Christ."

"What do you mean?"

"Well, it wasn't a shunt. It was a deliberate ram."

"Those bastards rammed the old dears?"

"The old dears rammed them. I was right there."

"Still, is it not more likely to have been a mistake?"

"They did it four times."

"Serious?"

"I was sitting with Jake at the rear of the Overgate. Saw the ladies sailing towards the entrance in an old Volvo estate, going about two miles an hour. We even had a laugh, this tiny woman leaning over the steering wheel, coming up to the queue. Then these morons, four of them in a custom Peugeot, come tearing up the middle of the road, all blue lights and boom box. They come screaming past, burning rubber, and she had to brake."

Nathan said, "Where are the other two?"

"Hospital. Anyway, Enid, that's the driver, toots her horn and you can imagine, they're giving her the finger. All they got for the stunt was into the queue before the Volvo.

"You could see the ladies were annoyed. I could see the passenger waving like she's saying go on and I'm thinking, there's no place to go on *to*. Turns out she's saying, 'Ram them Enid.' Enid lets them have it. Fucking bang. A ton of old Volvo, right into the back of the little hatchback. Guys can't believe what's happened, everybody thinking it was a mistake.

"I'm getting out as Enid starts to reverse. Gets far as she can go without touching the car behind, and comes at the hatchback again. Christ, what a mess."

"The young guys not get out?"

Piper shook his head. "Peugeot's bent so bad, the doors are jammed. Should have seen their faces when she pulled back for another go."

Piper was smiling now, but in a bemused way. "They were scared shitless. I mean she was hitting them *hard*."

"What did you do?"

"I'm at the passenger side, shouting stop, Police. Margaret, the passenger, keeps waving Enid on. I grab the handle. So, what does she do?"

"She locks it?"

"Locks the friggin door. Next time Enid hits the Peugeot, I dodge around the driver side."

"What about the tough guys?"

"Screaming their lungs out. Crying. Both cars wrecked by this time, but you'd think that old Volvo was designed for mashing up custom hatches. I got the driver door open and pulled the keys out."

"What happened to your face?"

"Enid didn't want me pulling her keys out."

"You going to do her for assaulting an officer? On top of whatever else."

"You must be joking. She's eighty and under five feet tall. I'd never be allowed to forget it."

For a moment the men stood in silence, then Piper said, "In the car coming up, they're all apologetic. For the trouble they're causing us, kept calling me dear. I say something like, what about the trouble you caused those young guys. Margaret says, oh no, the world would be a much better place if people of her generation rammed youngsters more often."

December 1976

David's parents were dressed for a Christmas night out, his dad wearing a paisley shirt with matching tie. David shook his head, but said nothing, because that's just dads for you.

His mother was wearing a skirt that was much too short for an old lady, with dangly earrings like miniature Christmas puddings. She said, "I couldn't help but notice you had a photo of a girl by your bed."

David had been expecting something like this. Had seen himself shrug and say something non-committal. Being cool, giving nothing away.

Now he said, "That's Angela. My girlfriend."

"Your girlfriend?"

"No need to sound so surprised."

He turned back to the television as his dad said, "Well, come on. Give."

He thought about saying, give what? Putting some irritation into it. Instead he said, "She's in my Psych class. Plays tennis."

"Was it her got you to dump that horrible Afghan thing? What a relief."

"No, it was not!" David glared at his mom. "Afghans aren't too practical, to be honest."

His dad. "Plus, they stink."

David's mother slapped her husband on the knee. "So, what's she like? Angela?"

David thought for a moment. "She's really neat."

"Well, of course."

"No, I mean neat. As in neat and tidy."

David's dad gave him a flat look. "You have a girlfriend who's neat and tidy."

His mother said, "She looks very pretty."

"She's not conventionally pretty, I don't think. But she has…she is." He blew his cheeks out. "She's really something. You have to meet her."

"Well we'd love to."

"No, I mean, you have to actually meet her, to know. She's got something about her that's really unusual."

Then he told them, anyway, I love her so that's that.

The term had ended on a sour note. Neil had been withdrawn on the train and they hadn't spoken since. His mother kept asking, when will we be seeing Neil? Till finally realizing something was up.

His dad said, "You know, you two probably need a rest from each other."

David thought there might be something more to it.

2016

They were in the Focus, Nathan driving towards the station, telling Dudek about Rose, how he was curious to look at Bernard's grave.

"What do you expect to see?"

When Nathan just shrugged, he said, "Go, if you like."

They drove in silence, Nathan thinking that he would just turn around and do it, now it was out in the open, Dudek agreeing that he should act against a direct instruction from Mackie. He glanced again at Dudek, thinking there was something more than usual eating the man. "Anything else happened, boss?"

Dudek didn't answer straight away. When he did, he was looking away from Nathan.

"You remember that journalist? Hilda Jarvis."

Nathan almost commented on what she looked like, but something in the man's voice stopped him.

"Sure."

"I've been getting information from her."

"Ok." Nathan thinking, the way Dudek was talking, it probably wasn't ok. If you didn't know any better, you'd think he was this smooth guy, cool and tough, good at his job. If you didn't smell the drink, and know about his wife. Roger Moore had somehow guessed at something there that Nathan still couldn't get to.

"Her father was a local hack, way back. Left and got famous."

"Not Jack Jarvis?"

"Yeah. She starts off telling me she was brought up here, talking about the place. Turns out her father left way before she was even born. Never looked back."

Nathan thought, so you've been looking into her. "Maybe he still had connections."

"He cut his connections, snip, like that."

"So, you don't think she's on the level?"

Dudek looked worried. "I don't know what she is."

After a few moments, he added, "I always thought that I got away too lightly, with the Hardy thing."

Nathan blinked in surprise but Dudek kept talking. "I mean the press, how they didn't come after me. So now, I'd be suspicious, except she's a business correspondent."

When Nathan stopped in front of the station, Dudek looked at him for a long moment. "You're going there now, aren't you?"

Then he simply climbed out of the car and walked away, not glancing back.

Nathan headed to the cemetery, stopping opposite the entrance. He had called Rose back, getting some directions and, seeing the size of the place, he hoped the old drunk had it right.

The afternoon was hazy, the air heavy with moisture. Figuring he had about an hour before it got dark, Nathan picked up the pace. The paths were wide and flanked by trees and gravestones, some of the older ones leaning, supported by posts with yellow signs warning they were unstable.

After about ten minutes, Nathan found the stone angel that Rose had mentioned, and slowed. Just ahead, a white truck was sitting with its engine running, and he figured Bernard's headstone should be right about there.

Coming up on the truck, he saw a man with a chainsaw, another loading logs into a trailer. Nathan nodded as he skirted the men.

"Taking a tree down?"

"It was dangerous. A nice willow, but it sickened."

The man loading logs straightened. "You from the Council yourself?"

"No, just looking for a grave."

The other workman dumped his saw in the rear of the van, the crash loud in the cemetery. "You look like police to me, pal."

Nathan frowned and turned away, spotting Bernard's grave only a few yards further on. The marble headstone leaned precariously, but no yellow warning sign on this one. He squinted, reading the inscription.

> Doctor Simon Menzies Bernard
> Academic
> 1935-1977
> Step softly, for he hath awakened

Another heavy crash made him start, and he looked back at the workmen, dumping the last of their gear in their trailer, hurrying to be done. Nathan watched the truck move away, its tail lights bright and checked his watch, seeing that it had taken him longer to find the plot than he had thought. The light was definitely failing.

He remembered his father telling him, on a camping trip, if you closed your eyes and counted to thirty you could see as well in the dark as you ever going to. He closed his eyes.

He could still hear the truck, and the sound of his own breathing. He held his breath so that he could hear better and there it was again; he was scared, like a little kid in a graveyard, the second time in a week. He had also stopped counting.

It struck him how weird this was, standing in a cemetery with his eyes closed and the thought came to him that maybe it hadn't been his idea to close them. And he had to wonder too why he wasn't opening them.

He stood as still as he could, listening, and heard movement, close by. His eyes came open by themselves.

A small man, wearing a puffa jacket, its color uncertain in the light, and a Dundee United baseball cap, his collie on a lead. As he came closer, he nodded to Nathan.

"Nights fair drawin' in." He stopped, and Nathan could see he was older than he first thought, maybe seventy.

"I still come here near every day, say hello to my Maggie."

"That's nice."

"Usually in the mornings. Can be lovely in the mornings here, but I had to pick up my pension, and next thing you know it's getting dark. You police?"

"No."

The man squinted up at him. "Aye well, you should be. I wouldn't hang about there, pal."

"Why not?"

The old man in the young man's clothes looked around, shrugged and said, "It's not the best corner in the place, that's for certain. Come on, Captain."

He nodded to Nathan and stumped off. Nathan called, "That's a good name for a dog. Captain."

The man waved, not turning, and there was nothing for it but to try to see what Rose had been talking about. Nathan was wondering, could it have been the just-felled tree, some creepy old twisted willow, the guy's booze-fried brain doing the rest.

He wondered about himself too, letting himself get spooked like that, maybe his nerves still jangled up after his embarrassing flight from Rankine Hall.

He made himself walk right up to the headstone, the inscription easily readable still. It canted heavily to the right and Nathan reached out, paused, then gripped it. It was colder than he had expected, but solid enough.

He had avoided standing on the grave itself, but now deliberately stepped onto it. Then he looked around, admitting to himself that he was looking for signs of disturbance, like might happen if something crawled out of the earth.

The grass was sparse, and the ground seemed unbroken for several yards around. He read the inscription again, out loud this time. Step softly, for he hath awakened.

He tried to imagine what lay under his feet. The box, collapsing inwards, the body. Shook that away and looked up, headstones and memorials all around, disappearing into the gloom; mainly plain stones or urns, with a few angels and squat tombs thrown in.

Nathan paced a wide circle, thinking about the drunk's nightmares of a creature, naked and white, squirming millimeter by millimeter through the earth, never stopping for forty years.

He tried to think like a policeman, but there was nothing for a policeman to see here. Here was a bush, leafless with winter coming on. He reached out and took a branch between his fingers, pressing it back with his thumb. It cracked easily, the wood dead and dry. Turf had been laid here too, but hadn't taken.

A sound, very close, froze him, prickling the hair on his neck and making the back of his head tingle. It sounded like an exhale.

Nathan listened but could only hear his own breathing. He stepped back, not wanting to take his eyes from the marble stone, because that's where it had come from. The sound again, a sigh that couldn't be a sigh. He listened, thinking, no, it was more like a whisper, and turned his ear towards the little marble stone; wanting to hear it now.

The sound was close, and he smiled, no longer scared. He closed his eyes again, trying to catch words. Stayed like that, listening as it whispered on.

Then there were words, real words, but they were harsh, ugly and unwelcome.

"Hoy. Big man. I've told you, get out of there."

Nathan straightened, suddenly feeling shaky and sick and opened his eyes to see the old man in the puffa jacket, his collie whining, straining to get away.

"This isn't a nice corner of this place, Son. Now come away."

"What?"

"Walk away. Across here."

Nathan could smell his cigarette, a roll up, in the corner of his mouth. The man wasn't coming any closer, and Captain was pulling hard to get away. Nathan couldn't think. There was too much in his head.

"What?"

The man struggled to hold the dog then gave up, shouting after it. "Captain. Stop at the gate. Mind me now."

Nathan heard himself say, "Captain. That's a good name for a dog." Felt himself nod, feeling the right of it.

The man put his hand out. "Come on. Time to go."

Nathan rubbed his face, his head.

"Come on, we've to see to Captain. He's a dog that takes a tellin', but he's spooked. Don't make me walk across there."

It was hard, taking the first step.

He stepped. Again. Then he actually ran, right up to the old man, who pulled back, surprised. He turned and looked back, scared to do it.

The stone was shining, seeming almost to float in the dark. Nathan realized that he was hyperventilating, too much oxygen making his head swim. He felt a hand, surprisingly tight around his arm, and let himself be led, the sound of gravel under his feet strange, like he'd never heard anything like it before. The old man stunk of smoke and old whisky, making him queasy.

They didn't speak until they reached the gates and Captain came running, making a noise, deep in his throat, like scolding. The man ruffled the dog's coat, quieting it before turning back to Nathan.

"You ok?"

"I feel like shit, to be honest."

"I've been here most days since I buried my Maggie. It's a nice cemetery."

Still ruffling the dogs thick coat, soothing it.

"But take my advice, never go back. Not in the dark, not in the light."

The man nodded, leaving him by the gate and he was surprised to find that he didn't want him to go. The cemetery was in full dark now, framed between the huge gate posts. Nathan turned and made his shaky legs move, hoping he wouldn't throw up in the car.

January 1977

Neil was limping slightly, having played rugby in Glasgow at the weekend, but was more worried about the loss of his coat, which had disappeared on the trip.

"One, I'm flat broke. Two, it's snowing. Three, it's really hard getting clothes that fit."

He was in Angela's room, sitting on the floor and it was almost time to go to classes. Angela and David were sitting on the bed, legs touching as usual, and Iris was in the only chair. She muttered, "Tell me about it."

Neil frowned, never sure how to take her since their disagreement. She was so loud sometimes, overbearing even, then the next moment so quiet. He had noticed that she seldom looked his way now, addressing herself to Angela or David.

So, he could look at her all he wanted, he thought. She was slumped in the chair with one long leg over the arm, again wearing a dress of some sort; a purple thing with an overlay of black lace. The sort of thing you might see in old films. He supposed it was stylish, in a weird way.

He wondered what she would look like naked.

As if she could hear, she turned to look at him and, not wanting to look away, he waggled his eyebrows. She frowned. "What's that with the eyebrows?"

"What?"

"All that eyebrow waggling. That an Aberdeen thing?"

Angela said, "Iris. Stop it."

Iris tutted. "You tried Oxfam?"

"Yeah."

"What about that one behind Markies. Cat's protection league."

"I don't know it."

"I'll take you, if you like. I know the ladies who run it. They like me."

Neil almost asked, why do they like you, but stopped himself. Instead he said, "Yeah, thanks."

"Meet me in the tower block at two?"

Neil nodded, and she looked away, still not smiling.

He was waiting at two and at ten past he saw a boy nudge another and when he turned to see what they were looking at, Iris was walking into the foyer. She was wearing a tailored coat he hadn't seen before with her hair was brushed out over the shoulders. Also Doc Marten boots, but still with the Lauren Bacall dress. She nodded to the door.

"Come on then."

They walked in silence, Neil shivering in his combat jacket. The sky was the color of zinc, flurries of snow blowing through. No snow was lying, not yet. He was relieved when Iris turned down a narrow alley, out of the biting wind, coming to a charity shop he didn't know.

An elderly woman wearing a pinafore, very small and with shortish white hair, looked up from behind a loaded counter and her face lit up. "Anna, it's our fine colleen back again, wearing Big Ag's dress, too. Och, it would look that much better without the boots. You never told us ye had a lad!"

Now another woman, clearly Anna and, just as clearly, the first woman's sister, appeared and both of them spoke at the same time, complaining that Iris hadn't mentioned a lad and look at the size of him.

Iris had to say it more than once before they accepted that he was just a friend. They were distinctly unimpressed. "I don't know what he's messin' about for, the loveliest girl in Dundee."

"Doreen. Anna. This is Neil. Think you might have a coat in his size?"

The two women looked at each other and said, simultaneously, "Doctor Carey."

Neil glanced at Iris and shrugged but both women crowded around him, looking him up and down and muttering. Finally, Doreen, he thought it was Doreen, said, "My friend's husband died a few months back. A fine big man he was."

She stood up as tall as she could and threw her shoulders back, looking sternly at Neil. "A Doctor, mind! A right good Doctor."

Neil nodded, feeling he was in trouble but not sure why.

Anna said, "When Bella heard we were raising money for cats she said, 'Anna! Anna, you can have the Doctor's clothes. He'd be pleased to see them going to a good cause.'"

Neil nodded, "So. Have you a coat in my size, do you think?"

Doreen turned to Anna.

"Have you put the Doctor's things on a rail yet?"

"Oh, not yet. But there was a raincoat, a car coat and a long dress coat."

She bustled into the back shop and Doreen turned to Iris. "Have a look at that green dress on the end row there, love. It's just your style and it would fit I'm sure."

Iris looked slightly embarrassed, but walked over to where the little woman had indicated.

Anna came back, struggling under the weight of three large coats. She threw them over the counter, and Neil picked up a light tan Mackintosh. It was clear that Doctor Carey had been very big. Neil pulled the Mackintosh on, feeling self-conscious. It fit around the shoulders and when he held his arm out the length was about right.

Iris made a face. "You look like a flasher."

"He does not! Iris!"

Neil looked at himself in the mirror. "Actually, I look like a thin version of my Dad."

He shucked the coat off and looked at the car coat. "I don't think that's for me." Then he picked up the long woolen dress coat. "This looks like the sort of thing that people wear to a funeral."

Anna shook her head. "It's formal wear, son. A very well-made coat."

Neil put it back down, but Iris called, from across the shop. "Let's see what it looks like."

Neil pulled the coat on and looked down at himself feeling silly, wishing he hadn't come. It was a long and heavy coat, coming down to his mid-calf.

Another woman had come in, as he had been trying it on, and now all four women stood appraising him. The newcomer, also short but much heavier than the sisters, stepped forwards and smoothed the front of the coat against his stomach, wiping it thoughtfully.

"That's a lovely coat, that."

Anna walked around the back. "Aye, it really suits him."

Doreen clapped her hands. "Would you look at that, Iris? He looks right handsome."

Anna agreed. "He's so tall, he can carry it off. All that dramatic way."

The new woman, to Neil's relief, had stopped smoothing the coat. "You would think it was made for him."

Iris looked at him, her head cocked to one side. "It looks good, Neil."

Neil checked himself in the mirror, thinking maybe it did look ok, also thinking that it would be way too expensive.

"How much is it?"

Iris said, "It would be lovely to think it would be going to another Doctor."

Doreen looked over, sharp and surprised. "What's that?"

"Neil's studying medicine."

"Oh!"

Iris looked across at Neil and didn't quite wink.

Anna. "Let's say, four pounds."

Neil looked at her, "Seriously? You only want four pounds?"

"Are you sure you're from Aberdeen?"

"Thanks, that would be brilliant." He turned to Iris, "You're sure I don't look like a poser?"

Iris was shaking her head as Anna asked, "What's a poser?"

"A show off."

"What you look is *classy*."

Feeling pretty good now, Neil turned in a circle, the tails of the long coat swinging around his legs. Anna, or Doreen, clapped with undisguised pleasure.

"Doreen take him round the back and see if any of the Doctor's other clothes will do. Iris, come on and let's see you with this dress."

Doreen took him by the elbow and steered him into a messy room at the rear of the shop. "This is the Doctor's pile here."

She picked up a pair of trousers, looked at Neil's waist and put them down again. "What about this jacket?"

Neil looked up as, out in the shop, Iris giggled like a little girl. "They're having fun."

"Anna loves dressing that girl up. The most fun she's had in years."

Doreen shook her head as Neil pulled the jacket on.

"You look terrible in that. Yeah, Iris came in here, only a week or so after we'd opened the place, lookin' like you lot always do. Just depressin'. We'd had a fantastic donation from another friend, Big Ag. Agnes Farrell. A great strapping woman but what a figure she had! People would stop to look at her when she sashayed past. Not just men either."

Before he knew he would say it, Neil said. "Iris sashays."

"She should! Big Ag had this amazin' figure, but she was only just pretty, on a good day. Iris is beautiful."

Neil allowed himself to be pushed into a heather tweed jacket.

"Now! That's more the thing."

Then she said, "Iris can spend an hour in here. I don't think she means to, but once Anna gets at her, brushing her hair and putting lipstick on. I like seeing the pair of them so happy. Look, this is a lovely dress shirt, heavy cotton. I'll let you try it on."

She scuttled away, and Neil pulled the shirt on. It was made for cuff links and a separate collar, but without either, he liked it. He tucked it into his jeans, pulled on the jacket and looked at himself. He looked...different.

"Pretty cool." He said, surprised.

He walked into the main shop, feeling self-conscious but also pleased, wanting to show Iris, he found.

All three ladies had gathered around Iris, who looked even taller. She was wearing the green dress, scoop necked, satin, cinched tight into her waist. Her hair was brushed out over her shoulders, which were shockingly bare and creamy white. She was also wearing pumps with a heel.

She was beaming, her teeth white against bright red lipstick. When she saw Neil, the smile disappeared.

Neil knew he was standing there like an idiot and staring, not even speaking. This went on for a few seconds, getting more embarrassing all the time, then Anna broke the spell, clapping her hands and saying something so densely Dundonian that it took Neil a few seconds to realize she was asking if he would agree to having some photographs taken.

"Photographs?"

"For the window. I have some of Iris, but the two of you together would be smashing. If you would hang on, till we close, I'll give you a discount on the clothes. Ten minutes."

He felt he couldn't refuse. "Sure. No problem."

Twenty minutes later, Anna had set things up with surprising professionalism and was looking through a large camera. Neil was sitting in a chair whilst Doreen brushed his hair.

"Ouch. I don't really like my hair brushed."

"Well that's obvious. The state of this, Anna! Honest to God."

The photo session turned out to be fun. Anna seemed to know what she was doing with the camera and she and her sister had an unconscious double act, honed over a lifetime.

Anna kicked off with Neil posing on his own, and he started out feeling self-conscious, not helped by the fact that Iris seemed to find the whole thing highly amusing. Anna had him sitting on a low chair, leaning forward with both hands on one knee, then asked him to tip his head back.

"Don't I look a bit…"

Anna was unfazed, "Hold still!"

Iris grinned. "You look sweet."

Then she had him standing up, looking noble. Iris was smiling at him and he realized he was enjoying himself. How had this come about, when all he had wanted was to buy a cheap coat?

Then it was Iris' turn. She took to it naturally, following Anna's instructions with a poise that silenced him. Anna was telling her to stand straighter now, shoulders back, head back, shove that bust out. Perfect.

Neil, standing behind Anna, agreed silently.

Then it was time for them both together. They sat. Stood side by side. Back to back with arms folded, looking over their shoulders at each other.

"Ok, now. Turn towards each other. A bit closer. Hold your hands together, about chest level. Good. Now smile. Come on, can't you smile, the pair of you? That's…actually that's pathetic. Smile!"

Neil, looking right into Iris's eyes, finally managed a smile.

"Ok now. Iris step right against him and look up. Neil put your other arm around her shoulder."

Neil could feel Iris' breasts just grazing his chest and was looking down into her eyes. He swallowed and heard a click in his throat. Anna said, "For God's sake, you two, move together. Together!"

2016

Hilda Jarvis met Dudek, this time in a bar. When she walked in, he was already there, checking his cell phone, a glass in front of him, close to empty. A good-looking guy, she thought, a man with something about him.

Dangerous too, someone who could break the rules. Nobody ever got to the bottom of what he did to Jason Hardy but, whatever it was, he made him tell.

He looked up and smiled, a proper smile that made her smile back. He stood and, without thinking, she leaned in to kiss his cheek. He looked surprised. Said, "What do you want?"

The way he said it made her stop.

"What?"

He waited a beat, definitely waited, before saying, "To drink."

"Glass of wine, please. Small, dry, white."

He drained the last inch of his beer and walked to the bar. She watched him go, thinking that he had meant to throw her, the flat way he asked, then waiting that moment. Thinking too that she liked how he walked, casual but confident.

When he returned, she sipped her wine and asked were things still crazy.

"Crazy hardly covers it. I don't know what's getting into people. Nathan has gone off sick with something."

"Is he properly ill?"

"His wife had to call me, he's so out of it. Apparently."

"Found out anything else about Haddow?"

He swallowed some beer, taking his time, then leaned towards her. "No, but I found some stuff about you."

"Me?"

"Spoke to a colleague of your dad's, she worked with him all those years back. Remembers him well."

"Ok."

"She was his friend, or so she thought. Wasn't surprised when he went away to work on the nationals, more surprised he moved here in the first place. A strange career move, for a Fleet Street high flyer."

She knew she was looking cautious, wondering what was coming. "Ok."

"When he left, though, he just left. Cut all ties the second he got on the train."

"Are you still in touch with friends from Exeter?"

"Actually, yes. And I never mentioned Exeter to you."

She sat back, waiting for what he had to say.

"Your Dad left in '78. Never looked back. This is your first time in Dundee."

She took a sip of wine. "Well done, Inspector Morse."

"So, why all the crap?"

"It gave me a place to start."

"With me?"

"Yes, mainly. But it's not that simple."

Now it was his turn to sit back, let her get to it by herself.

"My dad wasn't a happy man."

Dudek nodded, but didn't speak.

"He loved me, I don't doubt that. He loved my Mom, loved his job. But there was always *something*, hanging over him his whole life. I could never get to what it was, but one thing I did know, he hated David Haddow."

"You're saying Haddow did the dirty on him?"

"I just know he wouldn't talk about Dundee. Whatever was hanging over him, it had to do with his time here. I thought, maybe a woman, a bribe, something he was ashamed of."

"You speak to him about it?"

"Not until the end. I was getting on with my own life. Things were working out for me in the States, until they weren't. When I came home it seemed that things had gotten worse with my dad."

"Worse how?"

"He'd lost about twenty pounds, told me he had terminal cancer. Turned out that was a lie, but I bought it. He made me promise something. Two things."

Dudek said, "You would never go to Dundee."

She nodded. "Never. Wanted me out of the UK altogether."

"Did he say why?"

She shook her head. "He wouldn't. But he did admit he had lived his whole life under a shadow. Said it would do a lot more than just cast a shadow over mine, if I came here."

"But you're here."

"My dad killed himself that same night. Took pills."

"I'm sorry."

She leaned over, so that she could whisper. "Something terrible happened to him, John. Something he couldn't tell me about, even when he was preparing to kill himself. I don't know what Haddow did, but as far as I'm concerned, he killed my dad."

Her voice broke at last, her eyes tearing up, and Dudek took her hand, holding it tight. She looked away, visibly pulling herself together, but squeezed his fingers back.

Dudek gave her a moment before he asked, "What was the second promise?"

She sipped her wine. "He wanted to be cremated."

January 1977

Walking back to Rankine Hall, the snow was beginning to blow through more seriously, drifts building against walls. People were mainly walking hunched over, but Iris wasn't. It seemed to Neil that she kept staring at him, but not necessarily in a good way. Finally, he had to say, "What?"

Predictably, he was answered with, "What, what?"

"You keep looking at me."

"I just can't fathom you."

"How?"

"I mean, you're right wing, properly Conservative."

"Uh-huh."

"But you're nice. You're a nice guy."

"Can't you be both then?"

She shook her head, no. Her cheeks were high colored in the cold, snow catching in the red of her hair. More than anything, he wanted to reach across, brush them away.

He said, "Sure you can. I want people to look after themselves..."

She put up her hand, stopping him, shaking her head. "There's only one way this will work. I'm going to pretend you're not Tory at all. I'll just ignore it."

"Only one way what will work?"

She stopped him right there in the snow-blown street, taking hold of the lapels of the greatcoat. "This."

And kissed him.

When she stepped back he said, "Wow."

"You're not going to say you never saw that coming."

"I never..."

"Ah shut up, now, you did. Want to give it another whirl, maybe you can put some effort in yourself?"

He found himself smiling at her. "Let's give that a go."

2016

Nathan had spent three days in bed, barely able to stand, but on the fourth had gone back to work. Susan had been annoyed, telling him he needed to look after himself. She had much more to say on the subject of DCI John Dudek, none of it complementary.

She was right, of course. He still felt weak and strangely empty, but felt he needed to get back to the case, the one that Mackie had warned him off. Also, there was something about Dudek, all the stuff the guy had gone through, that was making him feel guilty.

Nathan walked to the Council offices, past the fountain and people eating lunch. At the Planning department he told the receptionist he was meeting a Mr. Oswald.

Oswald was around thirty, tall and very slim, with a shock of blonde hair and a straggling mustache. He had a bulging paper folder, which he set on the table between them.

"Glad you called. We always thought there was something off about the mill development."

Nathan, surprised this official was speaking so openly, just getting right down to it, asked, "How so?"

"It just never added up."

"But you gave it planning permission."

"There's no issue in planning terms." He unfolded a large schematic. "Too good to be true, in fact, very high quality, added affordable housing."

"So, what's the problem?"

The planner pointed to the plans. "The Tombstone Mill is a huge stone box, with massive windows, all the wrong size and place to light apartments. So, the architect included a giant central atrium, to provide natural light, look."

"I still don't see the issue."

"Then the clincher. The redirection of the underground river, the Scourin' Burn."

"That's what's causing all the road closures?"

"Biggest civil engineering project in that area for years. The commercial area to the West of the mill was bought out, just to make that happen."

"I still don't get why this is bad."

"None of it is bad. Crazy, is what it is. The cost to divert the stream…got to be ten mill. To break even, the flats would have to go for well over a million each."

"They won't, though?"

"Won't fetch a quarter of it. But here's the punchline. The diversion of the stream isn't necessary."

Nathan had been looking at the plans, but now he sat back. "What?"

"The development could go ahead without it."

"You sure?"

"No question. So, you have to ask yourself, why do it? The mill development is small scale, compared to the diversion."

"What's your suspicion?"

Oswald took a few seconds. "You'd have to say that this isn't about the development of the mill at all. It's about the diversion of the stream. I keep on asking myself, what benefit does that bring the developer?"

"What do you answer yourself?"

"I say, not a thing."

Nathan sat in silence, absorbing this. Then he asked, "You don't know anything about an old ruin out Perth Road, do you? Rankine Hall?"

Oswald smiled, impressed. "I guess that's why you're a detective. Well done, though, putting that together."

Nathan tried to look like he knew what the man was talking about. Didn't make it. "What?"

"I mean the same developer owning both of them. That Hall's been empty since the late seventies, but it could be a gold mine, and they let it rot. The mill is a terrible site, and they throw millions at it. Figure that one out."

Nathan stared at the plans, as though that could give him an answer. Finally, he said, "I don't think I can."

January 1977

It was Iris who came back with the flyer for the funfair and Neil was never going to say anything but yes, the way she lit up like a little kid.

David was less keen. "Seriously? Crappy rides and you'll be pestered nonstop to win goldfish and plastic hats."

"Angela's room could do with a goldfish."

They went that same day, getting on a bus in the dark. The snow had gone, but the wind still cut. David had stopped complaining in favor of an expression that Neil knew well, conveying that, he was going along with it, but they would soon see he was right.

On the bus, Angela surprised everybody with the information that she enjoyed fairs; liked the dodgems, being spun on the tilt-a-twirl. As they walked across a wide expanse of wet grass to the noisy, brightly lit group of rides and stalls, Iris broke into a skippy run, dragging Neil in his long black coat.

David called out, "Let's walk around, see what they've got."

"Fuck that!"

They had three straight turns on the dodgems, riding in pairs and taking it in turns to drive. Iris was a constant upset to the carney, determinedly driving into everybody she could at the best speed she could manage.

As they finally left the ride, Angela said, "I wonder if he's just pretending to complain. All the squealing Iris was doing, look at the queue now."

Neil could see that was true, and, after they had been on a few more rides he told Iris she should get them to pay her. "You're a one-woman advertising campaign."

They did the haunted house, mirror hall and came to the tilt-a-twirl. David shook his head. "Nah. I hate things that spin you round."

Iris shoved him, "Away, you Scots wimp."

Neil said, "He threw up all over my new Adidas Roms last time."

David put his hands up, "Go on, I'll sit it out."

Angela asked him, "How long since you were on one of these?"

"A few years."

"And you're not full of sweets or hot dogs. You've not smoked anything stronger than a cigarette either."

"What are you on about?"

She gave his hand a squeeze. "Be brave little one. We won't let the bad man spin it hard."

Ten minutes later, he was leaning against the side of a truck with his eyes closed, trying to get the spinning in his head to stop.

"I'll stay with him," said Angela, "You two go on."

Iris was bending over, the better to see how white David's face was. "So you should. It was you who made him do it."

Angela seemed stung, "I didn't make him do anything! I just suggested..."

"Keep your hair on. You sound even posher when you're drunk."

She leaned into Neil as they walked around the remaining stalls, then shouted, "Hey look. One of those sledgehammer things. Come on, ring the bell and win me a chimp."

I'll split your chimp for you. "A chimp?"

"Or a teddy bear."

The man was already calling out to them, handing the long-handled mallet towards Neil. Strong chap like you sir, let's see what you can do.

Neil took the mallet, looking at the cheap prizes ranged up. He pointed to a velour heart, puffy and garish red, feathers already coming adrift. "That's the one, Iris."

Iris put her hand on his. "Nah. I don't want you to win that for me."

Then she said, "I want to win it for you." Kissing him and pulling the mallet away in one movement.

She hauled back and hit the metal plate with everything she had, and the marker flew upwards, stalling about three quarters way to the bell.

Iris blinked in surprise. The carney was calling out how it was a good attempt for a lady, but it took a strong arm to ring the bell. Iris said, "Right!" and, despite the cold, shucked her coat off.

Behind her someone whistled, someone else clapped. A woman's voice shouted. "Thump that thing, red."

Iris shook her arms out and shifted position, blew out a couple of long breaths and brought the mallet around in a high arc, striking the plate with a loud clunk. Behind her a cheer rose and died as the marker stalled just below the bell.

Somebody called out, "Give that hammer to your man, doll. You've no chance." But that was followed by other voices, with different views.

Iris was standing in her jumper, breathing heavily. Now the jumper came off, causing more shouts and whistles. Iris spoke to the plate, "Bastard thing, that ye are. Come on then."

She walked round in a small circle, psyching herself up, muttering. She stepped forwards and threw the mallet to its full height, yelling as it came down.

Then, "I'm not giving up."

On the way back to the bus, David nodded to the heart in Neil's hand. "Shouldn't Iris be carrying that?"

"It's mine."

"But it's a girl's thing."

"Iris won it for me. Took her five goes." Neil grinned and pulled her close.

David, still looking, and feeling, slightly pale, said, "We've got to get on a Dundee bus. With Dundee people on it. Can Iris not hold it till we get back?"

Then. "Does that mean you're going to have that in your room? Where people can see it?"

Iris hopped, grinning, closer to Neil, pushing her face into his cheek. "Feel how cold my nose is?"

David rolled his eyes, but said nothing.

2016

The Tombstone Mill's massive wrought iron gates stood open and, from where he stood, Dudek could see a portacabin to one side of the cobbled courtyard, marked 'Site Office'. The courtyard was in shadow, despite it being late morning, the walls of the mill looming high over Dudek as he walked to the office. He thought again about what Nathan had told him about the project, wondering what was behind it. The final thing the planner had said, all that investment, you'd think the developer would be desperate to get his profit out. But the whole thing has stalled.

He looked at the building now and thought they'd be lucky give these flats away. Imagined explaining it to Hilda, the oppressive feel of the place, the smell of damp stone.

It felt deserted, apart from crows. There was only a single car in the courtyard, and Dudek automatically noted that it was a Skoda. A late model Fabia.

The door to the office stood open, a small man wearing a Hi-Viz jacket sitting behind the only desk. He smiled widely and clapped his hands together. "Ah! Inspector Dudek."

He was in his early forties, Dudek thought, searching his memory for the name he had been given.

"Mr. Hardy?"

"Well, come on in, why dontcha!"

The room looked like any other site office that Dudek had been in, the walls covered in drawings. On the desk, weighing down some papers, was what looked like an old sword hilt, an engraved pommel, heavily corroded, with an inch or two of rusted blade.

"What can I do for you, John?"

There was something achingly familiar about the man, but Dudek couldn't get there, the memory sliding infuriatingly away. "I'm investigating a sudden death."

Hardy winked, complicit. "That crazy lady. The one that drowned herself and her kid?"

Dudek's eyes flew open. "What?"

"Sorry, all I know is that somebody committed suicide. I'm not party to the details."

Dudek pretended to look around the room, getting himself back together. "The investigation isn't straightforward, and there may be a connection with another incident that happened here."

Hardy swung a fist in front of himself. "Whoda thunk it?"

"I just want to see one area, to be honest. The eastern edge of the Scourin' Burn. Where a body was found."

"We call that the dome pool."

Dudek sat back, surprised. "You know about the body?"

"Part of the mill's glorious history. That's where we've diverted the stream, so all you'll see now is the wall of the conduit. A massive concrete pipe."

"Still."

The man stood up. "Come on, then, Johnny boy."

"I don't need a Hi-Viz?"

"A what?"

He pointed to the man's own coat. "I thought I'd need a Hi-Viz, onsite."

Hardy sighed and rolled his eyes, but opened a locker at the side of his desk. It contained stationery. He opened the next one and cried, "Ah-hah!"

He handed Dudek a yellow jacket, and then left without a word. Dudek caught him up as he opened the mill door, still the original by their look, and stepped into the dark. A moment later a fluorescent light came on, only serving to underline how massive this place was. Dudek could just make out the shape of a huge and lumpen machine, the first in a barely visible line. Imagined himself telling Hilda, all the money that's been thrown at this place and it looks like nothing's been done.

Dudek hesitated and caught the way that Hardy was looking at him; amused, he thought. He said. "I can't believe this is going to be housing."

His voice echoed, so that his words were audible long after he'd spoken. Hardy just turned, walking away, again leaving Dudek to follow into darkness. He hurried after the man, shoes crunching and echoing on whatever muck covered the stone flags until they reached the east wall, and another pair of doors. When Hardy pushed them open it looked to Dudek as though someone had painted a black rectangle in there, the darkness was so solid. Hardy stepped through and was gone.

Dudek stood for a few seconds wondering what he should do. He couldn't hear anything from behind the door, Hardy had just stepped through and disappeared, Hi-Viz and all. The air coming out of there was frigid and smelled of a deeper, earthy dampness.

He stepped through the doorway and all light was gone, the darkness like velvet against his eyes. Then, from somewhere below him, a fluorescent tube flickered into life, showing a worn set of stone steps descending to a half landing large enough to park a car.

He took a shaky breath and started down, finding he didn't want to call for Hardy, or make a noise. The man was waiting at the bottom, in a dimly lit space that looked like an ancient underground station, with rough stone walls and a curved ceiling, but smelled like the sea. When he grinned at Dudek, that infuriating, unsettling feeling of recognition was redoubled. Dudek almost asked, don't I know you?

But, for the moment, his throat was too tight to speak. Dudek watched him turn to the edge of the platform, the dock, of course that's what it was, and then walk down a set of steps to stand on what must have once been the river bed, now a wide path of newly laid concrete, with the barrel shaped ceiling above.

Hardy pointed to a stone archway, under which the Scourin' Burn must once have flowed.

"It's through there. The dome pool."

The sound of his voice was different here, echoing still, but strangely flat. Dudek squinted, unable to make out his expression in the gloom. He walked down onto the old river bed and gave the man a wide berth, starting towards the archway, but Hardy wasn't following. He hesitated, looking back, and found that he could barely see where the man stood, despite the Hi-Viz.

Reaching the archway he slowed, because it was full dark under there. Electrical cable had been pinned to the wall, but he couldn't spot a light switch.

When he turned back, he couldn't see Hardy at all and that stopped him dead. He peered, feeling his skin prickle. Then he saw him, finding he could only just make out the Hi-Viz, with its fluorescent strip, even though Hardy was only about twenty paces back. As if darkness was somehow congealing around him.

Heart beating high in his throat, Dudek backed away, scraping his hand against the wall in hope of finding the switch. Hardy was coming towards him, and Dudek found that it *hurt* to keep him in sight. He searched with his hand, trying to keep a lid on the panic that threatened, and backed into darkness.

"Come on, come on!"

His fingers finally brushed something and, looking down, he saw a pickaxe leaning against the wall. He hefted it, in the same moment catching sight of a switch. It was ahead of him, not behind, closer to Hardy.

It was even harder to see him now, but there was no doubt that he was still coming. He opened his mouth, but found he didn't want to speak to him. Not one word. Dudek hefted the pick in both hands, throwing it hard at the fluorescent jacket, hearing a deep thud. He followed through and scrabbled, flicking the switch before taking several stumbling steps back, heart hammering like it might fail.

For a few panicked seconds nothing happened, then dim lights flickered into life. Dudek moved backwards again, trying to keep Hardy in focus, the man not hurrying, then turned and flat out ran. The light was even lower where the tunnel widened again, but he made out a recent excavation and, behind that, the curved face of the new concrete conduit.

A dead end.

Dudek ran to the edge of the excavation, peering into a deep hole ten yards wide, surrounded by a scaffold. He glanced back, squinting hard. If Dudek forced himself, hurt himself, he could just see Hardy emerging from the tunnel, ten yards away. As he watched, the shadows deepened, not just around Hardy, but everywhere, with a creaking noise that he thought might be inside his own head.

Fighting panic, he turned again to the excavation. It was hard to see clearly, but the scaffold seemed to offer a curving line of boards as a narrow walkway, just inside the perimeter of the hole. There was no handrail and the construction looked precarious, but there was nowhere else to go.

Dudek stepped onto the first board. It was only about ten inches wide and rocked badly as he shuffled forwards, arms out for balance. He kept going, feeling the board sink and bounce under his feet as he reached its middle, not a lot under there supporting it. Inside the hole he could just make out what looked like a large, angled rock, the fall enough to kill him, or break a leg. Stepping onto the next board, he suddenly saw a way out. All Hardy had to do was follow him.

If the man came part way around the circle, then it would be a straight race to the tunnel, he'd go one way, Hardy would have to take the other. The board under his feet shifted suddenly, and he waved his arms, crying out as he righted himself.

He couldn't see Hardy at all now, even though he heard the scrape of his shoe on the first board, only a few yards away. He kept going, arms out, then looked over his shoulder and narrowed his eyes, focused harder until he could see him. You had to take the pain and accept that Hardy wasn't really a man. He hadn't been a man, even when Dudek had taken him to find the boy.

The realization, flooding him like cold water, buckled his knees and almost tumbled him into the hole, but he straightened, unable to give himself the time to think about what that could mean. He tried to throw it away, but Hardy suddenly shimmered before him, grinning, triumphant and cruel, allowing himself to be seen now. And recognized.

When the creature spoke, it was like sand, running through feathers.

"You've always belonged to him, John."

Dudek fought his eyes away and overcame some terrible weight to *move*. Put out his foot, and pulled it back just in time, because the boards didn't form a full circle after all, the next one was missing, and he was trapped. Hardy made a sound that might have been laughter.

Hardy, fully visible now, stepped onto the board Dudek had just vacated. Ignoring the looseness of the walkway, Dudek turned and ran, bending to grab the board Hardy now stood upon. In the second before he straightened, Hardy's expression changed, the grin slipping. Dudek grunted, lifting and tossing the board into the pit, seeing the monster wave his arms and fall, like a normal man.

Now he used the scaffold poles to scramble across the gap, too scared to look down. Moving as fast as he dared, he reached the edge, and sprinted. He could hear noises behind him but kept going through the tunnel, racing up the steps into the main building, then into the courtyard and out of the shadow of the Mill. Actual daylight was shining on him.

Dudek risked a glance back now, but nothing was following, so he slowed, feeling his legs tremble, and his head swim. Crows rasped and cawed, but he ignored them to jump into his car, started the engine and hit lock. He sat shivering, staring at the mill entrance, getting his breath back with the car in gear and ready to go.

He was still wearing the yellow jacket. That was Jason Hardy in there. *His* Hardy, the guy who kidnapped the child, diverting him from Caroline when she needed him most. He had failed to recognize him, not even recognizing the name. Until the creature allowed it.

Dudek slipped the car into neutral. He still had the yellow jacket. When he swallowed, it hurt, and his heart still raced horribly, but he couldn't leave with the jacket. It wasn't his.

He killed the engine and listened, but the booming in his ears was still too loud for anything to be heard, except crows. He climbed out, shucking off the jacket, and walked slowly, checking as he went.

A crow landed beside him and made a rush for his leg. He kicked it and it took off, but he could hear the noise in the sky increasing so he hurried to the office.

At first it looked empty, but there was something, a disturbance, that made Dudek squint. He concentrated as hard as he could, feeling like his face might break, and there was Hardy, sitting once again behind the desk.

As Dudek watched, he began to smile, that infuriating self-satisfied grin he knew so well. His smile widened, and widened still. The man's mouth was so full of feathers that they tumbled from his lips, covered the desk, and filled the air around him.

Dudek threw the jacket down, and backed away.

January 1977

Iris' elderly music center had died the week before and, lacking cash to replace it, she had her radio on, playing low. Neil leaned over and kissed her and then sat back, just looking. She smiled and pulled him back and for a while that's how they stayed.

Then he sat back on his heels. "You know, that's Cliff Richards. I'm telling David. He'll make you listen to jazz, as penance."

"Hang on, it's changing." She kissed him but broke off, eyes wide. "I think that's Doris Day. Quick, cut the power."

She leaned forward, but he put his hands on her arms, stopping her from moving. Then, looking right in her eyes, he sang, along with the radio, *If I ever love*.

Iris covered her face. "Help! No!"

It must be a true love.

She peeked between her fingers. "You do know you can't sing?"

Then I'll know that love is real.

"Neil! This is embarrassing. Seriously."

He moved even closer and continued, *In a world that's in love with romance*

Quieter now. "Neil. Stop."

It can seem that true love is pretend

"You're a shit singer."

And our flickering flames of passion

She opened her mouth, but this time didn't speak.

Might catch fire and just as soon end

"You know all the words to a Doris song."

So give me all your heart

Now she whispered, "Neil."

Give it me forever

Still whispering, "Neil."

And I will forever

They were staring at each other, in the pause before the last line.

stay in love with you

Then he said, "You're crying."

She threw her arms around him and he kept singing, the entire song into her ear.

She sat back. "That was the cheesiest feckin' thing that's ever, ever happened to me. By miles."

"You're still crying."

"Is this something you read in a book? Ways to get a girl to go goosy."

"I meant it. If you say you love me. I'll love you forever."

She pushed him away, suddenly angry. "Nobody can say that."

He didn't answer and after a few seconds she rolled her eyes, dried them with her sleeve. She was still looking beyond him. Then she put her mouth, right by his ear so she could whisper it.

"Ok. But don't ever tell anyone about this. I love you."

2016

It took a few seconds for Dudek to recognize that he was in a bedroom, not one he knew. He tried to move, and his head immediately started to beat, as though his brain was a poor fit in there. Nauseated, he shifted, and pains around the rest of his body made themselves known.

Movement nearby, then someone leaning over him.

"I think you must win some sort of prize. For sleeping."

Hilda sat down on the bed, her room, he realized, the not-on-expenses hotel suite. He started to move, but the pain in his head beat him back.

"You seem surprised to see me."

"Uh-huh." It was about the best he could muster.

"You don't remember coming here?"

"Why did I come here?"

"I'm supposed to tell you why you came here."

He slid his hand down, encountering a cotton shirt. His boxers.

"What's the last you remember?"

He passed a hand across his face. "Feathers."

She didn't say anything, so he asked, "What happened?"

"I heard a car revving, hard enough to make me look outside, and it was you."

"When was this?"

"Yesterday afternoon."

"Damn! I've got to be at work. What time is it?"

"Seven-thirty. In the evening."

"Shit."

"Nathan called it in for you. You're off the hook. Do you want some water?"

Realizing how thirsty he was, he nodded. She helped him sit up to drink.

"So, I parked outside?"

"No parking involved. You ran into the bushes."

"Shit, that's an unmarked police car."

"Well, nobody can accuse it of being unmarked now."

"I don't remember."

He grimaced, the horrible feeling of black feathers blotting everything out again.

She whispered, "Crows."

That stopped him. She put a hand on his. "You remember now?"

"Some." If she hadn't been right by him, she wouldn't have heard him speak. He put his hand up and there was a plaster strip across his cheek. More than one. His hands cut up too.

"I got you in here and it was like somebody had pulled your power pack. You're a pretty heavy guy for a girl to carry about on her own."

He rubbed his eyes and for the first time noticed that the shirt he was wearing was lilac, with lace trim.

"This isn't mine."

"I've been trying my best to avoid saying, no shit Sherlock. But you're not making it easy."

She checked her watch. "Nathan should be here. Maybe half an hour."

Dudek was still looking at the lilac shirt. "Is that a bear?"

"A rabbit."

He thought about asking her, why did she wear a nightshirt three sizes too large, instead he said, "I still don't understand what happened to me."

"You were attacked by crows. And a vampire."

The same word Moore had used.

She put her hand on his arm. "That's where it's all been leading, don't you think?"

He squeezed his eyes tight, his mind sliding away from thinking about it.

"Is my shirt here? Nathan is supposed to look up to me."

"It was ruined. Nathan is coming here with some of your clothes. From your house."

"He's been here already? Shit."

"So, you ready to talk about it?"

"I'm not ready to *think* about it."

He took a breath. "I met somebody at the mill. The site manager. Remember leaving the car. The next thing…" He held on, trying to avoid being sick. "Feathers."

Hilda's cell phone rang, and she answered, saying no more than yes and uh-huh for almost two minutes.

"Nathan. He'll be here soon. We're going to have to move."

"Move where?"

"Out of here. We'll have to sneak away, so Nathan's rented a van. He's going to the other entrance."

"We don't need to sneak. We're the Police."

"There are about a thousand crows out there. You could arrest them, I suppose."

"Shit."

"That's what happened to your car. They're standing guard, now."

"What are you talking about?"

She leaned across him, put her hand on his cheek, the gesture making him catch his breath. "John. It'll soon be dark. I'm doing my best to act tough, but I'm really, really scared."

He didn't answer, and she leaned closer, saying it in a whisper, "Something is coming."

A vision came into his head. A little man, black feathers streaming from his mouth.

"How do we get away?"

"The kitchen has a covered delivery area. Nathan is going to drive the van into there. We'll try to get in, without the crows seeing."

"You hear what you're saying?"

"You're the one who drove halfway across Dundee with crows trying to rip their way into your car." She held up her hand, so he could see the cuts.

"This is from getting you inside."

"Jesus."

"And anyway. I can say what I like about crows. I've already used the V word."

A rapid knock at the door and she started to get up, stopped halfway and kissed him before going to the door. Nathan came into the room carrying a hold-all Dudek recognized as his own. He looked older. Thinner. The two men regarded one another, a long appraising look, Dudek in bed and the big man standing.

A strange expression crossed Nathan's face and Dudek wondered how he looked, but then saw the man's eyes drop briefly to the nightshirt.

"You ok, boss?"

"Been better. You?"

"Fine."

Hilda said, "He told me yesterday how he feels lighter. Less solid than before."

Nathan shrugged. "Think you can get up? Move at all?"

With both of them helping, Dudek got to his feet, ducking to avoid the worst of his headache. Catching sight of the nightshirt in a mirror he told Nathan, "You breathe a word of this…"

Ten minutes later, he was dressed, but still wobbly. Hilda had been out to the van twice, taking all her stuff, not intending to return. Now, dressed in a heavy jacket, with a baseball cap and gloves, she nodded to Nathan. "Ok?"

Nathan had the keys for the Focus in his hand and Dudek realized that the man was more than nervous, he was properly scared.

"What's going on?"

Hilda answered. "We're going in the van and Nathan is taking your car back to the station. The crows will go for the car, we think."

Dudek thought for a few seconds, failing to find another solution.

"And where are we going?"

"A hotel in the center, maybe."

He shook his head. "My place."

Nathan and Hilda exchanged looks and he said, "You think the crows have my address?"

Hilda blew out a long breath, seemingly wanting to get it over with. Nathan pulled his hood over his head and headed for the door.

Dudek stopped him.

"Nathan."

"Boss?"

"If it gets too..." He ran out of words. "I don't have any advice, sorry."

Even leaning on Hilda, it was tough going. She opened the rear entrance a crack and looked out to where the Transit was sitting inside a car port, then spoke in a shaky whisper, right into his ear. "I'll open the rear doors. ok?"

She looked at him closely, holding his eyes so he would know she was serious. "If you flake, we're done."

Hilda's first steps were hesitant, but Dudek could see how coiled she was, staring into the gathering darkness. She paused, then ran to open the rear doors of the Transit, hurrying back to get her arm under him. The adrenalin kicked in then, and he managed a run of sorts, all the time peering into the dark, trying to see if there was anything out there. Something a lot worse than crows.

Hilda helped him inside the van then pulled her cell phone, grimacing as it connected, then whispering, "Ready." A pause. "Good luck."

Almost instantly, the sky erupted as countless crows took flight, shouting about it. Hilda threw the door closed, shutting him in, and the engine roared as the van lurched forwards. Dudek tried to stay flat as they took a corner, fast and fishtailing, another. Paying the price for the adrenaline, he was soon was on the point of banging on the panel, telling her to stop or he would throw up over her fancy luggage.

She did stop, eventually, and the doors opened to show Kingsway retail park, a weirdly normal scene as shoppers wheeled their trolleys to and from Tesco. He peered upwards, searching for crows against a sky so black that it could be full of them, then let himself be helped into the passenger seat. Hilda checked her phone.

"Nathan's made it to the station. He's ok." She turned to him. "Where do you live?"

January 1977

David could hear a huge crowd, shouting, screaming, angry and cruel beyond belief. He recoiled from their infected thoughts, shrinking away. The shouting increased, hundreds of rough voices, vindictive and shrill.

And behind it all, something much worse, something huge and bloated, alien and knowing. He coiled away, further into himself.

"David! David!"

For a moment, as he came awake, aware of his surroundings and Angela holding him, he could still understand the voices, and their murderous intent. Then that faded into a confused racket.

"Crows." He said.

"They've been screaming like that for ages. Just a nightmare, love."

On some level, he noticed she'd called him 'love'. But he was listening to the crows. She held him tighter and told him again, it was ok.

"No, it isn't. For a moment, I understood them. They hate us."

"You're still half in the dream."

He shook his head and disentangled himself, standing naked and shivering in front of his ratty curtains. Outside, it was beginning to be light.

"Come back to bed, its freezing."

He took a step towards the curtains, but froze, not quite touching. Then he turned and pulled his jeans and jumper on, feeling the need to do it. Now, clothed but still in bare feet, he approached the curtains again, hesitating before peeling back a corner.

Something like an explosion, as though moving that inch of cheap curtain had launched a thousand crows, flapping and screaming into the sky.

Angela cried out, and he hopped backwards, dropping the curtain. The racket was huge, and furious.

He found he was sitting on the bed with Angela's arms around him, his around hers.

He whispered, "Get dressed. Quick."

This time, she didn't argue. The commotion outside continued unabated and he could hear other voices now, people waking. Imagined them peeling back their own curtains.

A flurry of feathers, *right outside*. An audible clack. Like someone had thrown a decent sized pebble at the window.

Another clack. Three more. He could hear the tremble in his own voice. "Unlock the door. Open the door to the bathroom."

He saw the question form, disappearing as she found the answer. The bathroom had no window. Looking properly scared, she opened the door and stepped out, coming back to grab his hand, leaving the door ajar. Together, they approached the window, but it was Angela who finally hauled the curtain aside.

Four crows, flapping and cawing, were fighting to stay on the window ledge. As they watched, one cracked its heavy gray beak against the glass, the sound so loud, so intentional, that they both hopped back.

Behind, the darkened sky was in tumult and, with shocking suddenness, a crow flew out of the confusion, hitting the window a shocking blow before falling away. Leaving the glass smeared with blood. And cracked.

David pulled back. "Let's get out of here."

But Angela stood rigid, her fingers tight over his. She stepped forwards, not back, and when she spoke, her voice was loud, and strong. It cut.

"Go *away*."

The crows on the ledge fell away and, for a horrible moment, David felt that swelling, alien thing again, right there in the room. Then it was gone, and the crows began to move off, boiling in the sky, but further away. Some took off from sills and ledges of Rankine Hall.

Moving away.

He gasped, having held his breath. "What just happened? What did you do?"

Angela whirled away to run towards the bathroom, not quite making it before she was violently sick. People were coming into the corridor, bed-headed, sleepy and shivering in the cold, asking each other, did you hear that? What was that?

He nodded self-consciously to one or two students and then froze, finding himself looking at Dr Bernard. The Brainiac was standing at the end of the corridor, clothes disheveled and comb-over hanging down the side of his face, like some dough-skinned homeless crazy. He was looking at David, ignoring the other students.

They stared at each other without speaking for what seemed like minutes, then Angela was there, pulling him inside, closing his door.

He asked again, gently and this time with his arm around her shoulders, "What happened?"

It took her a few seconds to answer, and when she did, she wouldn't look at him.

"You have your strange thing. Where you just know things."

"It's not that I'm exactly…"

"Hush, now. I have something too. More than the little thing I told you about, with my mother. In my head, it feels like there is something I can get hold of. Something solid, but not part of me. I can latch on, like grabbing a handle, and force a person to do what I want."

David was silent, thinking, strangely, about his Afghan.

She said, "It started when I was maybe thirteen. I couldn't use it on my mom, not one bit. I only used it consciously a handful of times before now, that I know of."

"That you know of?"

"It never went well. I put it away, because I was frightened, and ashamed."

"What did you do?"

She shook her head. "Don't ask me, please. This time, it was different though. I didn't know I could affect animals. In fact, I don't believe I can."

"But you shooed those birds away. All of them."

It took her a few moments to speak. When she did, her throat clicked with the effort. "I latched on, but it was strange, and I pushed, just wanting it all to go away. Not knowing what I was pushing at. I found myself, for a second, against something massive and horrible. Like I was a tiny child, pushing against a disgusting fat man. Totally powerless."

"But they went."

"Just for a moment, he pushed back. To show me he could squash me, like I was nothing. In that moment, I *saw* him."

She retched again, and some blood sprayed from her nose. He gave her a tissue, and held her.

"I don't know why he chose to back off, but it was his choice, not mine." Then she whispered, "Did you feel him?"

David took a few seconds to answer. "I felt him."

2016

Hilda was surprised to find that Dudek lived in a remote house, on the banks of the Tay, a few miles upstream of Dundee. Large and Victorian, it faced the river, maybe a half-mile wide at this point. In the wash of the Transit's headlamps, Hilda could see a grassed lawn, falling away towards coldly glimmering water.

She killed the engine and sat. Although there were no lights, there was a sickle moon and she found she could see surprisingly well. A small rowing boat bobbed just offshore, its rope line running to a cracked concrete slipway.

"I saw you more as a city sort of a guy."

"Maybe it's the job. I like to get outside."

"So, not your wife's choice?"

He thought about it. "Suited us both."

Hilda craned her neck, checking the trees, but Dudek said, "If we have to worry about every crow, we're in deep shit."

"You up to walking?"

He pushed the door open, grunting as he got to his feet. Following him into his house, Hilda wondered how much of the décor was down to Dudek and how much his wife, the woman who drowned herself.

He headed for the stairs, but stopped on the second step, looking like he might faint.

"Sit down, for God's sake. Where do I take my bags?"

"Spare room is first on the right."

Hilda walked up to a brightly decorated bedroom, but left the light off, stepping to the window, getting a feel for the place, seeing the orange glow from the city, car headlights moving along a road on the far side of the river.

Dudek had moved from the stairs, which she took as a good sign. There were five doors leading off the hall. The first opened onto a darkened room, dominated by a large dining table, crammed with books and papers.

On a sideboard was a framed photograph of a smiling, dark-haired woman, holding a baby. In the slanting light from the doorway, Hilda made out a crack running across the glass.

Dudek was in the kitchen, a bottle of Merlot in front of him. She thought about asking, is that a good idea, the state you're in, then took the glass he was offering and swallowed a mouthful.

"You ready to talk?"

Dudek looked older, beat up. He shook his head, "I want this, and sleep."

"You can still sleep?"

He took a large swallow. "Can hardly stay awake. Make yourself at home. I'm off to bed."

He topped his glass up, finishing the bottle. It had that rough taste of a red that has just been opened so he must have downed most of it while she was upstairs. She watched him get to his feet, not looking too steady, and go to the door. He turned at the doorway.

"Thanks. I'm fairly sure you just saved my life."

February 1977

Neil bought the acid, excited and proud that he had scored. Even the term scored making it sound like an achievement. Angela's view was different; Neil had met some seedy drug dealer in a pub. Not a mystical arrangement, just an exchange of money for illegal chemicals.

He had four tabs, saying they could each drop one but if Angela and Iris hadn't tripped before they should only drop half. Iris saying, get away with you, talking excitedly about previous trips, two of them, the boys laughing about her tales of inability to function like she was describing strokes of genius.

And, just like that, Angela was apart again.

They were in Neil's room, the intending trippers leaning forward, Angela sitting back. Neil and Iris were on the bed, the garish heart that Iris won for him, pinned to the wall behind them. Angela noticed a stray feather on the blanket, and found herself picturing a drift of them, collecting dust under the bed.

She glanced at Neil and caught him watching her before returning his gaze to the insignificant lumps, more like crumbs of ash than tablets. They looked too small to have the kind of effect they were suggesting.

David told her, "It'll blow your preconceptions apart! They don't call it a trip for nothing."

She wasn't going to take one, and everybody knew it. They were psyching themselves up, leaning towards the dangerous little tabs.

Neil said, "Friday night. Perfect man. We can blow our little minds and be back to functioning in normal parameters by Monday."

Iris. "Tuesday at the latest." And they laughed, a hysterical edge to it.

Iris looked at Angela. "How about it, Hon? Jumping with us?"

Angela shook her head and David put his hand on hers. "Tell you what. If you eat some dope, well, you'll not be up on our level, but you'll be someplace close."

Talking as though the chemical elevated them, on a higher plain rather than malfunctioning.

Iris said, "Angie. If you're not tripping, sorry but you're best out of it. You might even make us freak."

Angela was stung. "You mean, take a bad trip?"

"You don't approve, we all feel it. We might not be able to cope with your disapproval. Sorry."

"Fine!"

David was up, saying, "Angela, don't…"

As she left, she heard Neil saying, "Leave it, man. It's got to be just us, hasn't it?"

Back in her room, she couldn't settle. Irritated with herself, with Iris and Neil, but mostly with David, she put her coat on and hurried into the dying sunlight. The temperature had dropped again so that her breath plumed, and everything had a coating of frost, thickening on grass and walls.

Two hours of fast walking later and returning to Rankine Hall, Angela suddenly knew that something had gone badly wrong, like a nervy alarm bell had sounded in her head. She hurried through the gates, encountered a group of students, heading out. One, a tall and clearly drunk boy, told her, "I'd hang back, if I was you. Those two are totally wasted."

Angela skirted the group and saw the boys in front of the portico. David was jigging and ducking, as Neil tried to keep hold of him. They both looked scared and confused and she was momentarily scared and confused herself, as though her thoughts had dislocated. Then, she was herself again.

She thought, *David*, and his head instantly snapped around to look at her. He pointed in the general direction of the monkey puzzle tree and shouted at the top of his voice, "Can't you see?"

He struggled, but Neil still held him. "Nobody's there, Davie! Get it together, for fuck's sake!"

"He's got her!" David sounded way beyond scared, his teeth were bared, an expression she never thought she'd see on his face, and he was struggling hard.

Neil seemed just as close to panic. "Who's got her?"

"He's fucking killing her!"

By this time, Angela had caught up to them. She stood beside David and turned to where he was pointing, seeing only trees and bushes, glistening with frost. Was this what a freak out looked like?

He threw his arms around her and he felt the fear and panic coming off him like a wave. He looked at her, eyes scarily wild, and whispered, "He's right. Fucking. There. Right there. He's got Iris and he's killing her. Look. Ok? *Look*."

She was in his grasp, his hands painful bands around her arms, and she nodded, scared. The students at the gate still hadn't gone, in fact they were coming back. One of them shouted, "Hey!"

David pressed his face to hers and pointed and, for a horrible second, she saw. She saw Iris, standing as though in a swoon, held up by…

She cried out and looked away, feeling as though something had torn through her head. Something unspeakable, that could not be looked at or thought of again.

The students were moving towards them now, but uncertainly. One called out, "What you doing to that girl, pal?"

Reluctantly, Angela looked back across the grass. She could still see Iris, just about, and there was something else there, but she couldn't bring herself to see it again, not properly.

She said, "I see her. Something's got her."

Neil suddenly no longer looked remotely stoned. He said, "Well, let's get her."

And then, suddenly pumped up, huge and screaming, "Let's fucking get her!"

That stalled the other students, at least for the moment.

Angela didn't know the three of them would run until they did it. They sprinted, one each side of Neil who put his head down and charged like he was going through a line of defenders; a roaring, terrified charge that ended with them hitting something.

Or rather *falling* into something. Something so cold it stopped you breathing. And, as soon as it was begun it was over and they fell to the frozen grass and Iris was there. She was wholly and undeniably there, but she was still and unmoving and, strangely, Angela felt she couldn't move either. David was sitting stunned and blinking beside her. Only Neil was on his feet, roaring and throwing punches at random in the air.

And now he did punch someone, because the other students had had enough and there was a melee, people yelling and pushing one another. Angela shouted at David to get Iris on her feet, come *on*!

They retreated into the halls, with Neil's shirt torn and his face bloodied, David and Angela supporting Iris. David kept looking around, searching.

It occurred to Angela that maybe she wasn't thinking straight, that she had been dragged into David's hallucination. Except that Iris was there and she hadn't been before. And she was sick. They were in the grand hallway now, but the students had followed and they were angry, shouting about Neil breaking someone's jaw.

Angela didn't have time for any of this. She pointed. "Go. Just get out of here."

Turning on her heel, knowing they were leaving, she helped the boys carry Iris to bed. David slumped on the floor with his head in his hands and Neil just sat there, staring, blood smeared across his face.

Amazingly, it amazed Angela, she fell asleep. When she woke up, it was the early hours of the morning. She checked on Iris, who was pale but sleeping. The boys were gone.

2016

When Hilda woke, she lay listening to the quiet of the house. Stayed like that for a while, hoping to hear a dawn chorus but finally gave it up and pulled some clothes on, moving quietly to open her door, listening for any sound from Dudek. Satisfied, she crept downstairs.

This was a comfortable home, clean, but nothing new had been bought for a while. In the lounge, a professionally posed framed photo, the partner of the one with the cracked glass, lay face down. It showed Caroline and the baby, this time with a smiling Dudek, arms around them both. She looked at the happy man in the photograph, searching for the shadow of the person she knew.

She padded quietly upstairs, listening at Dudek's door before opening another door, stalling there. The nursery; cot, mobiles, soft toys, all still in place. Blue airplane curtains, pulled shut.

Dudek appeared in the kitchen around noon, wearing a smart suit and tie, but still looking exhausted and beaten up.

"You're not thinking of going to work?"

"There's somebody I need to speak to. What are you doing?"

"Cooking. You need to eat."

"I can..."

"Don't get used to it. Sit down before you fall down."

He watched her move around the kitchen, cracking eggs and frying bacon. After a while she stopped and looked at him.

"This freaking you out?"

He thought for a moment. "My wife drowned," He pointed at the river, an almost metallic blue today. "…out there. Taking my son with her. But you knew that."

"I'm so sorry, John. Post-natal depression…"

"It's called postpartum psychosis. Mothers have delusions, hallucinations. Maybe think their babies are the second coming. Or the devil. I didn't understand, till it was too late."

She put the pan aside.

"You blame yourself."

For a moment she thought that she had crossed a line, his face said that. Then he said, "I was on a case. You'll know about that too. I let it take over, desperate to find that little boy. And, all the time…" He looked outside again at the river.

She came to him. Put her arms around him then made him look at her.

"You're piling all this guilt on yourself."

"Caroline had this idea in her head about Shaun, being the wrong baby."

"What, like a hospital mix up?"

"No. She thought my baby should be special. More special than Shaun."

"Oh, John."

"She loved Shaun so much. I saw her crying and thought it was just baby blues. Told myself that. But turns out she was crying because Shaun wasn't the right baby. For me."

"So, she walked into the river with him?"

He stared outside. "She started seeing threats everywhere, got this idea about the river, that it was keeping

Shaun safe. Then, out of the blue, she phoned her mother and said, I hate him."

"The baby?"

"She loved him so much then suddenly hated him. I was out of reach, with Jason Hardy."

"That's terrible, but not your fault."

"When I checked my phone, I had six missed calls from Caroline's mom. Twenty-two from Caroline. I'm the guy who puts it together. And it was as if I was blind."

February 1977

David had insisted that Neil slept in his room that night and there was no reason to ask why. Neil had a feeling in his head as though important stuff had burned away. He could smell their charred remains, lining the cavities of his sinuses. His shoulder throbbed.

He smoked a joint to calm himself, watching David sleep. Then he arranged cushions across the floor, and pulled his long coat over his head.

He woke to sunlight and loud knocking, David stumbling to the door, being brushed aside by someone coming in. Mackie, the policeman, with another in uniform. Neil sat up, feeling sick and instantly guilty.

Mackie stood in the middle of the room, looking around. He moved to the table and picked up the tin foil containing the dope and his smile was suddenly genuine.

"Knew I'd see you boys again."

Two minutes later, he found the last tab of acid. Then they were being taken away, heavy hands on their arms. Bundled into a police car whilst faces at windows looked on.

Later, Neil was sitting in an interview room with Mackie opposite, smoking and smiling. His head still felt scorched and his shoulder ached badly.

Mackie said, "You're busted. You and your junkie pal attacked some girls in full view of about a dozen people. Poor bastard tried to intervene, and you broke his cheekbone. Creeping about before that, like the Man from Uncle. Completely out of your minds.

"And possession, not only of cannabis, but LSD. What do you say?"

"You're from Aberdeen."

"Seriously? You think that'll help you?"

"My dad's on the force there."

Mackie's smile dropped, and Neil added, "Chief Superintendent Kerr."

2016

When Roger Moore walked in, George trailing, he asked "Nathan not with you today?"

Dudek shook his head, "A lot on, Rod."

"You're…not quite yourself."

Dudek's hand went to a cut on his cheek.

"I met Haddow."

Moore closed his eyes. Opened them again. "I'd say be careful, but it's too late for that."

"And I've been to the Tombstone Mill."

When Moore looked away, Dudek leaned close and dropped his voice. "Something's happening."

"You think I don't know?"

George stirred beside him but said nothing, and Moore continued. "It's getting interesting in here. You having the nightmares George?"

George looked away. "I sleep just fine."

"I have to find Angela Murray, Rod."

Moore shook his head. "You don't want to find her."

"Don't you want us to get to the bottom of this? I know you loved your family…"

Dudek had to stop because Moore was laughing. "Don't you get it yet? I loved them. Still do. Love them to bits, no pun intended. But not half as much as I *hate* them. If I could get out of here, I'd dig them up so's I could cut them up some more." He had stopped laughing, and was leaning forwards, his teeth bared.

Dudek remembered what it was like, fighting him. He wanted to look across at George, but didn't dare break eye contact. George hardly seemed to be paying attention, different than before.

He hadn't meant to ask, the words just came out his mouth, "What you said, last time. About Caroline."

Moore just stared.

"It was like you knew something."

"Did her love turn to hate?"

When Dudek couldn't speak, he pointed to his dead socket. "His eye. On you, John. Has been, maybe for a long time."

"Who are you talking about?"

"I'm never talking about him. I'd die first. Who do you love, John?"

Dudek was surprised when Hilda immediately jumped into his head. Moore's face lit up. "Got yourself a special lady?" Saying lady like he meant whore.

He sat back.

"You think you're tougher than I was?" He tapped his caved in head. "Stronger in your mind."

"How do you mean?"

"You want to know, I'll tell you. I'll tell you where she is. Then, God help you, John Dudek."

Just before he left, Dudek turned a last time towards Moore "You asked me, who do I love? Who do you love?"

Moore didn't smile. "Angela Murray."

February 1977

David was anxious to speak to Angela when they got back, but the first thing he noticed was his and Neil's stuff piled up in the hallway, no one guarding it.

"My records!"

"They're kicking us out, Davie."

A door opened behind them and Tamblin, Brainiac 5's deputy, looked out, scowling.

"My office."

David was thinking, this is Bernard's office. Where's the Brainiac, with all this going on?

Once inside, Tamblin told them, "It's up to your course leader whether you stay on at university, but you're out of these halls. You were trusted, and you have broken that trust."

David blew out a breath. "We aren't going to be charged. We accepted a caution."

Tamblin took a moment, then turned to Neil. "What a waste. I understand that you were an outstanding student. Your keys."

He wasn't even holding out his hand. He was pointing to a spot on the desk, where they each placed their keys to Rankine Hall.

"Can we speak to our friends? Angela and Iris?"

Tamblin hesitated. "You don't know about Miss Colhoun?"

Neil had been hanging back, but now he stepped forward, looming over the man, his face stone. "What's happened?"

Tamblin stepped back. "Miss Colhoun is in a coma, I'm afraid. She's been taken to Ninewells hospital. They didn't know if it's drug related, or this meningitis thing."

David asked, "What about Angela?"

"She accompanied her. Five or six hours ago."

They walked outside in silence, David feeling like his legs had turned to rubber. The memory of last night was like a coating on the inside of his head, a taste at the back of his throat. He pushed it aside, dealing with the here and now and what his parents would say. He shook that last thought away, ashamed of it.

Neil, beside him, said nothing, but his glowering presence seemed bigger than it had ever been. Somehow heavier. Like his father, the thought came, unbidden. In the street, Neil pulled his long coat about him.

"I'm going to Ninewells."

"Ok, but where will we sleep tonight?"

Neil began walking, like he didn't mind if David followed or not, but he tagged along anyway. After a few minutes a green Triumph Dolomite, passed them and stopped at the curb. Minto, the archivist, started to get out but pulled back as a truck passed close, horn blaring.

Minto hurried around the front of his car, moving in that strangely uncoordinated way he did. He smiled uncertainly, looked as though he was going to put his hand out to the boys, then did a little half wave.

"Mr....em...Haddow, I b-believe?"

"Doctor Minto?"

"Yes. Of course, yes." Then, "Call me Ian." And, by way of explanation, "It's my name. And Mr. Kerr?"

Neil glanced uncertainly at David. "Yeah."

They stood on the sidewalk for several uncomfortable seconds, then Minto indicated the Dolomite. "Can I give you a lift?"

Neil frowned. "I'm going to the hospital."

"Of course. The young lady. I'll take you."

The car smelled of old leather. Minto, a skittish driver, pulled jerkily from the curb. "I was watching, last night."

David, in the passenger seat, glanced back at Neil. "Watching what?"

"I saw you attack the creature to save your friend. Quite unbelievable courage. I keep replaying it in my head."

For a while there was silence, apart from Minto crunching gears and muttering, giving himself driving advice. Then he said, "I had believed I was the only person who could see it, till last night."

David said, "We were hallucinating last night. We'd taken drugs."

Minto wrinkled his brow. "Hallucinating? So, you think what you saw…"

Neil told him, "I didn't see anything. He did."

"Why did you run then?"

"He told me to."

"But it was you! The other t-two were there, but it was you who shoulder charged the thing. You must have seen it."

David. "And you saw this?"

"Yes. I've been…I've been studying it, for a long time."

Neil took this in. "But it's invisible to everybody else?"

"Invisible isn't the right word. I believe it's there in plain view but that the mind just can't cope with seeing it."

"How come you can?"

"I concluded that it had to be there…wait, this…ah, fourth gear I think, no second, damned machine. I think you have t-to *want* to see it. Accept the p-p-pain as the p-price."

David said, "I've seen you, at the Tombstone Mill. Is that part of this?"

When Minto nodded, David asked, "Do you know what it is?"

"I have a theory."

He glanced in the mirror. "I can't believe you knocked it down. I wouldn't have believed that possible."

Neil rubbed his aching shoulder. "I believe you might be completely bonkers."

Minto took this cheerfully. "I understand you've been evicted? You are welcome to stay at my house tonight."

"Thanks, but…"

"Well, let's go to the hospital and take it from there, shall we?"

Minto lived on the higher slopes of Dundee's central hill, in a large stone-built house. The furnishings were old, and, although it was clean enough, it had a dusty, uncared for air.

Minto served tea and sandwiches in the large living room, himself taking a seat in a battered wing chair before a two-bar electric heater. It seemed to David that the man was too close to the heater, something about it making him feel anxious.

An extremely furry tortoiseshell cat hopped on Minto's lap, making itself comfortable. He smiled and smoothed its fur.

"Horace, you naughty boy."

The visit to the hospital had been less than successful. They had been told at reception that Iris was stable but critical, but that was as far as they got. The only visitors allowed, for the moment, were family members.

Now Minto told them, "I'm confident you won't lose your places on the course. Tamblin was simply being an oaf."

"But he can kick us out of the halls?"

"Oh, most certainly."

He had said it almost jovially, smiling at Horace. "It's really up to Simon, I mean Dr Bernard, but knowing him I can't imagine he'd hold a different view."

"You know Brain…Dr Bernard?"

"I count him as a close friend."

The boys exchanged a glance that said, that makes sense. Minto was speaking again.

"I tried to contact him this morning and couldn't. I'm really rather worried, to be honest. Have a look at this, Mr. Haddow."

He handed David a photograph, doing it almost casually, but David knew he didn't want to look at it. He held it in his fingers but kept his eyes on Minto. "What's this?"

"A photograph of the students Union. Taken at night."

"Why do you want me to look at this?"

"Why are you so anxious?"

David thought then that the man, for all his stammering and diffidence, had a hard center. Neil leaned over to peer. "It's just the Union."

Reluctantly, David looked at it, instantly dropping it, as though it had burned him.

Minto said, quietly, "I'm sorry. I know it hurts. But you see it?"

David nodded.

"Can you describe it?"

David opened his mouth, but it took a few moments before he could say, "Something that makes your whole head kind of wince, but describe it? No."

Then, "It might be black."

Neil, annoyed, picked up the photograph. "Look again, then."

"Didn't you hear? It *hurts*." Now to Minto, "Can you do it? Describe it."

"No. And I've tried to describe it out loud, whilst looking at it."

Neil glared at the photo, then at Minto. "You said you concluded it was there? How did you do that?"

"I suppose I'm an authority on the history of Dundee and, to cut a long story short, I concluded that the current epidemic wasn't medical. It was supernatural."

Neil snorted.

"It has happened before, Mr. Kerr. Many times, always after an exceptionally dry summer."

"I can't believe this shit! Iris is in hospital!"

Minto sighed. "I wouldn't expect anybody to believe this all in one go." He looked at David, "But Mr. Haddow can see it too."

Neil looked at David, who was suddenly on his feet. "Shit!"

"What now?"

"We need to find Angela."

When Neil just looked at him, he added, "I don't think she's safe."

February 1977

Alcohol seemed to be threaded through the lives of so many journalists, but not Jack Jarvis, who was pretty much tea total.

So, when he got the call from Simon Bernard suggesting they meet at the Scout Bar, he said, "I didn't see you as much of a drinker."

Jarvis had met the man only once before, at some stuffy black-tie event, but had no problem recalling him. Bernard was a seriously weird guy. Now the seriously weird guy, probably wearing bicycle clips like he had that evening, said, "It's simply a meeting place. Do you possess a motor car?"

Who called a car a motor car? "Yes, sure."

"Very well. Meet me in Brook Street eight pm on Friday evening, opposite the Tombstone Mill."

"Hold your horses, Doctor. You haven't told me what this is about."

"Are you aware of the illness?"

Jarvis took a moment, saying nothing. An old trick, if you were silent, people would oftentimes rush to fill the gap, telling you stuff they didn't expect to. Not so this strange academic. Jarvis got the impression he didn't even notice.

"You mean this syndrome thing?"

"Exactly. Do you know Doctor Ian Minto?"

Jarvis had to think. "The archivist?"

"He postulates that the illness is a localized, cyclic event. It has happened before, always following a hot summer. Do you wish to know more?"

Jarvis was scribbling this down, thinking he should go and see the archivist, thinking too that if Minto linked up with Bernard, they could do a comedy act.

"Why beside the mill? We could just have coffee."

"Eight o'clock, Friday. Opposite the Tombstone Mill."

When the line went dead, Jarvis wasn't even sure he'd go. But, something was going on; something that involved the phenomenally weird Bernard and this illness. How did he describe it? Local, cyclical. It's happened before.

He wrote the time and date on the pad in front of him. Then wrote the name Ian Minto, putting an oversized question mark beside it.

February 1977

David met Angela in the University tower block, almost as though they had arranged it. He had held her in his mind and there she was, waiting when he walked in.

He hugged her. "I was worried about you."

"We should all be worried."

"How's Iris?"

All she did was shake her head.

Now they were drinking tea in the archivist's dining room. Her update on Iris wasn't encouraging, and David thought Neil might blub. For the moment, he stood at the window, staring out.

Minto laid an old map on his dining table, moving Horace when he jumped onto it. "This is Dundee, in 1852. You can see it's a rather small town, a warren of tenements."

David said. "And mills"

Minto nodded. "Just so. Dundee was the jute capital of the world, back then. More millionaires per head of population than anywhere else in Britain. Jute Barons, they were called."

He followed the winding path of a road with his finger. "Witch's Knowe. Or Witch's Hill, now Lochee Road. Follow it down to this tombstone shaped plot is, as you've probably guessed, the Tombstone Mill. The name seems a bit melodramatic till you look at its closest neighbors.

"And here's the Scourin Burn. A river running under the great mills and through what became the university. Dundee's main watercourse, but over time, it was built over and eventually forgotten. Think of it, an actual underground river, only rediscovered when something collapses into it."

Neil bit out his response. "What's that got to do with Iris?"

Angela put her hand on his arm, but he didn't even glance at her. Minto paused, as though gathering his thoughts.

"Has your medical course touched on the Great Stink of London?"

Neil shook his head, once.

"Pity. The Great Stink took place in 1858, an exceptionally hot year in Britain. All the effluent from London went straight into the Thames back then but, in the summer of 1858, the river dropped so far it became a septic pond. The smell got so unbearable that Parliament stopped."

He turned to David, smiling. "Dickens mentioned it in Little Dorrit."

Neil was humming with tension. "Can you get to the point?"

"The attendant cholera epidemic killed tens of thousands, but only in London. No other epidemics that year. Except in Dundee, where it affected the West Port, Hawkhill and Crowhill areas."

Angela looked up. "Crowhill?"

"Gone now. Under the Tombstone Mill."

Neil sighed. "So? The same thing happened in the Tay as the Thames."

Minto shook his head. "The Tay at Dundee massive. An estuary, so the whole gigantic body of water changes daily. And Dundee was a tiny village compared to London. It wasn't cholera. Physician Dr James Lenzie described it as..." Minto picked up an ancient paper, "A baffling and intolerable horror. The patient simply wastes to death. Locals call it hot weather wasting and say it follows a hot summer like night follows day."

"Are you trying to link this with what happened to Iris?"

"There have been many other outbreaks. 1934 is the only one this century though, after a hot summer. Twenty-two deaths, again around the West Port.

"The point is that this has been happening for a very long time and it can be invariable tracked to unusually hot, dry years."

David said, "But you mentioned supernatural stuff."

"I've called someone who can explain much better than I. We'll meet her tomorrow, at my office."

Angela said, "But you can tell us what you think."

"I'd really prefer if she explained."

Angela leaned forward. "Still. Please tell us."

A muscle in his check twitched and he looked at her in surprise. "Very well."

He paused.

"I believe it is a kind of demon, from pre-history."

"Does it have a name?"

"It was once known as Curn Dhu. Or…" He looked around the room, and shifted in his chair, as though embarrassed. "The King of the Crows."

2016

The sea smelled of the sea, and the elderly, single tier ferry smelled of diesel. It seemed to Nathan, as he watched the churn of the water, that they were going on a much longer journey than the short hop to the island, Scriven.

Dudek peered towards the island, a distant smudge, the wind making his eyes water.

He surprised Nathan, asking, was he scared?

Nathan took his time over answering. "I'm scared. I keep thinking about…"

He dried.

"What happened with The Saint?"

Nathan nodded. "I want to say, you see me acting weird, hit me over the head with a baseball bat."

"But you're wondering, would that do the trick?"

"Yeah. And, before he did what he did, Moore wasn't even acting weird."

"No."

"Maybe I'll go away for a few days."

Dudek stared into the water. "You can stay at my place."

He was quiet then, and Nathan could see he had something to say, coming to it slowly.

"Come to the car. Something I have to show you."

The ferry was rolling in a way that made Nathan feel clumsy as he walked across its deck, wondering what Dudek had in there. The way he said it, working up to tell, made Nathan feel anxious as he got behind the wheel of the Land Rover, a beat up Discovery, his personal car.

Dudek picked up his briefcase, checking all around before bringing out a revolver, in a leather holster.

"My family, I ever tell you that there were a lot of military men? Army?"

Nathan shook his head, no. Dudek had never once spoken of his family. The name, he thought, sounding Polish.

"This was my grandfather's service revolver. He killed two Germans with this gun."

Nathan looked at it, the hatched butt and the long barrel, but didn't say anything. Dudek took another gun from the case, this time a Luger.

"One of the Germans was an officer. This was his gun. Grandad just took it."

"They work?"

"I stripped them last week and tried them out. I always thought older guns weren't accurate, but I hit a tree at fifteen yards, five shots out of six with the revolver, six out of six with the Luger."

"How wide was the tree?"

"Not as wide as you."

Nathan looked around, coming back to the guns. What he didn't say, aren't we police any more then? Everything they had done so far was legal.

Dudek asked, "What do you think?"

"She might force us to shoot each other."

"I could drop them in the water. I've been thinking about doing that."

"I'd feel better, though, being armed. I'm scared shitless."

Dudek nodded, like it was done. "You have a preference?"

"I'll take the Luger."

It fitted into the side pocket of his three-in-one.

Dudek stared across the water. "You heard about what I did? Taking Hardy out of custody?"

"I've heard some."

"You know, you get to have a sixth sense, after a while on the force? So many liars, you get to where you can almost guess what someone is thinking."

"Yeah."

"I've always had it. Even at school. Not telepathy, but I know stuff, sometimes. Stuff I shouldn't."

For a while both men were silent. Then Dudek continued.

"With Hardy, it was a different scale. I knew for absolute certain that if I took him out, he might not say anything, but I'd be able to home in. Like I was using him as a divining rod, to find the kid."

"How did you know?"

"I can't explain it any better than that. It worked."

"Where is he now? Jason Hardy?"

"His background, he seemed decent, an ok guy. Short, hardly above five feet. Family man. Then, suddenly, he wasn't an ok guy. Where is he now? I don't know. He doesn't even have a criminal record. My fault."

Then he said, "You know what this feels like, this boat trip? Moving out of real life into something else."

February 1977

David hadn't been sure of what to expect, this being his first time meeting a witch. They were sitting in a store room that seemed to double as the archivist's office, drinking tea around a long table, the mood subdued.

Minto had asked them to come to the council offices, bringing them down echoing stone steps to a long corridor and into this room with its jumble of artefacts and smell of old paper. Maps and ancient books lined the walls. A suit of armor stood in a corner, alongside a long cavalry sword with an elaborately carved pommel.

Scanning a line of books, David's eye lit on one which he read aloud, "A History of Scottish Politics. I. Minto and S. Bernard. Is that..."

"Yes, we co-authored this text."

Minto frowned. "Simon still hasn't returned my calls. He hasn't even been taking his lectures. It's extremely concerning."

David decided it was time to ask something that had been eating at him. "You never said why you were at Rankine Hall that night."

The man shrugged. "I've been tracking the creature. All will be explained when Mariel arrives."

At four minutes after ten, a tall thin woman rapped on the open door and called to Minto, telling him he had another visitor. The way she stressed the word 'another' and drew her mouth into itself, David wondered if everything was okay with Minto in these cold Council offices.

Minto smiled, sounding apologetic, as he often did.

"Ah. Yes. Thanks Mrs. Cory, send her through, would you?"

Cory returned a few moments later with the witch, Mariel Tanner, closing the door without a word. They all stood as Tanner walked in and Minto hurried across to usher her to the table.

She was a short, slightly round woman in her late forties, smiling at Minto as he bobbed in front of her, turning at his stammered introductions. She shook hands with each of them in turn, looking Neil up and down appreciatively.

Her hair was slightly longer than was the fashion for a woman her age, but there was nothing else to mark her as unusual. You would walk straight past her in the street, David thought.

She did wear a sort of cloak, he supposed, of the kind you might buy in Marks and Spencer. Under the cape she was wearing a print dress that his mother might have worn.

She was speaking again to Minto, shooing away his thanks.

"You sounded so serious. I'm intrigued!"

The witch looked from David to Angela and back again, eyes narrowing.

After a few seconds of uncomfortable scrutiny David asked, "What?"

"You have such a…" Tanner paused, "an intense aura. I can't really read it."

"Is that good or bad?"

"It could be either. With just a bit of help, I suspect you could do magic."

David started to laugh, but the witch said, "You are a seer, aren't you?"

It was Angela who answered. "Yes, he is."

There was silence for a few seconds, and then Minto jumped as though electrocuted, "Sorry. Do you want, tea? Coffee?"

She waved him away, bringing a can of Coke from her bag, "So. What's all this about?"

They took places around a table and there was a silence before Minto asked, "Do you remember the last time you were here?"

"Researching my book. Of course."

"Well." He puffed out his cheeks and held his hands up. "I've got some really rather bad news, Mariel. I'm afraid that the em...that Curn Dhu has returned."

The witch sat up straight, then began to laugh.

She didn't just give out a little giggle. She laughed so hard she had to get up and walk away, holding her sides. Minto started to speak but she waved him quiet, shaking her head.

They just had to wait it out, and when she finally came back to the table, David thought that anything could set her off again. Minto was blushing a bright red.

"Ian." She said at last, "You're truly priceless."

She put her hands to her face and parodied terror. "The King of the Crows has retuned? Well that's a proper nuisance, isn't it?"

It seemed she would go off again, but she managed to avoid it.

"Is this to do with all these crows?"

They looked at each other and David began to see that Minto had everything wrong.

Minto shrugged, still very red. "Well yes, in a way."

"That doesn't mean the King of the bloody Crows has popped back from mythology." She opened the Coke and took a long swig, then looked round at the four of them.

"I'm going to dine out on this forever. What do you all know about Curn Dhu?"

David. "Doctor Minto told us that he was probably the inspiration for Dracula. And that he had been trapped in a river near here."

She sighed, looked at Minto, "I'm sorry, Ian. Sometimes my sense of the melodramatic gets the better of me, I might have...misled you."

"Misled me?"

"It's a *myth*. I make a living from telling tales from the old Celtic legends, so I like to introduce a local angle, if I can. The Scourin' Burn is a good contender for being the Craw River, but so are hundreds of rivers."

"You don't believe in Curn Dhu?"

"If this gets out, I'd be out of a job, but no. For goodness sake, no. It's the scariest of all the Celtic legends, but of course I don't believe it. I've been working hard on it for the past couple of years precisely because it's not well known. It'll be the pièce de résistance of my little show.

"So, no. I doubt a prehistoric mythical being has made its return in 70's Dundee." Angela glanced at David. This wasn't going as anyone had anticipated. She asked, "What little show?"

"That's what I do. I work with two marvelous puppeteers, we have a travelling show, dramatizing Celtic legends."

Then, an edge of excitement in her voice, "You want to hear it? It stands up, even without puppets. You'd be my first ever audience!"

David glanced at Neil and Angela and saw they were as stalled as he was, but when Angela said, alright, the witch smiled like an excited ten-year-old. Neil folded his arms, stone faced.

Tanner took a deep breath, dropped her head and let it out. Minto mouthed a 'sorry' around the room.

Then the witch, slowly and melodramatically, raised her head to look at her audience. When she spoke her voice was different, deeper and stronger, a performer's voice.

"This is the oldest of all the tales of Celtic Legend, from before the Celts called themselves Celts. It took place at a time when faeries walked amongst us without fear or artifice and, even though they were dangerous and capricious, they were wondrous indeed.

"This was a golden age, when the faeries had a king to whom they owed fealty. This King of the Fae was named T'hu and he was the bravest and the best and it was he who made the two greatest mistakes a creature mortal or immortal has made on this Earth.

"There was also a great King of men in the North. A just and noble King was Kell, and the people thrived across the lands. But Kell had a son, Nikell, a willful and proud Prince. One cursed day, Nikell was hunting with his father's Captain when he chanced upon a meek and lovely wood spirit. Faeries inspire passion in the hearts of men, and Nikell fell in love in a trice, demanding she be his wife. When she refused, he was taken by a great anger and beat her until he could no longer lift his whip. He saw then that all his men had fled, but for his Captain, and knew his error.

"He hurried home, but the Faerie King was fleeter still and, on the steps of the keep, under his loving father's eye, T'hu slew Nikell. That deed, black and foolish though it was, was not yet one of his two great mistakes."

The witch paused to take a sip of Coke. David could see that the others had been pulled into Tanner's performance.

"On that moment, the age had turned. Kell raised his army, and set forth to destroy T'hu. But his Captain sent secret word to the faerie that he would speak. It was at this treacherous meeting that T'hu made the first of his mistakes. The Captain's name has not been remembered, for this is the man who would become the King of the Crows. He said to T'hu, if you make me an immortal, I will defeat Kell, and prevent the destruction of your race."

The witch paused. "How is it so far?"

The switch to her normal voice took them all by surprise, but David had to nod. "It's good." He glanced at Neil, who didn't meet his eye.

Tanner took a moment, getting back into character. "T'hu made his first mistake." She raised her hand, and dropped her eyes, dramatically. "He agreed.

"The Captain raised an army, and a terrible battle raged for three days, so that the fields were full of dead and dying and the rivers ran red. Only the carrion crows were happy. None could stand before the Captain's dread sword and, finally, he slew his own King.

"Black with the blood of old friends, he held Kell's head aloft and called on T'hu to make good his bargain.

"Through fields of crows, about their terrible business, T'hu came. He said, 'It can be done but one way. You must give up your heart.'

"The Captain cried, 'Trickster! How can a man do without a heart' T'hu pointed, 'You must take the heart of a crow, in its stead.'

"The Captain was furious, but T'hu would not be moved. 'You must take the heart of a crow.'"

This time, when the witch paused, the room was silent, so when she shouted, "Then let it be so!", all four jumped.

"T'hu snatched up a crow and hurled it at the Captain's breast."

She put her hands to her face, continuing in a whisper. "The air was full of black feathers, so thick that T'hu could not see what he had wrought. More feathers fell than could have come from one bird or a hundred such birds. Then, he caught a glimpse…"

She covered her eyes with an expression of shock and pain and was silent.

Angela, her voice low, asked. "What did he see?"

Tanner did not drop her hands. "The words for what he saw have never been spoken. For no such words exist."

She took her hands down and regarded them. "T'hu could not look upon his creation, and turned away. The King of the Faeries, the bravest and the best, flew in terror before Curn Dhu.

"Even the sun, who took no interest in the doings of men or immortals, said, 'T'hu. What have you done?'

"Then followed the darkest of times. If the man who became the King of the Crows had any good in him, it was gone with his heart. No man or faerie could stand before the terrible King, and the days were filled with smoke and carnage.

"Worse than death by far, though, the King of the Crows could inflict the curse of hatred, making men hate those they loved, with a passion that was not human. He raised an army of monsters, once men like him, who none could not look upon, even as they took their very spirit."

If Tanner noticed the look that passed between David and Angela, she didn't show it.

"T'hu asked the sun, 'Why have you deserted us? Can you not blast this abomination from the world?'

"The sun replied, saying that it would, for it hurt even its eye to look upon the creature. But crows are everywhere, and Curn Dhu heard the plot even as it hatched. He knew he could not stand before the sun, so never again ventured forth in daylight. He had a box hewn from stone, and slept throughout the day to rise when the sun left the sky."

The witch changed tone once again, sounding amused suddenly.

"So, Old Curn Dhu is in a coffin during the day, sunlight will fry him, and his followers are draining the life of their victims. I think Stoker lifted the main idea, threw in big teeth and bingo! He had the vampire."

Angela. "Is that the end?"

"Sorry, Dearie. Exhausted, and beset by crows, T'hu gathered his best warriors and finally gave battle below his own beloved faerie hills, where a spirit river met the sea. Ever cunning, T'hu attacked near the end of the night.

"The warriors, unable to look upon the monsters, fell one by one, but at last, the dawn approached, and the King of the Crows saw he had been tricked. He flew, with T'hu fast on his heels, and when the impatient sun finally rose above the edge of the world it determined to burn the creature from the face of the earth.

"But the sky was so full of crows that it could not reach the King. A million crows turned to soot, but the creature reached his stone chest and threw himself inside.

"T'hu smote the chest, but it was bound tight by the power of the King. In despair, he fell to his knees.

"Then the spirit of the river, a dreaming spirit indeed, appeared to him. It told him he had forgotten the simply power of earth and stream and, should he cast the casket into the water, the monster would dream, for so long as the river flowed."

"Em, Mariel? Sorry to butt in, as it were."

Tanner smiled, as though at a child. "Yes, Ian?"

"So, if the river were to dry, the creature would wake?"

"Shall I finish? I'm near the end."

"Sorry, of course."

"T'hu saw that she was right and, though crows attacked him grievously, cast the casket into the stream. The crows lost their purpose in a moment, becoming normal birds of sky and tree. And as for T'hu. He looked on the sun a last time, said goodbye to his own dear hills and gave up his ghost. The end!"

The witch took a sip of her Coke, smiling as Minto led a strange round of applause.

"That was wonderful. Well done."

"Thank you. You should see the puppets!"

"I'm sorry we've got you here on false pretenses." Then he leaned in. "But something is here, Mariel. Something that kills people."

Neil glared. "Iris is properly ill, and here we are, talking to a…an entertainer."

Mariel ignored Neil, but was immediately more serious, "A malevolent spirit?"

She turned to David. "Was it you who discovered it?"

"I saw it."

Neil had the photograph, and now he slapped it on the table, making her jump.

She peered. "What am I supposed to be looking at?"

David pointed. "Bang in the middle of the shot."

She shook her head. "Nope."

They looked from one to another and David said, "I'll do it."

He walked across to stand beside the witch.

"See, your mind just kind of slides around it. You have to force yourself to see."

He pointed along the curb. "See that line? Follow it close."

He winced and made himself focus. "See there? At that point, there's no curb."

"Yes, there is. Oh!"

The witch lurched to her feet, bumping into David.

The four of them watched her expression, the pain and revulsion. The disbelief. She shook her head, as though trying to shake something free, then picked up her cloak.

"I have to go."

"You can't! You have to help."

She looked at Minto as though he had gone mad. "Help? Ian, I'm..."

She pulled her cape on. "I'm sorry."

She was halfway to the door when Angela said, "Wait."

It wasn't spoken loudly, but the woman stopped as though a hand had been put on her.

"What is that thing?"

For several seconds the witch stood very still, then, reluctantly, she turned, looking at Angela with a less friendly expression.

"I see you now, girlie. Now you are showing your true colors."

"What is it?"

"I don't know. Something terrible."

"The King of the Crows?"

"Maybe...maybe his servant."

Minto said, "Every time there has been an exceptionally hot summer in Dundee, people die. For hundreds of years, the same illness. I believe when the stream drops, Curn Dhu wakes."

Tanner looked at him in horror, but Minto went on, "The line of hills behind Dundee. The Sidlaws, Gaelic for Faerie hills."

"I know."

"So, a dreaming stream under the Faerie hills."

Angela asked. "Do you know if we can kill it?"

"I don't know. *Nobody* knows about this."

She glared around the room, her eyes wet. "I've only seen a handful of auras in my life, that even hinted at the sight. Two in one room? Why is that? Why are you here?"

Angela asked, "What are you saying?"

"Maybe you were *brought* here."

"What for?"

Tanner shook her head, "I have no sight beyond the common ability to see auras. I don't know. But I do know that you should *run*."

2016

The metal ramp clanged when the Discovery drove onto the concrete dock at Scriven. Looking around the low houses and shops of the old fishing village, Nathan noticed a line of dead crows tied to a rail.

A man, wearing a grubby Hi-Viz, watched them as they passed him. A fisherman carrying a coil of orange rope stopped walking, following them with narrowed eyes.

They followed the road out of town and it soon became single track, lined by fields, and trees blown crooked. The sea, bigger than it ever looked from the mainland, stretched away to their right.

Dudek pointed out a farmer, walking his field with a shotgun in his arms, stopping to shoot at something, high in the trees. The dull pop reached them a second later.

They had to drive slowly, and every so often there were dead crows, tied to the fence that ran by the road. Dudek pointed. "The house, The Headland, should be on your right."

The dirt track was about half a mile long and dead crows had been strung every few posts but, by the time they reached the house, they were crowding the wire. The woman, Angela Murray, was already standing at the door, watching as the car stopped. Nathan could feel Dudek craning around him to look at her and thought how they would seem, two men sitting in a car just staring.

He thought about lowering the window, a single press of the switch, and as it dropped, bringing out the Luger and shooting her. Dudek had hit a tree at about the same distance, six out of six.

Dudek bumped his leg with the side of his hand, then the passenger door was opening, and Nathan found that he had to pause, wait till Dudek came around in front, between him and Murray. Thinking that he had always thought of himself as a brave man, but this was different. He stepped out, making himself walk alongside Dudek, seeing Murray look from one to the other.

She was a narrow woman of medium height, hair pure white and tied in a bob but with some wisps coming loose, wearing a lambswool cardigan over pressed trousers. She stood stiffly, her head high, fine featured and long jawed, her lips a thin line. She did not speak, or smile.

It took him a moment to make the connection. The way she stood, it was just like her mother.

February 1977

Minto drove them to Ninewells Hospital, giving Angela a key because it was understood that she was moving into the house with Minto and the boys. At least until Iris got out of hospital.

The hospital was new, a modern sprawl of concrete and glass, the entrance as wide as a basketball court, busy with people coming and going. The boys hung back as Angela, looking like Angela, marched up to the desk. A couple of minutes later, they were walking along a brightly lit corridor, long and wide enough to drive a car down.

They followed sign after sign, all the way into the astringent smell of Iris' ward. The background noise consisted of subdued talk and the squeak of shoe on vinyl. As they moved forward, two nurses passed them, laughing. David expected to be challenged, but neither glanced their way.

Now they could see bays with beds, patients sitting or lying on them, visitors crowded around.

A nurse, the one who had laughed earlier, paused and smiled. "Know where you're going?"

Angela said, "We're looking for Iris Colhoun."

"Second room on your left. We've just had her parents in. Sorry, but if they come back, two of you will have to leave. Three visitors max." She looked up at Neil, "You've got to be her brother."

Neil shook his head, "I'm her boyfriend."

Iris, when they entered the room, was very pale, and unconscious. She lay square on the bed, hooked up to a bag, hair brushed flat and arms over the cover, with her hands on her stomach.

For a moment, the three of them stood still, just inside the door. When David spoke, it was in a whisper. "She looks thin. Thinner"

Neil stepped slowly towards the bed, and David saw the muscles of his face jumping, realizing in that moment that he had never seen his friend cry. Not once.

He was crying now, tears pouring silently down his face as he stood, looking down at Iris. David felt a tug and turned to see Angela widening her eyes at him.

"What? Oh yeah."

He all but scurried out. Outside, the nurse seemed to understand. "There's a room along there if you want a place to sit."

Neil hadn't moved. He could feel his chin wobbling, tears scalding his face. He touched the back of Iris' hand with his fingertips, surprised at how cool her skin felt.

"I'm sorry. I'm sorry. I'm sorry."

He folded into the chair and took her hand in both his, trying to warm it. "Iris. Be ok. *Please* be ok."

Impossibly pale and painfully beautiful, her face did not move. Neil smoothed her cheek and touched her lips, surprised again at how cool she was. He stroked her hair, which seemed redder than ever, but was brushed flat. Under control. Neil stroked and teased it and soon it was spilling, wild about her head.

"Be ok, alright? I love you."

Iris lay unmoving.

"What is the point of being a great Irish lump if you won't fight. Come on! You're not just tall, you're *big*." He hit his chest. "In here. Fight!"

He had raised his voice and looked around, checking, then he leaned in, so his lips were touching her ear. "I give you my strength Iris. I give you mine as well. Together, eh? Come on."

But he couldn't give her his strength, that was just words, or the closest to a prayer as he had ever come. Her chest barely moved.

He whispered, "You still smell like you." And thought she might have reacted. The tiniest of movements.

He sat like that for a while, holding her hand. Unable to think of anything to say, he sang, quietly. Doris Day and a sad, under the breath version of 'Suffragette City'. After a while, the door creaked, and David looked in, looking almost scared. "Hey."

"Hey."

"How is she? Sorry, that was a dopey thing to say."

Behind Angela, the noises of the ward continued. An old man's voice rose now, quavering but still holding a tune, singing, "Run rabbit, run rabbit, run, run, run."

A woman's voice, scolding but good natured. "Will you change the record, Eddie Thomas?"

Iris stiffened, grimacing, her eyes screwing tighter. Angela, still in the doorway, said, "Should I shout for a nurse?"

Run rabbit, run rabbit, run, run, run.

Iris arched her back, lips pulled into a grimace. Neil stroked her face, "It's ok. It's ok. Please don't make it hurt. Don't let it hurt her. Angela, get help."

From outside the same line started again. *Run rabbit*...and David, operating on some instinct, pulled Angela *into* the room, closing the door.

Iris began to relax, and a second later was lying as she was before.

Neil looked up. "What just happened?"

David shook his head. "I don't know. But there was something about that old bastard's voice. I don't think Iris liked it."

They sat, struggling to find things to say that didn't sound stupid. Finally, the door opened and a heavy middle-aged woman with over-red hair stepped in, coming to a surprised stop when she saw them. Behind her was a large man. His face was covered in gray bristles and he had a thick mustache that straggled downwards at the edges. His lower face had the collapsed look of dentures unworn, and now it was jutting aggressively. It seemed to Neil that his chin sat immediately below his straggly mustache, as if the mouth had been somehow missed out.

They all stood, and Neil slid his hand out from Iris'. A thought crossed his mind and, ashamed, he pushed it away. About what she would look like in twenty years' time. But that led to another thought; did what Iris looked like in twenty years' time have anything to do with him? His answer – I hope so.

The man pushed past the woman, speaking loudly. Neil struggled to understand, the man's accent being stronger by far than Iris', the lack of teeth not helping, but it was clear he was angry.

He said, "I'm Neil Kerr, Mr. Colhoun. Iris' boyfriend."

He stepped forward, hand out, but stalled, still six feet away.

The man glared at him, his eyes wet.

"Didn't know my daughter was having any *boyfriend*." Giving the word a nasty twist of lemon.

Angela, standing by the window, said, "We're Iris' friends."

"The ones got her on the drugs? Put her in that bed?" The man's eyes were wild as well as wet.

Neil flinched, as though struck, then dropped his eyes to the floor. David said, "It wasn't like that."

The man turned his raw agony towards him, and it was David's turn to flinch.

"You saying you didn't get her on the drugs?"

Angela asked, "Do I look like I take drugs?"

"What do I know about junkies?"

"I've never even smoked a cigarette." The man opened his mouth, a pink slash below his stringy mustache. Closed it again.

"We're your daughter's *friends*. We love her."

The man nodded in Neil's direction, finding his anger again. "Look at the state o' creepin' Jesus there. You're sayin you and Iris were goin' steady?" The man glared at him, his chin tight under his nose, shoulders hunched and fists balled. He was wearing carpet slippers, blue polyester joggers and a crumpled shirt. Like he had dressed from anything that had been near to hand.

Neil, his voice tiny. "Yes."

"It was you with the drugs, wasn't it? You."

"We took drugs, but I never meant..." Neil ran out of words and the man took two long strides forward and pulled his fist back. Neil screwed his face up, eyes closed, but did not otherwise move and the man paused. Then slapped him, open handed across the face, making Neil's head snap back and his long hair swirl. He opened his hand again, sweeping it back for another slap.

Angela said, "Stop."

He stopped. Then she said, "Go and put your teeth in."

Colhoun stared at her, red eyed, teary. Confused. He turned to his daughter and laid his hand on her cheek for just a second, before shuffling from the room.

Now it was just them and Mrs. Colhoun. She spoke to Angela, sounding almost afraid, "What happened? For a moment there..."

Then she shook her head as though to clear it. Squaring her shoulders, she pushed past Angela and sat, smoothing her daughter's wild hair and kissing her forehead, like she did that first day, seeing her off to school.

"You better not come back here."

Neil. "I love her, Mrs. Colhoun."

"Just go."

Neil looked at Iris, feeling his heart clench, but walked to the door, David quick at his heels. Angela followed but turned before leaving.

"You know it's not drugs."

"They don't know what it is. Call it a syndrome. Words that hide their ignorance."

The she said, "But they do know that she's failing. My fine girl is fading away."

Angela waiting a moment longer, then left.

They walked in silence to the only bus waiting and climbed into the harshly lit, smoke smelling interior. One or two people were on board already, looking strained, cold, and unhappy, staring into the dark.

David led the way to the empty top deck and flopped into a seat, wiping condensation from the window before pulling his cigarettes out. Then he looked at Angela and put them away. Then took them out again and offered one silently to Neil. Both boys lit up as the bus lumbered noisily off.

David squinting through the smoke, said, "For a moment in there..." and paused.

Neil finished for him, "You wanted to leave the room. Go put your teeth in. Even though your teeth are all there in the first place."

"Yeah. For a moment there I did."

February 1977

David stood stock still, watching his classmates drift into the lecture hall, catching the way some of them were looking at him. There had been no contact from the University, no suggestion that there was a change in their status and so, when Angela had gone to her morning lecture, David tagged along. Neil, Mr. Straight-A, was already up when they arrived at the breakfast table but just looked at them when they said they were going in, like they were crazy.

David walked Angela to her lecture, kissed her goodbye and came here, where he was watching his last few classmates disappear. Asked himself, what the fuck am I doing here? A lanky student sitting nearby, jerked, snapping his head up in surprise, before putting his notes hastily in front of his face. David almost said, what, do I have to *think* quietly now?

He wandered outside, where a cold wind was blowing, some sleet in there. He glanced up at the crows, tumbling and croaking in the wind. Just crows, he thought. Please just be crows.

He walked, not knowing where he was going, but not surprised when his legs took the familiar route to Rankine Hall. He paused at the gates, then pressed on till he came to the portico, where he had first *seen*. He stood for a while, staring at the monkey puzzle, then dropped his eyes and paced, following tracks that must have been theirs, gouges that had to be the toes of Neil's boots, digging in as he drove forward. The ground was frozen hard, but those boot prints were clear.

This, then, was where they had hit something too awful to bring to mind. He bent to pick up something that glinted. An ear ring, seriously old fashioned. He nodded, remembering it dangling from Iris' earlobe.

And something else, pushed into the mud; a silvery circlet. He bent again but this time paused, not wanting to touch it. Straightened, still without picking it up.

No amulet of power, this. A bicycle clip.

2016

All the things that Dudek could have said to Angela Murray, what he came out of his mouth was, "You don't like crows?"

The woman stared at him, a hard, flat look, and Nathan found his hand tensing on the grip of the Luger in his pocket. He was thinking about Susan, Debs and little Sarah, thinking that maybe he had to get her now, before it was too late.

Then she turned, looking at the way her fence was stacked up.

"No. I don't like them." Her voice was cultured, but Scottish. The lady of the manor, in her cardigan and court shoes.

Dudek's voice sounded normal. "You wouldn't think there would be that many crows, on the whole island."

"There never used to be."

"Seems to be a year for them."

Dudek having a conversation with the woman.

"There's none on Scriven now. Not one."

Nathan wondered how she could know that, her sounding so sure, and Dudek mentioned the farmer, shooting into the trees in his field.

"He'll be shooting up old nests. Some people, once they get into a task, they don't know how to let go."

A cell phone went off, Nathan thought the ring tone was 'Suffragette City', a Bowie song from way back. The woman took a Nokia out of her pocket, speaking without taking her eyes off Dudek.

"No, that's fine." She broke the connection.

In the distance, Nathan heard a vehicle engine and turned to see the top of a tall vehicle, probably an old-style Land Rover, stopping at the entrance to the lane. Blocking it, probably.

She said, "I suppose you should come in, as you've come all this way."

She walked away and there was nothing for it but to either follow her or stay outside. Dudek glanced at Nathan, then walked into the house.

The interior was a strange mixture, old style furniture and décor but with a lot of contemporary looking paintings, a laptop on an old desk. She led them through into a kitchen, clean and surprisingly modern, and sat them down at a long pine table. Floor to ceiling glass doors gave a spectacular view of the sea. Keeping her back to them, she busied herself making tea, every movement brisk and efficient.

Dudek said, "Seems like you were expecting us."

She didn't look at them. "You spoke to Roger."

"How can you possibly know that?"

She turned. "Let's not pretend that everything is normal here."

Dudek took his identification out of his pocket and showed it to her, "DCI Dudek. This is DC Findlay. We're investigating the death of an old friend of yours. Neil Kerr."

She nodded. "That's where you started. Maybe you need to ask yourself, what has this turned into? You were Roger's friend."

"I'd like to think I still am."

"No, you're not."

Nathan asked, "Do you know what happened to him?"

Her eyes were on him now and he wished he hadn't spoken. He felt like somebody had poured cold water on him.

"Of course."

Dudek asked, "Were you responsible?"

Her expression didn't change. "Yes."

"So, might something similar happen to us?"

She nodded, once, up and down.

Dudek brought out the service revolver and pointed it at her. "What if I shoot you?"

She looked at the pistol, but didn't seem scared. Nathan brought the Luger out and now both guns were pointed at her.

"This is how police do things now?"

Dudek persisted. "What if I shoot you? Would I be safe then?"

"You've got this all wrong. But you know that, don't you?"

Suddenly her expression, looking at Dudek, changed. Like she had realized something that took her from relaxed to concerned. Dudek wasn't speaking, just staring at her. Nathan looked from one to the other, wondering what he should do. The gun was still in his hand, but it was no longer pointed at her. It was pointed at his own foot. Dudek's gun was on the table in front of him. When had that happened? Things were slipping out of control.

Murray said, "There's something about you, Inspector Dudek. Something I can't quite…I can't quite put my finger on."

"That's been said before."

"I imagine it has. But, there's something else. For just a moment there, I thought I saw something…"

The switch on the kettle clicked and she turned to finish making tea.

She said, "I wonder what's the best way to do this. I suppose we could start with you asking your questions."

Dudek said, "In 1977 you went to the Tombstone Mill with three others. Neil Kerr, David Haddow and Ian Minto."

She nodded, looking grave.

"Why did you go there?"

"To destroy a monster."

She sat at the table, prim in her lambswool cardigan.

"Why did you think there was a monster to destroy?"

"You know there is a monster. You've been brushed with him yourself, I see that much. What I can't see is how deeply you've been touched."

Dudek's eyes barely flickered. "Still, why were you bent on killing it?"

"The short answer is that it murdered someone we loved."

"Who?"

"I think we'll keep her out of it. What do you know about the creature?"

Dudek didn't pause. "It's some sort of vampire."

"It's much worse than that."

For the next twenty minutes they listened as the woman, Angela Murray, told them about the King of the

Crows. After she had finished, there was silence. Dudek took a long breath.

"How much of that do you really believe?"

"All of it. I have been touched also, more deeply than you."

"What do you mean by that?"

She said, "To tell you that, I have to tell you about the Tombstone Mill. And I can't bring myself to dwell long on that. What I can tell you is that, when we went there, we had no idea of the power of the creature, and were all destroyed by it, in one way or another.

"Those of us who did not die were changed. The monster seeks re-birth, Inspector, and chose me as the vessel. To do that, he had to open himself to me, and I found it within myself to resist. I take something from that, but I am changed, for good or ill. I can feel him, growing stronger, searching for me. But I can hide from him on this island."

"Is that what the crow killing is about?"

"They cannot be allowed to see me."

Nathan asked, "He doesn't notice that? His crows being killed?"

"It's nothing to him."

"Where did you go, when you disappeared?"

"I don't remember how I lived in the months before I came here, but the islanders took me in. The state I was in, insane, it's a wonder they didn't just have me hospitalized, but they didn't. Then I began to…I don't mean to, not always, but I bend people to my will. I'm like a wicked witch in a story and this island is in my thrall."

"As is Roger Moore?"

"Yes."

"You made him kill his children, kill himself, to keep your secret."

"In a way."

The policemen looked at each other. Nathan asked, "What way?"

"You fear for your own wife, Constable, your own children. You should. I told Roger to keep my secret. I *made* him keep it."

"And?"

"You can't comprehend the cruelty of the monster, or its power to make us hate the ones we love. With a depth that is alien to normal beings."

Dudek. "So, what happened to Roger?"

"Have you asked yourself, who employed him?"

Dudek's eyes widened. "Haddow."

She nodded. "When he returned to the mainland, he told Haddow he could do no more, as I bid him to."

"Did you know what would happen?"

"I suspected."

"So, you sent him away, to butcher his family."

She didn't answer. Instead, she sipped her tea and asked, "Are you hungry, gentlemen?"

It was later. Dudek had sketched a plan of the mill, showing the engineering works to divert the stream.

She pointed. "The monster's remains were in the dome pool, under thousands of years of mud. David will be driving the diversion project, taking the stream away to keep his master aware. All it needs now is a vessel." She turned to Dudek, "And a seed."

"Why are you looking at me like that?"

"Maybe you could be that person."

She waited a beat. "Or the one to destroy him."

"How would I go about doing that?"

She sat back, folding her hands onto her lap. "If he ever found me here, I intended to kill myself."

She said it calmly. "But just dead isn't far enough away for the King of the Crows. This house is rigged to burn."

"Why are you telling us this?"

Murray stood, then walked towards a large cupboard, returning to place a block on the table.

"Do you know what this is?"

Nathan's eyes widened. The woman had placed a block of PE4, the Army's version of C4, on the table. "Plastic explosive! This must have come from the military."

"It did, and I have a good deal of it. As did these." As Nathan watched, she placed two Heckler and Koch semi-automatics beside the explosive.

"You think we're going to...what? Blast our way into the Mill and blow it up?"

She pointed to Nathan's Luger, lying on the table. "You crossed a line, coming here. Let me make this plain."

She looked up, first at Nathan, then Dudek. "This creature is clever and more malevolent than either of you could comprehend. If he is reborn…"

She sighed, and rubbed her temple. "I used to have a dream. In that dream, cities were dark, and everybody was in terror. On every street corner there was a statue."

It took a few seconds before Dudek could say, "That nobody could look at."

She nodded. "That nobody could look at. You've had the same dream. Maybe that's what I see in you. I hope so. I could have stalled it, perhaps for hundreds of years. If I hadn't been weak. I hurt David, to prevent him being the seed. But I knew if I left him alive, that left the creature with a presence in the world. So, this is my fault."

Nathan asked, "Will you come with us?"

She shook her head. "An end of some kind is coming, and the odds are in his favor. If I come to the mainland now…it might not be in our interests."

Nathan noticed she had used the term 'our' as in them being together. She said, "When you are ready to make your move, and it must be soon, call me and I'll come. Once on the mainland, I suspect I'll be discovered. At best, I might be a distraction."

February 1977

"Ian!"

The man walking into Minto's office held his hand out, "Jack Jarvis. We met at the naval history exhibition."

Jarvis was short, with messy hair, sandy and thinning. He was smiling and that's how Minto had remembered him, a smiling man with a Yorkshire accent and an easy laugh, a tie that hung several inches below his collar.

Minto shook the man's hand, smiling uncertainly. It seemed rude to ask how he had gotten past Mrs. Cory.

Jarvis looked around. "So, this is your lair? Fascinating. The stuff you must have in here."

Minto shrugged, his version, an apology in there. "I'm the c-city archivist."

"You must let me buy you lunch sometime. You must have so much just rolling around in your noddle that would make a great article for *The Courier*. Everybody loves all that Auld Dundee stuff, eh?"

Minto dipped and smiled and shuffled.

Jarvis continued. "But, for the moment, I wonder if I could pick your brains? I'm trying to understand some local history."

Minto indicated a couple of chairs set around a large, messy table and they both sat.

Jarvis said, "This illness going the rounds, what's it called, PSS?"

"PMS. Pseudo Meningococcal syndrome seems to be the c-current name."

"That's the one! Current name?"

"Sorry?"

"You said current name."

Jarvis was smiling, leaning back, relaxed. Minto took a moment, before stammering a reply. "I understand the term to mean a group of symptoms. As in, similar to meningitis. But not meningitis."

"Okay." Said as if it was two separate words. Then, "Has there been a similar thing before, though? I'm asking you because you're a local historian. *The* local historian, really."

Again, Minto found himself pausing. He was thinking, it was surely a good thing that this journalist was taking an interest. Briefly, he imagined a conversation where he told the man everything he suspected, but no, that wouldn't do. He was also wondering how he had put this together.

"Interesting you should ask that, Mr. Jarvis."

"Only my bank manager calls me that. Jack, please."

"Jack. Actually, there have been similar clusters, going b-back. In 1858 there was something that was termed the Summer Sickening."

"The same symptoms?"

"It's hard to say."

"Have you told the medical officer of health?"

"Yes, but I don't think he put any store in it."

"Do you?"

Still smiling. Still leaning back.

"I have to say I'm surprised you're asking me. I'm hardly the first person to speak to in relation to a health issue. Unless you'd heard there's a historical pattern."

Jarvis leaned forward. "So, there is a pattern?"

"I didn't say that. I asked, had you heard there was such a thing."

The smile was back. "A man like me hears things, Ian. I heard you contacted the medical officer. Wondered what you had to tell."

"Well, that's about it really. Any good?"

"As we say in Yorkshire, its neither use nor ornament."

Minto nodded, thinking to change the subject. "You came here from Yorkshire?"

"I was in London before here to be honest."

"What paper?"

"*The Times.*"

"You moved to *The Courier* from *The Times*?"

Jarvis smiled. "I was hoping to work for the *Beano*. What do you know about David Haddow and Angela Murray?"

The question, fast and out of the blue, took Minto by surprise. "What?"

"David Haddow. Angela Murray. Know them?"

"I thought you were looking into the illness."

"I am. Iris Colhoun. Currently in Ninewells. Murray and Haddow are close friends."

Minto was thinking hard. "So, you're trying to find friends of ill people?"

"Sounds like you ducked the question there, Ian."

"But what a strange question it was."

Jarvis smiled again and put his hands out wide. "Just journalism Ian. I can't help but notice you've stopped stammering."

Minto and Jarvis looked at each other for a few seconds. Minto asked, "What year did you come to Dundee, again, Jack?"

"I never said, but it was '69."

"I remember that year well. Another sunny summer, I had to water my geraniums just about every day."

Jarvis nodded but didn't say anything. Minto cleared his throat and stood. "Now, if you don't mind..."

"Of course." Jarvis stood also. "But look, I get the feeling you think I'm fishing for something unsavory here. Not a bit of it, I'm just trying to help." He put a card on the table. "You might get around to thinking you need some of that and if so..." he tapped the card.

2016

It was dark but much too early for Nathan and Dudek to have returned from Scriven when Hilda heard the car turn into the drive. She killed the light and stood in the gloomy kitchen, peering out.

There was a car sitting behind her rental, clear in the moonlight. A Skoda Fabia, with a man sitting inside.

It was strange, though, that he was just sitting there. It wasn't too late for anyone to visit, just a little after nine, but she didn't like it. Not one bit.

She wondered, could he see her looking out at him, and decided no. Not with the light off. The front door was locked, but only with the Yale. One good kick would burst it.

Trying to keep her breathing easy, Hilda walked the length of the hall, hurrying the last few steps to turn the key in the mortice. Then she pushed a heavy old bolt home and ran to the back door, thinking this was probably silly but not really caring. There was a bolt there too, that she managed to force home.

The windows were all modern, and locked.

The man was still there, sitting in his Skoda, and that surely wasn't right. She grabbed her cell phone and was about to call Dudek when the driver door opencd and a short man got out, holding a clipboard and a measuring tape, like a surveyor would use. She pulled back, but he smiled, friendly, raising a hand as he walked towards the front door.

Seconds later, the doorbell rang. There was a pause and the bell rang again, followed by a rap on the knocker.

Hilda took a step closer, beginning to feel foolish. It seemed rude to ignore someone, perhaps a friend of Dudek's. She walked to the door, listening.

The letterbox flap came open and she skipped out of view as the man spoke through the gap.

"John? It's Jason, with those figures you wanted."

She called back, "John isn't here just now. He'll be back…" She hesitated, "…later."

The answer came after a brief pause, "Ok." Spoken slowly, the man showing how patient he was being. "I'll leave them with you, shall I?"

"Could you just pop them through the letterbox?"

"I've got some samples here."

"Just leave them at the front door, thanks."

Another pause, then the man spoke again, annoyance in his voice, "Look, I'm doing John a favor here. I'm not leaving expensive samples outside."

Feeling ridiculous, Hilda put her hand on the key.

"What samples are these?"

"Double glazing."

She had been about to turn the key, but now she stopped.

"The house is already double glazed."

"It's an upgrade. Look, are you going to let me in?"

Hilda turned the big key, but went to put her cell phone down to undo the heavy bolt, and the sight of it stalled her. Instead of putting it on the floor, she hit call. Dudek answered almost immediately.

"Hilda?"

"I've got a guy called Jason outside. Says he…"

"Don't let him in! Where are you?"

"By the door."

"Lock it and get away quick. Far into the house as you can, and keep speaking to me. Don't speak to him. Don't listen to him."

Jason was calling through the door again and she found that it was hard to walk away. It just seemed so wrong. She wanted to do what Dudek said, but there was such a buzzing in her head. She dithered, beginning to turn back.

Dudek was shouting down the phone, shouting walk away, do it. Do it.

Showing him she was calm even if he wasn't, she said, "I can't just leave your friend out there. Be reasonable."

Dudek was shouting, trying to get her to listen, saying Hilda that is a vampire out there. The word caught her, and she froze, finding herself with her hand on the bolt, trying to let the nightmare in.

She turned and ran. "What do I do?"

"Go upstairs. Stay on the phone and whatever you do, remember nothing is important enough to let him in."

"Shit! I'm crapping myself."

Upstairs now, she looked over the banister.

"We're not far away. If we put the foot down, we can be there in about an hour."

"Will your cell last that long?"

A pause. "I've got maybe twenty minutes. Do you hear anything?"

"No. I'm going to the window, look outside."

"Stay away! That thing can get into your head."

"I've got to look. See what it's doing."

She slipped into Dudek's bedroom and crept to the window.

Dudek spoke into her ear, making her jump, "You ok?"

She whispered back. "I'm in your bedroom."

"Your breathing is scaring me. Slow it down, if you can."

Hilda tuned into her breathing, hearing what Dudek meant and taking a long, shaky breath. "I can't see him."

"It's not a him. Remember that."

"Can't you get a cop to come?"

"He wouldn't know what he's dealing with. Might even let it in."

She pressed her head to the window, trying to see as much as possible, gasped, and Dudek wanted to know what it was.

Her whisper was tiny. "I heard rustling. From downstairs, I think."

"Inside or out?"

There was no reply and he asked again, "Inside or out?"

"I'm not sure. I'm going to look."

"Don't go out!"

"I'm on the landing."

Then, "It's in the house!"

"Did you lock up?"

"Yes."

"Hilda, think. Nothing can break in without making a lot of noise. What does it sound like?"

A pause. "I don't want to say."

"Feathers?"

"Don't! I'm going downstairs. Make sure I locked the back door."

"Please, please stay upstairs."

"Ok. I'm going down."

Hilda went down, one step at a time, listening hard. Mostly, she heard her own panicky breathing.

"I'm downstairs."

"Stay in the middle of the house, Hilda."

She stood undecided, then felt a run of ice, running over her whole body.

"Something's scratching on the hall door. It's inside!"

"It's a trick! If something's in the hall, why isn't it opening the door?"

"It's in the house! I've got to get out."

"Stay inside!"

Hilda nodded, backing up fast. "You're right. I've got to get out."

"Listen to my voice. Stay *in*side. Inside, Hilda."

"Ok. I'll sign off. Save batteries."

Hilda was back at the front door, car keys in her teeth, struggling desperately with the bolt. Panicking, she tore at it and it finally came free. Unable to swallow, she pulled the door inwards, enough to peek out.

Nothing. Telling herself if she was going, just go, she stepped out and ran, but stalled halfway to her rental, hearing something she couldn't make sense of.

The sound made her wince, and it was coming from a point immediately in front of her, which wasn't possible. It sounded like laughter, or rough feathers, scraping against stone.

The creature that called itself Jason was suddenly there, right there in front of her, only a few steps away. She realized then that she hadn't seen it by herself. It had shown itself. There was enough human left to show that it wanted her to see how easily she had fallen into its power, and it wanted her fear. It was gleeful.

She tried to peel away, but couldn't. Her legs were shaky but might, she thought, agree to move forwards, towards him. They would not move back. The creature opened its arms, not wide, an understated gesture and she felt suddenly like she was on ice, a steep and slippery slope that led straight to him.

Hilda inched forwards. He laughed again, this time a proper human laugh and she was angry suddenly, the way this little shit was looking at her, expecting her to fall under his sway. Another slippery half step forwards. She shook her head, trying to come to herself, and twisted her neck to see the moon shining on the wide river. Dudek's wooden row boat bobbed off shore, a picture postcard scene.

For a second, she felt something let go, as though she had been underwater, getting her head up for a little sip of air. Then she was moving, turning clumsily and trying to run but not quite making it, her legs doing that dream thing, where they can't make progress. She tripped and fell, hearing it come for her, but got back up again, managed a stumbling run onto the concrete slipway, stepping off into a foot of icy water.

The shock drove the breath from her, but her mind was instantly clearer. She thrashed forward, the water cold enough to hurt as it came over her thighs. Then she turned to look.

The creature was at the edge of the river. A ripple lapped at the shore and it stepped back. She watched it, her eyes widening.

"Can't do it, can you?"

It looked directly at her and, feeling as though she had been slapped, she looked away, but made her eyes come back.

"You can't step in the water."

Hilda inched backwards, putting more river between her and the thing. It stared at her, hard, and she felt it, like a pressure, had to put her hand to her head to push it away.

"Nuh-uh. You can't do that either."

Its face contorted with very human rage and she surprised herself by snarling. She pointed. "Fuck you."

She turned, pushing further into the freezing water and eventually having to swim, reaching the boat in a dozen strokes. She pulled herself in, hurting from the cold, shivering so much that her hands were waving around.

It wasn't in sight now but something was there, a ripple in the air just a few steps away from the rope that could simply pull the boat to the shore. In the silence, there was a tiny trilling noise. Her phone.

The next sound Hilda was conscious of was a car engine. She came to, shivering in the boat, aware that she had flaked out. She made herself concentrate, and saw the creature, moving from the water's edge.

The Discovery slewed into the drive, spraying pebbles, and Dudek was out and running towards the house before it even stopped. She tried to call out, warn him, but the noise that came out of her mouth was tiny. At the door, he paused, casting around. The thing was moving towards him and she thought, he can't see it.

The first Hilda knew about the pistol was when he fired it, sparks coming out of the muzzle. The creature stopped, and then came on. Dudek wasn't running away, he was walking *towards* it, shooting the gun. Fired again and again, the thing getting closer, being knocked about but not slowing. She just had to watch as the distance between them closed.

February 1977

Neil heard that Iris was dead the following morning. He got up early, even before Minto, and made breakfast, everything feeling weirdly normal. Called the hospital but received no news, then hung up and thought about calling home. Imagined himself speaking to his father.

And telling him what?

Had Mackie been in touch with him? Of course, he had. That meant he knew that Neil was out of Rankine. Maybe he was even here in Dundee, searching for him. Hearing that Neil had stopped attending classes.

He sipped his tea, biding his time till the others came down. First Minto, then Angela, neat and groomed as usual. Finally, David, looking spectacularly ungroomed and near exhaustion.

Looking back, he couldn't recall anything that happened that morning, just the phone call, which Minto picked up. His expression was grave as he said, "I see." Said it three of four times then finished with "Not at all. Many thanks."

Iris had died in the night, life just fading out of her. She had regained consciousness briefly but had made no sense, saying "Run rabbit run", the song the old guy had been singing. Then that big heart just stopped.

David tried to console him, but he pushed him away and stumbled out of the door. He walked fast, hunched over, not seeing where he was going, but coming eventually to the hospital, following the route he had taken when Iris had been part of the world. Her room was empty but he looked around, trying to find some last thread of her in the medicinal air. He put his hand to the mattress. There was nothing of Iris here.

A nurse pushed the door open. "Can I help you?"

When he shook his head, she stepped into the room. "You're Iris' friend, right? Her boyfriend?"

He nodded, feeling his chin begin to wobble embarrassingly.

"Where is she?"

"Downstairs. Waiting for the funeral director. Her parents are taking her back to Ireland."

When Neil turned, the nurse put a hand on his arm. "Don't go down there. She was such a pretty girl. Remember her that way."

He blundered out, eyes tearing up. Walked, then ran out of the hospital, ran until his lungs were nearly bursting and he was outside the Tombstone Mill.

The Tombstone Mill. It seemed to get heavier as the sun got lower, gathering shadows to itself. Like it was such a weight, it should sink into the earth. The circling halo of crows sounded to Neil's ears like they were laughing today.

It was beginning to snow again, and he recalled how flakes caught in her hair, how he had wanted to put a hand out to brush them away, and didn't. But she kissed him anyway.

He shook the rusty gates. "I'm coming for you. Going to fucking *kill* you."

But, crazy angry as he was, he was gone before darkness fell.

Back at Minto's house, Neil said, "We have to destroy it."

Angela nodded, emphatic, but David shook his head. "Nobody will believe us."

"I mean that we have to do it. Us."

For a while they were silent, then Minto said, "I don't know how one would go about that."

Angela frowned, "If we can't, it will keep killing."

David moved uncomfortably, coming to a decision. "I have an idea who it is. The servant."

The room was silent, and he had to continue, tell them how he had found the bicycle clip in the grass. How he couldn't bring himself to touch it.

Neil. "So?"

"A vampire wearing a bicycle clip? Who do you know wears one of them and doesn't even know it?"

"You're talking about Brainiac."

Minto looked confused. "Brainiac?"

"You're great friend, Bernard."

Minto paled visibly. "You believe that Simon is the creature?"

"Yes."

The silence was of a different order now. Minto rubbed his face. "I think it more likely that he's a v-v-victim. He's d-disappeared, you know."

Neil stared hard at him. "You never properly explained why you were there that night. Why Rankine Hall?"

Minto blew out a long breath. "The Tombstone Mill was built in 1812 by..."

David's eyes widened. "Roland Rankine? The miserable bastard in the painting."

"Exactly. Rankine was by far the wealthiest of the Jute Barons, but there were sound reasons for him looking so miserable, as all his family, including his wife and children, died soon after moving into Rankine Hall. Not unusual for Victorian times, of course."

"So, there's a link, between the mill and Rankine Hall?"

"There is indeed. The same man built both the mansion and the factory. After Roland died, Rankine Hall had a sad and checkered history, gained a reputation as a house of ill fortune, and fell into disrepair."

"Haunted? Is that what you're saying?"

"No, it's more than nobody who lived there thrived. It became synonymous with tragedy and I'm fairly sure it would have been demolished if the university hadn't bought it. It was, in my view, a site most worthy of watching."

Neil took a long moment, staring at him, before turning to David. "That photograph. You need to see if it's the Brainiac."

David and Angela approached the table, holding each other tight as they tried to force themselves to focus, but it seemed it couldn't be done. Angela cried out, for the fifth time twisting away, eyes screwed tight. She stayed like that for a moment before turning to David. Put her hand to his face as she stared into his eyes.

"I'm sorry."

He frowned. "Sorry for what?"

"I hope you can forgive me. I've got no choice, love."

His eyes widened, and he shook his head, but she told him, "Look at the photograph and describe the creature."

David's looked hurt, like a little boy who had been scolded, but still he turned to the photo. His whole body trembled for a second or two, before he twisted away, covering his face with his hands.

Angela was by him, stroking his hair, telling him again how sorry she was, but he pushed her away, hard enough to make her skitter across the room.

"You *did* that to me."

"I'm so sorry."

"When you see it, really see it, it can see *you*. You've no idea what you've just done."

Neil put his hand on his friend's shoulder.

"Was it him?"

David nodded, pressed his lips together "It's him."

Angela stepped towards David again, but stalled, seeing how he glared. Almost as though he hated her now.

It was later. Minto had been quiet, thinking, but now he cleared his throat. "I could talk to him."

They all looked at him, and he continued, "I think, somehow, Simon is still there. Before I knew it was him, I wondered why the creature never seemed to notice me. I think now that it did, but Simon didn't want to harm me."

Neil frowned. "What are you thinking?"

"I'll try to speak directly to him."

Neil looked out at the darkening, snowy sky. "I don't want to talk to him. I want to kill him."

"Simon's a good man, under the thrall of a monster. If we can help him find himself, it might weaken it, more so than destroying him."

"What if he attacks us?"

"We simply retreat to the car and drive away."

David shook his head. "We can hardly set eyes on it and you want to have a conversation."

"But we've all seen him, *him*, not it. Like a guise that can be taken on and off. If I help Simon fight the monster, all this might stop."

Angela looked towards David, but he kept his face turned from her.

Neil said, "Ok. But if that doesn't work, I'm going to kill him."

2016

Dudek had stepped out of the car before it was even stopped and started shooting, but there was nothing there to be shot. He was walking forward and aiming, firing his grandfather's revolver. The next shot, Nathan noticed a strange discontinuity, something not right.

It was the same as in the cemetery, the same feeling. Dudek had a look on his face that wasn't like any expression Nathan had ever see him use and he was still moving, still firing. Nathan saw *something*, then, material puffing into the air from nowhere. He floored the accelerator.

Suddenly a man was right there in front of him, turning to look his way, and Nathan lifted his foot in shock, but the heavy car hit with a sickening crunch, spinning him through the air to smash against the wall of the house.

Nathan sat, staring at the body of the man he had just killed, unwilling to believe what he had done. Then the man started to get up. As he watched, Dudek put his revolver to his head. Shot him, from a distance of inches, knocking him down again. Tried to shoot again, but the gun was empty.

The man lay still now. Nathan got out of the Discovery, feeling shaky, and hurried to Dudek, the Luger in his hand.

"Is he dead? You think?"

Dudek shook his head. "No. I don't think."

"Me neither."

"You feel him? In your head?"

The same as in the cemetery. "Yeah."

"We've got to find Hilda."

Dudek was shouting for her as Nathan ran to close the tall wooden gates, thinking maybe somebody had heard the shots, or might drive by. He came back, seeing the dilemma on Dudek's face, wanting to find Hilda, but not wanting to let the creature recover, maybe get into somebody's head.

Nathan opened the boot of the Discovery, coming out with the semi-automatics that Murray had given them and handing one to Dudek.

"What do we do?"

"Let's drag it down to the shore and incinerate it."

"What about Hilda?"

"I'll look for her. Could you drag it across there, start piling…"?

Nathan felt his gorge rise. "Touch it? No way."

Dudek rubbed his temples. "Ok. Watch it for now, but don't get too close. I'll look in the house, see if she's there. Anything happens, fire of a couple of rounds."

Nathan said, "Wait."

He turned and stared out over the water, thinking he had heard something.

"Listen."

Both men stood still, then ran to the water's edge when they heard her call. Dudek started pulling the rope, hauling the little boat to shore. Nathan could see her face, luminous in the moonlight.

They pulled her out of the boat and Dudek held her close, rubbing her arms and back.

"We've got to get you out of these wet clothes and…"

She shook her head. "It's not dead."

"We know."

Dudek picked her up and hurried inside the house, then Nathan was on his own, looking down at the creature. It looked like a small, very dead, man, its body crushed, and its skull shattered. He watched as the thing's remaining eye flickered and opened. Its head turned to face him.

Then Dudek was back, carrying a coil of rope.

Nathan whispered, "It's looking at me."

"I'll grab his cuff, pull his arm up, you slip the rope on and we drag him to where we can burn him. Ready?"

"Not really."

Dudek put his hand out very slowly, but pulled it away is if he was burned. He walked in a tight little circle, shaking his arms out.

The next time, he grabbed the coat sleeve and Nathan slid the loop over, pulling it tight. They backed up a few paces, under the stare of the creature. Dudek froze, an expression of horrified surprise on his face.

"Boss?"

Dudek turned to Nathan.

"You know who that is?"

Nathan shook his head, wondering where this was going, but all Dudek said was, "Never mind. Let's drag him onto the shingles. Burn the fucker."

Hilda lost more time. When she came to herself, she was waist deep in Dudek's bath, warm water pouring over head, down her shoulders. A pause and then it happened again, Dudek filling a plastic bowl with bath water, tipping it over her.

She turned to him. "I'm still wearing my bra and pants."

"You think I'm some kind of weirdo? How are you?"

"Is this a recognized way of treating hypothermia?"

"Just seemed the quickest way."

"What about the...you know?"

"Burning. I've piled my entire log pile on it, and all my coal. It's a very hot fire."

He poured more water on her and she closed her eyes.

"I want to see."

"It'll burn all night. You think you might be able to drink something? Hot chocolate?"

She nodded. Dudek stood.

"Where are you going?" Her voice sounded all wrong. Too high.

He pointed to the door. "Hot chocolate."

She shook her head. "Oh, no. No being left on my own."

"What?"

"You see these horror films, people being scared shitless and then getting left on their own. Well, not me."

"I don't think you've thought this through."

He helped her into a robe, still shivering. "I need warm clothes. Out of these wet undies."

She gripped his arm and walked him into her bedroom, then he turned his back as she dressed.

Nathan was standing as close to the fire as its heat would allow, which wasn't close at all, the stubby semi-automatic cradled, ready. He turned as Dudek and Hilda arrived, arm in arm, Dudek looking embarrassed. Hilda just stared at the fire.

Nathan asked her, "How are you?"

"Still cold."

"It's not cold here."

The fire was much hotter than a normal bonfire, and she stepped closer, but soon had to shuffle backwards, the heat beginning to hurt. Dudek brought brandy and they sat on sun loungers, handing the bottle around and watching the flames dwindle, the fire becoming white hot and forcing them further back. Hilda sipped, feeling the liquor working in her.

"I'm surprised nobody called the fire brigade. Or the police."

Dudek shook his head, "You hear something in the distance, popping. You think it's probably fireworks."

They were silent for a few more minutes before Hilda asked, "You reckon it's still alive?"

Dudek shook his head. "It's gone."

"Maybe we wait till it cools, scatter any bones in the water. It didn't like the river."

Dudek stared hard at the water.

"We've not told you yet, about Angela Murray."

She listened quietly while Nathan and Dudek told the story. "You get how weird this is, don't you?" Then, "I need to sleep." She tapped Dudek's arm. "You have to come too."

Dudek turned to Nathan, "What are you going to do?"

"Sit here, till morning."

"You don't want to get some sleep? This'll burn all night."

"I keep wondering, could it get up, even now."

Dudek handed him the bottle. "It's gone, Nathan. But stay if you like. Something weird happens, don't mess about, shout or shoot."

"I'll do both."

Hilda was unsteady getting to her feet and Dudek had to help her to the house and upstairs. She patted his shoulder. "I need to pee."

He nodded but she was looking at him as though she expected something more, so he said, "That's nice."

"You have to come with me."

"What? In the toilet?"

"I told you. I'm not going to be on my own. Not for tonight at least."

"Can't I just stand outside?"

She shook her head. He frowned, "But I need to go too."

"Well, that's fine, then."

"I can't, in front of someone else."

"Men's rooms have communal peeing, don't they? Urinals?"

"Yeah, but that's other men."

"John."

She pulled him into the bathroom. He closed the door and stood looking at it as she went through her routine and flushed.

"Your turn."

She was standing at the wash hand basin, squeezing toothpaste onto her brush.

"You're standing right by the bowl."

She rolled her eyes and stepped away, facing the door as he had done, brushing her teeth.

After a few moments he said, "It's no good. I can't, with you standing there."

"Oh, for God's sake." She leaned to the washbasin, turning the tap on. "See if that helps. What are you doing?"

She frowned, looking at how he had placed his right hand to screen himself. Muttering, she stepped back to the door.

"It's still no use."

"Why don't you sit down?"

"Men don't sit to pee."

"They do sometimes."

Dudek shook his head. "No, they don't."

"I can't believe it. You're actually indignant."

When he didn't reply, she said, "My boyfriend, ex-boyfriend, used to pee sitting down sometimes."

"I bet you made him do it."

"Well, no, but I did prefer it. Most of my girlfriends, agree. We like a man who sits down to pee."

"Why?"

"None of you are exactly fool proof in the aim department. You get distracted."

"You make it sound like it's running down the walls and...ah."

The situation seemed suddenly funny to Dudek. He laughed and shook his head, watching the stream going into the bowl.

"What is it?"

He couldn't answer, but was laughing harder now, having difficulty keeping his aim from wandering. He had to put one hand on the cistern as his legs were going. Hilda was laughing too, an edge of hysteria in there, for both of them.

She managed to get out, "See what a mess you've made." And fell to her knees, holding her sides.

Five minutes later they were in Dudek's bedroom, and Hilda was still struggling with bubbles of laughter. Dudek looked around, like he wasn't sure where he was.

"I've got an inflatable mattress."

Hilda staggered to the door, opened it before closing it again and coming back to fall on the bed. Dudek stood uncertainly, watching her wiggling around, tears streaming down her face.

After a while, it seemed she had finally laughed it out. She said, "Let's just go to bed. I've never felt so tired. Can I use one of your tees?"

He got her a faded NYPD shirt, and turned away, stayed turned as he pulled his own clothes off, down to his boxers. Hearing her climb under the covers, he flicked the light off.

There had been one other woman here since Caroline died, but that hadn't been any good, and wasn't repeated.

It was dark, but he could see her well enough, feel her warmth, even from his position at the edge of the king size. He listened to her breathing, wondering could he touch her, and she said, "It would be nice, if we could maybe hold each other."

She turned then, and he slid towards her, his arms going around. She leaned her head into his chest and he pulled her in.

When Dudek woke, he briefly forgot that his wife was dead, and this was Hilda Jarvis reversed into him, still inside his arms. He was aware of his hand under her shirt, resting on her stomach just below her breasts. He was aware also he was poking out of his boxers, pressing into her behind, and thought she had to know that too, if she was awake. He thought she was awake.

Holding his breath, he moved his hand, sliding it across the edge of her breast, over her ribs to her hip. He had tormented himself in the brief period before falling asleep, wondering whether she had worn pants under the Police T-shirt. Now he knew.

She wriggled, pushing her butt out, making him gasp, then pushed her arms out into a long stretch, yawning and breaking the contact. She rolled out of bed and he quickly covered himself, embarrassed at having misread her signals. Frustrated too.

She yawned and stretched again, arms right over her head so that the shirt rose up.

"You slept ok then?"

He nodded, "Pretty well."

"Pretty well? You were out like a light. Snoring like a wildebeest."

"Really? Sorry."

"It was ok. Nice, actually."

She walked to the window and opened the curtains, blinking in the sunshine.

"You have to work today?"

He shook his head, "Tomorrow. Nathan too."

She leaned into the window recess, trying to see down to the water and the shirt rose again. He closed his eyes, thinking she had to know what she was doing to him, playing another little game, then couldn't help himself and opened them.

She was on her tip toes now.

"John?"

Something about the way she said it had him moving, rolling out of bed. Nathan lay on the lounger, seemingly asleep beside the smoldering fire whilst a large crow stood only feet away. Dudek hauled on his jeans and ran downstairs with Hilda following. The crow cawed as he burst from the house, and flapped lazily into a nearby Oak, joining a dozen others who shifted around, a rustle going through them.

Dudek stalled between the house and the bonfire. He looked back, at Hilda standing wide-eyed in the doorway, and up at the roof, where a few more crows stared down. He shook Nathan's shoulder, saying his name quietly. Nathan didn't move, but he didn't feel dead either. Dudek shook him harder and he came awake, sitting up with an abrupt movement, but looking confused.

"What?"

Dudek pointed to the tree.

"Let's do this nice and slow. Get inside."

Nathan nodded, fully awake now. The crows shifted around as they walked to the house, but nothing more than that. Back inside, Hilda asked, "Couldn't they just be normal crows?"

Dudek thought about it. "Maybe. Maybe we're just more aware of them. Let's eat. We'll be able to think better after a coffee."

Hilda was still staring outside. "What's left in there? A skeleton?"

Nathan shook his head. "You can't see a long bone. Let's bag what's left when it gets cool, dump it in the river."

Dudek spooned coffee into a large cafetiere. "If the crows let us. Bacon sandwich?"

After two rounds of sandwiches and several mugs of strong coffee they were feeling better. Dudek found that he could hardly believe what had happened last night, had to keep walking to the door to look at the glowing mound of ash. Finally, he asked, "What now?"

Hilda put her cup down. "We have to stop Haddow."

"You think that will be easy?"

"We killed that one."

Nathan yawned hugely. "Murray thought there would be another servant, that's what she called it, but not as powerful as Haddow."

"There are three of us."

Dudek looked at her. "Three?"

"You think I'm going to stay here by myself?"

"So, you're going to fight a vampire because you're scared to be on your own?"

"I mean I'm in. Part of it."

"You ever used a gun?"

"I spent a year in L.A. Girlfriend of mine used to take me to the practice range."

Dudek nodded, but didn't look happy. "Ok. We're going back to Stirling House. This time, we're going there to kill him."

February 1977

David wanted them to stay in the car, talk to the thing like that, so they could drive away if it came for them. But Minto said that when it moved, it moved slowly. Even after Neil had knocked it down, it got up and moved away slowly. Called it a defining characteristic.

David said, maybe you've never seen it when it wanted to go fast.

They were on their way to the mill and it was still light, just about. David wouldn't look towards Angela, staring instead out of the side window.

He told them, "None of you are thinking straight. You've no idea what this thing can do."

Minto stopped the Dolomite near where Brook Street met West Port, with an amount of gear crunching that might have surprised them, days earlier. It had snowed through the night and everything was under a light cover, the roads turned to muddy slush.

Neil opened his door "Ok. The Doc and I will walk fifty towards the mill. Angela, be ready in the driver seat in case we have to run."

He turned to Minto. "You try to communicate, and we'll see what happens. If it comes too close, we run back to the car."

David asked, "And what if it doesn't know it's meant to be slow?"

Neil brought a length of solid iron, about two feet long and as thick as his wrist, from the foot well.

Half an hour later, Angela was sitting in darkness in the driver's seat, with David beside her. They had turned in their seats so that they could see Neil and Minto, looking cold and scared below a street lamp.

For the twentieth time, she said, "David. I'm sorry."

Finally, he looked at her, his expression flat. "Never do that to me again. Never make me do something."

She shook her head. "I won't. It's just that we..."

"Never mind that shit. Promise me, you'll never do it again. No matter what. Promise me."

"I promise. No matter what."

He nodded, but didn't move towards her. Then the expression drained from his face. She leaned over and grabbed his arm.

"It's *stirring*."

Neil was looking stiff and cold, the long weight hidden inside his long coat. Beside him, the much smaller archivist shifted nervously, rubbing his hands together.

David straightened. "I've just realized. They're doing what you tell them."

Angela glared at him and turned back to the street. Then, her voice suddenly much higher, "It's coming!"

"Shit. Start the engine."

When she turned the ignition, the two men started, looking their way, and then looked around, tension clear in their stances. The street was almost empty, an elderly couple walking away, but at a distance. A group of young men crossed in front of the Dolomite, heading towards town. Normal.

David said, "Oh."

"What?"

He pointed. "There it is."

"Where?"

He threw the door open, jumped out of the car and shouted, pointing. "Neil! You see him?"

Both men looked confused. They hunched down, as though making themselves smaller, then appeared to rally. The creature was on the other side of the road, walking slowly along the sidewalk. David watched it, then had to give himself a break, look away.

He heard Minto call out, in a voice that was shaky but surprisingly strong, "Simon! Simon Bernard! It's Ian."

David looked up, trying to keep Bernard in his peripheral vision but, as Minto had warned him, found that didn't work. Minto was looking directly across the road and Neil had one hand on his shoulder. The metal bar, looking lethal but useless, hung by his side. Neil, David noticed, was staring hard at his own feet.

Minto called again, "Simon. Can you respond?"

David made himself look again and what he saw dumped frozen water into his chest. Bernard had stopped and was looking directly at his friends.

Minto, his voice shaky, called, "I want to talk to my friend, Simon."

It was several seconds after the creature began speaking that David recognized that's what it was. He found himself wincing, as though something was gouging out the inside of his head. It left him feeling shaky and he could see that Neil and Minto seemed dazed.

All the creature had said, "Minto. Kerr."

Angela. "This isn't right."

David nodded, "We have to get them out of here."

Bernard started across the road towards Neil and Minto, moving slow, but it wasn't a very wide road. David jerked as Angela burst out of the car, running towards them, shouting at them to run. After a second, he hurried after her.

Bernard paused, and David realized he was looking right at him and it stopped him cold. The creature smiled, or its mouth widened. Till it was simply too wide. He spoke again.

"Murray and Haddow. You were called."

Angela reached Neil and Minto but had to step right in front, shake them before they noticed her. "We have to run!"

"What?"

Bernard was moving again. She glanced over her shoulder and screamed, "Run!"

They jerked and stumbled, slithering in the slush, clumsy footed as they tried to get away from Bernard, who suddenly was no longer moving *slow*. Nobody would describe him as moving slowly at all, and he was coming for them.

Angela shouted, *run, run*, and Minto broke into a confused totter, looking like he was drunk.

Neil shook his head as though to clear it. Angela, clearly terrified, got her face in front of his, he seemed hardly bigger than her at all, and shouted, "Neil! Wake up!"

The creature was almost on them and David could feel it freezing his mind, caressing his skin with frozen feathers so he wanted to sit and weep. Neil seemed to unfurl, then, up to his proper height. As the creature reached out, he lifted the iron bar, forgotten in his hand, and threw it with all his strength, hitting the creature's head with a dull thump. It stumbled only slightly, but now they were all running properly, slithering pell-mell to the car.

Minto jumped into the driver's seat, revving wildly. Neil and Angela jumped into the rear and David threw himself across them. A second after Neil hauled the door closed, the creature struck the window. Everybody was screaming as the car lurched forwards, fishtailing crazily. The crows struck the car in a fury of wings and beaks. David saw the side window crack and curled into a ball. Neil was shouting, floor it, floor it!

The car picked up speed, but inside a furious ball of wings and feathers. They hit the curb and lurched to the right. "I can't see!"

"Go! Go!"

Although the crows were still hammering at the car, suddenly the windscreen was clear, and Minto took the West Port roundabout at a speed that would be crazy, even if the roads were dry, horns blaring at him. He weaved madly, straight through the lights, accelerating until he hit the brakes and threw the Dolomite into a right where it skittered and slid horribly before picking up speed, flying along beside the river now, overtaking cars. The windows were cracked and scratched, but the onslaught had lessened.

Neil looked around. "We've got to be through. They can't fly this fast."

The crow came out of nowhere and struck the windscreen with such a thump that everybody screamed again. It was cracked, top to bottom.

Several more crows hit the car, one shattering a headlight, but they reached the dual carriageway to Perth and, after about ten minutes at eighty, during which David got himself sitting upright, Neil said, "I think we've outrun them."

Minto barely slowed till they reached the outskirts of Perth. He crawled through traffic, across the bridge and into central Perth, and no crows attacked them. Finally, he pulled in and stalled the car across two parking places, roughly facing the Tay, which was only a hundred yards wide at this point, and dropped his head onto the wheel.

Neil looked around. "People are wandering about, normal."

David opened the door and climbed out, ready to dive back in. "I think it's ok."

They all got out, cautious, and then leaned together on the railing overlooking the river. Lights from the town reflected in the water, trees and roofs on the other side shining white under linings of snow.

Minto said, "It's beautiful, isn't it?"

David surprised himself by agreeing, although he didn't say anything. The beauty of the normal world was breathtaking.

Minto bent over and vomited in the snow, then straightened, catching sight of his car. They circled the scratched and dented Dolomite, crazily stickered with blood and feathers.

Minto sank onto a snowy bench. "I want to go home. I've never been so exhausted."

Neil shook his head. "Let's go to a pub."

They went to a small bar, cozy with its coal fire, and Minto bought four cognacs. Then he bought four more.

"That's better. A little."

It was, shockingly, just after seven and there were only two other drinkers, both older men, sitting at the bar. David noticed that the barmaid kept glancing over and wondered how they looked, if what they'd been through had left some noticeable trace.

In the end, they cleaned the worst of the mess from the Dolomite and drove back, taking it easy. Reaching the city, they searched the skies as Minto took a staggered route, keeping well away from the Tombstone Mill, kept searching until they were safely inside the old house.

2016

It was midday when Nathan rolled the Discovery to a stop outside Stirling House and, for a while, nobody said anything. Hilda looked at the crows, a lot of them flying around, then at the house with its darkened windows.

Dudek brought the semi-automatic into his lap, put an extra clip into the pocket of his jacket and turned to look at Hilda. She was white and kept licking her lips.

She said, "If you guys have a plan, I never heard you talking about it."

Dudek looked at her. "I thought we could go in there and shoot him."

Then he added, "And burn the house down around him."

Hilda looked at her pistol. "I'm worried that I go to shoot him, find out I'm shooting one of you."

Dudek made eye contact with her, holding it for a second before stepping from the car. Hilda had been trying to watch all the windows at once, and now she was the only one left in the Discovery.

She made herself move, catching them on the front step, three people with guns.

Nathan whispered, "You think he's in there, phoning the police?"

Dudek took a long stride to the front door and kicked it as hard as he could. The sudden violence, the speed and the noise, echoing around the gardens, shocked Hilda, nearly making her drop the Luger. Crows took off around the trees, hundreds of them.

The door didn't even rattle.

"Well, he knows we're here now." said Dudek. "We should have brought a sledge."

Nathan kicked the door three times, quickly, making no better impression on it.

Dudek pointed. "I noticed steps going down the side. Maybe an easier door."

They ran now, around the side of the house, and down a flight of steps leading down to a damp little landing and a small green door. Dudek put his shoulder to it, and it instantly shuddered open. Inside, it was dark and smelled musty. Dudek drew a breath and leaned in, feeling in the darkness for a switch. His expression was set, but Hilda could feel how scared he was. He stepped into the dark and there was a loud click, lights flickering into life.

The cellar was a low, wide space, filled with moldering furniture and expensive looking junk. They crossed slowly, coming to another door, so close to each other they were touching.

Hilda had to keep reminding herself not to let her Luger point at the others. Feeling ridiculous, she pointed it upwards, like an agent in a film. Dudek glanced back, taking a deep breath before opening the door to more darkness.

Again, Dudek found a light switch, this time showing a carpeted flight of stairs, going up. Hilda stayed at the rear as they climbed, but kept twisting to look behind, thinking maybe Haddow had been in the cellar. The hair on the back of her neck crawled, and the muzzle of the Luger was waving as much as an inch side to side.

Dudek waved them close, to whisper, "This is the hall, at the front of the house."

Hilda followed as he crept to the front door, then suddenly grabbed a handful of curtain to haul it bodily, and noisily, from a window. They blinked at each other in the sudden sunlight.

She hissed, "Why'd you do that? He'll know where we are."

It seemed that Dudek had no good explanation. Nathan, still in a whisper, asked, "So. How are we going to do this?"

Hilda stepped between them. "Don't even mention splitting up."

"Room by room. Working front to back. Then upstairs."

The first room was a lounge, massive and seriously dusty. They switched on the light, checking behind couches and chairs. Closing the door quietly behind them.

Next was a study, clearly well used, with screens and laptops and many files, papers covering a large desk, then a dining room, with a table set for around twenty people, a thick layer of dust over everything. They made their way methodically through room after room, searching carefully.

The last room on this side was the kitchen, looking exactly as Dudek remembered it. He pulled a cord and the blind slid up, letting in more sunlight.

"I didn't notice, when we were here. He kept all the blinds closed."

Hilda was going to say, vampires are like that, but found she didn't want to use the word here, even in a whisper.

Dudek pointed to the cups that he and Nathan had drunk from, nastily congealed now, the plate with breakaways and wagon wheels, everything still on the table exactly as they had left them. Coming back into the hall, Dudek did the same as before, rattling curtains open. Hilda jumped at the noise, but got the idea. It was worth it just to have some sunlight in this place. She suspected there had been none since old Canfield popped his clogs.

The next room had double doors. Dudek cracked one side and hissed, "There's something here."

Hilda was trying to keep her breathing in check, as the policemen got themselves into position, guns ready, then they were going through, peeling left and right, moving fast. Peering around the doorway, Hilda could just make out the backs of a line of chairs.

She stage whispered into the darkness. "It's Fraser Canfield's cinema!"

Nathan's whisper. "You smell that?"

She could smell it alright. She glanced behind her, at the front door, then the kitchen, with the cups still sitting there, thinking didn't we close that door? Then she thought, I'm on my own here, and walked stiffly into the dark.

She could just make Dudek out, sliding along the long his arm moving in sweeps as he searched for a light switch. Two shuffling steps further and her eyes were adjusting already. The smell was stronger, and she could see the last couple of rows of seat in the dim light. She blinked, frowning, trying to make sense of what she was looking at.

Such an everyday scene; a cinema, white screen floating ghostly ahead of rows of seats. With people sitting in them.

She wanted to scream but it stuck in her throat. Nathan might have seen the same thing because she heard a bump from that direction. Then, her brain working slow, she thought maybe something else was happening and turned that way, her pistol coming up, finger squeezing.

The light went on. Not bright overheads but muted wall lamps. Nathan stood with his mouth hanging open, one hand still on the switch and the other pointing the semi-automatic. The cinema was about half full, maybe fifty people in there.

Dudek was beside her now and she jumped when he touched her, then he was past, edging towards the nearest figures. She wanted to scream, let's get out of here, but then she understood. All these people were dead.

Dudek was kneeling by one of them now, a man with short black hair, slumped in the plush chair. Hilda felt her panic rising again, just managed to keep it in check as she squeaked, "Not so close."

"Look at this guy's face."

The man might have been in his thirties, but it was hard to tell. His skin had yellowed and dried, pulled into heavy vertical wrinkles, and his face had a strange shape to it, as though the skull beneath the flesh had sunk away.

Nathan said, "It's like they've been mummified. Except they look...bendy. Like the bones are soft."

They walked in a frightened knot towards the front of the room. The figures were spread randomly around, mostly sitting upright, but some slumped to the side. One or two lay on the floor. There seemed to be no pattern to the type of person here. Most were male, but there were females too, all ages. Hilda found herself staring at a little girl, maybe eight or nine years old, wearing a school uniform. Some wore business clothes, a few looked like they had come straight from a construction site.

Then she reached out to Dudek, grabbing his wrist.

"I know him. This guy sitting there."

"Who is it?"

They were still speaking in whispers. She turned to tell him but the thought of saying his name out loud was too frightening, like maybe it would summon him. Wake him up.

She beckoned both men close to her and spoke into their ears.

"Karl Bayer."

Dudek frowned, like a distant bell had been rung, but Nathan said, "The Banker who went missing a year ago? Stole a couple of mill."

"More like three years. He'd been involved with Haddow, doing a lot of business, some of it started getting looked into, and he disappeared. Everybody thought he'd gone on the run."

She turned back to him, a man with an expensive haircut on his collapsed skull, wearing an expensive suit. "I interviewed him twice. Nobody who knew him could believe he was crooked."

Nathan looked around. "What are we looking at, a collection?"

Dudek said, "We need to check every single one." Adding, "In case Haddow is sitting here, watching us. We're not picking him out."

It took them several anxious minutes, starting at the front row and working back. Once they were sure none of the bodies were Haddow, Hilda slid the Luger into the pocket of her jacket and took out her phone.

She was standing in the center, right at the front, concentrating on taking a picture, getting it framed right, when Nathan whispered, "You sure you want to do that?"

She stood for a second, then dropped the camera back into her pocket.

They checked the rest of the ground floor and moved upstairs, finding themselves on a wide landing, with corridors going to both wings. All the doors were closed, except the nearest one on the right, and Dudek made for it.

It was a bedroom, dominated by a huge bed with cherry wood posts, carved into spirals. There was a dent in the blue cover, as though someone had lain on it. On the floor beside the bed was a pile of clothes, a tweed suit of some kind, and a shirt, both badly torn up.

Dudek stepped into the room and his foot hit something, a metal ball the size of a large marble.

Nathan said, "The same shot as Kerr's."

Dudek nodded, moved to the center of the room as Nathan checked possible hiding places. Dudek bent to pick up the tweed jacket, but straightened without touching it. He pointed instead.

"Recognize this?"

Nathan nodded, "The material Barry got from the university. That jacket's been ripped up pretty bad."

Hilda grimaced. "Canfield's clothes. He just put them on, didn't he? Never mind they were made for someone twice his weight."

Dudek prodded the shirt with his foot, an expression of distaste on his face, spreading it out to show the holes the shot had made. Then he knocked something aside.

Hilda looked at it. "What's that?"

"What's it look like?"

"A chunk of bone."

"Kerr must have hit Haddow, maybe nearly destroyed him. That must be why he's in such a state. If he'd got a clean shot first time, maybe Haddow would never have gotten control. Made him do what he did."

Nathan said, "Before getting hit, he could have driven to Dundee. In that Mercedes."

"How do you think he got back, that night?"

Nathan compressed his lips. "He got a taxi. Made the driver take a walk onto the bridge after."

Hilda finally said what they were all thinking.

"He's not here."

Dudek nodded, "I would've felt him. You think we should hide the car? Wait for him."

"You want to be in this house when it gets dark?"

She put the Luger back in the pocket of her jacket and flexed her hand. "Let me get some photographs. And we can get out of here."

Hilda photographed the suit and shirt. Then they went back downstairs, moving faster now, wanting to be out of there.

"I've got to capture that cinema. Sorry."

"Nathan and I can."

"How about we open the front door, to the house I mean. Nathan can guard it while we do the biz, then we leg it back to the car."

Nathan walked to the front door, turned both locks and opened the door a crack to look outside before opening it wide. They all stepped out for a minute, just to be out of the house and breathe fresh air, surprised by the brightness. Dudek checked his watch, said it would start to get dark in around half an hour.

Hilda took his arm. "Let's get this over with."

They walked back down the hall, Hilda noticing again how heavy the gloom was. Catching the smell from the cinema, she gagged.

He took her hand and she squeezed tight. "You okay?"

"It seems worse. Now I know what it is."

They opened the door to the cinema, to let light in, both sides at once this time.

Hilda sniffed the air and coughed. "I don't remember us turning the lights out."

"Let's open some of those curtains. Let some real light in."

Dudek went to disentangle himself, but she pulled him tight to walk through the darkness to a window. Hilda took a handful of curtain, but a sound behind her made her freeze, a soft noise like cloth against cloth. The sound of movement, it went on for several seconds. Dudek tensed, pointing his gun in that direction and breathing hard.

There was a pause of a few seconds, then a thump. A series of thumps, from different parts of the room. Hilda flapped desperately, catching hold of a cord and pulling hard. The curtains, maybe fifteen feet tall, slid open with a rough rumbling sound, but it didn't get any lighter.

There was another noise, closer this time. Hilda was panicking, and she knew it, could hear it in her own throat, and it felt like Dudek was about to spray the place with bullets. She could see the doors to the hall, but they had all but closed, hardly any light getting in that way.

Why was there no sunlight from the window? She grabbed at the material that was there and pulled desperately, putting everything she had into it, stumbling back when heavy black-out blind tumbled down around them, along with a crashing burst of near-blinding light.

The dead sat in their seats, as before. Then, one of them moved.

Hilda heard herself scream, as a woman a few yards away shifted slowly to the right and slid to the floor, as though her skeleton had become too soft to support her. She grabbed onto Dudek and they watched as another, and then another body collapsed.

Dudek's pulled her close and they scurried out of the room. Once outside, he said, "It must have been something we did. I mean to make those things collapse."

"I think it was sunlight. And I think he's done with this place."

Nathan nodded his agreement. "Everything coming to a head, like Angela Murray said."

"Where do you think he is, then?"

Dudek stared at the crows for a moment. "I'd say the Tombstone Mill."

Hilda, after a pause said, "Me too."

February 1977

David and Angela slept, heads together, and arms around each other. They woke together too, eyes flying open in the same moment. And they whispered together, the exact same words. "He's here."

Angela's internal clock told her it was around three. For a few seconds they just stared at each other.

Angela whispered, tiny, right into his ear. "Do you think he's in the room?"

Cautiously, David looked around the darkened bedroom, before shaking his head. They crawled from under the covers, wincing at every bump or rustle. David stepped to the door and listened, asked a question with his eyes.

She shook her head and they stood there as minutes passed and a decision had to be made. David put his hand on the handle but had to take several breaths before he could bring himself to turn it.

It squeaked, the mechanism clicking horribly in the quiet of the house. He peeked into the hallway, glancing back at her and pulling a face that was mostly just scared.

Clutching together, they inched into the hall. David pointed at Neil's door, which was ajar. They pushed it open.

It was lighter in here and they could hear Neil's light snore, see a long leg poking out from under the cover. Angela shook his shoulder, hushing him as he woke.

"It's here." She whispered, bringing him fully awake.

Neil felt down beside his bed and picked something up, a hatchet he had found in Minto's tool shed. Three of them now, they crept into Minto's room. He sat up instantly.

"It's here. We can feel it."

"In the house?"

David said, "I don't think so. Close, though."

Minto took the time to tie his shoes on – I simply can't face a vampire in my bare feet – and then they looked into the hall.

Minto asked, at a normal volume. "Why are we in the dark?"

"We're scared to put the light on."

"I think it does rather better in the dark than we do. And this is my house."

Minto snapped on both upper and lower hallway lights and then they crept downstairs.

They tried every room, lighting every light, but not finding Bernard. The outside doors were still locked. In the kitchen now, Minto said, "Could it be a mistake? Just a case of the heebie-jeebies?"

David and Angela shook their heads.

Neil walked to the window and pulled the curtains and there he was, lit by the light from the room and standing quite still, only a foot from the glass. Simply standing there, looking in.

Angela felt her bladder go. It occurred to her then that she hadn't known it was possible to feel this scared. The thing had followed them, and only a few millimeters of glass stood between it and them.

She shouted, "Back! We need to get as far away as possible."

David moved but the others didn't, and she had to tell them again, putting something into it, so they came into the hallway. She shut the door.

"We should stay here."

David hissed, "All that's keeping it out is glass."

They shivered in the cold, as minutes passed.

Neil said. "Where can we go, barricade ourselves in? All of the downstairs rooms have windows."

"Upstairs then. Barricade ourselves into one of the bedrooms."

"That would just trap us. We could wait here. Make a run for it if we hear him coming through the window."

Angela shook her head. "You're forgetting about the crows." Then she said, "Did you see his face?"

David touched his own head, just above the eye. "His skull is caved in, where Neil thumped it."

Neil straightened. "So, it can be *hurt*."

"He didn't look bothered, though. He looked…" he searched for the word.

Angela finished for him. "Satisfied."

David nodded. "Like everything's going his way."

Minto said, "Things are changing. You can see him clearer now and recall what you've seen."

Neil said, "Doc, do you have anything else that could be used as a weapon?"

"There's a shotgun in the cellar."

Neil looked frustrated that this was the first time the guy had thought to mention the gun. He said, "Well, great!"

"But the shells are in a lock box in the garage."

David and Angela had been looking at each other quizzically.

David said, "He's not so close, is he?"

Angela shook her head.

Dawn found them in the kitchen, strung out, and drinking tea. Minto stared at the lightening sky, "I'm going to turn in."

David turned to him. "I don't think we should be here tonight, after it gets dark. I get the feeling that we're right where it wants us."

2016

Even before Dudek walked into the station he knew that something was badly wrong. A traffic car was parked right outside, its front wheel actually on the first step.

The scene in reception was pandemonium, more people in there than he had seen before, a lot of shouting and pushing going on, both police and public. It seemed like everybody was shouting at the same time.

He ran quickly upstairs, over typed pages scattered on the steps. Nathan was already in his room, waiting. "Another three murders, boss."

"Three!"

"Mackie said none of them needed much in the way of investigation."

"Mackie's looked into them? How does that work?"

"I'm not sure how anything's working. That isn't the worst though. You were once partnered with Gerry Devlin?"

Dudek frowned, knowing this would be terrible. Nathan went on, "He's one of the cases. He shot somebody."

"An armed…"

"The guy wasn't armed."

Dudek thought of the way the man's finger tightened on the trigger, sighting on crows. Still, he shook his head. "No way."

"Sorry, boss, he emptied his gun, the entire clip, into some guy who confronted him in reception, about a case that had nothing to do with Devlin. Took him out front and pretty much executed him. In front of about half the station."

Dudek had to sit. "He say what he killed him for?"

"Sorry, but he did. He said it was for impudence."

Dudek had dropped Hilda in the city center before heading for his office, a crowded area being the only place she would accept being left on her own. She wandered the shops for a while, but there was a strange mood in the air. She could taste it.

Gap was astonishingly messy, discarded clothes on the floor and rails in disarray, no staff. A middle-aged business man shucked off his trousers, pulled on a pair of jeans and walked out, leaving his shoes and trousers behind.

In a coffee shop, she took a seat at a window with her Americano. Most seemed to be acting normally, but she watched as a proper fist fight broke out between a young man and an older woman. Other people gravitated towards the scuffle, including an elderly couple, and joined in rather than break it up. She eventually counted seven people in the melee, which fell apart all by itself after a few minutes.

Dudek had been summoned to see Mackie, and he was anxious. He wondered what that said about him, all that was going on, and he was still worried about his career.

Mackie sat behind his desk, the mess of which had increased. The state of it, it had to be deliberate on some level, a document volcano.

"Know what this puts me in mind of, John?"

"'76?"

"I'm the only one still around from then. None of the old stagers left."

"Was it this bad?"

He grimaced. "Worse now."

Dudek thought, to hell with it, and said, "The case you didn't want me to look into…"

"Took a chance on the Kerr boy."

Dudek couldn't read the man's expression.

"He was a medical student, you know that? Dad on the job too, a super in Aberdeen."

"You remember what happened, boss? In the factory."

"Nothing much to tell. Stupid bastards dosed up and broke into the mill."

"But the archivist…"

"Guys like that don't take drugs? Anyway, we had to go in there, search for the missing girl. That was no fun at all."

"No?"

"No. All we knew was that they broke in, went crazy, and the girl was missing. So, we had to go down there."

Dudek had started this, but now he didn't want to hear it. Mackie was looking into the corner of the room, deep in his own memory.

"We went through the main building, following footprints. You could see where Kerr had come back, dragging something. Probably Haddow. Blood trail. We go down and end up on a stone landing, pitch black. Just me and two uniforms. Scary, I don't mind tellin you. And here's a fuckin' river! Underground."

"Any sign of what happened?"

"We're standing there, in the dark with our little flashlights, and one of the uniforms screams. Shouting there's something in the water, he's jumping about all over the place like a prick, so I says prick, calm down."

"Did that calm him down?"

"None of us were calm. Anyway, upstream, the river goes through this arch. We waded through and came out in another area. The Arch Pool?"

Dudek made himself say it. "The Dome Pool."

"The Dome Pool. That's where it got really weird. We found a body. Not the girl's, but some other guy. Unconnected. Dead for ages."

"What killed him?"

"A heart attack, coroner said. Natural causes."

Dudek thought about Bernard's head, cut from his shoulders, but kept quiet.

Mackie frowned. "No sign of the girl. The only crime was breaking into a derelict factory."

"So, that was that?"

"That was that."

Mackie stood, and walked to the window. "Should've retired. The problem is that everybody's bastards."

Dudek had no idea how to reply, and after a while Mackie straightened. "This is better, though, a good old tidy up."

"Tidy up?"

"Look at them out there. Millions of the bastards. Drivin' cars and on their iPad. Thin them out, this will."

He pointed at Dudek, "You go and organize it down West Port. Anybody steps out of line, don't take any shite from them."

But when he stood to go, Mackie said, "That body, the one we found."

"Bernard?"

"Couldn't make myself touch it. None of us could."

Hilda had moved to Riverside Drive, so she could lean on the wall and look at the river. The Tay was flowing fast at this point, high up on the wall. Behind her, cars drove in and out of the city, as if nothing strange was happening.

In the end, the atmosphere in the center had driven her away, but it felt safer here, by the river and its cool, clean breeze. It occurred to her that if she had a boat with an engine, she could sail it straight to Dudek's house.

Her cell phone trilled. Dudek.

"Everything's going nuts. Even Mackie's lost it."

"You got stuff to do?"

"He told me to get down to the West Port, organize things from there."

"Organize what?"

"He wasn't too clear on that. Point is that everything has gone to hell."

"You think this is to do with...you know?"

"I don't know what else I can think. Where are you? I've given up being a police officer for now, let's go home."

She noticed he was calling his house home. Thought about commenting on it, but just asked, "Nathan with you?"

"Gone to look after his family."

"I can be there in fifteen minutes."

February 1977

Morning. Minto opened the window, the one that Bernard had stood outside only hours earlier, and put a dish of tuna on the sill. Outside, everything was under a fresh blanket of snow. "Puss, puss, puss. Horace, you fat pudding, where are you?"

David said, "I know it's weird but I'm starving."

"Well, the cupboard is bare, unless you want pickled eggs. I'm not used to visitors."

Neil stood, "I'm going to the bakers. We need to keep our strength up for what we need to do."

In the end, Neil and Minto left together. It was just after midday on one of the startlingly bright but freezing days that Dundee seemed to specialize in. Neil followed Minto down the steep path that led through his garden, stopping when Minto stopped. Horace lay, under a smattering of white.

Minto stood for a while, not saying anything, then reached down to his cat, but didn't quite get there. He straightened, without speaking, and Neil touched his shoulder, pointing to an ambulance parked several doors down, a group of worried neighbors clustered a respectful few yards behind it.

Minto said, "That's the Clarke's house."

They hurried across and a small round woman wearing an apron under her heavy coat frowned briefly at Neil, then came to hold Minto's hand, looking earnestly into his face.

"I'm awful sorry, Ian, but Sandy has passed away."

Tears came into her eyes. "Just like that. Eileen woke up and he was lying beside her, gone. Maybe it was the cold."

"Is there anything I can do, Agnes?"

"Oh, son, there's nothing anybody can do now."

Neil noticed that she was no longer looking at Minto, but over his shoulder, a look of puzzlement replacing the grief.

"Would you look at all those crows on your roof, Ian! I've never seen the like!"

They buried Horace in the garden, having to use a pick to break the frozen ground, and came back around the kitchen table.

Angela said. "We have to stop it."

David looked at her, "You still believe we can? Didn't work so good yesterday, did it?"

"Neil damaged it with what was basically a lump of iron."

"It didn't look too troubled, though, did it?"

"It's the servant of a prehistoric demon and they didn't have guns in prehistory. What if we got that shotgun, went to the Tombstone Mill in the daytime and shot it?"

"I'm not sure if that would work."

She was suddenly angry, "What do you want to do? Just let it keep killing?"

Minto said, "If the myth is accurate, then Bernard is effectively a conduit, providing sustenance for the true monster. And facilitating his rebirth"

Angela was nodding. "I've felt him. Much stronger than Bernard."

Then she said, "I have dreams." David looked up, as Neil asked, "What, dreams where you see the Curn Dhu."

"Not exactly. The streets are rivers and I'm looking down from a second-floor window. The rivers are black and boiling, and they aren't made of water."

Neil grimaced. "This would give anybody nightmares."

"I had the first one this summer. Before I came here."

Minto thought about this, frowning. "I'm trying to work out the implications of what you just said."

"My mother asked me a hundred times, why Dundee? I never had an answer."

David threw up his hands. "Come on! You're saying, what, it's fate? Your destiny."

"Like the witch said, what were the chances two psychic people would come here at the same time? Why did you?"

David pointed at Neil. "'Cause he did! And that teapot's more psychic than him."

Neil's voice, when he spoke, sounding nothing like him. It was like listening to a much older man. "It was the other way around, Davie. I came because you did."

He leaned forwards. "A monster killed Iris. It's killing people and we are the only ones who can do anything about it. We either run away, or we kill it."

"Why did it just stand out there last night?"

"It was you that told me that it was cruel beyond anything we could imagine. It doesn't think like a human."

Angela repeated. "We have to do it, because there is nobody else, David."

"It said we were *called*, Angela."

After that, nobody spoke for a while. Minto left the room, returning with the shotgun case. "I've also got this." He put a long knife in a sheath on the table.

"I can also get my hands on a Crimean cavalry saber. It's in my office."

David said, "From the charge of the light brigade? The dopiest attack in history. What's happening to everybody?"

He stared at his own hands for almost ten minutes before saying, "Mackie."

Neil frowned. "The cop?"

"We should at least try. He knows there's something going on. I saw that in him."

"David..."

"He *knows*!"

Minto said, "Maybe if all four of us speak to him."

2016

When they got back to the house they went to bed, running upstairs and shedding clothes. Dudek couldn't remember a time when he wanted to have sex as badly. Hilda seemed to be thinking along the same lines exactly.

Afterwards, they lay side by side for only a few minutes before doing it again. It grew dark and Dudek locked up before coming back to the messy bed and a long, amazing evening of sex.

At some point, they fell asleep and, when he awoke, Dudek realized he was incredibly hungry. Hilda groaned and moved in his arms and he asked, "Did we eat anything last night?"

She laughed, a dirty laugh, and he said, "Food. Did we have any food?"

She sat up and blinked and he felt himself getting aroused again.

"I don't think we did, John. All we did was…oh."

It was around an hour later that Dudek went down to the kitchen. He had to admit that he was in some discomfort, but was pretty pleased with himself. Catching sight of his reflection, he told himself, "Didn't know you had that in you."

He made coffee and toast, snapping on the radio. Radio Tay had a feature on the spike of violent crime, and a sound bite from Mackie himself, talking, of all things, about statistics. Saying also that there was an investigation underway and that he would be in a position to say more shortly. Everything was under control. He listened for some sign of madness, but heard none.

It gave him a strange feeling, all this going on and he was hiding out, going for an Olympic medal in screwing.

He heard the sound of the shower running, thought about joining her there, but ended up eating instead, staring out over the water.

When Hilda came downstairs, she was walking gingerly.

"No more of that for a while. I'm a bit…tender." Then she laughed and hid her face, genuinely embarrassed. "I can't believe I did that!"

He came to her and they kissed, a long slow kiss. She looked at him thoughtfully. "You know, all that last night, I don't think we kissed."

She put a finger on his chest. "Kissing is good. We ought to kiss."

"Why does that feel like a lecture?"

She whispered in his ear, "Because you are a beast."

Then, much louder, "My God. Toast!"

Dudek got a text from Nathan later that day, saying everything was ok. He was going to be away from Dundee for a few days. He texted back, look after yourself. And your family.

All day they stayed together, talking, eating and talking some more. The night before, Dudek had drunk no alcohol at all, an unusual event. They kissed a lot and, when it grew dark, they went to bed again. Hilda snuggled up to him and whispered, "We can't do it again, you've *wrecked* me."

Then she moved against him. "Well, maybe if we do it gently."

The next days followed the same pattern; they didn't have sex again with the intensity of that first night. Hilda said, "What we're doing now is making love. That first night we were just fucking."

On the third day Dudek got a call from Superintendent Walker, his official line manager, asking where he was.

"I need to take a few days out."

It was an uncomfortable call, Walker clearly annoyed, saying all leave had been cancelled and needing all hands to the pumps.

When it finished he slumped at the table. "I'll get fired for this, probably."

"Everything still going mad?"

"Yeah, but, at the same time, it seems like things are functioning."

"We've been hiding out, haven't we?"

He nodded, then his expression changed as he got to his feet. "That's a car, coming into the drive."

It was Nathan. He had taken his wife to her family in Shropshire. "She thinks I'm going nuts." Then he was staring at Hilda, a long look.

She glanced down at herself. Back at him. "What?"

"You look...different."

"How so?"

"In a nice way. You look...I don't know. Different."

She gave him a sideways look. "I'll make more coffee."

Dudek frowned, saying nothing. Nathan had said 'in a nice way', but that didn't fit his troubled expression. Dudek raised his eyebrows and opened his hands in query, but Nathan just shrugged, looking uncomfortable.

February 1977

Mackie watched from his window as the mismatched group walked away, on their way to God knows where. Fucking freaks.

Kerr and Haddow he knew, of course. Junkies. He shook his head, thinking of the decent guy he had spoken to days earlier, Kerr's Dad. One of the good guys.

Wondered should he call, tell him about this new bit of craziness. Probably not.

Murray. What was she doing with the long hairs? Like some stiff old auntie with her blouse and slacks, till she looked right at him and he found himself jolted, as if he was an insect she was thinking of pinning. He remembered the relief, when she looked away.

Yeah, on second thoughts, she was freaky enough to be with those weirdos.

And, the city archivist! *Doctor* Minto, if you please. Blinking and stuttering like a silly prick as he backed up the crazy story of illness and monsters. Asking Mackie hadn't he noticed...

Mackie spoke to the rapidly disappearing group, loud enough so that somebody in another room asked, what was that, Mac? "I've not noticed fuck all!"

Now the journalist, Jarvis, came to mind. The guy collaring him a week ago, asking weird questions, and coming eventually to the illness. Jarvis not mentioning any monster, but talking about all the same things.

2016

On the night that Haddow came for Hilda, the first Nathan knew about something being wrong was when Dudek looked up and said, "Something's coming."

It was just getting dark, rain spattering against the window. Nathan looked at Hilda, came back to Dudek and asked what was coming. "I don't know. Can't you feel it?"

Hilda shivered, looking scared. "I think so. I don't know"

Dudek picked his semi-automatic up into his lap, sat like that.

That was the first thing. The second was the crows. Nathan noticed the noise first, a strange shuffling and scraping, and looked outside. He frowned, at first unable to make sense of what he was looking at. Then he took an involuntary step backwards. Hilda, who had been watching him, asked, "What is it?"

Dudek turned on the exterior floodlights and they stood by the window, stunned into silence. It looked to Nathan as though every crow in Scotland had to be out there. As he watched, even more arrived in a flurry of rainwater and feathers, jostling for space even on the ground. Drenched crows fidgeted on the window sill, their feathers rubbing the glass, smearing it with grease and water. One tapped its hard beak on the pane, looked at Nathan with its clever little eye.

"They're not saying anything. None of the usual racket."

They hurried around the house, and everywhere it was the same. Crows, fidgeting and jostling on every possible ledge or surface. Upstairs, the sound from the roof was unnerving.

They had their guns in their hands, but Hilda said, "A fat lot of good these things will be, if they decide they're coming in."

Nathan, speaking to Dudek, sounding angry, "What do they want? Why now?"

"How should I know?"

"You knew they were coming."

Dudek shook his head. "The thing I was talking about…it's still to come."

Seconds later, the doorbell rang. Nathan asked, "You think a crow did that?"

They walked in a huddle to the front door, the whole house murmuring to the sound of crows. The bell rang again.

Dudek called out, asking who was there.

Haddow's voice. "You know."

They looked at each other with wide, scared eyes.

"What do you want?"

"You know."

Hilda looked, one to the other.

"It's me, isn't it?"

Haddow spoke again. "You all know."

"When I said you were different," Nathan asked, "What did you think I meant?"

Terrified now, she shook her head, but didn't speak.

Dudek opened his mouth but Nathan went on, pointing at him. "What did *you* think I meant?" His tone was harsh, not like Nathan at all.

"I didn't know."

"Don't shit me. I saw it in your eyes."

"What are you talking about?"

"Both of you know!"

The door shuddered under a heavy thud and it sounded as though entire the house was being scraped and scratched; slithering, scraping noises from every point.

"I want the woman."

Nathan had raised his semi-automatic. It was pointing at Hilda.

Dudek aimed at Nathan, pulling his gun into his shoulder.

"Nathan! He's in your head! You're aiming at Hilda!"

Nathan shouted back, having to shout, with the noise of crows, beaks hitting stone, wood, and glass. "She's pregnant!"

"Shit she is!"

Hilda had her head in her hands, saying over and over, "Oh my God. Oh my God."

"Her dad was desperate for her to stay away. Something happened to *him*. Infected *him*. But she had to come. And you…how did you get out of the mill?"

"I escaped!"

Nathan was shaking his head, no. The noise of the crows was everywhere but loudest of all was Haddow, in their heads. "I want the *woman*."

Nathan brought the gun to his shoulder. "We have to, John. She has the…thing in her."

Dudek was sighting on Nathan, putting pressure on the trigger, "Don't you fucking…don't you…"

The crash, when it came, came from the kitchen, and crows poured in like a solid black arm. Dudek only had time to turn and they were on him. He fired the gun, spraying bullets, but Hilda was right. A fat lot of good that did.

They were on him and around him, pecking and slashing, beating and thrashing. He was driven into the lounge, encased in feathers and claws. Trying to shield his eyes, he used the gun as a club, swinging at the birds, kicking them, stomping on them. He stumbled around, crows gouging at him, dropped the gun and snatched up the poker, hitting out again and again.

It seemed to go on forever, and his strength finally ran out. He felt it go. There were still crows, lots of them, some injured and still trying to crawl after him. The room was littered with bodies. His hands and arms were ripped and gouged, blood spraying with every strength sapping swipe. His breath was ragged, and things were turning gray around the edges of his vision. He struck a crow off his face, stomped on it when it hit the ground. Another slashed his temple and he lurched sideways, no longer moving fast. A beak caught his eye, he felt it pop. Screaming, he dropped the poker, grabbed the crow from his face and ripped its head from its neck.

He could barely see. Only one eye was working, but it was filled with blood and sweat. Another crow was at his face and he caught it, feeling it scratch and bite his hands. He fell, hammered the crow on the floor. Another was on the back of his head. Others on his back and legs.

With what felt was the last of his strength he threw himself backwards, trying to crush them. Another crow was on his face. He batted it away, but it came back. This time he caught hold of it and hit it against the table leg.

Minutes passed and he started to think he'd killed them all. Feathers and dead crows were everywhere. One or two were moving still, but he couldn't do anything about that, not anymore.

2016

Nathan was still living with Dudek, for the moment, but it seemed the man he knew was gone. Since getting him home from hospital he just sat there, without speaking.

Nathan's own face, when he looked at it in the mirror, was badly misshapen, swollen so that he couldn't close his mouth properly. He was covered in gashes and cuts, some stitched and some still bleeding. His nose was packed with cotton wool and, four days later, still sometimes dripped blood.

He still had both eyes, though. Nathan wondered if it was the loss of the eye that had affected Dudek so that all he would do was sit and stare at his own bandaged hands. Or maybe shock. He could detect the symptoms of shock in himself. In normal times, they would never have allowed them to leave hospital.

But, Nathan thought, for Dudek, it was the pure horror of *everything*. Starting with Caroline, and his child; his inability to save them.

Since the night of the attack, it had rained incessantly and the chill it brought seeped into the house. Into Dudek. On the fifth day, a BMW pulled into the drive. Nathan, hearing the sound of tires on gravel, hurried to the window with the semi-automatic ready. The car door opened, and Mackie splashed across the gravel and into the house, opening the door and marching in without being asked. Nathan, knowing he would have seen the dead crows piled outside, hid the gun and went to greet him.

The two men looked at each other in silence for several seconds, Mackie taking in the state of him. "Where's Dudek?"

They walked into the sitting room, and Dudek glanced up for a moment, before returning his gaze to his lap and his bandaged hands.

Mackie bent low, squinting. "He got an eye behind that?"

"No. Sir."

"What a mess. Jesus Christ!"

Mackie looked around the room, then frowned and Nathan turned to see what he was looking at. He said, "Oh yeah."

Realizing now that his brains weren't working too well, either. The wall was badly shot up. Some of the holes had black rims, pieces of feather in there.

Nathan shrugged, thinking to hell with it. "You ducked it in the seventies, Chief. Now it's back."

Mackie pushed the bigger man and Nathan winced. Some of the wounds in his chest were still bleeding.

"There's nothing *to* come back."

He paced around the room. "You're fired, the pair of you! Useless pricks. How's a man to do a job when all he's got is a set of useless pricks? You're finished in the Police."

He stomped off and Nathan sighed, feeling a strange sense of relief. He had spoken at length to Sue, a lot of talking over the phone. She had said, just come. We'll start afresh. He had looked in the mirror and told her, I can't leave yet. Maybe a couple of days.

Now he could hear Mackie thumping around in the kitchen and, after a few moments, he came back with what looked like a cup of whisky.

He sat down opposite Dudek, staring at him.

"He was brilliant, Dudek. Had this way of figuring things out. Not like the likes of you with your fucking fast track. Look at him now."

Then he stood, almost looking like he might cry. "None of this was my fault. That fucking Kerr, going on about supernatural fucking forces. What was I meant to do with that? Didn't know what it was then. Don't know what it is now."

With one last look at Dudek, he shook his head and walked away. A moment later the BMW fired up.

February 1977

Snow crunched under the wheels of Jack Jarvis' car as he parked opposite the mill and climbed out. He could hear crows, making their horrible noise up there in the freezing dark. A lot of them.

Jarvis buttoned his coat and looked up and down the street. His was the only car and there were no other pedestrians nearby.

"Hello, Mr. Jarvis"

Jarvis jumped. Bernard was standing beside him, and he was at a loss to understand how that was possible.

"You're light on your feet! I don't know why we have to meet out here, in the middle of the night."

Bernard didn't respond, and Jarvis looked at him properly, thinking he had forgotten how weird the guy looked. Thinking he had gotten a lot weirder.

"We can sit in your car, if you would prefer."

It occurred to Jarvis that he would very much prefer to be in his car, but not with Bernard.

"Can we just get to it? You sounded like you had something to tell me. This illness, some connection to the archivist."

"What do you know about the illness?"

"I-"

Bernard talked straight over him. "Nobody knows. Minto is getting close. Why did you come to Dundee, Mr. Jarvis?"

Jarvis blinked, thinking this was close to the question Minto had asked. "What's that to do with anything?"

"You are an ambitious man, correct?"

"What?"

"You were on a good path. Had a career plan."

Jarvis rubbed his temple with his fingers, feeling irritated, a headache coming on. It seemed to be getting darker. How could that be? Bernard was speaking again.

"You could still have it all. Everything you dreamed of. You are a good journalist, are you not?"

"What kind of…"

Jarvis could not think of what should lie at the end of that sentence. It was definitely getting dark, but the darkness was right by him. He could still see the illuminated sign of the Bay Horse bar, everything normal just a hundred yards away, but the air around him felt like it was turning to oil.

No, not oil. He couldn't see Bernard. His car was right there, but he couldn't move towards it. In his head he heard a voice, whispering. Promising him things he wanted, everything he wanted. All he had to do was nothing very much at all.

2016

Nathan looked up at the sound of gravel crunching, wondering if this was Mackie returning. But it was a sleek black van, ghosting past to halt hard by the front door. Nathan hissed at Dudek, who didn't react. Swearing steadily, he ran, getting into position at the end of the hall, gun at his shoulder.

Something entered his head then, a weasel thread about how important it was to open the door. That he had to do it *now*. He half stood, then shook his head, shouting.

"John. We're under attack!"

If Dudek heard, he showed no sign.

Then his cell phone rang. He held his position, but hit answer and Angela Murray said, "Open the door."

She came in quickly, closing the door, then looked around.

"Haddow came for the woman, I assume."

"We couldn't stop him."

She waved it away. "I saw something in Dudek, but wasn't sure. Or maybe I didn't want to believe. How much of him is left?"

Nathan turned and opened his hands, meaning look for yourself. Angela followed him to where Dudek sat.

"Chief Inspector?"

He blinked and looked up, then dropped his gaze again. She put her hands to her face, seeming suddenly shaky.

"May I have something to eat? I've been driving all day."

Nathan was about to turn, but had to ask, "Does it know you've come?"

"I can't be sure, because he's tricky. But I think, not yet."

When Nathan returned with sandwiches, Murray was sitting across from Dudek, staring at him. She was wearing a sweater and knee length skirt. Her hair was neatly combed. Her backpack lay on the floor beside her.

She looked up at him. "I know you have been through things that nobody should go through. But you have more to do."

Nathan felt his throat tighten. "I'm done."

"It's not fair. But it has to end."

"Can't you end it?"

She shook her head. "I can help. But I can't do what needs to be done."

"Miss Murray..."

"There is only you. And him. You need to finish it."

"Look at him!"

She sighed, looking suddenly more than her age.

"We repeat the same mistakes, it seems. I knew what I had to do back then, but couldn't bring myself to. I truly loved David. And then with your boss. I let myself believe."

She leaned towards Dudek, her eyes sad. They hardened then, visibly, like a whole new person was sitting there, one you should be afraid of. "John."

For several moments, it seemed that Dudek did not hear. Then he raised his head.

"You knew what I had in me."

"If I had, you would never have left the island."

"Caroline wasn't sick."

Murray closed her eyes. "If you'd had a child, he wouldn't have wanted that."

"The whole thing with Hardy..."

"You were a pawn in a game you didn't know existed. It's been going on for thousands of years."

Dudek blinked his one eye. "What are you doing here?"

"You have a job to do. Kill the creature that murdered your wife. Your child."

Dudek's face was stone.

Nathan said, "We wouldn't have a chance."

She turned to him. "We almost beat it once before, Neil and I."

"You stalled it."

"With a cavalry sword."

Now she picked up the backpack, showing the weight of it.

"My house is no longer rigged to blow. Because it's all in here."

Dudek touched his bandaged eye, looking exhausted, defeated.

"We're not finished yet, are we?"

"No."

"Can we save Hilda? Save her life?"

Angela looked at him, a long look, empty of sympathy. "No."

2016

Angela Murray parked the black van in the same position that Nathan had stopped his Focus, a couple of weeks earlier. She took a moment, just looking at the old gateposts.

Rankine Hall. Only five months of her life had been spent here, but it was at once the best and worst time she had ever known.

She climbed out, and didn't hesitate, using bolt cutters to snap the chain and walking straight through the gates. The grounds were in darkness, but she followed the familiar curved path to the portico, its white pillars seeming to float in the gloom. Crows took flight from the monkey puzzle, but she ignored them, walking to the entrance with her flashlight.

She stood in the doorway, playing her light around the hallway. She had to compress her lips, seeing this place so unchanged; the telephone booths and the grand staircase. She listened hard, but heard only crows. At the foot of the stairs, she splayed her fingers the full width of the banister, just as she always had, and started up. Rowland glared from behind his thick film of dust and Angela told him, "Cheer up, you miserable old bastard."

At the last step before the first floor, she paused, checking the position of her feet. Yes, this was it. The exact spot they had made shocking love that first night, right out in the open. It had certainly shocked David.

High above her, something rattled.

She continued into the corridor, pausing at David's room, but not going in, not yet. Instead, she entered her old room.

It was still just about furnished, but the bed was upended against the wall, and the wardrobe was broken. She waited a moment, hoping to feel something but there was nothing for her here. Next door was Iris' room, and that looked strangely the same. No posters, but the same. She checked inside the wardrobe, searching, and found the sticker she was looking for, a cartoon dog wearing a red hat. She remembered Iris sticking it there, calling it Motley, or Mutley. It was hard to tell, with her accent.

Was it in here they had sat, Neil with those idiot crumbs of LSD? No, it was Neil's room. She recalled him and Iris, sitting under the ridiculous feathered heart.

She spoke out loud, but in a whisper. "I'm so sorry, Iris."

Neil's room meant nothing, but she went there anyway. It was empty apart from the bed, without even a mattress now, and she had almost closed the door again, when a thought hit her. She hauled the bedframe from the wall, just enough to shine the flashlight and get her hand in there.

Not one, but two feathers, still bright red. She smiled, but sadly, blew the dust off and slipped them into her pocket.

David's room seemed almost unchanged, except for newer posters; Harrison Ford as Han Solo, and *The Exorcist*. The same iron radiator, the same tall window with its stained-glass top panel, the pane cracked, from a crow's beak. Behind it, there was only plywood.

Someone had left a tattered copy of *The Grapes of Wrath* at the side of the wash basin and she picked it up, tossing it onto the bare mattress. Then she changed the flashlight setting, so it became a lamp, put her bag down and sat on the bed. Probably the same one. She struggled to remember their love making, but could remember waking in the morning and feeling him warm against her, his wavy hair across his face as he slept. She would sweep it gently aside and he would twitch his nose but not wake. She had, she thought, been entirely happy in that moment.

Angela checked her watch. Three hours until daybreak, a morning when the two policemen would make their final, desperate, throw of the dice. One neither would walk away from.

This was the night she died, too, one way or another. She let out a long, shuddering breath, and brought the machine pistol out of her bag. Then she took out the block of explosive, fitted the detonator with fingers that shook only slightly, smoothing her skirt to cover it. The gun was hidden by her bag. She closed her eyes, and searched for David, immediately feeling his surprise.

He was in the Tombstone Mill, of course he was. She saw it clearly through his eyes. The dome pool had been excavated and lights installed, just as Dudek had described. She could see the curved face of the culvert, diverting the Scourin' Burn. At the base of the excavation lay the ancient tomb of the King of the Crows.

There were other people there, some alive, some dead. With a shock, she recognized the corpse of an older Neil Kerr. Then the attention of the King turned to her. There was no anger there. Instead, something colder, more malign than could be properly understood.

She closed herself off as best she could, having to push hard. Maybe her involvement would prove to be a disaster, and the policemen would be torn to pieces before they could even leave Dudek's house.

She hoped to turn Haddow's attention long enough for them to reach the mill and within moments she was sure that he was coming for her, at least. She checked the gun's safety was off, avoiding looking at it.

If she could destroy David, it would not stop all of this, but it would change the odds. She emptied her mind.

February 1977

It was a freezing morning, well below zero outside the Tombstone Mill. Crows wheeled and circled against a sky the color of frost, too many of them up there. Minto shaded his eyes, shaking visibly.

"They don't appear interested, for now."

The gates to the courtyard were around fifteen feet tall, elaborate, but rusty and peeling. Ridged icicles hung from its iron curves and the gutters and ledges of the mill itself.

The gates squealed on their rusty hinges when Neil pushed, but juddered open. David took a step into the courtyard, iced over snow crunching and popping under his boot. It seemed to him that the air in here was different. They were still in the open, but even though it was just as cold, he felt he was inside.

He was about to tell Neil to get a move on when he saw what his friend was staring at. Crows, hundreds of them, some alive but most long-dead and frozen over, lining every perch around the courtyard. The dead crows were heavily sheathed in ice, their feathers dark shadows beneath layers of frost.

Neil whispered, "How come didn't notice them before?"

David took a step forward and a shifting, a rustling of feathers, passed through the birds, the ones still living. The heavy doors of the building were twenty yards away, hanging slightly ajar.

David stepped again. The crows watched, rustled, but did not take off. Three steps further and they were becoming more agitated, cawing, restive on their perches. Reaching the middle of the yard the crows were noisier still, flapping their great wings. Another, more horrible, sound now, a creaking and cracking, as ice splintered around the frozen birds. Still, they kept going, trying to keep it slow and steady.

Ice fell in splinters as dead crows shook their wings free. Only yards from the doorway, every crow burst into the sky and they rushed into the dark interior and banged the door closed, the sound reverberating in the silence.

Inside, it was darker, but not so they couldn't see. The smell was musty, sharp with the smell of massive iron, rusting. Looking around, David saw that the mill was mainly one colossal box, with huge stone pillars holding up the ruined roof.

Crows circled lazily in and out of the shattered windows, ignoring them now. David watched them, expecting them to take notice, but they didn't. He could make out the shapes of gigantic machines, but they were lumpy and misshapen, as though organic. It took him a few seconds to work out that every surface was covered in bird droppings, sometimes six feet deep.

Minto said, "Many generations of pigeons have done this."

"I don't see any pigeons."

Even whispers bounced and echoed unsettlingly around the huge space. Minto pointed. On the floor, camouflaged by the mottled grays of their own droppings, were hundreds of feathered bundles. Feathers were everywhere.

David's eyes were getting used to the gloom, but still something was wrong, he thought, because the floor wasn't quite still. Angela stepped backwards, then did a rapid spin, seeing what David was just realizing. Despite the cold, the place was alive with cockroaches and beetles.

"Can we hurry it up, please?"

Minto pointed. "This way."

They walked through the living mess to an open door, a rectangle of solid blackness. Neil pulled the Cavalry sabra from his bag, buckling it around his waist.

"Can you believe any of this?"

Minto checked the shotgun, looking awkward and embarrassed; an unlikely gunman. David put the long knife in his belt and Angela, holding the hatchet like a tomahawk, said, "Let's go."

Their flashlights were powerful, but there was an awful lot of darkness behind that door. They descended a flight of stone steps, worn by the passage of years, the only sound their own shaky breathing and the scrape of feet. David, bringing up the rear, kept swinging his flashlight behind himself, scared of what might be following.

Angela stopped, and shone the flashlight on his face. "What do you feel?"

He was feeling plenty. Bernard was down here someplace. But there was something else, something much worse. It seemed to be…

"Everywhere." Whispered Angela.

"I was going to say amused. Laughing, in fact."

At the bottom of the stairs, they found themselves on a wide stone landing. The smell of the river was very strong, and David could hear running water.

Neil whispered, "My God, this is a dock. Underground."

Above them was a huge curve, a long barrel of stone under which the river ran, maybe knee deep and glinting in the shaky light of the flashlights. The rotted skeleton of an old boat lay tilted below them.

David and Angela were staring hard at each other, because it was so much worse here. Massive and malignant, the weight of its watching was like a physical pressure.

David whispered, "We should get out of here."

In answer, Angela pointed her flashlight at a flight of steps, leading down to the water. "We have to walk upstream."

She had spoken in a normal volume, and her words bounced around the space, like they had taken on a life of their own.

Neil checked his watch, shocked to find it was almost midday. "We've been in here for almost two hours! How is that possible?"

Angela started down the steps and there was nothing to do but follow. David was shocked at how deep and cold the water was, pressing hard against his legs. His head, though, was a little clearer.

They walked, lights bouncing from river to the arched stone roof, and every step David took increased his sense of dread. He stopped checking behind, because the thing he had to fear was dead ahead.

2016

The first Angela knew about David's arrival was when she looked up and saw him, saw him clearly, even though he was standing on the other side of the closed door. That wasn't good. She had overestimated herself, or underestimated him.

He had brought no light and she recollected Ian Minto saying, I think he does rather better in the dark than we do. As the door swung open, Angela braced herself for the impact of setting eyes on him, but the shock was greater than she could bear, and she had to look away.

He said, "You've forgotten what it's like, to see the face of his servant."

Then, in a voice so much like that of his teenage self, "Where's my posters?"

When she looked up it looked like no more than a wrecked and ruined man standing, the remains of the only one she had ever loved. Was he being kind? It didn't seem likely.

"They might be there, still. Under Han Solo. Come in."

David took a step into the room and she saw the extent of the damage.

"You're a mess."

"That's unimportant. You came back for the birth. He knew you would."

David was still too far away to be completely certain that the explosive would destroy him as utterly as it had to. He stepped again, dragging his other leg, then stopped.

"You're closing off your mind."

"Can you remember the first time we saw each other?"

He smiled, his old smile. "In the library."

"I felt someone looking and it was you. Looking gorgeous, in a goofy kind of way. Do you recall our first night, here?"

"I remember it all."

She told him. "Come here."

He began to move and then didn't, but the strain of refusing her was showing. Suddenly he was no longer a man, but the creature, breaking her focus. She gasped and looked away. Then, slowly, she turned her head to give him her full attention, all in now. She cried out with agony.

"Come here!"

"No." But he took another shuffling half step towards her.

"Come here." Blood was running from her nose. Not just a drip, it was pouring, splattering the front of her blouse.

"What have you got there?"

It felt to Angela as though the entire room was vibrating, deep thumping pulses, as though the walls were shifting in and out. She could feel it in her chest, and in her head, her eyes.

As if in slow motion she lifted the gun, but something was pushing against her, iron biting into bone. Maybe David, maybe his master, it was stronger than she. Everything shivered and went dim, and she had to fight like a drowning swimmer, back to the surface of herself.

Angela screamed with the effort of trying to bring the gun around. It was coming, but it felt like she was bursting every membrane in her head to do it. She choked, coughing and spitting blood across the floor. The gun was almost pointed towards David and she pressed the trigger, sending a spray of bullets across the room. In the shock of the noise she let it drop and grabbed the block of explosive, leaping up and towards David as her thumb found the button.

"I'm sorry!"

She pressed down hard, but nothing happened. She reeled, blinking down at what she had in her hand, trying to make sense of it.

The dog-eared copy of *Grapes of Wrath*. She turned, looking for the explosive and there it was, on the bed. She screamed again, with terror and because she had been tricked. But still she would not give up. She twisted, thinking she could throw herself and slap the detonator. But she was moving slow, as though she was underwater.

For the first time in forty years, David Haddow put his hand on Angela Murray.

2016

Early morning, bright and clear. A hundred yards back from the factory, Nathan stopped the Discovery, glancing at Dudek who was looking upwards, frowning hard.

Following his gaze, Nathan could see that the sky was blue, but there was something dark up there. Something black.

A huge disc, seething in the sky.

Dudek said what he already knew. "Crows."

Nathan nodded, feeling himself shrink with the terror of it. Not thousands, but tens of thousands of crows flying in a great ragged wheel.

"Like the star at Christmas."

Dudek laughed, but no humor in there. A man who had already lost one eye to crows. "And we're, what, two wise men, bearing plastic explosive?"

"Angela Murray makes three."

"If she's still alive."

They sat for a few minutes, mesmerized by the great wheel of the crows.

Nathan pointed at the gates. "I could drive straight through."

"What do you think the crows will make of that?"

"I guess they'll see it for what it is. Once we're through, we have to get into the building fast."

Dudek nodded and touched his eye patch, the movement becoming a habit. "Ok. Let's do it."

They pulled heavy gloves on, and riot helmets, face shields down. Nathan clipped the heavy backpack around his shoulders. Then there was nothing left except to go, but Nathan had to take a minute, get his breathing under control.

He accelerated hard, the engine revving high as they roared forwards, bracing himself as they hit the old ironwork. The crash wrecked the front of the Discovery but they were through, skidding to a stop and sprinting for the building, bursting through the doors. Nathan switched his flashlight on, the one on top of his gun, and swung it back and forth. They took a few seconds, getting their breath. Trying to.

Dudek pointed his light towards the door that led to the stairway and they followed the beam, angling across the factory floor. Dudek had warned Nathan about the cold, but hadn't mentioned any smell. Nathan gagged.

Dudek, grimacing, whispered, "I don't think that's an actual smell."

"Smells like a smell."

"I think that's the only way to make sense of it. I think it's something else."

They dumped their helmets and crept down the steps, noticing it getting brighter, a little, lights on down there somewhere. Reaching the bottom of the stairs, the smell was much stronger, horribly so, but Nathan could understand what Dudek meant now. He could smell it even if he held his breath. He could hear something too, almost like voices chanting, but too low, more vibration than sound.

Aiming along their rifles, they crept down to the old river bed. The chanting grew louder as they walked the tunnel, and the smell so bad that Nathan had to fight the urge to turn and run.

Dudek, acting more like Dudek than any time since the attack of the crows, led the way. Nathan had to remind himself, the man had been here before. He could hardly imagine the courage needed to come back.

Nathan knew what lay at the end of the tunnel; the conduit that diverted the Scourin' Burn, and an excavated tomb. The tunnel opened out, like Dudek had said, but Nathan could make little sense of what he was looking at. There were human forms in the gloom, a confusion of limbs and naked bodies, knitted together in a weird lattice that curved above the excavation, almost like some kind of structure.

Suddenly there were children, a dozen or more between five and ten, walking towards them, climbing out of the hole to do it. Nathan sighted on them, but didn't fire as they closed in. Just kids, they were even smiling as they surrounded them. Then they had hold of the gun, and it was out of his hands. The children took both guns and simply put them down.

They turned their backs on Nathan, ignoring him, and surrounded Dudek, ushering him towards the excavation and whatever was there. Nathan still couldn't persuade his mind to decipher it. He stood forgotten, and it occurred to him to run.

The smell was overpowering and the vibration made it hard to think. Nathan thought he could catch words as it rose and fell. He shook his head, for all the good that did, as if his mind had forgotten how to handle information from his senses.

He closed his eyes, but then all that was left was the reek, and the sound, which he understood now was coming out of the mouths of the people in the dome pool. He opened his eyes again, seeing Dudek at the edge of the hole. Curving above him was a high wall of people, naked and linked in impossible ways, through crooked elbows and legs and around necks and torsos.

No, Nathan corrected himself, this was no wall, it was a massive egg-shaped construct, rising from the hole and made entirely of people. Even after all that had happened, the wrongness of this monstrous thing was the worst.

Things began to shift, then, legs and arms folding and reorganizing like a flower opening to create a gap for Dudek. Nathan could see the interior of the lattice now, understanding that it lined the walls of the hole, all the way down, and that everyone faced inwards, eyes closed, chanting.

Nathan thought, why don't these people tear and break? Why do arms remain in sockets, and bones fail to crack? It was horrible and impossible, and it made him sick and dizzy. He forced himself to walk to Dudek, who stood stock still, staring down into the interior.

Nathan saw then that some of these people were alive, and some dead. Telling himself out loud to stay sane, he took another step forward and caught sight of a canted rock at the bottom of the hole. Hilda was lying on it.

Except that this was no rock. David Haddow stood beside the tomb of the King of the Crows, smiling up at Dudek. Nathan shook his head, made himself refocus. Directly opposite him, twenty feet off the ground, he recognized Mackie. The old policeman's eyes fluttered in what looked like bliss and his arms were locked through a woman's to the right and a dead man to the left. His distended belly hung horribly and his mouth was open. The sound coming from him was too deep for a man to make.

Kerr was there, Angela Murray's arm crooked through the hole in his shattered chest. Searching now, Nathan found Roger Moore, and George. Hilda lay with her clothes torn and her arms and face bloody, legs bent in a position to give birth. She screamed, and he realized she had been screaming all the time. When Haddow spoke, Nathan winced.

"Ah. The Father. We feared you would be late."

Nathan saw Dudek unclip his pistol, watched as it was taken from him.

Hilda screamed again and Haddow said, "He comes."

Nathan turned to run, but recalled suddenly what was in the backpack, what he was there for. He turned back, and locked eyes with Angela Murray.

Alone in the wall of people, her eyes were not closed, and they stared at each other for seconds that became minutes. Then, he stepped past Dudek, who seemed in a trance, and tentatively put his hand out to touch a man. With a shock he recognized this man as Charles Rose, the mortician's assistant, now making an inhuman sound and locked into people around him. Rose didn't react in any way.

Nathan leaned out and put his foot on his thigh, caught hold of a young blonde woman's ankle, and stepped away from the floor. The lattice sagged slightly, adjustments were made, and the structure held, barely registering his two hundred pounds. He moved to his left, shifting hand and footholds, and found himself face to face with Rose. The man didn't open his eyes.

The weight of the backpack dragged, but he kept moving, finding hand and footholds on arms and shoulders. From time to time he glanced at Angela Murray, the woman looking like she was part of it, but wasn't.

It was a nightmare climb, with the sound of Hilda screaming and the weird vibration making him want to scream himself, having to put his hands on one person after another, expecting eyes to fly open. He wondered, was Angela Murray helping him? Or forcing him.

Finally, he reached the far side. It was a struggle, getting the pack off, and he jerked around so much that he could hardly believe that the people he clung to didn't open their eyes and see him.

One by one, he brought out the bricks of explosive and, leaning between a dead man and a young girl, stuck them to the curved concrete of the culvert. He got the last piece in place in the second that Hilda's screams changed and he arched to look. What he saw almost made him fall.

February 1977

David was walking behind Angela when the tunnel opened into a circular area with a high ceiling, a rotted wooden platform to one side. A small fiberglass boat was tied to the platform, a pedalo for God's sake, painted in purple glitter. Bernard stood on the platform, his ruined face doing its best to smile.

He said, "Welcome."

For a moment, everybody froze, nobody speaking. Then Angela shook herself, and turned to Minto.

"Shoot him."

Minto said, "Ah-um."

David found himself looking around, with a feeling that he had forgotten something important, but he couldn't force his muddy mind to think what it was. This domed place felt sacred. No, the opposite of that.

Angela stepped up to Minto, and said it again. "Shoot. Him." Putting a lot into it.

Minto nodded. "Yes, of course. Yes." He shook his head, shook it again, as though there was a fly annoying him in there, took a couple of drunken steps to the side, and the gun went off, deafening in the space, sparks flying and small shards of stone falling from above. It exploded again, this time into the water.

Minto screamed like David had never heard anyone scream before. He had no idea a person *could* scream like that and for a second, he glimpsed what was inside Minto's head. Before he could close it out, he screamed too.

Neil began shouting now, thrashing around the river. David shone his flashlight on his friend's face and it was unrecognizable, almost. The face of someone lost in terror and madness.

Only two flashlights were still working now, his and Angela's. They shone on each other for a few seconds before coming back to Bernard, who stood smiling, just as before. His head was caved in, his comb-over hanging down to his shoulder.

Neil was thrashing and screaming still, but hoarsely as he had ripped his vocal chords. Minto was on his back, gurgling.

Bernard said, dismissively, "Those two were not welcome."

David could hear Neil struggling and he knew he should care, but he didn't. His mind felt hollowed out, like a husk. For want of a point of reference, he wondered if somebody had spiked his drink with LSD.

His perspective was widening out, changing. He knew he was still standing in the water, but that was a distant awareness. The mud at his feet was mud, and he couldn't see through it, but at the same time he could; everything was transparent and broadening out.

Beneath his feet, and the build-up of millennia, there was some*thing*. The first real thing that he had ever encountered in his pointless, vacuous life. It was terrifying and glorious and everything else paled into a lesser existence.

It seemed to ask him who mattered, and he quickly thought of and discarded Neil and Angela and John Lennon. The absurdity of his regard for them was in sudden sharp relief. He felt his old self bleed away, as though from a wound, and was happy to see it leave.

The King of the Crows, the monster of the ages, was opening its mind to him and he went fearfully, gratefully. He saw himself through its eyes, how tiny he was, but tears of gratitude poured down his face when he saw that he could be of use. He was standing now as though on a plate of glass and the universe expanded below him and at its center was the terrible King. He knew his purpose now, the honor of the great service he could offer his Lord. He could provide the seed.

That gift had been bestowed on him the first night of his return to Dundee. He had locked his window in terror, before letting the servant Bernard through the door.

He understood it now, why he had been brought to this City. Like Angela, some of the blood of the faeries ran in him yet. The body of the King had long since rotted into the silt, but his will inhabited this place. David could provide the seed and thereafter die, as he would have ceased to matter. The girl had been chosen for a vessel, he sought her name and it came. Angela. He felt for the physical change in himself and found it. Knew that when he gave his seed to Angela what would be born.

The great wings of the King unfurled, and he fell into them, shedding his old self like rotted cardboard. Then its searing focus shifted to the girl, and the boy felt a great sadness as its eye left him.

Angela stood beside him still, her flashlight on Bernard. David remembered his own flashlight and shone it on Angela. To be embraced by the King, to be his vessel, he had to open himself to you, sharing himself, his knowledge and his immense will. He had opened himself to David and now he did so to the girl. But Angela was fighting.

David saw much more than he ever had. He saw into Angela's heart, her own powerful will and her gift of bending others to that will laid bare.

Angela pushed, pushed with everything she had, and he felt himself rock back, even though it was the King who was pushed and not he. The King was still weak, yes, and opening to the girl had weakened him further. And strengthened her.

David heard her then, surprised by how loud her voice was under the stone. She shouted, "Neil! Neil Kerr!"

Neil instantly stopped thrashing. She shouted again, "Destroy him."

David turned his flashlight and found the boy Neil, lurching to his feet, but swaying. His hands were clamped on his head and his teeth were bared in agony.

She spoke again. "You have to destroy Bernard. For Iris."

It took Neil a few seconds to pull himself upright, but, bit by bit, he did it, up and up until it was hard to believe he was only the size of a man. The next thing happened very quickly.

Neil ran, water flying as he vaulted the platform. David saw him come as if from Bernard's eyes, saw him rise up, huge and too powerful to stop, saw the sword, its tip six feet above my head and...

Neil brought the sword down with enough brute power to cut Bernard's head from his shoulders, but Bernard did not fall. Instead, with his head hanging by a strip of flesh, he attacked the big man, fought him.

Struck again and again by the sword, Bernard finally fell into the water and David felt the cold shock, the water finishing the job for the monstrous warrior.

The water. Now he understood the strength of the river and knew that he had to get the girl onto the platform.

"David."

He looked at her, but said nothing.

"David, fight. Come back to us."

He had to get her out of the water.

"David, please. I love you. Come back to us."

He felt her push, and pushed back. He searched for the King, but the King was far away, for the moment. Robbed of his servant, he had faded.

David ran at her, thinking to drag her out of the water, but the fool Neil had him now, and the three of them wrestled and fell.

"David. Fight it. Please!"

Her voice was like dirty metal, pressing at him, gross and indecent and almost impossible to resist. How long the fight went on, he couldn't recall afterwards. But, at some point, Angela realized that the boy was gone, and in the madly dancing light of the remaining flashlight, she stepped away and fixed him with those terrible eyes. She told him to take his knife from his belt, and he did. She told him what he must do.

The last words he heard her say. "I love you, David."

After he cut himself, consciousness came and went. He saw her run, light bouncing ahead of her, throwing water patterns on the stone wall and leaving them in the dark. Warm blood poured down his legs.

Then there was a gap in his consciousness. He could hear Minto muttering, over and over. Wessex, Norman, Plantagenet, Tudor.

In a move he understood as pointless cruelty, he reached out and took that from the archivist, heard him gasp, his mouth working till he grew quiet.

The next thing, he was being lifted into the arms of the stupid boy. A wave of love for him rose in his chest and then dissipated, replaced by raw, visceral hatred. He hated Neil Kerr. The boy he hated carried him through darkness, following the breeze that ran along the river.

2016

Dudek had no idea how long he stood, helpless as Hilda writhed and screamed, but it seemed just as she was tiring, something was coming. Something black and hideous protruding from between her legs. Wrenching his eyes away, he saw Nathan clinging onto the far side of the terrible lattice of people. Saw him sway and begin to lose his grip.

Haddow held something the size of an ostrich egg, jet black, whilst Hilda lay, perhaps dead. Dudek shifted his gaze towards Angela Murray, just as she slumped, and closed her eyes.

Haddow changed, then, staring first at Dudek, then at Angela. He pulled the black egg into himself and screamed, in sudden fury, "A bomb?"

The whole structure started collapsing, folding into itself so fast that Dudek had to steady himself as children poured past to join the sudden confusion of bodies. He watched as Nathan was dragged into the new structure forming around Haddow, layer upon layer of bodies making a tight ball.

Across the gap, Dudek could see a red light, blinking in the plastique. Nathan, just before he disappeared, yelled, "Run!"

Dudek picked up his semi-automatic and aimed at the mass of bodies. Looked from that to the winking red light. Then he turned and, for the second time, sprinted the length of the tunnel, was leaping onto the dock when he was tumbled across the stone by a sudden rush of sound and heat.

He might have lost consciousness, but only for seconds, because he looked up just as water came roaring through the tunnel, churning and frothing and full of limbs and faces.

It filled the channel, overflowing so that he had to grab the rifle and scurry backwards. The lights flickered but stayed on, and the water rose to a peak, then subsided slightly, still flowing fast and hard.

From time to time, a body would float past. Sometimes it seemed as though the person might not be dead, but mostly they were. A minute passed, and the water sank further, although it was still deep, and fast.

Dudek suddenly fell to one knee, sighting on two figures walking from the tunnel, chest deep in water. For a moment, he let himself hope it was Nathan and Hilda.

But the couple were clearly dead, and the man was Neil Kerr. They moved as though stuck together, but all four hands were cupping something, holding it with extreme care.

Something black.

Dudek watched as they approached, face pressed to the gun, but did not shoot. Watched as they reached the stairs, only feet away. Bending, they placed their precious load on the step above the water, then melted into the river.

Dudek stood very still. The egg, his child, sat on the precarious step just above the water, which churned angrily, frustrated. Let it be frustrated.

He let the gun barrel drop and moved closer, till he was standing above it. It wasn't pure black after all, but marbled. It shifted, as though it was translucent and inside an inky storm was taking place.

His son. His son at last. Caroline had been right all along, *this* was his son.

He stepped closer, careful not to knock it from its position. He smiled. He would have to take it someplace safe, away from the river.

Dudek knelt, and the surface changed, black on even blacker. Then something came to the surface, as though the egg was deep, and something huge could swim up from its depths, to look out at Dudek.

It moved right to the surface and he jerked back, losing his footing and crashing into the river. Thigh deep in freezing water and the egg was there, right in his eye line. Inside, something shifted, and this time he had to look away, repulsed. The smell of it was in the air, vile, disgusting beyond belief. A smell that was not a smell at all.

Dudek made himself look back and that *thing* came to the surface again, the thing that killed Caroline, killed his real son, and he screamed, bringing the gun up. Screamed as the entire clip emptied, pieces of stone and egg and bullet flying in all directions.

2016

Dudek woke in his own house, on his couch. Behind his eye patch, something throbbed redly and he was aware of other pains around his body. He lay full stretch on the couch, still wearing his riot gear, gun heavy on his chest. It was light outside.

He was damp, but no longer wet. What did that mean, in terms of time? He couldn't bring himself to think about it.

Someone was in the house.

The door was open, and he could hear movement, whoever it was not trying to be quiet. There was a smell in the air too, the sharp tang of petrol. He told himself to move, forced himself to sit and point the gun towards the door.

Hilda came in, limping badly, carrying a metal jerry can and a Glock pistol. Maybe his. She pointed it at him, stopping for a moment to catch her breath.

He asked, "How did you get out?"

When she spoke, her voice was strange. Everything torn from screaming, probably.

"All the people crowded around to protect our son. It saved me. You destroyed him, didn't you?"

He nodded and watched as she started pouring petrol in big splashes, keeping the pistol pointed vaguely in his direction.

He said, "Everything down there must have been blown up or drowned."

She kept pouring petrol, till it was empty. "I wasn't."

She straightened and looked around, wincing.

Dudek asked, "Did you see what happened to Nathan?"

"Pulled down. Didn't see him after. Do you have a lighter?"

"So you can set fire to the house?"

"So I can set fire to you. Watch you burn."

He thought about getting up, making himself do it. She pointed the Glock.

"If you try to get up, I'll shoot you in the leg."

They stayed like that for a while, pointing their guns at each other.

He said, "I love you, Hilda."

Her chin trembled, and tears slid down her face. "I love you too. I really do."

"But not so much as you hate me?"

"I want to kiss you. Make love to you. It hurts so much to see you hurt like this. I want to make you all better. But more than that, I want to see you burn. Alive. There are no bullets in your gun."

He dropped his arm.

"Couldn't hold it up anyway. Do you think we could make another one of those things? You think we've still got that inside of us?"

For a moment he thought she would scream. Her expression was of someone screaming. Then he thought she was going to shoot herself, the way she was pressing the pistol against her face. With an effort, she came back.

"We are the horror, John. You think I should let you reload? We count to three and start shooting?"

She smiled. A sad smile that he felt himself returning.

Then she said, "That won't work, though."

He pushed himself to a sitting position, gasping and swearing, and got to his feet. Ignoring Hilda and her gun, he limped towards the mantelpiece, fishing around before holding up a box of matches. Gave them a shake, then pulled one out and struck it, standing on a petrol-soaked carpet and watching it flare.

"You're right. It wouldn't work."

He dropped the match. "Because just being dead isn't far enough for the King of the Crows."

Epilogue

It was a bright morning in late January and there was snow. Although not far above zero, there was no wind and a warmly dressed person would not be cold. Two young people, tall and holding tightly together, were walking along the wide pavement of the Nethergate.

Anyone who saw them, maybe driving past or glancing up from their desk, could not help but mark them. They might even turn to their passenger or colleague and comment. Look at those two.

Look at her with that red hair and those eyes, she fills that jacket, eh? Now, that is what I call a beautiful girl. And the size of the pair of them! Him with that coat. It would look silly on a normal sized guy, a long black thing like that.

They can't get their eyes off each other, look. It's a wonder they don't walk into something. What must it be like, to be in love like that. I've been in love, sure, but *look* at them.

What? Change places? In a heartbeat. Even if it meant I only had a week left to live. That's living, that is.

Iris kissed Neil, right there in the street. A long and deep kiss that made them slow, fall together even more, but not entirely stop walking. Then she said, "You know what I am?"

He didn't bother thinking. "Gorgeous. Beautiful. Sexy. Fan-"

"I'm happy."

"Yeah, me too."

She put her hand over his heart. "Well, stop a minute, and appreciate it."

"I'm appreciating the hell out of it."

"No, you're not, and I mean it. I've had a few good times before. Like when I've been having fun. I've gone through periods of feeling things were just tickety-boo."

"Tickety-boo. That should be our word."

"I've even thought I was kind of in love before. I can look back and say, I must have been happy there. But I didn't know I was feeling properly happy *at the time*. Are you getting this, you great lump? I'm happy!"

"I get it, I just don't know what the fuss is about. I'm happy too."

They paused, and Iris used his lapels to turn him towards her, then stepped away so they were looking at each other. They were both smiling so it might hurt their cheeks.

"Well, whether you get it or not, take this moment. This one right now. This is the moment. Look in my eyes and know, right at this point in time, we are both properly happy."

Neil smiled down at her and was surprised to find that his eyes were wet, and he had a lump in his throat.

"Don't you make me cry right in the street."

"Why would you cry?"

"You know why."

Now she leaned in and whispered. "You have to say."

Neil looked up at the enormous blue of the sky, still with that wide, dopey smile. Then he moved suddenly, dipped and lifted her, laughing, straight up above his head.

"Because I am *happy*!"

Acknowledgments

So many thanks to Michael and Rebecca at AM Ink, for believing in this book.

About the Author

Bill Davidson is a Scottish writer of mainly speculative and horror fiction. His debut novel *The Orangerie* - a psychological thriller - was published in 2021 by Close to the Bone Publishing. His collection of short stories *New Gods, Old Monsters* was released by Dark Lane Books in 2020. He has had many short stories published by good publications around the world including Ellen Datlow's highly regarded Best Horror of the Year Anthology and large distribution magazines. Find him on billdavidsonwriting.com or @bill_davidson57.